UNCROWNED EAGLES

Witold Ułan

DEVOLICA
PUBLISHING CO.

ISBN 0-9699181-0-0

CONTENTS

PREFACE

I had thought of writing this book long before I left Poland. It was to be a true picture of the nation I loved, written for North Americans. It had to be in English rather than Polish in order to express ideas in terms well understood by the readers. To achieve this I had to put myself in the position of the reader, rather than write the book in Polish and have it translated. Apart from the danger of poor translation, the latter option could have caused me to treat some issues as obvious (as they are often obvious to my fellow Poles) which would have resulted in producing a book not readable to many North Americans.

'Uncrowned Eagles' describes conditions under social and political systems which were completely different from those in the USA, Canada and other western countries. These are systems which no longer exist in Eastern Europe but whose legacy will remain for many years. The book is based on the fundamental premise that human values and feelings in the East and in the West are very much the same, and because of that, one can explain Poland and Polish thinking to any North American reader.

I knew I needed to find an editor who had been born in North America, not only to take care of the finesse of the language, but also to make sure my book would be comprehensible to people living here. I met a young graduate of journalism Adrienne Scott, who volunteered to be my editor. She is a Canadian with no Polish background whatsoever, but she sympathized with the Polish Cause. Writing, editing and rewriting took more than four years, every weekend and many week day evenings. At the same time I worked full time to make a living. The book was written out of passion; this took care of the emotional side of the story. At the same time I had to include some historical information and a lot of descriptions and comparisons to make the reader feel like he/she was right there. Even such things as swear words used in dialogues were painstakingly chosen to retain their Polish character while being comprehensible to North Americans.

By writing the book in the third person I think I avoided producing a pseudo memoir, which Uncrowned Eagles is not, despite containing many true events. Also, I felt that this approach would allow the reader to identify himself/herself with the main character, which would have been more difficult had the story been told by Konrad Dymowski himself. This format also made

1

it easier to leave the protagonist from time to time and to have a look at other important characters in the novel.

'Uncrowned Eagles' provides the reader with a microcosm of the Polish experience over three generations through the characters of the protagonist's grandparents, parents, and his own generation-the one which ultimately led to the 'Solidarity' movement. The novel covers the period between January 1978 and December 1981 and describes events during that time as seen through the eyes of Konrad Dymowski, a young university graduate living in Warsaw. While the events in the novel progress in a chronological fashion I have made some use of flashbacks, characters' reminiscences, and other techniques to supply readers with some sense of the history behind Poland's social and economic decline and the reasons behind the birth of 'Solidarity'.

The 'Solidarity' period can certainly be described as the one during which the Polish People achieved their highest moral level after the end of World War Two. While reading 'Uncrowned Eagles', one can see workers, intelligentsia (professionals), peasants and intellectuals, solidly united in their struggle against the communist system. Such a unity, difficult to achieve in the West, or even in today's post-communist Poland, was the result of the working of the so called Real Socialism which had deprived everybody of almost everything, except for the military, the police and the Communist Party officials.

The novel is divided into four parts, with a large portion of Part One being devoted to the protagonist's experience in the Polish army during his compulsory military training. The extent to which the military served as a powerful propaganda tool for the Communist governments of both Poland and the USSR is fully illustrated. The military provides the crucial link between the beginning of the novel and its conclusion, since many of the characters introduced in Part One reappear in Part Four as the architects of Martial Law. The book is not all about politics, many timeless human qualities such as love, friendship and solidarity have been given attention; there is sex and humour too.

Who would read 'Uncrowned Eagles'?
Michener's 'Poland' has often been accused of providing a simplistic and erroneous image of the Polish Nation and Polish problems. However, there is no other popular novel on this subject and 'Uncrowned Eagles' could well fill the gap. The second or third generation of Polish North Americans who may have lost their mother tongue but still retained their Polish roots could be potential readers of this book. Also, with increased business contacts between Poland and Canada and the US, many other North Americans might be interested in reading this novel.

The Author
April 1994

2

ACKNOWLEDGMENTS

Adrienne Scott has been the main Editor or Co-author of 'Uncrowned Eagles'. In addition, Miss Veronica Low and Mr. and Mrs. Wcisło proofread the whole novel and made important editorial comments. Mrs. Scott, Mrs. Low, Mr. Jacques Bourbeau and his parents provided invaluable moral support during writing/editing of 'Uncrowned Eagles'. In 1988, author Linda Manning made important editorial comments to first two chapters of the novel.

Throughout 1994, Mr. John Archer Houston provided linguistical guidance in the final stages of editing of the manuscript.

Last but not least, Mr. Janusz Rychter made creative suggestions for final layout of the manuscript for typesetting.

All of the above help was greatly appreciated.

The Author
December 1994

DEDICATION

Today it appears that ordinary Polish people attached more importance to 'Solidarity's' ideals than did the Union Leadership who achieved political power in Poland in 1989. The phenomenon of Poland's 'Solidarity' impressed countless people around the world during the eighties.

This novel is dedicated to those who believe in freedom and justice and to everyone who lit a candle for Poland in December 1981.

The Author

P A R T

Good Soldiers

CHAPTER 1

The line-up slowly advances. Ahead of him a young, dark-haired woman, her large figure tightly wrapped in a thick sheepskin coat, collects her passport from the officer on duty. He sits behind a counter inside a small, glassed-in booth. As Konrad waits impatiently for-his turn, he watches the passenger pick up her luggage and pass through the customs clearance area with ease. From there, she makes her way toward the airport security check. He is overcome with weariness and his eyes feel wretched and painful from the effects of a sleepless night, the last night he would spend in the country of his birth, the country that is his life with all its memories and tears. He yearns to be on the other side of the barrier.

"Your passport please," the Border Zone Defense officer requests tersely. Konrad faces the man and feels his deeply set brown eyes survey him carefully. His eyes are penetrating, sharp, even ruthless - the eyes of a professional, an indifferent examiner.

As the precious green booklet is opened Konrad feels his whole life being laid bare for the man's perusal. He mentally lists the personal information on the passport's first pages:

> PA 352000
> Obywatel Polski-Polskeey Grazhdanin-Citoyen Polonais
> Dymowski, Konrad
> 174 cm; eyes blue
> Characteristic features - none

The photograph on the inside page depicts a thick-set man with a straight defined nose, rounded full chin and closely cropped, medium brown hair. It bears only a mild resemblance to the thin, apprehensive man before the officer. Seemingly satisfied with the vague similarity between the two, the lieutenant checks the validity of the visitor's visa to Canada and stamps both the passport and a border crossing card.

Konrad reaches forward, expecting the passport to be returned promptly, and when it is not he looks up questioningly at the officer. The man, still holding the booklet, casually asks,

"Your military rank?"

"Second Lieutenant of the reserve..." He surveys the expressionless figure in khaki, bewildered by what appears to be an irrelevant inquiry. Silence. His chest pounds - the nervousness he has managed to suppress up to this point, surfaces. He waits.

"Do you have your Military Record Book with you?" the lieutenant asks. Again puzzlement. Why all these questions about the military? Konrad asks himself. Then he remembers - the country is now being run by a general who holds three top government posts...

"Do you have it or not?" the officer demands with clear military precision. In his nervous frenzy, Konrad reacts automatically. His feet snap together and his backbone stiffens.

"No I don't," he answers firmly. "It is prohibited to take this document out of the country. I am well aware of that fact, Citizen Lieutenant."

Konrad isn't sure but the slight hint of a grin seems to twist the corners of the officer's lip as he pushes the passport slowly out of the wicket.

Konrad takes the booklet, heaves a sight of relief and his eyes meet the officer's one last time. Only then does he realize that he is standing at attention and that he has just answered the man in true Polish military fashion. He, a man who spent a year as a military draftee and not once willingly followed the regulations of the People's Armed Forces. A crushing sense of subordination, heightened by the fact that it was self-inflicted weighs heavily upon him. It tears away at his ever-present conscience.

Six khaki coloured trucks with roaring engines sat in a single row outside the railroad station. A few uniformed officers, as well as drivers in light fatigues and padded jackets, smoked cigarettes as they waited for another load of new draftees to arrive. In the cold air, their warm breath intermingled with the greyish tobacco smoke.

As his train approached the worn, concrete platform ahead, Konrad felt overcome by a wave of anxiety. He gulped and tried to concentrate on the scenery outside the train - a river bed, its frigid contents covered with a fresh cushion of snow. It was spanned by a narrow, ramshackle-looking bridge. He reluctantly joined his friend Roman in the aisle and waited for the train to come to a full stop. As the door opened, the cold winter morning poured in.

Most of the people leaving the train were young men, all wearing the same apprehensive look on their faces. A somewhat stout officer, with a shallow jaw and disproportionately long arms, clumsily raised two fingers to the visor of his cap and nodded to them in greeting.

"Gentlemen. Are you here to join the army?" the man shouted. "Welcome".

Roman nudged Konrad.

"Here we meet our first corporal," he whispered "moreover, he is a military academy cadet."

Konrad, surveyed the white bordered epaulets on the man's shoulders and nodded.

"All right," the corporal yelled as the last newcomer joined the group "get in the trucks."

"Are we far from the barracks?" Roman asked; the cold interior of the vehicle wasn't encouraging.

7

"On foot it is only ten minutes," the young officer paused and smiled, "however, it takes twenty minutes to drive there".

And before any questions were asked he continued.

"The reason is simple, as you approached the station you saw a wooden bridge. It is very old and can handle pedestrians but not trucks. We've got to detour down the river to a steel bridge."

As they bounced along the frozen road in the open-backed truck, Konrad wished that he had simply walked to the garrison. The driver seemed to have forgotten his passengers in the rear and, as the truck roared around a sharp curve, Konrad clung to the cold steel bench. Snow covered hills beyond the open end of the vehicle danced a bizarre ballet as he was thrown back and forth across his seat.

The truck rolled to a stop. Their ape-like corporal quickly jumped out of the vehicle and they followed his lead. They were standing in a garrison, totally enclosed by a steel-mesh fence. In front of them lay what looked like the garrison's roll-call square. A red and white striped flagstaff with similarly coloured Polish national banner flew prominently over the snow cleared area. Around this rectangle was an asphalt running track. An enormous placard loomed just beyond, with stylized hands intertwined in a firm grip. Polish national colours decorated one arm's sleeve, while the other was red with a yellow overlay containing a crossed sickle and hammer. Tall, black, shiny letters dominated the bottom of the poster. "Long Live Perpetual Friendship between Socialist Poland and the Soviet Union."

Konrad glanced at Roman and they both smiled bitterly. Any illusion they might have shared about the political character of their new home, were gone, after only a minute.

The chatter of the conscripts echoed through the empty, high-ceilinged hall. The gymnasium was one of the largest buildings in the garrison and Konrad sensed that it must have been the pride of the regiment. Separated into three zones, it contained space for volleyball and basketball courts, gymnastic equipment and Ping-Pong tables.

They approached a white fabric screen for a medical examination. A uniformed nurse motioned for Konrad to step onto a scale. He recorded his weight, 87 kilograms, his height, checked a small number of boxes and then yelled, "Next." Roman followed.

Six career officers were seated along a table, each joined by a corporal.

"O.K. Soldiers," a thin, sharply featured lieutenant announced. "We will be reading out names and you will file in front of your respective officer. Understood?" The draftees nodded.

"Babowicz, Aleksander."

"Cybulski, Roman." Konrad's companion smiled and walked toward the shouting lieutenant.

Konrad sighed. We are being grouped alphabetically, he thought with relief. The chances of being placed in the same platoon were good. It occurred to him that he and Roman had always been together-through most of school and university. Though Roman had his faults - he could be a bit overbearing and overconfident - still, Konrad valued his friend's company highly.

Roman grabbed a chair in front of the officer and quickly sat down. The

8

man had the most peculiar eyes, pink-lidded with blotchy, discoloured eyeballs. They were set off by his dull greyish pallor.

He was asked the usual run of questions -birth date, address and occupation. Roman noticed that most of the items on the bureaucratic form in front of the lieutenant had been entered by somebody beforehand. The officer was simply verifying the information.

"O.K. Cybulski, we need to know one more thing. What are your convictions?"

Roman glanced back towards Konrad and then to the bottom of the form. He stared at the officer with bewilderment.

"Didn't you hear me Cybulski? I need to know this information so that I can put the answer in the appropriate box. What are they?..." The officer's pinkish eyes blinked erratically.

"I'm sorry, lieutenant, but I can't answer the question", Roman said meekly. "My convictions aren't perhaps unique, however, it would take me some time to explain them."

"Don't be ridiculous," the lieutenant said with a sigh. "I am only interested in one thing and nothing more. Are your convictions 'scientific' or 'non-scientific'?"

"I'm sorry, but I still don't understand what you are asking me, Citizen Lieutenant," Roman replied, now understanding the intent of the inquiry.

The officer eyes twitched. He sighed again. It was obvious that Roman was not the first person to have trouble with the answer.

"All right Cybulski. Do you believe in God? Yes or no?"

"I do," Roman answered curtly.

The lieutenant wrote the 'non-scientific' in the 'Convictions' box and Roman was quickly dismissed.

"Dymowski, Konrad."

Konrad sat himself down in front of the same pink-eyed officer. He decided at that moment to play dumb and further aggravate the man. The lieutenant shuffled in his chair impatiently. He seemed determined to get the conscription registration over with quickly. To Konrad's disappointment he simply asked him whether or not he attended church.

Konrad rose out of his chair He could see Roman standing in a far corner of the gym waiting for him.

"Did I say you were dismissed?" the officer snapped.

Konrad stiffened. He turned quickly around to address the officer.

"I'm sorry," he said."I thought you had finished with me."

The officer raised his voice and continued.

"I have finished with you, yes, but you must go for a short interview with lieutenant Zabłocki," his pinkish eyes glared at the draftee.

Konrad heard the sound of clumping footsteps enter the gym. They belonged to a heavy man who took long, careless strides. When he approached the table, Konrad recognized the man as the military academy cadet who accompanied them in the truck. The gangly man's coat and cap were lightly dusted with snow and, once stopped, he stretched his long arms out, cleared his uniform and stood at attention.

"Citizen Lieutenant!" he announced as he saluted, "Cadet corporal Kowalski reports that he is ready to take orders."

"Thank you, stand at ease," the lieutenant shouted back.

"O.K. Kowalski," the pink-eyed officer continued. "You can take this group to the bath. That is everyone except private Dymowski. Comrade lieutenant Zabłocki requests a visit with him. Come back here once you are finished. There will be others to deal with after they have registered. Understood?"

"Yes Citizen Lieutenant," the ape-like Kowalski yelled. He stood at attention and saluted curtly.

Outside, the roll-call square was covered with a soft blanket of fresh, wet snow. The corporal strode resolutely across the square, motioning to the forty or so draftees behind him to follow.

Kowalski greeted a duty officer in the front hall and then led Konrad down a long, grey corridor. They stopped at the third door on the right.

"Follow me, Dymowski," the cadet corporal said as he knocked on the door. "This is the office of lieutenant Zabłocki, the assistant company commander for political affairs."

The room was narrow and dimly lit by a small window in the far corner. Zabłocki was seated behind a massive, wooden desk. Poland's coat of arms, a white eagle on a red shield hung on the wall close to the man's head. Beside, there was a large portrait of Lenin.

"Good morning cadet Dymowski," the lieutenant said.

Konrad surveyed the man's face closely. He shuddered as his eyes followed past the rows of fat lining Zabłocki's chin and neck, to his thin nose and shallow, greyish complexion. The man smiled incessantly.

"I suppose you are wondering why I wanted to see you," he said with a grin.

Konrad remained motionless. The lieutenant's eyes were dark and bead-like; so dark that he could see his own reflection as the man's eyes shifted continually from left to right.

"O.K. Let's make things simple." Zabłocki pulled one of his desk drawers open. He took out a single sheet of paper and placed it on top of the desk. It was a questionnaire.

"You probably recall, cadet Dymowski, that you were required to fill out this form during your military classes at university. Do you recognize this?"

Konrad nodded silently. He remembered filling out the form two or three years before. The handwriting was certainly his own.

"This," Zabłocki said, tapping the sheet of paper, "is the reason why I summoned you today." He leaned over the desk and handed the new draftee the sheet of paper. Three questions on the form had been encircled in red pen.

"You will notice, Dymowski, that the first question pertains to your relatives and their service in the Polish army before 1939. The other questions refer to their involvement in the Polish army in the West, and in the Home Army or any other organization that took orders from the Polish government in London during and after World War Two. You have answered 'Yes' to all of them."

Konrad had always been proud of his family's military heritage, however, he knew perfectly well that he had to be careful about that sentiment in front of the political officer.

"I believe that I filled out the form as requested," he remarked as he handed the form back. "As far as I know the information is fully accurate."

The officer smiled.

"Of course it is," he paused. "However, I would like to have you expand on it a bit..."

Konrad shuffled his feet impatiently.

"I am sorry," Zabłocki said. "take a seat." He barely raised his gaze from the questionnaire. "Now - Dymowski, I see that you have quite an extensive military tradition in your family."

Son-of-a-bitch, Konrad murmured quietly to himself thinking about the treatment the non-communist military men received after the war. His grandfather Robert had been a lieutenant colonel, had fought in three wars, yet under the Communist rule he was almost penniless in his last years, forced to live on a meager pension. Konrad glanced at the officer's face and their eyes met for a fraction of a second. The bastard must know what I am thinking of him-of all of them, he thought. He then realized that he was allowing himself to succumb to the officer's mild provocations. He took a deep breath.

"I am glad that Citizen Lieutenant appreciates the extent of my family's involvement in the military." He attempted to curl his mouth into a pleasant smile. "What further information would you like?"

The overweight lieutenant opened his desk drawer once more and pulled out a thick, black notebook. He opened it, flipped through a few pages, and then looked over to Konrad.

"Now, why don't we start with your answer to the first question. When did your grandfather Robert first join the military?"

"I am not sure. You see, I have never been interested in his military achievements," Konrad replied caustically.

Zabłocki leant back and laughed briefly. Konrad watched with disdain as the fat in the man's lavish chin began to shake uncontrollably.

"Dymowski - I think you do know," the officer commented with equal sarcasm. "Your grandfather died just a few months ago and I can hardly believe that he didn't tell you about his past. You may correct me, but it is my impression that the younger generation likes to learn from its elders."

Konrad shrugged. He avoided Zabłocki's gaze and concentrated on the red and white Polish coat of arms on the wall.

"Listen cadet Dymowski," Zabłocki continued calmly - he was obviously not all that bothered by Konrad's reticence, "I will tell you one thing before we go any further. What your grandparents did was their business, not yours. Why don't you just tell me what I have to know - frankly - and we'll get this over with. I do have to talk to about fifty other cadets just like yourself some time today."

At least I'm not the only person going through this, Konrad thought with relief. He glanced at the officer's sardonic smile and it dawned on him that Zabłocki didn't need to ask him these questions. Zabłocki merely wanted to monitor his emotions, his attitudes, his reactions.

"All right Citizen Lieutenant," he answered. "As I said earlier, I don't know much about my grandfather's affairs but I do recall that he joined the Czarist Russian army at the beginning of World War One. His regiment was manned by Polish troops."

11

"Good," Zabłocki commented marking the information in his thick notebook. "Now. Did your grandfather join the Polish Legions when Józef Piłsudski[1] moved them to central Poland from Galicja[2] in 1915?"

"No," Konrad replied. "His regiment belonged to the Puławski Legion and later to the General Dowbór-Muśnicki's Corps."

"Right. The Russians organized these divisions expecting them to fight the Germans but..." Zabłocki looked at Konrad attentively "at the end they were fighting somebody else..."

Konrad shrugged. "That is a well known historical fact," he said indifferently, "Dowbór-Muśnicki turned his divisions against the Bolsheviks."

"You certainly know your pre-war military history," Zabłocki commented. "Now–did your grandfather fight in the war Poland waged against the Soviet Russia in 1920?"

Konrad nodded and Zabłocki made another entry in his book.

"What happened to your grandfather in 1939 when the Soviet army moved into Poland's eastern provinces?"

"You know all too well what happened to him," Konrad mumbled. He stared angrily at the portrait of Lenin near Zabłocki's head.

"I'm sorry, what did you say?" the officer asked.

Konrad's mind raced with images of his grandfather. Calm down, calm down, he told himself. He took another deep breath and answered firmly.

"He was arrested, sentenced to eight years in a labour camp and deported to Russia."

Zabłocki recorded Konrad's answer, smiled and sat back in his chair.

"O.K. Dymowski, that's it for the first question." He leaned forward and pointed to the form one more time. "When did your grandfather Robert join the Anders' Army?"

"When it was formed in 1941."

"Did he fight in Italy? In Monte Cassino?"

"No, he was just stationed in the Middle East."

"After the war... When did he return to Poland."

"1946."

"Was he arrested by the Polish authorities when he got back?"

"No," Konrad replied quickly. He knew that Robert had managed to escape persecution only because he was bed ridden and more often in the hospital than at home, but he didn't feel compelled to explain that to Zabłocki.

"Very well. The last question now," Zabłocki said, seemingly pleased with the interrogation so far. "Your maternal grandfather Jan served in the Home Army during the Second World War, didn't he?"

"That is what I wrote down."

"Yes, and what happened to him after the war?"

Konrad lifted his eyes towards Zabłocki and gazed squarely at him. This time the lieutenant's eyes were motionless.

---

1. Józef Piłsudski (1867 - 1935) Polish politician and military commander involved in the struggle for Poland's independence. 1918 - 1921 the head of the Polish State.

2. Galicja (Galicja - read: galitsya) Austrian name of the region of Poland occupied by Austria during the country's partitions, 1772 - 1918.

"He was arrested," Konrad said loudly. "He was arrested and held in prison for five years while he was being investigated for charges that never materialized."

"And then?" Zabłocki asked quickly.

"He was released in 1956. When he died, a year later, he was only fifty two years old."

"That's very sad," Zabłocki commented indifferently as he noted a few more lines in his book.

"You can join the others in the bath now, Dymowski. Tell the next draftee to come in."

Konrad took a large gulp of air when he got out into the hall.

He walked across the snow - filled square and he felt the sky opening up above him but it was not uplifting. Numerous low-lying clouds cast a shadow on the snow. His grandfather Jan died when Konrad was very young. All he remembered was that the man was tall, grey-haired and very quiet. It was Konrad's mother Tina who had told him about her father.

With Robert it was different. Konrad realized that up to the interview with lieutenant Zabłocki he had never thought of his grandfather as of a dead person. Zabłocki and others like him had been careful to record Robert Dymowski's death in my military file, he thought bitterly.

Robert had always been so close to Konrad, and so was Julia, Robert's wife.

Konrad could never forget the day, almost a year before, when his grandmother suffered a massive stroke. It was Robert who had called and asked him to go to the hospital. Konrad and his girl friend Klara rushed to Warsaw's Child Jesus Hospital. Once inside the glass doors of the faded yellow admissions building, they saw signs directing them to the neurological ward. It was located in one of a few separate buildings within the medical compound.

The buildings were old, with weathered and greyish bricks, surrounded by a tall fence. It looked like a forgotten town for the ill, a wasteland separated from the rest of the city. Konrad sensed that those within were not meant to return to the outside world. The glaring light of fluorescent lamps hanging from the ceiling reflected sharply on the glossy, yellow-coloured walls.

Klara waited on a bench near the nurses' station while Konrad walked slowly down the worn corridor, past single files of hospital beds and cots. The neurological ward was overflowing with silent patients, many of them lying immobile on their makeshift beds. He noticed that most of them were elderly women with pale, yellowish faces.

One patient, apparently unconscious and uncommunicative, started to shudder violently as her throat filled with ugly gasps. A passing nurse looked down and methodically, without hesitation, placed a rubber nozzle in the woman's mouth. Then she flicked a switch with her foot. A motor roared and Konrad watched saliva and vomit seep into a glass jar connected to the machine.

As he stared at the woman's face, he heard his father's voice and saw Eryk at the far end of the hallway. I'm really surprised he is here, Konrad thought. As always when they met, Konrad instinctively searched for some evidence of booze. Eryk's eyes were slightly pink and the unmistakable smell of alcohol was noticeable a couple of metres away.

13

"Babcia[3] is conscious Konrad," his father said as he led him into a hospital room. "But she is partially paralyzed.

Inside, six beds were crammed into a small, box-like room. Julia looked deathly still on her white hospital bed; two bottles of intravenous liquid were suspended over her head. Before he let tears overcome him, he bent over the bed. "Hello Babcia. How are you feeling?" he asked, trying to be cheerful.

"I - feel - well." His grandmother spoke very slowly and he noticed that the right side of her face remained completely still.

"I'm here now Babcia. Everything is going to be all right."

He took her hand. It was lukewarm and trembling and he squeezed it gently.

He found it difficult to concentrate as he waited for the next crucial forty eight hours to pass. Invariably he thought of the same and, invariably, he tried to suppress these thoughts with passionate prayers.

The following morning, he ran through the entrance of the hospital and down the crowded corridor. Lord Jesus, he repeated silently, let there not be an empty bed...

He sighed when he saw her slight figure under the covers and two intravenous bottles still attached to her arm.

Konrad was with Robert when he first came to the hospital to visit Julia. As they walked slowly down the hospital corridor together, Konrad couldn't help thinking how the older man's increasing age had become more noticeable lately, especially since his wife's stroke.

Robert leant heavily on his cane as he stood beside Julia's bed.

"How are you feeling?" he asked.

Julia smiled and lightly squeezed his hand. "I feel better. I am not going to die. Not this time."

Robert bent down and kissed her cheek. "You are not going to die now or any other time," he said in a shaky voice. "You're going to be a healthy woman again... soon."

"I am feeling much better... besides, enough of me. You should rest a while until I come home," she told him. "You'll be busy when I do. I won't be able to walk," she added quietly.

Robert kissed her hand.

"I can't wait until you are back," he said.

"I will be home soon Robert, the doctor said so."

Konrad watched as she gently caressed her husband's almost bald head with her one good hand.

After the showers the new recruits were issued fatigues and ordered to pack up all their civilian clothing and send home. "Hurry up, your moms are waiting for this stuff," sergeant Bochan shouted trying to penetrate through the thick voices of the draftees.

Their sergeant major was a short, middle-aged man with a protruding belly and a pleasant enough personality He stood in the midst of the steamy dressing room and urged them to assemble in the corridor outside.

"All right guys, does everybody know their platoon number?"

3. Babcia (read: babcha) - Polish for granny, grandmother.

"Yes sir," a tall youth behind him answered eagerly.

Bochan turned around and looked at the soldier with well pretended disgust.

"No 'Sir'! No 'Sir'!" he declared, "remember that 'Sir' was used before the war. There is no such word in the People's Armed Forces. When you address me, you say 'citizen sergeant', understood? "

"We had better start remembering our university military classes-fast," Roman remarked.

They heard a piping voice behind them call out. "I have always thought, comrade sergeant, that it is optional to use either 'citizen' or 'comrade'. Am I right?"

Konrad turned to look for the owner of the sarcastic inquiry. A short, wiry man with curly blond hair stood his ground and stared at Bochan resolutely. The sergeant blinked his small, brown eyes, but chose to ignore the caustic tone of the short cadet private's comment. He smiled and answered, "When we go to a Party meeting you can call me 'comrade'. But for now 'citizen' is good enough." He pointed at the new draftee. "Do you know your company number?" he snapped.

Private Janek Wytwicki shook his head.

"You are Company Zero of the School of Officers for Reserve, SOR for short. Understood? Now everyone to the barber. We will make soldiers out of you yet!"

CHAPTER 2

"Get up. It's six o'clock," a brutally commanding shout roared through the barrack building. During the seconds that followed, he collected himself and to his surprise, managed to climb down from his upper bunk and find a pair of wrinkled fatigue trousers.

"First platoon!" corporal Kowalski yelled once more. "Proceed to the barrack corridor for the morning run. Time-one minute."

He must be out of his mind, Konrad thought. The barracks room that he and Roman shared with thirty others was full of scrambling, half-clothed bodies. Sixteen bunk beds were arranged in two rows down either side of the linoleum floored room. Dingy lockers filled the aisle.

Konrad desperately scrambled to lace up one of his boots. He bent down and ran his hands along the floor underneath Roman's bed. When he looked up, he saw that both of his friend's boots were neatly done up and he was pulling a sweat shirt swiftly over his head.

The tall dark-haired Roman peered down at him, self-assured as usual; his long-lashed eyes, freckled nose and mischievous grin giving him a boyish appearance.

"Time's up," corporal Kowalski barked. "Turn right and follow me."

They ran into the roll-call square. The soft, wet snow of the day before had welded into a hard crust overnight. A sharp, crunching sound under their boots, was breaking the quiet of the still dark morning. Loudspeakers hung from the lamp poles squeaked and then spit a loud, penetrating beat.

"They're playing that new hit song by Maryla Rodowicz," Roman yelled back to him.

Konrad frowned as soon as he heard the singer's voice. He thought the lyrics were cliché and meaningless.

"Board any train, don't worry about the luggage,
Don't even bother about the ticket,
… just watch the scenery as it passes by…"

I wish I could, Konrad thought as he struggled to keep up with the more athletic and confident Roman. I have to slow down or this fucking stitch is going to kill me…

16

Most of the conscripts tagged behind Kowalski and herded into the barracks building, but Konrad decided to stay out. He pulled a cigarette out of his back pocket and sat down on a bench to one side of the building entrance. He found himself facing a framed company billboard, set up along the sidewalk and protected with glass and wood enclosure. Its lighting system illuminated the written message and the sidewalk in front. Faded cardboard letters filled the upper half of the billboard. "Our thoughts, hearts and deeds belong to the People's Armed Forces," Konrad read out loud. He burst into laughter. "Welcome to the Army, SOR cadets," read another message. He spat on the ground in disgust. His image reflected unsteadily on the glass panel as the fluorescent light flickered.

He was startled by what he saw. Most of his once thick, brown hair had been lopped off. He remembered the ordeal in the garrison barbershop the day before. His hair fell in great bundles to the floor as the clip, clip of the barber's scissors created well-trimmed circles around his ears. He had emerged from the operation feeling like a grotesque, inferior being.

"Shit," he yelled and spat again. "I really am stuck here. I won't be allowed outside of this fence for the next forty days while I train for their stupid oath..."

"Cadet Private!"

Konrad turned around and found a stout captain in his early thirties a few strides away.

"Yes, what do you want, sir?"

"First of all no 'sirs' here," the captain shouted without hesitation, "and secondly, stand at attention when you talk to your superior."

Konrad reluctantly stuck his neck into the air, straightened his spine and quietly faced the man.

"What the hell are you doing here, cadet?" the captain yelled. Why does the S.O.B. have to shout, I can hear him, Konrad thought angrily.

"I am taking a break after my morning run," he answered.

"Put your fucking cigarette down," the officer yelled with fury, as he noticed Konrad's right hand for the first time. The cadet stamped the butt underneath his boot.

"Listen private. You are a soldier now and the place for a soldier at 6:30 in the morning is ON the company. You have to keep order ON the company, understood? So, right now you'll go ON the company and put your fucking bed in order. I will check it myself".

Konrad understood the military jargon. He had heard plenty of it during his military classes in university. The military had a peculiar way of extending the meaning of the word 'company' to the section's headquarters. As for the grammar, the most beloved preposition that Polish military used to describe a location was ON. It made little sense to an average Pole, it was carry-over from the Russian language. Well, let's go ON the company, he laughed to himself as he climbed the few steps at the entrance door.

The garrison gymnasium was filled with new conscripts seated in rows. A small podium covered with a soft, purple cloth dominated the room. On it were two chairs and a large table. Roman elbowed Konrad. "It looks like a May Day celebration at grammar school," he whispered.

17

Konrad shrugged. "There aren't any political placards."

"No?" Roman said, "so what's that?" he pointed to the gym's entrance. A squad of soldiers carried three, enormous red posters into the room. "What more do you want Konrad?" Roman snickered, "Now we can celebrate May Day officially".

Konrad nodded and then read one of the slogans out loud. "By increasing our battle readiness we shall contribute to the well-being of our socialist motherland. Ha!"

"The other one sounds even better," Roman added. He pointed to the board on the left. "Comrade Gierek," he mimicked, "Polish cadets can too! Hilarious isn't it?" A few soldiers around them laughed.

"Shit, it sounds ridiculous," a tall cadet beside Roman commented, barely able to hold himself in his chair. "What the hell do they mean we can? We can what? Fuck?"

Roman winked to his neighbour.

"Just think of any major construction site in the country," he suggested, "what posters do you see all over the place?"

"O.K., I've got it now," the man laughed briefly, "A Pole Can! isn't it?"

Konrad did not join the conversation. As he looked at the poster his thoughts flashed back to the early seventies, the beginning of the Gierek era. He remembered a day, a few years before when he and Klara had visited the newly opened Warsaw Central railroad station. The large hall had a posh marble floor. They had climbed a set of wide stairs and entered the station's cafeteria.

A West-German made conveyor belt ran around the restaurant collecting dirty dishes. They sat down near the window which overlooked the two-tiered driveway in front. Below, red and white Berliet buses from France periodically entered and left the terminal.

Back then, few people bothered to question the government's indiscriminate purchases of Western licences and equipment. It was a part of the modernization of the Polish economy promised by First Secretary Edward Gierek in 1970. Konrad smiled bitterly. Just the day before, on his way to the garrison, he had met Roman at the same cafeteria. It was offering only three dishes from its once lavish menu and the West-German conveyor belt had long since been out of order. Beyond the window, they had watched a meatline form in front of a store that wasn't due to open for at least two hours. Yet, right above the escalators that led to underground platforms, there was a large billboard displaying the country's new industrial plants and the Warsaw Central itself. "A Pole Can," the red tall letters on the sign read.

"Are you with us Konrad?" Roman turned his smiling face to him, "Look!"

Two officers quietly mounted the podium. One, a colonel in his early fifties, had reddish hair, a light freckled complexion and smiled continuously. He was accompanied by a much younger officer with a heavier frame and crude facial features. Konrad immediately recognized a captain who caught him in front of the barracks that morning.

"My name is Marek Gapa," the colonel said. "As a commander of the 17th Infantry Regiment in the Military District of Warsaw, I welcome you to the ranks of the People's Armed Forces. Our Regiment has an excellent record in our Military District." He paused and surveyed his audience.

"Two years ago," he continued, "we had the opportunity of meeting First Secretary Edward Gierek when he visited the garrison."

"Lucky you," Roman commented quietly.

"The First Secretary was very impressed by what he saw here, and," the colonel picked up a single sheet of paper from the table, "I have kept a copy of a speech he delivered at our casino club back then. Today, I am going to read you a short excerpt that specifically refers to you, the cadets of the School of Officers for Reserve." The colonel coughed and cleared his throat.

"Dear comrades, officers - commissioned and non-commissioned, Party members and non-Party members, my friends. I would like to congratulate you on the exceptional order and enthusiasm I witnessed in your garrison. It is you who provide us with a feeling of security, you defend our country against the greed and enmity of the reactionary circles of the capitalist world. Thanks to you, we all can build the new, rich, industrialized and happy Poland; the Second Poland as we call it. You also train Poland's young engineers, the SOR cadets, so that they will become highly qualified and ideologically engaged officers of the reserve, that the modern army, the modern socialist society need."

Both Roman and Konrad tried to suppress laughter. Many other draftees were going through the same ordeal, some simply yawned. The colonel seemed oblivious to his audience's reaction.

"Dear cadets," he continued warmly. "You yourself heard the First Secretary's simple and outspoken words. On your second day with us, I wish you the best results in your military training. It will benefit not only you but also the socialist motherland of all Poles, the Polish People's Republic. And now..." he continued with a smile, "I am honoured to introduce you to the commander of Company Zero, one of the most able young commanding officers of our regiment, Captain engineer Henryk Gugawa."

The colonel sat down and at precisely the same moment, Gugawa anxiously shot up from his seat. Konrad eyed the upright figure closely. The officer looked distinctly uncomfortable, even embarrassed. The cadets chatted among themselves and waited for him to begin.

"The show is going to take ages," Roman remarked and yawned loudly, "Our captain must be very shy."

"I doubt it, he was a real bastard with me this morning."

"That was just with you," Roman remarked sarcastically, "Now the poor man is facing his entire company and a superior."

"Soldiers," the captain announced finally. "I am your commander. As your commander I am responsible for the order ON the company. I want to be well understood. ON the company must be neat and orderly. No mess, no breaking of regulations..."

The colonel rose from his seat behind and whispered in the captains ear. Most of what he said was picked up by the microphone on the podium. "Why don't you tell the cadets about the various servicemen they will encounter here. Not that I underestimate the importance of the order ON the company... platoon commanders will be filling them in on those details, though..."

Captain Gugawa nodded dumbly and turned his face to the cadets once again. The colonel motioned him to begin and the captain took a long, deep breath.

19

"Cadets, in this regiment there are a number of different types of servicemen. First of all, there are people like myself, career military personnel - we are usually called army cadre. Next, there are the academy cadets in ranks ranging from corporal to sergeant. They wear white bordered epaulets, not white and red like yours. They came here from another regiment, a professional Officer Academy. They will remain your platoon commander aides until you take the oath. Not only will their proper military virtues be an example to you, the cadets themselves will benefit from this valuable command experience."

"Now he's never going to shut up, what a speaker he is," Roman whispered to Konrad.

"I would like to stress," Gugawa continued clearly and with confidence, "that you must show respect to academy cadets and obey their orders. I mention this, because in the past some SOR's didn't want to follow academy cadets' commands. This must not occur again! When the academy cadets graduate, they will become engineers as you are. And they enjoy higher ranks than you do, now." Gugawa sat down and engaged in a quiet conversation with colonel Gapa.

"Why is he bothering to tell us this?"Konrad nudged Roman with his shoulder.

"There must have been some friction between SOR cadets and 'puddings' in the past."

"Puddings?"

"Academy cadets. That's their nickname. All of national servicemen call them that."

Konrad smiled. "Are puddings really going to be engineers?"

"Shit, no; engineer-commanders. Their degrees won't be recognized by any civilian university or industry. You must admit, though, that engineer-commander sounds nice. It probably helps the army lure away high school graduates that failed their university enrollment exams."

Gugawa finished talking with the colonel and stood up. "Finally," he continued after clearing his throat, "there is the regular draftee or the national serviceman. He serves his two-year draft term only, and will never become a commissioned officer. Some, however, have higher ranks than you and therefore you must honour them with a salute, in the same way you do an academy cadet or someone like myself. Until you are promoted, you have the lowest rank of all, hence you have to salute everyone."

It was a dull, long morning and the 'second breakfast' issued at 11 o'clock hardly improved Konrad's mood. Seated at the yellow laminate top table in the canteen, he looked down disdainfully at the meager meal in front of him. A tough, two-day old bun sat alone, a small island, in the middle of his plastic plate. In addition, each squad was allotted a single bowl of strawberry jam. Konrad grabbed a clumsy spoon and slathered his share of the sweet spread on his hard roll. He gnawed through it, and methodically licked the sticky substance from his fingers. He could still feel a trace of its persistent stickiness and wiped the seat of his pants brusquely. There was no washroom in the canteen and he headed outside to clean his hands in the snow.

Two national servicemen loitered in the deserted square in front of the canteen. They were sharing a cigarette and some talk.

One of them pulled a long, coloured measuring tape from his pocket. He cut a small portion off the end of the tape with a knife and handed it proudly to his younger friend. "Look Cat[4]. I've got only 101 days left. 101 days and I'll be a free civilian again. Can you believe it?"

Hidden behind the door Konrad smiled to himself. He had been told about this special measuring device known as 'fala' or 'wave'. As a draftees' discharge day approached, each usually bought himself a 150 centimetre long tape measure. The 'falas' were often skillfully painted and inscribed with witty poems praising civilian life, girls and booze and were full of ridicule for career servicemen. Officers maintained that 'falas' violated the principle of pride of serving the socialist motherland and the colourful tapes were confiscated whenever found. The very next day they appeared in the barracks again.

Hand-painted maps and glossy placards decorated the walls of the garrison's Hall of Tradition. Konrad, Roman and the rest of the first platoon of Company Zero sat behind desks arranged in even rows like a vegetable patch. Corporal Kowalski placed small booklets in their hands.

"These are the People's Army Regulations," he said. "You must go through the chapter on tradition. After that, the lieutenant will begin your political training. I'll be back in 40 minutes. You had better be quiet while I am gone," he warned, "Colonel Gapa's office is right across the hall." Kowalski saluted and strode out of the room in his usual way. Konrad sighed. The booklet lay unopened on top of his desk. He noticed that Roman was casually flipping through his, but wasn't bothering to read anything.

"Have you noticed the decor of this place?" Konrad remarked, pointing to the large map to the left of their desk. Battle lines in 1939 were depicted in red and blue on the map. He shook his head and shrugged when he saw that the Polish forces were marked by red arrows and their attackers, the Germans, in blue. The colour red for Poland seemed ridiculous to him. We weren't Communist then, he thought stubbornly.

There was something else about the map that puzzled him even more. Its eastern side was free of arrows, as if nothing had happened there.

"Roman," he said pointing to the empty section of the map. "It looks as though they've neglected to remember that Poland still had her eastern half, back in 1939."

Roman glanced at the map and nodded. Then he looked back at Konrad and smiled mischievously.

"It will take them more than forging a map to brainwash this platoon, however," he said quietly. "Of course if you help me..."

Konrad smiled widely. "A lecture... like in the high school?" he asked.

"Exactly."

Roman sat up in his chair.

"My friend," he said loudly, raising his eyebrows and wrinkling his forehead. "Your idea of Polish history is incorrect, it is distorted." Everybody in the room turned his head toward them. Konrad began laughing hysterically

---

4. Cat - a nickname given by more senior national servicemen to junior draftees.

21

as Roman paused for a moment and gave him a stern glance. "I am sure you have heard," Roman got up and stood in the middle of the room, "that Poland was invaded by the Nazis on September 1, 1939. That is of course correct," he turned to the rest of the class. "But," he continued, "I bet that this man was also told that the Russians invaded Poland's eastern provinces on September 17, that same year according to the Ribbentrop–Molotov Pact, that hundreds of thousands of Polish officers and civilians were deported and put in the concentration camps in the USSR. And this..." he faced the class again, "this is an abominable lie."

Some cadets laughed. They saw a caricature of a Polish Communist before them. Roman's voice and mannerism closely mimicked many of the country's leaders who spoke regularly on television and radio.

"I also suspect, that he has been misinformed about the slaughter of thousands of Polish officers in the Katyń forest, and I wouldn't be surprised if he, like many other Poles I met, blamed the Soviet Army for that atrocity." Roman then lifted his index finger and shook it in Konrad's face. "Nothing could be more erroneous," he insisted, "Nothing. Just look at this map. Can you see anything in the East? No, you can't because nothing happened there in 1939. Poland was attacked by the Germans that year, that is all."

"But dear leader," Konrad said mockingly, pointing in Roman's direction, "I don't understand. I thought that two hundred thousand Polish soldiers and civilians left the USSR with General Anders in 1942. Where, the hell, did all of them come from?" Roman raised his eyebrows and pursed his lips. "Well, many of them fled their country and sought refuge in the USSR. The Soviet Union moved peacefully into the east part of Poland to protect its predominantly Ukrainian and Belorussian population against the Nazis. The Polish army, which had been formed in the USSR, was expected to fight the Germans alongside their hosts and benefactors, but instead of doing that, the notorious General Anders ordered his men to withdraw from the Soviet Union to Iran. Fortunately," he continued facing the class, "some soldiers, the true patriots, stayed." Roman turned and pointed to another map, dated 1943. It showed Poland sadly shrunken to its postwar size.

"Look," Roman said. "With the help of the true Polish military men, the invincible Soviet Army liberated Poland's territory. They stood behind their comrades and helped them make the triumphant march to Berlin in 1945."

"Hurrah," Konrad murmured half-heartedly and a few other cadets clapped their hands briefly. Roman looked at his audience and concluded that the mood for jokes simply wasn't there. The room turned quiet as they reluctantly started to read the regulations.

Konrad still surveyed the maps on the Hall of Tradition's walls, 1939, 1943 and 1945, seemed to be the only dates the Communists wanted the Poles to remember. "The fraternal aid from the USSR helped the Poles to defeat the Germans in Berlin," one of the map's slogans read. At that moment he felt relief, genuine relief, because he knew more.

Konrad could still remember the sound and tone of his grandfather's voice as he told the story.

... It was second half of September, 1939. Most of the Polish troops were fighting the Nazis. Other units, including my regiment, were ordered to move into Lithuanian territory after offering some resistance to the Soviets. The Polish government hoped to use the large number of fresh outfits on the Western Front to defend the capital from the Germans. That remained the top priority.

The Soviets came early in the morning and within hours of their arrival in Wilno, all military and public buildings had been taken over by the Red Army. The NKVD, that was the KGB back then, made their headquarters in the huge, classically-designed building which housed the Wilno District Court. It was not far from Łukiszki prison.

About two weeks later, our government, which had evacuated to Rumania, ordered all Polish outfits to disband and form the underground. It was then that I managed to escape from the Lithuanian camp, and I returned home to Wilno.

The following night, two officers wearing navy-blue-ringed caps pounded on the front door of our house with what sounded like the grips of their pistols. I put my clothes on quickly. Before I left I kissed your father and your uncle Bib who were still in bed sleeping, and then moved towards the door. Julia embraced me and we stood like that for several seconds before one of the men pulled her away and pushed me down the porch stairs.

I was taken to an inquiry room in the District Court building. It was almost empty except for a desk in the far corner and a lone chair in the middle. They seated me in this chair, tied my wrists with a piece of rope and pointed a desk lamp straight in my face.

I sat there alone, trying to avoid the glare in my eyes.

"Noo gospodin powkovnik, pogovorim," I heard a voice behind me say. Translated that means: 'Let's talk Mr. Colonel... sir...' The voice was deep and bore an unmistakable tone of ridicule and irony. A minute later, he faced me - a tall, blond man, with unusually heavy-set shoulders. He wore a loose blouse, without epaulets, but I could tell he was a captain from the insignia pin on his collar. A long barrelled TT-pistol dangled in the shiny leather holster suspended from his belt. The man's left cheek was marked with a long scar. Only a saber, Konrad, could have left a scar like that... I also noticed that another soldier, this one was shorter, with dark hair and narrow, slanted eyes, had seated himself down at the desk in front of me. He was filling out a sheet of paper.

They started off by asking me about my superiors. I told them that I knew nothing. The tall captain approached me, playing with the gun at his side. 'You don't know anything?,' he remarked with a twisted smile. 'Why don't we talk about your achievements then.' When I glanced up at him, my eyes met a malicious stare.

Then he asked me why I had been involved in fighting against the USSR in 1920. I told him, quite honestly, that I fought because there was a war. 'But if you had refused to fight, if all of your fellow officers had done that,' he said, 'there would not have been a war. Am I right?'

I told him that what he was describing was desertion, and that the penalty for that crime in any army was death. I watched the officer. His scar turned purple and became even more obvious on his pale face. He began walking around my chair. By that time, he was holding his gun by the barrel and swinging it left and right. Then he smiled at me once more - a long, foul grin.

'Well, Lord Pollack, back in 1920 you obviously thought that you had already defeated the Soviet Union.'

The lamp was so bright that it was beginning to blind me. I had to close my eyes for a few seconds but when I did that I felt a creeping sensation in my bones - a foreboding. I sensed that our conversation was becoming more heated, that something was definitely going to happen soon. The officer's antagonism frightened me. He was like a wild, unpredictable creature. I was convinced that I wouldn't leave that room alive, but I told myself that whatever happened, I had to endure it with dignity. He would not triumph over me completely.

The blond, athletically-built devil confronted me again. The gun was in his right hand.

'I got this near Warsaw...' he hissed, pointing towards his scar. 'When your fucking marshal Piłsudski and his army repulsed our brave troops in 1920, you never thought that we would be back. But we are,' he said, 'and where are your soldiers now? Where is your Piłsudski and his war machine? Where is your famous cavalry, Mr. Pollack?' His hatred burned me - it seared my flesh, but I held his gaze.

'Where is your Polish army, you son-of-a-bitch?' he shouted again. 'The Germans have decimated your military and we'll finish you off. No more Poland, Mr. Pollack. That bastard of Versailles Treaty is dead - forever.'

Konrad, you can't imagine how I felt then. I tried to jump of my chair, but the ropes around my hands wouldn't give. I became hysterical. 'She is not dead,' I screamed. 'Poland is not lost yet!'

I crumpled to the ground, the chair on top of me, after the third blow. I remember feeling something in my mouth and spitting it out. Two of my teeth fell on the floor.

But that wasn't the end of their fun. The captain and his aide kicked me furiously, in the stomach and mouth. When I think back to it now, I can only remember that at a certain point the room started to whirl around me. Soon after, everything was quiet and dark.

When I regained consciousness, I found myself in a dim cell along with two other officers from my regiment. I remember trying to talk to them, but I couldn't utter a word - a pink foam was the only thing to come out of my mouth.

A few minutes later, a guard came into the cell. He splashed all of us with icy water from a bucket and ordered us out. Just before dawn, they forced us to walk through the town square and down to Łukiszki prison. About sixty of us, for the most part Polish officers, were escorted by two platoons of NKVD armed with submachine guns and pistols. The walk seemed to last for ages. We passed a nearby hospital and then walked through the prison gate. They then hoarded us into an enormous hall. Even today I remember its huge, barrel-vaulted ceiling.

From there, they took me through a labyrinth of steps and corridors to my cell. While I sat there, I learned that I had been found guilty of being 'an enemy of the people' and sentenced to eight years in a labour camp.

I ended up spending two months in the prison. It was only bearable because your grandmother was allowed to come and see me a few times, and would send in food every day. From the small window in my cell, I could see women lining up at the guardhouse with food parcels every day. This was very convenient for the Soviets. By allowing families to bring food, it cost them nothing to keep us there.

But then, one night, at two o'clock in the morning, they took us out of the prison and we were hoarded into freight cars. They fed us potatoes in iron bowls and gave us wooden spoons to eat them with. The potatoes had been boiled God knows when, were cold, semi-rotten and stank like hell. I left my food and began scratching my name and address on my spoon with a nail. I wrote one last thing on it, 'eight years,' and then I tossed the spoon out of the train by pushing it through the barbed wire which covered the window-like openings in the ceiling of the freight car. Many of my fellow soldiers did the same thing. I learned later that a woman had found the spoon and delivered it to your grandmother.

I have to admit that I wasn't very experienced when it came to handling Russian soldiers then. For some reason, once we were out of that prison, I let my guard down. The first night, I had noticed a peaked-looking guard with an annoying dry cough, eyeing my new boots with interest. He even told me that he liked them and offered to buy them, but I refused. He didn't seem to take much notice of me after that, or so I thought.

The second night, I took the boots off and fell asleep. When I woke up the next morning and reached for them, they were gone. Then I looked at the guard's feet. He was sporting my new boots, the boots that he had tried to buy from me! I screamed and demanded that he give them back. His response was a number of hard kicks to my belly. I knew that without boots I wouldn't last long. Fortunately, your grandmother managed to pack another pair of boots in the bag on which I slept. I put them on and never took them off while on the train...

... When the Germans violated the 'friendship treaty' in 1941 and attacked the USSR, the Polish government in exile in London resumed diplomatic relations with the Russians. The envoys from Britain came to Moscow and soon after an agreement between Polish Premier General Sikorski and Stalin was reached. This was all going on while I was in the labour camp in Vorkuta.

The camp was located beside a rock quarry. I remember that they used to feed us two meals a day - usually two bowls of salty oatmeal soup, and two measly slices of hard, brown bread. The work was difficult. We had to make our way down into a rocky canyon with a wheelbarrow and axe. Our days were spent quarrying the rock by hand and carrying it up the hill, making sure that our rusty wheelbarrows were well filled. The target was twenty loads a day, but I remember all too well having to bring three or more extra loads up the hill because my wheelbarrow was not always full enough. The guard at the top never neglected his duties... I wasn't all that strong back then either, Konrad. It was hard on me and often my younger colleagues would help me push the damned wheelbarrow up the narrow trail.

One day, when I was hauling my load of stones up the path, I heard a guard shouting. We lined up side-by-side in front of him. I think that most of us were expecting a firing squad to be there. But instead, the guard said, 'Well, you're free to go now. You aren't our prisoners any longer, you are our allies. You will be sent to join the Polish army and we'll fight the Nazis together.'

I was stunned. They just let us go. Before I knew it, we were boarding a freight train heading south. It took us two weeks to get to the assembly area in Kirgiziya. General Anders arrived a few days later.

The Russians supplied us with almost everything. We were issued Polish uniforms, probably the same ones that they took in 1939 when they had invaded us. There were enough of those to go around, but not arms. Luckily, because I was a Lt. colonel, I received a pistol, but most of the soldiers got nothing at all.

The situation was so bad that General Anders confronted the Soviets. He made it clear that if we didn't get arms, we wouldn't be fighting the Germans with them.

At about the same time, four of their spies were spotted inside our camp and Anders ordered them to be executed.

The situation wasn't good. There we were, in the USSR, former prisoners dressed in Polish uniforms with no weapons - troops without arms...

Konrad knew the rest of the story. Anders ordered his army to leave the USSR and they went on to fight battles in Italy and Africa, using arms supplied by the British. They battled for the Western cause.

When the mass grave of Polish POW's, murdered by the Russian NKVD, was discovered in Katyń forest, the Soviets broke off diplomatic relations with Polish government in London.

"Didn't some Poles, fight with the Soviets, after Anders left?" he had once asked Robert. "Who were they?"

"By and large, they were soldier-prisoners just like us. I was in the camp in Vorkuta near the White Sea and that meant that it didn't take me all that long to reach the assembly area. But some of the Poles were in labour camps as far away as Sakhalin on the Pacific coast. They just didn't make it back in time to leave the USSR with us. They grouped in Sielce on Oka and were organized into what is now known as the People's Polish Army. Not many of those men were officers, but they were Poles. That second army went straight back to Poland. On their way, they were decimated by the Germans and brainwashed by Soviet political officers... "

Roman interrupted Konrad's roving daydreams with a light tap on his shoulder. "You had better open the book," he reminded him. "The regulations are waiting for you, and Zabłocki is expected soon."

Konrad quickly opened the booklet, but just reading the first paragraph made him squirm. 'The military tradition is an important factor in the upbringing of a conscious soldier of the People's Armed Forces. This tradition comes from the fraternity in arms between the Polish Army and the invincible army of the Union of Soviet Socialist Republics.'

"Get up! Attention!" corporal Kowalski yelled.

The soldier took three large strides, assumed the attention position and reported:

"Comrade Lieutenant, corporal Kowalski reports that the first platoon is ready for political training. All soldiers present."

"Thank you, comrade corporal," the short, corpulent Zabłocki replied. "At ease!"

The lieutenant then turned his rather disproportionate torso towards the class. His puffy face was marked with a wide grin.

"Nice report, wasn't it comrades?" he said. "It will take you some time before you are able to report as well as the comrade corporal just did. Don't worry though, we are all here to help you become great soldiers." He smiled again in their direction.

"Well, comrades engineers. I think I should introduce myself. You know my rank, or at least you should have spotted it," he said. "My name is Włodzimierz Zabłocki. I am the assistant company commander for political affairs. "

The classroom fell into a deep, ominous silence.

"First of all," he said as he paced round the desk in the front of the room, "you should forget that you are engineers." He paused. "No, no, don't worry comrades. You will return to your degrees and titles eventually. But for training purposes, just forget about it. Comrade Gugawa is an engineer. You can talk to him about any technical problem you may face. If anything is wrong with the hardware, if the Kalashnikov should seize, Gugawa will help you. Should a tank fail to function properly, Gugawa will fix it."

Konrad sat back in his chair. He and Roman looked at each other and sighed.

"I am not an engineer," Zabłocki continued. "I am a political officer. That is something else comrades, isn't it?"

The room remained fixed in its silent trance.

"My profession? A lawyer. I completed three years of law at the University of Wrocław before I joined the army. I managed to finish my remaining year at the legal faculty at the Staff College and, as you can see, I remained in the army. One of my duties here is to integrate your political and historical knowledge. As one might expect, our draftees come from a variety of backgrounds. Before you can take the oath, everyone must meet the high standards of consciousness required by the People's Armed Forces. I do hope that you will cooperate during our training". He paused. "You will, won't you?"

There was no response from the class.

"Well dear, comrades, you certainly must be asking yourself a fundamental question right now. That is: why am I here? I suppose that in civilian terms you are officers of our industry. You may wonder, why you were taken out of your offices, factories and away from your families. Well, comrades, the answer is simpler than you suspect. You are here to become officers of the People's Armed Forces. That is fair enough, isn't it? But what does it mean to be an officer? That is the question, as Hamlet says."

The lieutenant glanced quickly through the room, and Konrad sensed that he was almost expecting a bit of laughter following his Shakespearean quotation, but the classroom remained more quiet than ever.

"Well," Zabłocki said, as he took a deep breath and readied himself for more persuasion, "the basic difference between a civilian and a soldier is that the latter must obey orders. Right now you have got to obey orders." He paused and looked squarely at the cadets. "But that, is not our real goal, comrades. Our objective is something more than that, something more tangible and everlasting."

The word 'everlasting' surprised Konrad. It reminded him of his Sunday mornings in church, but as far as he knew, religion had been thoroughly weeded out of the army.

"What will last forever," Zabłocki declared in a solemn voice, "is your obedience to the people's motherland. Yes, comrades, this must last. I ask you to consider this: who gave you your jobs? The people's motherland did. Who paid for your university training? The people's motherland again. And, who pays for your socialized medicine? The people's motherland does."

Konrad and Roman looked at each other in utter disgust.

"You'd better believe it," Roman whispered in his friend's ear.

"However," lieutenant Zabłocki continued, "our socialist Poland did not emerge overnight. You should realize that, comrades. For hundreds of years, the working class has struggled against extortionists, against the gentry and the capitalists. As you know, the struggle was not really successful until the working class established its own party. It was the Party that made the dream come true. The Party," he said, slowing down a bit, "is a force that successfully directs our socialist motherland towards its ever greater achievements. But it is not an easy path. There have often been obstacles, but the Party has always managed to remove distortions and, when necessary, get rid of individuals who were enemies of the people... The next question to consider then, comrades, is this: why was the Party able to resist the enormous pressures from both inside and outside class enemies?"

Konrad sat quietly and waited for Zabłocki to answer his own rhetorical question. Instead, he heard a voice from the back of the room. It belonged to Janek Wytwicki, the cadet who had called sergeant Bochan 'comrade' just the day before. Wytwicki stood up and calmly asked for permission to speak. It was obvious to everyone in the room that the officer was not pleased by the sudden interruption. Zabłocki's sharp eyes swept through the hall, resting for a second on Konrad then behind him to the short private. Wytwicki had followed the People's Army rules. Zabłocki had no choice but to agree to his request.

"Yes, you may ask a question Wytwicki," he replied impatiently.

"Will comrade lieutenant elaborate on the idea of inside and outside class enemies. I think we should understand these terms before you go into more detail..."

"Very well, Wytwicki. You can sit down now," Zabłocki said, forcing a smile on is face. He circled around his desk methodically. "I have been asked a question and I will answer it promptly. However, this lecture was meant to spell out the objective of political training. Private Wytwicki's question is somewhat out of context." The lieutenant's eyes darted from row to row.

"Starting tomorrow, we will go through the entire history of Poland from 1914 to 1978. I think this is an important facet of your training. I am sure many of you might have been exposed to some version of history outside of school. Am I right?"

Konrad sat frozen in his chair. Hatred for the political officer began swelling inside his breast. He turned away and gazed intently on the shiny wooden floor.

"So, as I said, I will be teaching you the true history of this country during the next four weeks. You must understand it if you want to become conscious soldiers of the People's Armed Forces." Zabłocki looked once more at Janek Wytwicki. "As for the question about inside and outside class enemies, let's begin by examining the latter term." He circled his desk once more. "Outside class enemies were of course capitalists and those people who supported them before and during World War Two. All of the pre-war bureaucracy, including the army and police forces, were outside class enemies of the working class. During and after the war, outside class enemies were involved with the Home Army and the Polish government in London. This group also includes Polish troops who fought in the West. No matter how bravely they fought, they were in fact serving the enemies of the people."

Konrad felt his face harden with strain and anger as Zabłocki's voice floated through the hall. Roman grimaced sourly.

"Of course outside class enemies still exist. Even after thirty four years of Socialism in Poland, we still find individuals who would befriend the United States before the USSR. If they had their way, history would be turned back, and the crown placed once again on the head of our Polish eagle. Now there are very few outside enemies still living and as the old generation dies out, there will be even less."

Konrad saw his grandfather's wooden coffin being carried slowly into the graveyard. He heard the priest's prayer over the crowd of mourners. His hatred for Zabłocki blossomed. He wished he could punch him, just one fast blow. The thought made him grin openly.

"Well, comrades, I think that I have clarified the term 'outside class enemy' successfully. What do you think, Wytwicki? "

The private murmured a quiet "Yes, comrade lieutenant."

"All right. Let's turn now to inside class enemies. I should emphasize at this point that the entire issue is very complex but very important. Inside class enemies are individuals 'in' the Party who pretend to be true Communists. They are really enemies of the working class. An example? The Party was purged of Zionists in March, 1968. Before then, these people, these scheming agents of the CIA, pretended to be members in good standing of the Polish United Workers' Party. They caused a great deal of social unrest in the country. Some people associated with Władysław Gomułka could also be put into this category. They were responsible for the riots on the sea-coast in 1970."

Suddenly, Janek Wytwicki jumped out of his seat and began yelling hysterically at Zabłocki. "Comrade lieutenant! When Gomułka was the leader in the 'Sixties, he and his cronies were all touted as true Communists. Now you are saying that they were class enemies?!"

Zabłocki walked quickly down the centre aisle of the hall past Konrad and Roman.

"You have asked me one question already, Wytwicki," he said angrily. "I couldn't question the motivation behind it because you complied with the People's Army regulations. But now, you interrupted your superior without permission. I order you to be quiet now. I am going to ignore your outburst. Our Party, comrades," he continued, "can always rely on the fraternal help of other Communist parties, including the great Leninist Communist Party of the Soviet Union. And, only its proletarian and internationalist character allows our Party to avoid destruction. No matter what happens to the damned world, we can always count on fraternal assistance."

Konrad was relieved when the lunch bell finally rang. Corporal Kowalski issued his customary commands. The cadets began rising out of their chairs when Zabłocki turned to them once again.

"Remember comrades," he said, "if you ever have any personal problem or you find you are having trouble dealing with your conscience, you can come to see me directly. You don't need to notify captain Gugawa or anybody else."

Platoon Commander, lieutenant Suka, visited his soldiers late in the afternoon.

"Well, cadets," he said, pacing around the classroom. "You have one hour to learn a good, patriotic marching song. Read the chapter on singing in the regulations' book so that you will know what to sing and why. Then learn an appropriate song".

The People's Army regulations devote an entire chapter to the practice of singing. According to the dictum, soldiers can sing post-war songs composed by strictly Communist authors. Left-wing partisan songs, dating from World War Two, are also recommended.

Konrad found the chapter depressing. "According to this chapter, we can't sing 'The Red Poppies at Monte Cassino'," he commented to Roman.

"Well," Roman pointed out, "the men in that song died opening up Italy to the British and the Americans. It's not the kind that I would pick to stress the fraternity-in-arms between the USSR and Poland."

Janek Wytwicki walked up to them and placed a single sheet of paper in Konrad's hand.

"Do you have a problem?" he asked. "We'll be singing this," he said, tapping the paper. "I am sure everyone recognizes the melody. Just learn the words."

"I know them already and so does Konrad," Roman said. "My father taught me the First Brigade when I was still in grammar school."

"Good, then you won't need the lyrics," Wytwicki said, grabbing the paper from them. He handed it to the cadets in the back of the room. "You see, Konrad, there's nothing to worry about. Our friend Janek has found a song for us."

The First Brigade was composed and sung by the Legions, the Polish military units formed at the beginning of World War One. It was first sung in 1914 by Legion troops led by Józef Piłsudski against Russia. In 1920, Polish troops under Piłsudski's command managed to defeat the Red Army.

"I don't really think it's a favourite song of our superiors," Konrad said with a chuckle.

"Well," Roman said, leaning back on his chair, "at least, there's the Russian connection that they want so badly."

Corporal Kowalski finally rose from his chair.

"First platoon," he said, striding back and forth in front of them, "Form up."

Beyond the hedge, a platoon of national servicemen was returning from field exercise training. They marched in a neat column with Kalashnikovs resting on their shoulders. Konrad could hear the tapping of their boots on the gravel paths.

"Just watch," Kowalski yelled.

The platoon emerged from the hedge. Konrad heard the corporal heading the detachment let out a loud shout, "Platoon... sing! Three - four!"

At the command "four," the soldiers began to sing - so quietly at first that Konrad could hardly hear the melody. But the chorus quickly became strong and imposing. They interrupted each verse with emphatic pounding on the pavement.

"O.K.," Kowalski shouted above the din, "now, you'll try to follow the example. First platoon - sing, three four!"

For the first time since he had left Warsaw, Konrad felt almost happy. The platoon was singing with confidence and The First Brigade echoed across the yard of the camp as they marched toward the canteen.

"We... the First Brigade...
Soldierly family.
At the pyre... we tossed our fate
Our lives and stakes... at the pyre... at the pyre..."

As he led the detachment through the yard, corporal Kowalski gleamed with satisfaction. Under his command, the new recruits shone.

"Platoon... halt!" Zabłocki yelled as he ran up to the draftees from the opposite side of the yard. "Corporal Kowalski," he shouted, slightly out of breath, "what are these soldiers singing?"

31

"A song, citizen lieutenant," Kowalski answered with astonishment. He seemed to be genuinely shocked by Zabłocki's angry reaction.

"Yes, that's right corporal, it is a song," Zabłocki said. His face was red. "But - tell me what song they are singing!"

"I don't know, comrade lieutenant. This is the first time I have heard it myself."

"Well, Kowalski, it looks as though you need some extra tutoring in politics! After supper, I want you to report to me in my office. Bring private Wytwicki with you."

"Why me?" Wytwicki screamed.

"How dare you interrupt your superior? You will report to me with Kowalski right after supper. Dismissed."

Kowalski saluted and stood at attention until Zabłocki disappeared through the canteen door.

Kowalski called the entire platoon to the empty TV hall that evening. He did not look pleased.

"I am warning you," he said. "If I had known what song you were singing tonight, you can be sure that I would have treated you accordingly. I am not eager to punish you - to order you to crawl under your beds... but I could do just that if I wanted to, and if I do, you have to follow my orders. I am staying in the army for a long time," he said solemnly. "You are not. You will be leaving eventually. But your time here will be a lot more pleasant if you are fair with me. This is only your second day here," he continued. "I've been with the army for three years now. I'll warn you about one thing. The army can do anything to anybody. Some officers are worse than others, though. Make sure that you watch yourselves with the 'Civilian'. Zabłocki is the worst of all."

Roman asked him why Zabłocki had left his civilian university.

"The son-of-a-bitch was kicked out," Kowalski answered in a ridiculing tone of voice.

"Just tell us one more thing," Konrad said quickly. "What is going to happen to Janek Wytwicki?"

"That I don't know but the Civilian is really furious about the mouthy little jerk. If I were you, I'd warn him to keep quiet until Zabłocki calms down."

At that moment, the door squeaked open and cadets from the other platoons herded into the room and sat themselves down around the company's television set. Watching the evening news was another mandatory part of army training.

Polish television was born in the mid 'Fifties. One of the first programs broadcast on a regular basis was called "The TV Daily[5]." It had its heyday after the political thaw of 1956. Back then, it was simply a news program with little political commentary.

By the time Konrad and Roman were old enough to watch it, The T.V. Daily consisted of a lot of propaganda with a small amount of genuine news.

---

5. The TV Daily - the official name of Polish TV News till 1989.

Konrad remembered watching the government's reporters praise the First Secretary of the Party Władysław Gomułka continually. They called him a great and courageous leader. The United States was severely criticized for its role in Vietnam. Anti-Church commentaries also accompanied the news. Konrad had hated the program from the beginning. "I can't stand Gomułka and his T.V. Daily," he confessed to his grandfather one evening.

"The program has gone downhill," Robert acknowledged, "but be easy on Gomułka, Konrad. We owe him a lot."

"But why? Isn't he a Communist?"

"Yes, but at least he is a Polish Communist. He proved that in 1956. That year, in October, the prisons were opened and thousands of people were released. That is when I met your mother's father Jan for the first time." The older man paused for a second to think.

"It was an exciting time," he said with a wistful look in his eyes. "The Stalinist era was finished - gone forever. Everyone in those days talked about freedom... the students, the workers, the school children. Censorship was slackened. Gomułka had control of the Central Committee of the Party. The Committee officially condemned Stalin and began approving reforms. And then..."

Konrad could remember how his grandfather's eyes lit up as he continued his story.

"... Krushchev flew into Warsaw. He wanted to keep an eye on the Central Committee's activities. And do you know what happened? Gomułka met him when he got off the plane and told him to go back home. I heard that he told Krushchev he wasn't welcome."

Gomułka's reputation soared after that. But things went sour quickly. He began taking advantage of his popularity, and slowly the reforms were rolled back one, by one.

The T.V. Daily mirrored the changing political winds. In 1968, it covered the controversial banning of "Dziady"[6], a patriotic drama by poet Adam Mickiewicz. Protests by students and intellectuals followed after the popular 19th Century anti-Russian play was banned.

Soon after, Konrad also witnessed the government's harsh campaign against the Jews on the TV screen. Two years later, the government announced an unexpected 40 to 70 percent price increases for food. Soon after, Poland's Baltic coast erupted with strikes, which twined into riots following brutal intervention by the police.

Prime Minister Józef Cyrankiewicz appeared on the TV Daily. Konrad watched him sternly warn that the government would do whatever was necessary to crush the 'counterrevolution'. By that time, tanks were rolling into Gdańsk, Gdynia and Szczecin. Machine guns seemed to be the best argument...

Konrad watched the new leader of the Party, Edward Gierek, on television a few days later, following the resignation of Gomułka and his administration. Edward Gierek promised that the Party would soon be trusted again by the

---

6. Dziady - "The Forefather's Eve"

33

country's workers. He also promised to embark on a daring modernization program.

Gierek acted quickly and announced a number of reforms. Konrad remembered feeling excited about the new political thaw. "Isn't it great?" he said to his grandfather. "Things are really getting better."

Polish television began broadcasting a new series of programs. There were different faces on the screen, new formats. Konrad watched one program in particular in those days called "The Citizen's Tribune". One week it featured Stefan Olszowski, a member of the politburo. Olszowski spent 45 minutes on the show, answering letters sent in by the general public.

One of the first was sent by a Lenin Shipyard worker from Gdańsk. Olszowski read it out loud for the television audience. "Could you please explain why the people who are responsible for the deaths of scores of innocent people are not in prison for their deeds? On the contrary, many of them are being sent abroad by the government. Must Poland be represented by butchers?"

And Olszowski's answer? Konrad could still remember his carefully guarded words. The politburo member smiled into the camera and said, "Well, we have to take into account the entire career of those in question, their merits and contributions, not just their flaws."

Konrad was stunned. Olszowski smiled and began reading another letter.

"Is that it?" he exclaimed, looking at his grandfather who was sitting beside him. "No more explanations, no responsibility for the corpses on the pavement?"

His grandfather smiled down at him. His face was at the same time, twisted with bitterness.

"A crow will not peck out another crow's eye."

"Konrad, are you sleeping?" Roman asked, elbowing him. "You are not supposed to do that while TV Daily is on."

"I was just daydreaming, and thinking how much the program has changed over the years."

"I think it has gone over the deep end lately. The commentaries can't get much worse," Roman said with a sigh, stretching his legs and putting them on the empty chair in front of him.

"I think you are underestimating our propagandists," Konrad remarked with a brief laugh.

"Cybulski and Dymowski! Shut up, sit up straight, and keep your eyes on the television," lieutenant Suka yelled from the back of the hall.

The figure of the TV Daily reporter Ryszard Kwapień appeared on the screen. As the camera pulled back slowly, he introduced himself. Konrad could see the wheels of an enormous truck in the background.

"Ladies and gentlemen," the reporter said, smiling confidently. "Today we are at one of our country's major construction sites for a celebration. The second stage of Poland's largest steel mill complex, Huta Katowice, has been successfully completed. We can look at this project for proof that 'A Pole Can!'"

The camera pulled back quickly and the journalist pointed to printed placards posted on the side of the truck. In the background, viewers could see shapes of broad, massive buildings. "Now let us move on to the celebration.

We've been joined by a delegation of Soviet government officials, led by the Prime Minister, comrade Aleksei Kosygin."

Six men stood on a decorated podium. The camera focused on one of them, then moved away from the tribune toward a man wrapped in a thick fur coat. He awkwardly tried to unfold a piece of paper. The reporter's voice continued in the background. "Here," he said, "is the true representative of the Polish workers. He is now going to express the working class' strong feelings of fraternity towards our Soviet friends."

The fur clad man walked slowly towards the tribune. He was so short that his face was barely visible behind the speaker's podium. Konrad could see that the man had short, cropped hair, a wide forehead and a long, bulbous nose. A "real" Polish worker, he thought to himself. Everything fits the image, except for the fur coat.

"Dear comrade Kosygin and friends," the man said. "Today, we are here to celebrate the completion of stage two. I am only a simple worker so I don't intend to take up much of your time this afternoon..." the man gazed nervously at the Soviet guests in the audience and then down to his prepared speech. "I am only a simple worker..." he repeated. "Sorry, I've said that already..."

Company Zero burst into laughter.

"Shut up!" lieutenant Suka barked. "The TV Daily isn't over yet."

The camera remained frozen, focusing in closely on the man's face. "I would just like to tell you," he said, "that we, the Polish workers are thankful to our brothers, the Soviet workers, for the effort they put into the manufacture of the machinery we are erecting here. I would also like to thank the great Communist Party of the Soviet Union and its Secretary General, comrade Brezhnev."

Applause thundered through the yard. Polish and Soviet banners waved amidst the snow that was just beginning to fall lightly upon the site.

"And now, dear comrade Kosygin, we would like to sing a song for the absent comrade Brezhnev and please, do convey this song, the song of the Polish working class, to him."

The fur wrapped man began to sing "Sto Lat" (May You Live a Hundred Years), a song used during special occasions to honour celebrities.

Polish television credits began filling the screen as the camera pulled back slowly, displaying a crowd of singing workers at the construction site of Huta Katowice.

Konrad sighed and began rising out of his chair slowly. He felt stiff after sitting so long in one place, and started moving and stretching, one limb at a time. Roman sat motionless in his chair.

"What's wrong with you? I thought you liked the show?" Konrad remarked to him with a bitter chuckle. Roman wore a look of resentment and disgust on his face.

"I don't want to laugh any longer at this, Konrad. Do you know what I'd like to do? I want to puke."

Before taps, the conscripts had some free time. They could do what they wanted, as long as they didn't lie down on their beds which was prohibited. Many of them polished their boots and washed superficially in icy water. They heard that the water was supposed to be heated, but apparently, due to a coal shortage, the command decided that they needed hot water for their weekly baths only. Their superiors only checked their boots, buttons and the length of their hair. The barracks were virtually empty except for Janek Wytwicki. Konrad found him sitting at the end of his bed.

"So, what did Zabłocki tell you?"

The short cadet gave him a wry grin. "He told me a little story. He explained how he became an officer."

"Well, aren't you going to tell it to me?"

"O.K., I don't really think he tries to hide it. In a way, he actually seems proud of it. The story without all his rhetoric is quite simple. Zabłocki was indeed a student of law, but he was also a chairman of the ZMS, the Union of Socialist Youth, for his law faculty. According to comrade lieutenant, the dean of the faculty interfered with his political activities and was extremely spiteful towards him. The dean engineered Zabłocki's dismissal from the university."

"When did that happen?"

"After his third year."

Konrad was surprised. Political activists almost always received support from their organizations. Some even helped them improve their academic standing.

"Zabłocki maintained he had been a great student," Wytwicki remarked. He then lit a cigarette and sat down on a bench in front of the lockers.

"All right, what happened next?"

"Well, Zabłocki joined the army but he never forgot the insult. He called the dean a dangerous class enemy."

Konrad heard footsteps at the far end of the barracks and he urged Janek to finish his story quickly.

"... Zabłocki eventually arranged for the dean to be drafted, for routine retraining. The man must have had some cardiac problems because he died during an alarm march. Zabłocki said he lasted only two weeks."

"Not a nice story, but I don't understand what it has to do with you, Janek."

"A lot, I'm afraid," Janek said, in a serious tone of voice. "Comrade lieutenant Zabłocki asked me about the condition of my heart. He says he envisages some marches which, he thinks, will help me understand the army a bit better – 'You Wytwicki,' he told me. 'You may have ten degrees and yet if you don't do what the working class and the Party want, you'll always be a little shit in our society, just a little shit.' "

Konrad sat there and imagined the slight, blond Janek, standing in the Zabłocki's dim office and being terrorized by the officer. He shrugged and got up off the bed. Tapping Janek on the shoulder he tried to reassure him.

"Don't worry. Just keep your mouth shut and everything will be O.K."

After taps, he felt restless. The night hours passed by slowly. Over and over again, the advice he had given Janek Wytwicki dominated his thoughts. Yes, that's very convenient, Konrad, you don't risk much that way. I am against the rhetoric, against the Party, and Roman is too, but what do we do? We limit ourselves to sarcastic comments and jokes in secret. Konrad could sense the approach of dawn, but still rest eluded him. If I hadn't told him to keep his mouth shut and stop being so bold, I would have had to change my own behaviour...

36

CHAPTER 3

Klara stood in the large hall of the local post office. The once majestic building, constructed before the war, was in disrepair, but still boasted dignified high ceilings and marble floors. She faced a grey-haired woman who sat behind the wicket marked "Poste Restante". The woman frowned as she leafed through envelopes, all neatly categorized and separated by cardboard sheets labelled with different letters of the alphabet.

"I'm sorry, miss, but there doesn't seem to be anything here for you," she said to Klara. She smiled at her somewhat apologetically.

"But there must be a letter. My friend called me yesterday. He said he mailed one over three days ago."

"Oh, you impatient young people," the woman muttered. "What is your name again?"

"Klara Kossowska."

The woman began flipping through the letters, this time, much more slowly.

"Here you are," she exclaimed, placing a fat letter in Klara's palm. "You've got your letter after all. It was placed under L not K."

Klara fingered the envelope and profusely thanked the postwoman. She left the building through a set of double brass doors which hadn't been polished for years.

I'm glad the Poste Restante service still exists, Klara thought as she began walking along the snow-covered sidewalk outside. She came to an intersection, and for a second, hesitated. No, I won't go home, she decided. I have to read this letter first. At home I... Klara sighed and continued along the street, passing a number of small shops and restaurants.

On her right, was a small, inconspicuous coffee house. She pulled its familiar door open.

A woman sat in the front cloakroom. She seemed engrossed in a magazine, but smiled when she saw Klara standing there with her coat and hat. After handing them over to her, Klara carefully unfolded her pride, a silver fox collar.

"Will you hang this with my coat? Just thread the hanger through this," she said, pointing to a large safety pin attached to the collar.

I can't stand it, she complained as she gazed at herself in the hall mirror of the café. She struggled to run a comb through her mass of rich, blond hair; it was in total disarray. Whenever I wear a hat it has a mind of its own. She looked through her purse for a lipstick and began to pull it open, but just as quickly, put it back into her purse. My lips and eyes will do, she thought, glancing at the mirror for a final inspection.

Klara was a handsome woman in her early thirties. She had a well shaped face and unmistakably large, deep blue eyes. Her chin and other features were fine, except for her nose which was not entirely straight. It ended with a small ball at its tip, giving her face a slightly jolly look. It was not her favourite facial feature.

She sighed and walked into the café proper. A few tables were occupied by students from the nearby university. She sat herself down at a small table made of mock ebony. It was dark and heavy with a glass top.

"Your usual?" the waitress asked her. "A little black?"

"Yes, a little black as usual," Klara said, smiling up at the woman.

The waitress delivered a small demi-tasse of strong espresso coffee. No milk.

"Is your friend writing an exam now?" the woman asked.

Klara smiled again and let out a small sigh. For five years, she and Konrad had been meeting at the same coffee house and the café staff knew both of them very well.

"No, he has graduated. He's serving in the army now," she revealed sadly.

The waitress patted her on the shoulder with sympathy.

"Oh, you poor souls," she said, and left to clear another table.

Klara sat there, nursing her coffee and watching the other customers chatting amongst themselves. For the first time since Konrad had left for his garrison, she felt really alone, even solitary despite a husband and a daughter.

Her romance with Konrad was really nothing exceptional. He wasn't very handsome, nor did he have much money. She sometimes wondered why she had anything to do with him at all.

And yet, she wanted Konrad badly. Year after year she had led a double life; all her spare time had been his. I wish he was still here going to school, she thought to herself. We didn't spend many nights together, but the days were ours...

She lit a cigarette, laid it down on an ashtray, and pulled the letter out of her purse. Her hands shook slightly as she slowly ripped it open.

"...We had to crawl up a mock battlefield for two hours. Our fatigues got completely wet. Then they made us do target practice. It was so cold that after an hour, I could barely move. My uniform was completely frozen solid.

The next day, I woke up with a very high fever. I guess I must have been pretty sick because I fainted during roll call.

Dear Klara, it is only now that I have time to sit back and think of you..."

Klara stopped reading and took a sip of her coffee. She looked back to the top of the letter to find out when it was written. So, he hadn't bothered to write me for ten days, she thought. She shrugged and returned to the letter.

"... Roman and I are surrounded by a fence nicely decorated with barbed wire... One guy in the fourth platoon wanted to stay out of the compound and go for a beer but his pudding caught him and made him come back immediately. This one pudding is a tall, red-haired guy. He's a bastard when he deals with us and is a perfect example of an obedient soldier when he talks to the 'zlewy' (sinks)..."

What is he talking about? Klara asked herself. He must have had a high fever when he wrote this. She ran through the letter quickly and found dictionary-like definitions of the military slang at the bottom of the first page. She smiled and read:

"Pudding — a military academy cadet. The name was created by the national servicemen here, because the cadets get desserts, mainly pudding, and the regular soldiers don't. Others say that academy cadets' brains look like pudding. No sign of mental activity."

"Zlewy (sinks) - these are career commissioned or non-commissioned officers. I don't really know why they're called 'sinks.' If I had my choice, their nickname would be a lot worse than that."

Klara laughed to herself, glad that Konrad had not lost his sense of humour. It was this sense of humour, along with his at times crazy behaviour, that still attracted her to him. He was impetuous, he often kissed her in public. Sometimes when he was really in a funny mood, he would do silly things like lifting her up and carrying her in his arms across a busy street. She always scolded him and told him to stop, but she knew that she really liked it. He made her feel younger and she was pleased that he was always ready to show his love for her so spontaneously. When she thought deeply about their relationship, she knew that she felt proud to be his first, and his lasting love. She turned to the next page of the letter, and began reading again.

"Generally, I'm glad that I got sick," Konrad wrote. "I think that this is probably the first time I have ever said that. My fever did go down quickly, but right now I am beating the thermometer against my palm so that my temperature still looks high. Antek Zakucki, the draftee-nurse here, showed me how to do it. The best thing about being in the sick ward, is that I don't have to attend the mandatory political training. Believe me, it is at least a hundred times worse than crawling in the snow. The political officer in our company, his name is Lt. Zabłocki... well his rhetoric is just too abominable.

I'm not the only person in our platoon who is missing political classes. Janek Wytwicki, another cadet, is the shortest guy in our company, but I have to admit, the most brave. He challenged and ridiculed Zabłocki to his face, during the first lecture. He's paying dearly for his courage right now. Zabłocki is forcing him to run each day for punishment. That's not really too bad, but he has to run the distances during our political class which lasts only one hour, carrying a fully-packed knapsack, wearing a helmet and sporting an unloaded Kalashnikov. The poor guy has to run five kilometres, report to an officer at a post and then get back to class before Zabłocki is finished talking. Before I got sick, Zabłocki told Janek to do the march all over again because he came in five minutes late...

Klara - you can't imagine how much I miss you right now. I would love to kiss your beautiful nose, embrace you and make love. I want to see you so badly. On Sundays, family and friends are allowed to come to the barracks. I wish you could. Take care of yourself and if you write me a letter, remember that our correspondence will probably be tampered with...

Klara read the last page of the letter over carefully, and stuffed it inside her purse. Just as quickly, she pulled it out again and methodically ripped the paper up into small tatters. His letters can be controlled at my place just as they are in the barracks, she thought smiling bitterly. She took a last sip from her coffee and got out of her chair.

"Come again. Come again... with him," the waitress said. Klara smiled at the girl and went out into the street. She wouldn't be able to visit Konrad at the garrison, she knew that. Sundays belonged to her husband only.

It was an hour after taps. The lights in the sick ward were switched off, and only the long and dreary corridor was dimly illuminated. A large washroom was situated at one end of the hall. It contained a number of cubicles, four washbasins and two mirrors. For some reason, the door to the room had been removed, leaving it open to the hallway. Konrad was washing his hands in one of the basins, facing the glass mirror in front of him. His fleshy complexion reflected the hospital environment - pale and lifeless. Behind his image, he could see a small section of the corridor and the open door of the nurses' room. It housed two beds belonging to two national servicemen, assistant nurses at the sick ward.

He was surprised by voices coming from the room. He knew that one soldier was away on holidays for a week. Konrad decided that it was none of his business anyway and began to walk down the corridor in the direction of his room. He could hear Antek's voice echoing down the deserted hall. "No, I don't want you to stay here tonight!"

Konrad heard a murmur in response. Antek's voice grew louder, "I don't care if he is on duty tonight or not. Please don't come here anymore."

Konrad was about the open the door to his room when he heard a clacking sound against the sterile floor. He turned around sharply and saw a handsome woman clad in a dark-coloured dress, walking in the opposite direction. The mysterious silhouette vanished as swiftly as it had appeared, this time through the exit door.

Antek emerged just as the door slammed shut. He stared at it silently for a few minutes and then turned to go back into his room. He stopped when he saw Konrad, standing there in the hall.

Konrad smiled at him nervously. "I didn't hear or see anything. I was just in the washroom cleaning up."

His friend laughed wildly. "Don't worry. Why don't you come to my room for a nightcap?"

Konrad looked enviously around his friend's room. It was more like an apartment than an army barrack. The walls were covered with colourful photographs of the Rolling Stones, Elvis Presley and other stars. A bottle of Stolitshnaya vodka and a pack of Marlboro cigarettes sat on a small table near Antek's bed. Antek smiled when he saw Konrad's reaction.

"To serve at a sick ward is probably the best posting you can find in the army," he admitted.

He motioned Konrad to sit down and proceeded to pour some vodka and coke into a glass.

"To your health, cadet private," he said, laughing and grinning. "I wish you a prompt discharge."

Konrad sipped the drink slowly. He wasn't particularly fond of Russian vodkas. They were often poorly purified and they always gave him a rotten hangover. Antek quickly read his thoughts.

"I'm sorry, I sometimes have Polish vodka, but this is what she brought tonight," he explained, and passed a pack of cigarettes over to Konrad.

"...she is the wife of a 'sink' in our regiment," Antek explained, with a shrug. He looked almost more puzzled than proud of himself. "I have often wondered why the women here are so man-hungry, quite a few of them have passed through my bed during the past two years."

Konrad took a long drink and paused. "I don't really know anything about this military society," he conceded. "My grandfather was a lieutenant colonel but that was before the war. I'm pretty sure that nothing like that ever happened. My grandmother was a perfect wife, she and my grandfather attended balls at the garrison casino, went to church on Sundays. Things seem to be a bit different now..."

"A bit different? Your grandfather was in an army that was supposed to defend the country against the enemy. This army is allied with an enemy or, one could say, 'a dependable friend'. Nobody goes to church either."

The two men quickly downed another glass of coke and vodka.

"I think," Antek said suddenly, "that the women are so loose here because we, the soldiers, are only around for a short period of time. That way there are no ties, no shame. We come and go. Once we've left, they forget about us and others come to take our place."

When lieutenant Zabłocki was satisfied with his rendition of Poland's history, he turned his attention to the oath that all the draftees would be required to take forty days after joining the regiment.

During one of their classes he said, "In 1943, scores of the best Soviet officers joined the newly formed first division of Polish People's Army in the USSR. They schooled the Poles in battlefield skills and in the ideology that they needed so badly."

Zabłocki then raised his voice. "My friends and comrades, you are expected to take the oath, one similar to that taken by the first division which was truly devoted to Poland's working class. In 1943, the Polish soldiers pledged to be faithful to our allies. There is one thing though, they said, 'so help me God'. Back then, a trace of the old order still existed. You, dear comrades, don't have to mention God in your oath. We are a modern and developed Socialist society."

Zabłocki smiled amiably at the draftees and lowered his voice to a mild and tender tone. "I am sure that most of you have been baptized," he said. "No, don't be ashamed. I was christened myself, my mother did it. It was not my fault, nor is it yours. But dear comrades, you are lucky you don't have to swear to a non-existent God. All you have to do is pledge to be faithful soldiers, faithful to the Polish and Soviet armies and be ready to defend the freedom and happiness of our people..."

Next, Zabłocki asked them all to open their books to the appropriate section and repeat each sentence of the oath after him. "I, a citizen of People's Poland," he began, "joining the ranks of the Polish army, do pledge to be a courageous, good and obedient soldier. I swear to fulfill the orders of my superiors and to be always faithful to the Polish United Workers' Party. I do swear to remain in the fraternal alliance with the Soviet army and other armies in the Warsaw Pact. I will always be ready to work and fight for the benefit and happiness of the people. However, if it should happen that I do not live up to my solemn pledge, may I be punished by the severe hand of the people's justice."

The next day, Janek Wytwicki joined his platoon in the Hall of Regimental Tradition. Zabłocki greeted him with a triumphant grin.

"Well, Wytwicki, did you enjoy your active political training?"

The short private stood at attention in front of him according to the regulations, yet he lifted his eyes up to Zabłocki and looked at him squarely.

"The marches helped me to improve my readiness for battle, yes, but I regret that I missed your lectures. I heard that they were exceptionally good."

Zabłocki's eyes swept through the class. For a second they rested on Roman, then Konrad, and eventually back to Wytwicki. The class was on the verge of breaking out into laughter, and Zabłocki seemed reluctant to begin another verbal duel with the stubborn Wytwicki. Instead, he addressed the draftee in a restrained, calm tone of voice.

"Don't worry, we will be having political lectures after the oath," he said. "Classes will be held only once a week, but your interest in further political knowledge and understanding will be catered to. You may sit down."

It was the night before the oath-taking ceremony, about thirty minutes after taps. Enveloped in quiet darkness, Konrad, Roman and the other cadets slowly settled down to sleep.

A small light shone into the room from the corridor, and cascaded on to the glossy, linoleum floor. Konrad could barely discern the slight murmur of a conversation at the far end of the hall, and a soldier's racking cough. Silence graced the barracks for a moment and Konrad felt sleep slowly overtaking him.

Then a voice filled his ears. It was deep-throated and loud. He thought that it was coming from the hall. "Tomorrow, during the oath... when Gugawa reads the sentence about the Soviet army, we shall not repeat it," the peculiar voice announced. "I repeat, we shall not vow to be faithful to the Soviet army."

The strange voice appealed to their hearts and minds. Despite Zabłocki's determined effort, somebody had decided to fight back. Excitement kept Konrad from sleep as he puzzled who it was.

General Nikolai Ivanovich Lebiedyev was a faithful soldier of the Soviet army. He was genuinely proud of the twenty odd years he had spent as a guardian of his motherland, the last ten years of which had been spent outside of the USSR. He had lived in Czechoslovakia for three years and his commanding skills were used to help quash the counterrevolution in 1968. This task earned him the prestigious rank of colonel. After a two year assignment in East Berlin, he was promoted once again, this time to the rank of general. During the past five years he had served as the commanding officer of a Soviet armoured division in Poland.

Soviet troops were a common sight in Czechoslovakia and East Germany and Lebiedyev was content to be tolerated by the civilians there, but Poland was different. There, the Soviets controlled garrisons in remote areas of the country.

He had never felt very comfortable in the streets of Warsaw or any other Polish city, even though he could speak and understand Polish well. Most of the time he took advantage of his Tshayka limousine and driver. One day though, he happened to be walking through the streets of downtown Warsaw fully dressed in his general's uniform. He passed a mother and child on the sidewalk. 'Who is that big, fat man with the funny cap?' the child squealed. 'His uniform is strange. Is he a fireman?' Lebiedyev turned around quickly, just in time to see the woman scurrying down the street with her child in her arms.

Now, as he walked toward the 17th Regiment's roll-call square, he felt his face turn red as he recalled that day. The Poles never let him forget that he was from the Soviet Union. That was the one thing about them that he hated the most. The Czechs and East Germans might dislike the Russians, but the Poles went a lot further than that. Lebiedyev knew that they looked down on his country with disdain. They call us Asiatic boors, he thought, the nostrils of his nose widening with anger. Ot Polyatshki![7] If we went ahead and stationed sixty more divisions here, they might act a little differently!

Back at home, he continually pushed for an increased Soviet military presence in Poland.

Zabłocki is pleased by the sight below - Company Zero in the ranks with well positioned caps and shiny boots. He smiles openly. That Gugawa is an idiot, he thinks, but at least he knows enough to check their boots thoroughly. He glances quickly at the Kalashnikovs resting on the cadets' breasts and their new dress uniforms.

Kowalski and the other puddings stand in a single row to the right of Konrad's company. It is their last day at the regiment. On both sides of the square, the national servicemen are positioned.

All are solemn as the flag is slowly pulled to the top of the flagpole. The regimental band sputters out the national anthem of Poland. All eyes are on captain Gugawa.

7. Ot Polyatshki! - (Russian) damned Pollacks!

"I, a citizen of People's Poland," he says. The soldiers repeat his words in unison.

"I do swear to remain in the fraternal alliance with the Soviet army..." Gugawa announces. He pauses, and waits for the chorus to echo the phrase. Konrad takes a large gulp of air and purses his lips. The yard is completely silent. One second, two seconds... the silence persists. He is ecstatic. We have done it, he thinks joyfully.

Zabłocki's expression transforms instantly. His eyes widen with disbelief and incredulity. A scowl has replaced the smile on the Soviet general's face.

Captain Gugawa waves his hands violently at the platoon commanders and the academy cadets. They manage to utter a slim chorus and repeat the phrase.

Zabłocki's face reddens and his hands tremble, as Company Zero dutifully completes the rest of the oath.

Black caviar, smoked salmon, tenderloin, pork chops and other delicacies lined the tables in the regimental officers' club. Glasses of Polish vodka and frozen Soviet Stolitshnaya clinked together in celebration of the oath-taking ceremony.

General Lebiedyev though, was not impressed by the festivities. He sat in silence between his Soviet aide and a Polish general. They emptied three glasses of Stolitshnaya, and Lebiedyev lit a strong Soviet Bielomor Kanal cigarette. The Polish general struggled to keep from coughing.

Colonel Gapa took the floor and greeted everyone. He assured the Soviet general that all of the officers and the soldiers of the regiment appreciated his presence at the ceremony. He was about to continue when Lebiedyev stood up.

"Despite all that you are saying, these Pollack soldiers of yours don't like the Soviet Army."

Gapa's face immediately turned red and he was lost for words. The room became deathly quiet. Captain Gugawa held a glass of vodka midway between the table and his mouth and didn't move.

Zabłocki promptly approached the general. With a solemn expression on his face, he requested permission to speak.

"Dear comrade," he said earnestly. "I teach politics at the regiment. I taught the soldiers who took the oath today. It is me, I am solely responsible for the quality of their training. Therefore, dear comrade, please don't blame the other officers here. Colonel Gapa is certainly innocent, I am to blame. The ringleaders will be found and punished and am going to ensure that this never happens again." With that, Zabłocki invited the general to his apartment to speak about the matter in private.

Lebiedyev listened closely to Zabłocki's nearly perfect Russian and smiled for the first time that afternoon.

"Well Zabłocki, you speak very well. I can't refuse your offer."

"Thank you very much, comrade general," Zabłocki replied. He noticed a look of immediate relief on the faces of the other officers in the club.

He excused himself and headed for the nearest phone.

"Hello, Emma? Look, I am bringing a visitor home. I want you to dress nicely. Perhaps that black dress of yours. All black, OK? Don't ask stupid

44

questions, you'll see when I bring the guest over." He hung up the phone and slipped easily back into the celebrations.

Lebiedyev's black limousine stopped in front of Zabłocki's apartment building. The general got out of the car slowly, and then dismissed the driver. "Go and get a bite at the club," he said.

Following Zabłocki, he was led up the apartment stairwell to the second floor. The lieutenant's wife opened the door.

"Please come in, comrade general," she said, greeting them in perfect Russian. Before he could express his surprise she cut him off and added in a calm voice, "I was born in Kransnodar, USSR, comrade general."

Lebiedyev was absolutely bewitched by his hostess He took a seat in a comfortable chair and gazed at his beautiful compatriot with obvious delight.

"Would you like a Stolitshnaya or a Żytnia to drink?" Emma asked him politely.

"Żytnia."

A telephone rang in the adjacent room. Zabłocki took his time answering it. When he returned to the living room, he explained to the general that he was needed at the barracks. "But," the lieutenant added, "if you would like me to stay with you and explain the whole issue of today's unfortunate incident..."

The general shook his head. "Not at all, comrade lieutenant. If you have to go, you must go. When you are available, I will talk to you with pleasure. Now, you can go."

Zabłocki closed the door silently behind him, and headed towards the regimental club.

Emma smiled as she filled Lebiedyev's glass as well as her own. The general inhaled the strong scent of her perfume as she handed him the glass.

"How long have you been here, in Poland?" she asked him.

"Over five years now," the man answered, staring at her lustily. He felt the warmth of the vodka streaming through his veins gently. It was a nice sensation.

The room was quiet and the light dim, as the short winter day signed off for the night.

"Don't you feel somewhat solitary here, comrade Lebiedyev?" she asked, sitting down in the chair facing him. "What city are you from?"

"Moskva," he answered. "I was born and raised there."

"Ah, Moscow," Emma said sighing, "a gorgeous city. Why don't we drink to it," she added, replenishing the general's glass. "Let's drink to our motherland's prosperity, comrade general. Long live the USSR!"

"Long live," the general said, and raised his glass. They emptied them quickly.

The general began surveying the room. On the shelf he noticed a brass Russian samovar.

"Do you like it, comrade general?" she asked pleasantly. "I visited my home last year and decided to bring it back with me."

"Yes, I do like it very much," he answered. "But, must we be so formal? Call me Kolya."

"Good. Call me Emma then," she replied with a smile.

The general couldn't help staring at the woman in front of him. Dressed in black, her eyes and hair matched her clothing. He thought she was beautiful. Like many Russian women, she had high cheekbones, but even that feature was subtle and fine. Emma stood up and walked gracefully across the room to the window looking out to the street. Her large buttocks and breasts seemed to caress the inside of her dress. After a brief glance outside, she walked back and stood in front of the general. She stared squarely into his eyes and lifted one of her legs on to the coffee table in front of him. He could see just a hint of flesh above her black stockings. She mesmerized him and he sat frozen in his chair. Emma looked at him with some annoyance.

"Noo tshevo zhdyosh, Kolya?"[8] she asked.

Lieutenant Zabłocki was promoted to the rank of captain a few short weeks after Company Zero took its oath of allegiance. Gossip and rumours swept through the camp.

"If my wife were Russian, I could easily become a captain too. I've served longer than the Civilian has," lieutenant Suka complained to sergeant Bochan.

Bochan smiled at him knowingly. "You should be promoted on the basis of your merits," he replied, "but a nice wife is also an asset."

There were two schools of opinion about the promotion. Some officers sided with lieutenant Suka and his suspicions about Zabłocki's wife. Others maintained that his advancement had nothing to do with her at all. They pointed to Zabłocki's first promotion in the garrison, from second lieutenant to lieutenant. He was single at the time.

Many officers gnashed their teeth when they talked about that promotion. It had happened two years before, but nobody forgot it. The cold water in the barracks was a constant reminder.

First Secretary Edward Gierek was visiting the regiment. After supper, Zabłocki stood up, toasted Gierek and promptly announced that he and the rest of the officers and soldiers were ready to contribute significantly to the country's modernization program, while at the same time improving their battle readiness. "Dear comrade First Secretary," they remembered Zabłocki saying, "here at the camp, we burn a lot of coal in vain. As soldiers, we should be ready to stay clean and efficient on the battlefield, and there, hot water is not available. I'm sure that I am expressing everybody's feelings here when I tell you, dear comrade Gierek, that we are proposing to give up at least fifty percent of our coal quota. Perhaps it is not much, but please take it, and export it for the benefit of our Socialist motherland of all Poles - the Polish People's Republic."

Gierek seemed touched by the gesture and accepted the gift eagerly, saying how much he appreciated the unit's generosity. The result was a promotion for Zabłocki and cold water in the barracks. Those who suffered most were the junior officers, cadets and draftees. The officer apartment buildings and the Command headquarters had natural gas water heaters.

The oath ceremony over, Konrad and Roman and the rest of Company Zero were suddenly eligible for regular passes. Theoretically, each soldier was supposed to receive a day pass twice a month.

8. " Noo tshevo zhdyosh, Kolya?" - (Russian) "What are you waiting for, Kolya?"

Janek Wytwicki though, seemed doomed to rot in the barracks. The officers singled him out and his requests for leave were always ignored. He didn't seem to care all that much. He knew that his army service was short-lived. "I can survive these six months, or even the entire year, without a pass. If they think I'm going to become a fucking Communist to receive their fucking passes, well they're just fucking wrong!"

All of the draftees looked eagerly to the day when they would be discharged but none more than Janek Wytwicki. One day, he noticed a tall, overly thin soldier cutting a piece off his personal tape measure. "60 days left. Who's got less?" the happy soldier shouted. He tossed the cut portion into the remains of his muddy soup and handed the tray over to the garrison dishwashers. Janek followed him outside.

The next day, he showed Konrad a colourfully painted, custom made tape measure.

"How do you like it?" he asked, with obvious pride. Konrad grabbed the 'fala' and turned it over slowly, running his hand down its length. Numbers in centimetres covered the front. They were overlaid with small sketches showing international flags, bottles of booze and girls. The opposite side was covered with graffiti.

Janek unveiled the 'fala' for the entire company that night, after taps.

"Gentlemen! The 44th day of Company Zero is over," he announced solemnly. A unanimous chorus responded to the declaration with "Fuck it!" Wytwicki eagerly cut the tape. "Only 139 centimetres left. Only 139 days before we leave the regiment," he proclaimed.

"Oh, whore! Too, fucking, long!" the company screamed.

Another day of service for Company Zero was over.

It was a quiet Sunday morning in the garrison. Konrad sat in the canteen munching on a slice of bread and savouring the mug of cocoa that each draftee was allowed once a week.

He had requested a day pass so that he could go to Warsaw to visit his grandmother Julia. After breakfast, lieutenant Suka checked the length of his hair and the cleanliness of his boots. The pass would not be granted unless his uniform met the officer's requirements.

"O.K., Dymowski," he said indolently. He blinked his reddish eyes and then sighed. "This is only a 12 hour pass, remember!" he yelled. Konrad was already beyond the garrison fence. "I know, you bastard, I know," he grumbled.

Many of the soldiers hitch-hiked into Warsaw and most of the time they were lucky with rides. Only five minutes after Konrad had reached the main highway, he heard a truck passing him gear down, and its brakes grind to a stop. A smiling, dark-haired driver leant over, opened the passenger door and beckoned Konrad to get in.

The soldier found himself inside the cabin of an old truck with a dreary, faded interior. He guessed that it was probably made shortly after the war. The controls and the dash were primitive and the only decor was a collection of photographs of nude women the trucker had taped to the ceiling and sides.

"Where are you going?" the stranger asked.

"Warsaw."

"Good. I can get you there. You're lucky today. There aren't many trucks on the road on a Sunday morning."

Konrad offered the man a cigarette and they began to chat. He found out that the trucker had been a draftee at the same garrison ten years before.

"Is that red haired bastard with the freckles still there?" the man asked him, his face hardening with distaste.

"Do you mean colonel Gapa, sir?" Konrad asked.

"Yes, that's him. He was only a major back then, though, Major Marek Gapa, the commander of the Second Battalion of Tank Mechanics," he snarled. "But," he said, his expression becoming more pleasant, "he was my problem and that was a long time ago. By the way, you don't have to call me 'sir.' Bolek's my name." They shook hands warmly.

Konrad liked the look of the ribbon of razor-straight pavement in front of him. He was far away from the crowded barracks. The truck streamed past small settlements separated by bare fields still covered with patches of snow. Despite his initial reluctance, Bolek seemed willing to tell Konrad his story.

"Major Gapa," he began, "he and his fucking son, cost me a lot of nerves. Young Gapa was a pudding and he practiced his commanding technique on our platoon. You know... before we took the oath. He was a damned malicious pudding. He made us crawl almost every day. But what pissed me off more than anything else, was the way he treated one of my friends Karol. He was pretty deaf and I don' t think that he should have been drafted at all. Well, Gapa scolded him like hell. One day he even went as far as calling him a 'deaf swine'. I couldn't stand his gall any longer and I slapped him hard across the face."

The tired, old truck jumped on the uneven pavement. Konrad shrieked when his head hit the roof of the cab.

"Watch it," Bolek said laughing. "This old piece of junk can be dangerous."

"What happened to you after that?" Konrad asked gravely as he rubbed the top of head. "Did they court martial you?"

Bolek produced a wide-mouthed grin.

"No. There weren't many witnesses. Karol wouldn't say anything and Gapa was too ashamed to tell anybody about the incident. And, as you know, it's hard to try an unsworn conscript. According to the regulations, you aren't officially a conscious soldier..."

"So you got away with it? Unbelievable!"

"Well, not really. The younger Gapa left the unit and went back to his officer school not long after we took the oath. But his father took care of me. During the two fucking years I was there, I made it home only once! And I lived so close to Warsaw... Gapa wouldn't even let me go home when my mother was dying - only for the funeral," he said.

The truck crawled past a gray 'Milicja' police car and entered the outskirts of Warsaw. Konrad's heart was warmed by the sight of red streetcars and buses criss-crossing through the city.

"O.K. Konrad," Bolek said, "I have to drop you here. No, don't pay me anything. You need it more than I do."

Konrad thanked him and put the coin back in his pocket as he stepped out of the truck's cab. Once he planted his feet on the sidewalk, he straightened his cap, checked his coat and began walking toward a large cemetery. He had been thinking of visiting his grandfather's grave for weeks.

Nobody rushes at a graveyard. People linger at the small benches near the burial lots and enjoy the flowers blanketing the stone or concrete frames encircling the tombs. Some lay fresh blossoms down and sweep out fallen leaves. Many bring small lamps with them and illuminate the graves with a soft glow. It's just as well that I bought two, he thought as he walked towards Robert's grave. His great-uncle Wiktor lay beside his brother in the same lot.

Konrad stood solemnly in front of the graves for a few moments and then gently laid the carnations down on the tomb. Then he lit the small lamps.

Despite the cold, he appreciated the sunny weather and relished the fresh air. He knelt, took off his military cap and prayed for the souls of the two men.

Konrad had been away on vacation when Robert died, but his uncle Bib had detailed the events that preceded the elderly man's death.

"I remember that Julia was feeling poorly that night and I decided to stay with her," Bib explained. "Eryk came in at about one o'clock in the morning. He was drunk and fell asleep quickly. The Police came for your father at five o'clock. Eryk dressed quickly, kissed Julia good-bye and left with them.

I stood in the hall with your grandfather. As the constable walked by, Robert stopped him and asked why his son was being arrested. The policeman told him that Eryk was accused of petty theft.

Robert began to shake just after Eryk was taken away. He went back into his bedroom and sat in his canvas armchair for over an hour, without saying a word to anyone, not even Julia. The next day, he broke his leg. Three days later, he was gone..."

Konrad had been given the task of delivering Robert's best suit and shoes to the hospital mortuary.

"Don't forget to pin the two small medals on his jacket lapel, Konrad," his grandmother said to him as he took the suit out of the wardrobe. "He cherished them so much."

He nodded and opened the top drawer of his grandfather's dresser. Amidst neatly piled letters and documents, was a small, square box which contained the eight medals that his grandfather had collected during his thirty years of military service. On the top, lay the two miniatures.

His grandfather always wore them on his suit on special occasions. One was a cross with a circular centre suspended on a royal blue ribbon. It was the silver Cross of Virtuti Military, the most important medal granted in pre-war Poland for bravery in the course of battle. The other was a thinner, brass cross decorated with black enamel and hung on a purple and white striped ribbon. Konrad knew that it was the 'Independence Cross', an award granted to those Poles, who like Robert, conspired against the Russian Czar and the Emperors of Austria and Germany before 1914.

He pinned the miniatures on the suit and carefully closed the box. Before he left, he closely embraced Julia and kissed her warmly. She didn't cry, instead, she seemed intent and alert.

"Go now Konrad," she told him. "Get Robert his best suit on time."
The ladies were all dressed in black. Konrad, Bib and his great-uncle
Fryderyk wore suits with a simple black band around the arm. As the priest's
voice droned on, Konrad mulled over his grandfather's death. There was a
sense of unfinished business about the whole thing. It was as if his death was a
terrible mistake, an error of fate, happening so quickly and unexpectedly, he
couldn't quite convince himself that Robert wouldn't be around to tell him
stories or answer his questions. The quiet resonance of Chopin's funeral march
echoed in his ears.

As Konrad, the uniformed cadet, stood up and saluted Robert's grave, he
felt a flood of warm tears flowing across his cheeks. A few people walked past
the saluting soldier but paid little attention.

He saw Roman that night in the barracks and he quickly noticed that his
friend was in a particularly jocular mood. The room carried a slight scent of
beer.

"Where have you been?" he asked Roman. "Did you manage to leave the
compound?"

"We were considering jumping over the fence, but then sergeant Bochan
arrived ON the company. You know Konrad, of all the sinks, he's the best."

Konrad laughed silently to himself, thinking that Roman must have
sampled quite a few beers that evening. He asked the slightly drunken cadet
about the sergeant.

"Well, Bochan said that Suka was an idiot, the way he's so uptight about
marching and the rest of the crap, so he issued garrison passes to all of us. We
spent most of the afternoon sipping beer in the cafeteria by the river." He
smiled. "And what about you, what have you been up to?"

Konrad pulled up a small stool and lit a cigarette.

"I was at the cemetery, visiting my grandfather's grave. Then I went to
see granny Julia and my great-aunt Agata at their apartment."

Roman knew Konrad's family well, and he inquired about Julia's health.

"She can't really move on her own. She's virtually paralyzed for the rest
of her life. Outside of that, she seems all right. She watches TV and has fun
chatting with visitors."

"And Agata?"

"Oh, she hasn't changed. She still grumbles and scolds about the meat
shortages and doesn't have a kind word to say about the Communists, but
she's O.K. too. She liked the tarts I bought for her. She still has a real sweet
tooth," he said, thinking about his great-aunt popping one cake after another
into her mouth.

"Those two ladies are priceless," Roman said quietly. "When you think
about it, I suppose they and your grandfather were really the ones who brought
you up. You owe a lot to them, certainly more than to your parents."

Konrad nodded silently in agreement.

He had trouble sleeping after taps. Roman's words about his relatives
lingered in his mind... "they brought you up, you owe them more..."

Konrad spent part of his childhood in a communal apartment that his
family shared with others. After the war, there was shortage of accommodation.

One room of the joint apartment was occupied by a man. Konrad thought he was crazy and avoided him as much as possible. The other belonged to a married couple. They all shared the kitchen and bathroom. Konrad remembered little of his parents' stay in the apartment. He did recall though, that his father was seldom at home.

Eryk was imprisoned for the first time when Konrad was seven years old. While his father was under investigation, he and Tina were forced to talk to him through a mesh in a tiny wicket in the prison visiting area. Later, after his sentencing, Eryk was able to see them in a small room. Konrad squirmed when he thought about the sharp bristle on his father's cheeks, of the sound of jingling keys carried by the prison guards, and the hours he and his mother spent in the dingy waiting room.

"Mom - why is Daddy here? Why doesn't he come home with us?" he always asked his mother when they were outside in the street.

Tina would always smile bitterly and tell him he was too young to understand. She used the same explanation when he asked her why a strange man was sleeping in her bedroom. Month after month the same 'uncle' came to the apartment. He always brought a bottle with him.

Konrad's hatred of booze and of his 'home', drove him away. His grandparents' door was always open to him and there, he found himself in the midst of a caring and kind family. There were so many people to love then – one was his great-grandmother, a tiny woman who placed great importance on compassion and sympathy. Even after her death, that legacy seemed to continue through her daughters, Konrad's grandmother Julia and her sister Agata.

As he grew older, he learned that his family represented an unusual mixture of denominations in the overwhelmingly Catholic Poland. His great-grandmother was a Moslem - her daughters Lutheran, and all the others attended Catholic services. These differences seemed insignificant, however, as all of them kept pictures of Jesus Christ and Saint Mary in their rooms, and celebrated the holidays together.

On Christmas Eve, his favourite day of the year, his grandfather Robert, despite his bad leg, used to stand by the front door and greet the multitude of guests arriving for the traditional holiday meal.

Seated around the table, elbow to elbow, the family always enjoyed a traditional holiday supper - carp in jelly, herring, beet soup and baked, savoury dumplings stuffed with mushrooms.

Those days were also filled with familiar Christmas carols sung by his great-uncle Fryderyk and his wife Barbara. A large spruce tree occupied one corner of the living room and gingerly touched the ceiling. It always had to be very tall. Konrad smiled. Christmas was a day belonging to his family and to the baby Jesus.

Pleasant memories receded from his mind and he began to think back to the gloomy day of 1965 when his father moved in with Robert and Julia. He arrived at their door one morning and dropped two suitcases in the hallway. Julia greeted him as she always did, with a welcoming kiss. Agata though, frowned upon Eryk's return and she interrogated him about his own apartment and furniture.

Konrad remembered how his father's face changed several shades of red. Agata's questions made him distinctly uncomfortable. He told her that his girlfriend Lili had kicked him out of the apartment. "The flat belongs to her now. All I have is packed in these two suitcases," he explained, looking down at his luggage.

During the 'Fifties, Eryk had made a small fortune buying cars and selling them for a profit, which was illegal. Tina divorced him while he was serving his first prison term. When he got out, he met Lili, a woman who worked as a bar-maid in Warsaw's Europejski Hotel. Lili was blond, attractive and quite jolly.

At that time, Eryk still seemed to have a lot of money, but Robert worried about him. "Your father believes in his lucky star," he would often complain bitterly. "I don't know what it will take to get him back to earth."

Eryk was sent to prison for the second time. Following his release, he returned to the apartment he shared with Lili, but their relationship soured. He was disillusioned and instead of working, he drank.

One day, Lili presented him with a list of expenses. It included everything she had covered, his food parcels in prison, laundry bills, and the booze she bought each week. "From now on Eryk, we are even," she told him firmly. "My contributions have matched yours. If you don't want to work, if you want to drink at my expense, the apartment and everything in it will be at stake..."

Eryk liked elegant hotels and expensive liquor. Lili would give him money whenever he wanted it, but she demanded that he sign a note for it each time. He did.

Two years later, she showed him their accounts. "This is my apartment now," she told him. "Go back to your parents." They had been supporting him ever since, paying for his clothes, food and booze out of their small pensions.

"He's not good, but he's our first born," Granny Julia would always say.

Tears left Konrad's eyes once more that day, as his thoughts melted together - thoughts of abandonment and compassion, anger and love. Perhaps forgiveness is the way to help those lost in a ruthless world, he murmured. He felt one, last tear stream down his face.

CHAPTER 4

The sun rose over the horizon and as it approached its highest point in the blue sky, it sent ever-warmer rays onto the regimental compound.

Small droplets suspended tentatively on the grass after the morning rain shone and gave a pleasant freshness to the air. Clusters of yellow wolfbanes and buttercups punctuated the green meadow.

Beyond the compound's enclosure, a small hill dominated the landscape. From the knoll, the large fenced square housing the barracks was visible as well as the steel bridge joining the compound with the mainland in the distance.

To the north of the hill, stood a cluttered garrison settlement with a number of four-storey apartment buildings, a post office, stores and, close to the river, a cafeteria. From that point, a wooden bridge linked the garrison with the nearby town and railway station.

A single road nicely split the compound in two. On its left, a number of two-storey buildings, the command headquarters and the roll-call square, gymnasium, and officers' club. To the right, a parking lot cluttered with tanks, trucks and jeeps and more buildings used to house the overflow of soldiers. A canteen sat directly beside the parking lot. The meadow separated the barracks from the officers' living quarters.

"It looks pretty good," sergeant Bochan said after he had finished scrutinizing their work.

Company Zero was following captain Gugawa's instructions and building new curbs along the compound road. First they peeled grass from the road's surface. Then two narrow trenches were dug on either side. Bricks were brought in by wheelbarrow and arranged carefully, with soil added to fill in the gaps. The final touch was the whitewash the draftees from the Tank Mechanics Battalion used on the bricks.

"You've done a good job boys," Bochan said, adding to the praise. "I don't think I've seen this road look better."

May Day was approaching and the unit was preparing for the annual 'Party Deed'. As tradition dictated, Party members joined soldiers to do a token amount of work and complete the upgrading of the compound two days before the holiday.

More road work was pledged for the Party Deed. Captain Gugawa decided that the circular lawn in front of one of the garrison stores needed a curb as well.

Two aging T-34 tanks rested on the lawn. They were the first vehicles to arrive at the garrison in 1945. One bore a red star and the other a white eagle. Together, the Red Army and the allied Polish forces had launched offensive and expelled the Germans from the island. Konrad heard that the tanks arrived unexpectedly after crossing the frozen river and the Germans surrendered.

They sat, rotting with disuse, their paint peeled back like skin swept by the wind and baked by the sun. They had been repainted many times, but not always in the military khaki. That day, they sat motionless, sporting a bright tomato green.

The day before the Party Deed, Roman and Konrad began digging the trenches around the tanks.

"Well, we've certainly done a lot of work for the sinks," Roman said as he wiped ribbons of sweat from his forehead. "A whole week of this and who is going to get credit for it? The Party."

Konrad shoved his spade into the ground and shrugged.

"I don't really care," he said, "as long as they give us the passes." He yanked the spade off the ground and resting one elbow on it, lit a cigarette.

"What time do you think they'll actually let us leave?" his friend asked.

"Well, Gugawa says the annual Party Deed will probably last until noon and then we'll be free to go. Imagine, 36 hours away from this shit, isn't that great?"

"I think you're going to be the happiest cadet here," Roman remarked with a smile.

Konrad grinned back.

"I think you're probably right. I can't remember the last time Klara and I spent a night together. I think it was about two years ago... no, two and a half."

"Is she coming to your mother's apartment?"

"No, I'm going over to her place. Her husband is leaving for a five day business trip in Czechoslovakia..."

"What about her daughter?"

"That's worked out too. Ania went on a trip with her class. She'll be gone for two days."

"Oh, what a happy lover you shall be," Roman said, raising his eyebrows surreptitiously. "What time are you meeting Klara?"

Konrad looked down at his watch.

"Well, they say they're letting us out at one o'clock. I'll probably get to Warsaw by about three and assuming it takes me 40 minutes to take the streetcar and a bus home, I should be dressed by about four o'clock. Then Mr. Dymowski meets his woman and they go out for supper together.

Roman's eyebrows leapt up into his forehead. "And, after supper? "

"Shut up! It's none of your business," Konrad said and gave his friend a shove into the mound of dirt they had just dug up. They both laughed.

Konrad noticed their new aide to platoon commander, Wiktor Gran, running in their direction. Roman saw him too. The tall cadet sergeant yelled "Wait!" and stopped in front of them. He was out of breath and his face was strained with anger.

"What's going on, Wiktor?" they asked uneasily.

"Our 36 hour passes have been postponed," he gasped.

"What?!" Konrad screamed. He felt as if someone had stepped up to him and punched him squarely in the gut. "What did you say?"

"It's the Civilian," Wiktor answered.

"O.K., the Civilian is a son of a bitch, but what do you mean?" Roman demanded.

Konrad stood in silence, gnashing his teeth forcefully. He glanced at the ground carelessly, downhearted.

"Zabłocki invited a television crew to come in and shoot the Party Deed here, at the regiment. The earliest they can come is 1:30, so our passes won't be issued until 7:00 P.M. "

Konrad sighed with relief. Well, I can forget about the supper but at least the rest of the night is spared, he thought.

Roman grabbed his spade and tossed it in the air.

"My girlfriend lives outside of Warsaw, in Wólka. I have to catch the 5 P.M. train from Warsaw or I might as well not bother going until the next day. Why the hell do we have to stay?" he yelled.

"Sergeant Bochan asked the bastard the same question," Wiktor said. "He told him we could go right after doing the job and let the cadre stand up for the newsmen."

"And what did the Civilian say?" Konrad asked.

"He said simply no, that they needed to have all of the cadets there, working on the Party Deed."

"I really wonder what I'll do to that bastard one day," Roman said, clenching his fist in the direction of Zabłocki's office.

"You'll probably do nothing," Wiktor said sadly. "Just like the rest of us."

It was 12:30 P.M. The curb around the tanks was completed and the soldiers were finishing up with weeding, lawn cutting and clearing bush. Sergeant Bochan operated a wheelbarrow and Gugawa picked up a spade with the rest of them.

A fast food stand was set up to sell beer and fried sausages. Zabłocki and the high ranking officers hoped it would help to lure younger officers to the site of the Party Deed. Most of them had made plans for the afternoon and were just as reluctant to work overtime as the draftees. Four cases of Warka beer sat near the counter. The tall, brown bottles shone brightly in the sun.

Once he had resigned himself to the postponement, Konrad found the work in the fresh air even pleasant. The leaves of the old horse chestnut trees unfolded and bees buzzed around its blooming white flowers. He took the handles of the heavily loaded wheelbarrow and began wheeling it to the road when someone elbowed him in the ribs. It was Roman. He was smirking and pointing to his right.

"Come here, I want to show you something," he said. He led Konrad past the beer stand and stopped behind a set of bushes. "Look."

Captain Zabłocki was sitting on a bench. He held a paintbrush in one hand and a beer in the other. He was methodically dropping the brush in and out of the paint can beside him but nothing was painted.

"Our politruk[9] is really working hard," Konrad whispered. "How long has he been sitting here?"

"From the outset. He's been like that for three hours now!"

The Polish Television reporter was dressed in an attractive tweed jacket. He was tall and lean and fit everyone's ideal image of a T.V. newsman.

The news team was preparing for an interview with Zabłocki. They had the captain stand between the green tanks on the circular lawn. Konrad watched the cameraman position his equipment, and the sound technician lower a mike down to the reporter and the officer on an extension boom.

"It's O.K. with me," the technician yelled.

"Will you move a bit to your right please," the cameraman said to the reporter impatiently, "I want to have you and the eagle on the tank together. Then you'll move toward the star and then turn to the captain. Is that clear?"

The reporter nodded and took two steps.

"Am I O.K. now?"

"Perfect. Let's go," the cameraman said with a smile.

"Ladies and gentlemen," the reporter said, smiling into the camera. "Today, in Poland long and wide, from the seacoast to the Tatry mountains, the members and candidates of the Polish United Workers Party are building the Socialist motherland. They work every day, but today is special." He paused and then smiled again. "Today, Polish Communists are devoting their leisure time to contribute to the annual Party Deed."

"Stop," the cameraman yelled. The sound technician flicked his microphone off. "Now move to the star and turn to the comrade captain when I signal."

The reporter shifted beside the Russian tank and wore a smile once more.

"Today, T.V. Daily comes to you from a small garrison outside of Warsaw. We're here to watch the Annual Party Deed. The 250 metre road and the beautiful lawn I am standing on right now, were given new curbs."

The camera moved quickly to the left and swept its view along the road. The reporter stood quietly nodding to the soldiers in the crowd until the camera settled on him again.

"This project ends here, with the two tanks which helped to liberate this area 33 years ago. One tank is Polish and the other Soviet. A very meaningful connection, don't you think?"

Konrad couldn't help laughing. Roman struggled to keep a straight face. Under his breath he warned his friend to keep quiet. "Zabłocki is watching you."

"These two tanks is monument to the fraternity between Poland and our friends, the Union of Soviet Socialist Republics," the reporter added, "This is especially relevant today. Thanks to the invaluable aid from our allies, we completed industrial projects which will take us into the 21st Century, all leading us to a new, happy Poland – the Second Poland."

The cameraman motioned to the reporter to pause and he focused on the front of the Polish tank for a few seconds. Then he motioned to the reporter to continue.

---

9. Politruk (Russian) – a political officer in the army.

"To be able to build the Second Poland, the first Poland had to be liberated. The Party Deed at this garrison, the care and tending of these tanks, these monuments to those who spilt their blood 33 years ago, is a great gesture." With those words the newsman turned to face Zabłocki while the camera pulled back slightly. They shook hands and exchanged hellos.

"Comrade captain," the reporter asked, "Who is responsible for this project?"

"Our commander, colonel Marek Gapa and I."

"And who did all of this work?"

"The army cadre, with considerable help from the S.O.R. cadets who are in training here."

"How many Party members, would you say, are among them?"

Zabłocki smiled cheerfully and cleared his throat. He glanced uneasily at Janek Wytwicki who stood in the front row of the attending cadets.

"I know that a good percentage of the cadets belong to the Party," he answered. "Even more are expected to join its ranks before their training is completed."

Konrad's heart sickened as he listened to Zabłocki's rehearsed lies.

"So this really is a Party Deed then?" the reporter queried.

"Of course non-Party members do some work," Zabłocki stressed. "We don't try to discourage anyone from building the Socialist motherland, but here, at the 17th Regiment, it was the Party members who did the bulk of the work..."

"That son of a bitch," Roman whispered, as he glanced down at his blistered palms.

The television crew's truck roared but it's engine refused to move the vehicle.

"What the hell is going on with this piece of junk?" the reporter yelled angrily. "I've wasted enough time in this stupid place!"

His cameraman, who had some difficulty walking, limped to the front of the vehicle.

The driver jerked the hood open below the dashboard and helped the cameraman lift it up. Then they bent down and looked into the engine.

"It looks like all the connectors are burned," the driver announced confidently. He turned to the reporter. "It's probably going to take some time to fix it, Mr. Kwapień."

"How much time?"

"How am I supposed to know? Maybe 30 minutes, maybe an hour..."

"An hour! Are you crazy? I really can't stay here any longer. I'm supposed to be meeting the boss."

"So go and get a cab," the driver snapped, "but the vehicle is registered in your name. You'd better bring the truck back to Warsaw."

Ryszard Kwapień was tempted to argue with him but decided against it. The driver was right. Instead, he looked at the large, white truck with anger and kicked one of its tires.

The truck was decorated with red, green and blue circles and an inscription 'Telewizja Color'. It carried a fortune worth of imported television equipment. Kwapień knew that on any other day he could have left the truck and driver and gone to Warsaw on his own, but he realized that the vehicle had to be brought back safely for the May Day parade broadcast. The boss would not be pleased if I disrupted tomorrow's transmission, he thought.

He turned to the driver and urged him to fix the truck as soon as possible. Then he asked the technician if there were any restaurants in the garrison compound.

"I think there is a cafeteria by the river," Michał Jankowski answered.

"Let's go then. I'm not going to stand here in the middle of the road like an idiot."

A blond waitress approached them in the restaurant. Her cheeks, nose and arms were speckled with very noticeable freckles.

"What would you like?" she asked courteously.

"Give us a bottle of Żytnia and two servings of herring," Ryszard replied without a smile.

The waitress left to fill their order and to tend to the other customers in the restaurant.

"Did you notice how unattractive that poor girl is?" the reporter remarked in a somewhat haughty voice.

"She may be a bit plain but not everyone can be as handsome as you, Mr. Kwapień."

"Don't be sarcastic, Mr. Jankowski. You know what I mean," the reporter said. "You've travelled to a number of small communities like this one with the crew. They're so boring and unaesthetic," he said throwing his hands up in the air for emphasis. Michał shrugged indifferently.

The waitress placed two dishes and a bottle on the white tablecloth.

"Thanks and bring two cokes," Ryszard said, barely acknowledging the woman.

"Sometimes I wonder," he said, picking up the conversation again, "why the hell we spend so much time on bullshit like we did today? That idiot with his two tanks..."

"We make a good living because of it, don't we?" Michał said with a smile. "At least some of us do anyway."

"All right, I agree with you there. Without the existence of 'Second Poland' there wouldn't be as many opportunities. No, I'm not against the propaganda itself. It's great for us. Our budget was just doubled. Why don't we drink?"

"A hundred years!" the sound technician blurted out. The two men clinked their glasses together and drank heartily.

Ryszard put his glass down on the table brusquely and sighed. "I really don't know," he said. "Why did we have to come here? I don't know who cooked up this trip. We might just as well have interviewed some idiot in Warsaw."

"The boss ordered the trip himself, didn't he?"

"Yes, I know that, Mr. Jankowski, I just wonder why?"

"The colonel at this unit, Gapa, is supposedly a good friend of the boss. I've heard that he has a very prestigious place in the Party."

"You mean? Oh, well..." the reporter said sheepishly. "If that's the case, take back everything I just said." He paused and took a bite of his herring. "This is salty," he commented. "Why don't we drink? I'm paying..."

The technician looked at him with a sneer. "So, how was your weekend in London, Mr. Kwapień?" he asked.

Ryszard seemed oblivious to his colleague's antagonism. "Great," he said, smiling with contentment, "absolutely great. The boss spent most of the time with his mistress so I was pretty well on my own. Imagine, 500 British pounds and a weekend to myself..."

Michał raised his eyebrows feigning interest. "It must have been nice," he commented. "What was this trip supposedly for?"

"We were negotiating the purchase of a new sound recording unit from the E.T.C.," Kwapień answered with a chuckle.

Michał pondered his colleague's words.

"Well," he said, in a slow, deliberate voice. "I think I should speak to the boss soon myself. I really think I could have gone as well. I'm the expert in technical matters. That seems reasonable, don't you think?"

The reporter's face curled with a smirk. "Mr. Jankowski, we didn't talk technical at all. The E.T.C. invited us for dinner, the boss said O.K., and that was it. The rest of my time was spent with beautiful women and boys."

Michał could tell by Ryszard's voice that the reporter was revelling in his memories. He decided to bring him back down to earth harshly.

"You should like it here then. There are all sorts of boys to choose from." The reporter didn't acknowledge the comment. Michał continued. "I don't understand," he said. "In the past, the boss has always distributed the foreign trips fairly among the staff, but since my trip to Japan last February, I've been sitting on my ass in Warsaw. You, you've been away almost every weekend... Paris, London. Where did you go last month? Vienna, wasn't it?"

"Don't be jealous, Mr. Jankowski," Ryszard said smugly.

The technician slowly added more vodka to his glass and sat back casually in his chair. "You don't understand, Mr. Kwapień," he said. "I'm not jealous at all. But," he continued, leaning forward and facing the reporter squarely, "some people just cannot handle having too much. Some people become demoralized, ungrateful even. They can hardly put up with a trip to an army garrison after a wild weekend in London, England."

Ryszard anxiously filled his glass with more vodka.

"... Some people," Michał continued, "think that reporting on colonel Gapa's regiment and the Party Deed is boring." He smiled at the reporter confidently. "I think I might just have a talk with the boss..."

Ryszard swallowed his drink in one gulp. He looked nervously around the crowded restaurant. The blaring rock music coming from the jukebox in the far corner irritated his ears. "Listen, Mr. Jankowski," he said, breathing heavily, seemingly gulping for air. "I'm still closer to the boss than you are."

"That could change..."

"Yes, but why should it?" the reporter asked, fidgeting with his glass. He looked up at Michał and smiled openly. "Next week a trip to Madrid is planned. I think - no, I'm sure that the boss wouldn't mind assigning an experienced sound technician to our T.V. crew."

Michał silently took his glasses out of his pocket and began rubbing them with a napkin. He held them up to the light, looked through them and then placed them carefully on his nose.

"You are a very intelligent reporter, Mr. Kwapień," he said with a grin.

Konrad stood nervously in the hallway knocking on the door. Why isn't she answering? he thought.

After a few more taps, Klara opened the door. She wore a lavish purple velvet dress. Her eyes were made up with a delicate shade of blue. When she smiled and said "Hello," her deep red lipstick made her teeth gleam. Konrad kissed her gently and stepped into the apartment's small vestibule, murmuring how disappointed he was about their planned night out.

"You know it's too late. Anyway, it doesn't matter," she said. "I've made a wonderful meal for us. It will be just as good as we could get in a restaurant, you'll see." She smiled warmly and led him into the apartment. "Why don't you sit down and relax? I'll bring the food in when everything is ready."

He sighed and slumped down on the comfortable sofa. He noticed a delicious smell emanating from the kitchen and smiled with contentment.

The apartment was rather small but cozy, with a large room serving as both the dining room and the living room. Klara and her husband occupied a small bedroom located on the opposite side of the apartment's walk-in kitchen. Their daughter had a tiny alcove to the side.

The main room was furnished with taste, and Konrad thought, even luxury. The plush sofa bed was accompanied by twin armchairs and a coffee table of dark walnut.

One wall was covered with a shelving unit. It held books, knickknacks and had a special cabinet which doubled as a bar. Klara had placed a variety of plates and vases on the shelves. Most of them were white with delicately painted blue flowers.

Klara likes Włocławek plates, Konrad thought. He remembered how happy she had been when he gave her two of them on her name day.[10] They were made in Poland but most were exported. Finding and buying one of them was like discovering buried treasure.

"You look very nice tonight." Klara commented as she walked back into the room. She carried a heavily-laden tray.

Konrad stared with disbelief at the dishes in front of him and murmured a quick "Thank you." Filet mignon, mushrooms, French fries and other vegetables filled his plate. "Is this really 1978?" he exclaimed. "I haven't eaten a meal like this in years!"

"Let's eat it while it's really hot," she urged. Konrad could see that she was obviously pleased with the way the dinner had turned out. The steak was a bright pink and smothered in juice. She had cooked it medium rare, just the way he liked it.

"Don't eat so fast, you always rush," she said as Konrad eagerly gulped down his food. "Try to eat slowly. Dining in a civilized manner is an art.."

Although he consciously tried to chew more slowly and take smaller bites, he finished his meal well ahead of Klara. "Where did you buy this meat?" he asked as he wiped his mouth with a napkin and sat back contentedly. "I didn't think that filet mignon even existed in Poland."

"You can buy it sometimes in the 'komercyjne (commercial) stores', but even there, I had to line up for over an hour."

---

10. Name day – the day on which a person, bearing a particular first name, celebrates a holiday. It will be explained in more detail in Part 3.

At the mention of the 'commercial stores', Konrad pursed his lips with displeasure. The government added them to the bizarre spectrum of Polish food markets in 1976. That year, a staggering increase in meat prices triggered massive strikes and protests. The government then rolled the prices back but the better cuts of meat disappeared from the regular stores and new outlets were opened where prices were more than three times higher.

"Who shops in the 'commercial stores'?" he asked Klara. "Party members, policemen...?"

"I haven't seen any military or police officers. I imagine, most of them shop in their own meat stores where prices are much lower. Our neighbour's father," she continued, "works with the Central Committee. I'm not sure who he is or what he does but he manages to bring his daughter a large ham and pork tenderloin every week!"

Konrad chuckled bitterly. "Everything seems to be so well organized for our elite," he commented. "But, who were the people who lined up with you for over an hour when you bought the filet? I'll bet they weren't someone like Agata or Tina."

"I think most of them are small entrepreneurs. They seem to have money but don't have access to any of the special stores."

Konrad sensed shame in her voice. Klara's financial situation was better than most. She and her husband had recently begun a small toy company and they were doing surprisingly well.

"You can be sure that Agata hates the 'commercial stores'," he said.

"I don't really like them either," Klara replied with an anxious shrug, "but it was the only place I could go to get the right thing for you."

Konrad noticed the deliberate intensity in her voice, especially in her last two words. He was pleased that she had gone to so much trouble just for him.

He poured two glasses of brandy and for a few moments they sipped them in a state of contented silence. Klara got up and walked over to her stereo console. He heard a record drop on to the turntable.

She walked back to the couch. "Do you remember this song?" she asked.

She and Konrad embraced while they listened to Zdzisława Sośnicka sing, "The Home I Have."

"I love her voice. It's so deep and rich," Klara said. "Do you remember...?" she said, looking straight into his eyes.

He sat back and savoured the song's melody and lyrics. Memories began flooding back. The song was a hit when they first met each other.

"Seven years," Klara murmured. Tears were swelling in her eyes.

Konrad embraced her tenderly and kissed her wet cheeks. "My love, my only love," he whispered. "Why can't I have you to myself forever?"

Klara began caressing his hair. She lightly kissed his face. "I am yours, I've always been," she said quietly. Konrad heard the song fading out and the stereo click off automatically. It was a painful transition. He felt the charm of the evening fizzle and begin to drift out of the apartment.

Gently, he lifted her arms off his shoulders and rose from the sofa. He refilled their glasses and lit two cigarettes. One of them he handed to Klara.

Then he walked over to the window and opened it slightly to let some fresh air into the room. The street below was dark, but he could make out the faint outlines of a few people walking along the sidewalk. On the far side of the road, a streetlamp gave off a feeble light. Behind it, there was a gathering of benches around a small lawn.

"Do you know how many times I sat there waiting for you?" he said in a voice mixed with sadness and pleasant recollection. "I would wait until you came out and then we'd each walk in a different direction to make sure your husband wouldn't see us together."

"Klara," he said approaching the sofa once more, "I want you to get divorced and marry me. I want you to be mine, only mine."

Klara's eyes blinked quickly and she feigned a weak smile. "But where would we live?" she asked. "With your mother? Perhaps with your drunk father?"

He slumped into one of the armchairs. There was nothing more to say. He realized that his offer of matrimony, just like the others he had made to her, was hollow. He desired her, but he also knew that it was virtually impossible to do more than dream.

His frustration quickly grew into heated anger. "What can I ever offer you, Klara?" he cried. "I've spent years at university but that doesn't seem to count for much. If I had been born into a family of Party bosses or private entrepreneurs I would have been rich for my entire life without much effort at all..."

"You studied very hard at university," Klara said. "I've always been very proud of you. I know you were one of the best students."

"But where the hell has it gotten me? You're right, I was a good student but I can expect meager wages for most of my life and I won't get an apartment of my own for at least ten years. I'm from a poor family, and that's never going to change. I can't even think of having a woman like you because I don't have any money and you do..."

"We don't have much really," she said sheepishly. Then she paused briefly and looked at him closely. "You're forgetting something else, Konrad. When I met you I was married and had a child. Even if you did have money, it wouldn't make the situation very easy for us."

Konrad watched her pour some more brandy into her glass and drink it quickly. "I know the Communists have deprived people like you of opportunities," she continued, "but you can't blame them for the state of our relationship. That's ridiculous."

He sensed a slight suggestion of scorn in her voice and lashed back. "You can make fun of me if you want," he cried, "but you know, as well as I do, that I don't have and probably never will have money here, in Poland. In America or Canada it would be possible. There, you could be my wife. I could get a good job there..."

Klara sighed deeply. "Konrad," she said, shaking her head, "perhaps you could, but let me ask you one thing - were you happy when your mother divorced Eryk?" She stared closely at his face.

Konrad eyed her sternly and took a long, casual drag from his cigarette. "No, why?" he remarked slowly.

"Well, Ania wouldn't be happy either, would she?"

Whenever he began talking about any form of permanency in their relationship, the conversation inevitably ended with Klara pointing out all the reasons why they could never really be together.

He felt helpless. He couldn't refute her arguments. Unlike him, she was being logical and realistic. He got up from the couch suddenly and doggedly began to pace around the room. He paused briefly and looked down at her. "O.K.," he said, "but if you want to be with your husband forever, there's no place for me. I can't be your lover for the rest of my life. I want something more..."

Klara sat on his knee and embraced him tenderly. "I love my daughter," she said in a low voice. "I didn't say anything about my husband. I don't love him." Konrad kissed her lightly on the lips. "Will you ever divorce Czesiek?" "Maybe - one day - who knows," she said. "I think you expect too much of me, Konrad. I know you want me to be perfect, to be strong, to shed my weaknesses. Well, I'm not perfect." She stared at him woefully with her large, beautiful eyes. "I want you and I think I love you too. But I'm not strong enough to make any big changes. I can't plan anything... or be what you want me to be. Maybe someday," she repeated. "Who knows? My life could change dramatically any time. Perhaps I'm just waiting for something to change it for me. I've often told you that I think there's little anyone can do to change the course of the future. I'm a believer in fate..."

"And I am supposed to wait for this, right?" Konrad said angrily. Her vague statements were frustrating. Without answering, Klara bent over him and flicked the light switch on the wall behind her. The soft orange bulb in the bar cabinet provided the only illumination in the room. Konrad watched her slowly unzip the front of her velvet dress. She smiled and stretched her arms out toward him.

It was going to be Company Zero's last night at the unit.

"Can you believe it?" Wiktor Gran said joyfully.

"You're right Wiktor, it's great, but it would be even better if this was our last day in the fucking army," Roman said pessimistically. "It's going to be hard coming back after our holiday to face another six months."

Wiktor shrugged and anxiously paced around the room, seemingly oblivious to soldiers lounging on their bunks. It was one of the last acts of defiance they could muster against the People's Army regulations.

Konrad looked up at the tall, blond cadet whose cheerful blue eyes gleamed with obvious joy. He knew that the man had a right to feel relieved. Lieutenant Suka had appointed him platoon commander-aide after the oath and the departure of their pudding, corporal Kowalski. Wiktor wasn't an opportunist and he hated the army. But, he was a commanding figure, over two meters tall and Suka seemed to respect him for that.

Almost all of the S.O.R. cadets defied the rules and regulations and they didn't try to conceal their real feelings about the People's Armed Forces. Wiktor tried to be loyal to them, but at the same time, he was responsible for their behaviour. When anything went wrong in the First Platoon, he was the one who had to stand at attention in the lieutenant's office.

The day before, Konrad and the rest of the company were given their graduate cadet service orders and told to report to their designated units. Konrad was assigned to a small outfit outside of Warsaw while Roman, to his disappointment, was heading south.

63

He found himself looking around the barracks; the beat-up steel lockers, the gray blankets they were allotted on their first day.

"What's the matter with you?" Roman asked him. "You look a little sad. Don't tell me that you'd rather enlist for life?" he said, playfully elbowing him in the side.

"Don't be an idiot. I was just thinking that after our furlough there won't be a Company Zero. We'll all be split up. We'll still be in the army, but not together. Don't you guys find it a bit depressing?"

Most of the soldiers nodded.

"It's not a big deal, Konrad. We'll be seeing each other again. In six months, we'll be back for our promotion," Wiktor said and tapped him on the shoulder.

"I wish that were happening tomorrow, " Roman repeated.

Konrad stood up quickly. "Let's get out of here," he said. "We have to get something to drink for our celebration tonight."

Roman followed him out of the building. They were about to start down the road when Janek ran up behind them.

"Good news!" he yelled. "Come back with me to the barracks and I'll tell you."

Janek strode quickly into the building with Konrad and Roman close behind.

"O.K., Janek, what happened?" Roman asked.

"Zabłocki was censured!" he said gleefully and pranced around the room.

"What do you mean?" one of the cadets asked impatiently.

"Just what I said," Janek answered. "An officer from the GZP, Central Political Command was very outspoken in his criticism of Zabłocki's marvellous political skills. It happened at the Party meeting in the command building earlier today."

"How did you find out about this?" Konrad asked with disbelief. "You couldn't have been listening..."

"Well, Bochan was and he told me. I can just picture Zabłocki's face going beet red. Bochan said he didn't know what to say."

Roman stared at Janek with a puzzled expression on his face. "What did they tell him? I would think that by their standards he is a perfect politruk, wouldn't you?"

Janek flopped on his bed and laughed wildly. "Do you know how many S.O.R. cadets in Company Zero joined the Party during our six months here?" he gasped, slapping his knee.

The cadets shrugged.

"Only one S.O.B. out of 200 draftees joined. Not many..."

"All right, but what does that have to do with Zabłocki?" Wiktor asked him.

"Bochan said the major from the Central Political Command brought the results of the Party recruiting of the other S.O.R. companies in our military district. At least five people enlisted with the Party on average. The major said that only one Party member from the 17th Regiment was unacceptable and he advised colonel Gapa to look into the quality of our political training."

The entire barracks erupted with laughter.

Konrad and Roman tried once again to get to the liquor store. They walked down the garrison road, past the veteran, green tanks. The store was right beside them. Roman shook the front door with frustration. "Can you believe it, it's closed," he said, peering with disappointment into the dark and empty building.

They decided to head to the neighbouring town just beyond the river. To get to the bridge, they had to walk close to the riverbank surrounding the garrison. Konrad sensed that they were entering one of the oldest sections of the compound, one they hadn't seen before.

A small cluster of desolate-looking buildings huddled together at the crown of the river bank. Most were badly dilapidated and had only a tentative hold on the ground. The overgrown trees surrounding them seemed like old friends.

They managed to scale a wire fence and then almost stumbled upon an old building which was surrounded by dense brush. Like the others they had just seen, the building was empty, it looked like it had been deserted for years. Dust, spider webs and the corpses of a multitude of insects clotted its every crack and opening. Most of its arched windows were open to the air. They've probably been broken for years, Konrad thought. "Look," he said, elbowing Roman impatiently

A small corner of a marble plaque peeked out from the weeds and undergrowth. After pushing the brush aside, he found that the stone was badly cracked, but still legible.

"It's the garrison church of St. John, erected 1920 A.D.," he said quietly.

Janek Wytwicki mounted a stool in the barracks later that evening, amidst a mass of drinking and smoking cadets.

"O.K., go ahead," Wiktor Gran yelled.

The cadet pulled a small piece of his measuring tape out of his back pocket. Throwing it into the air he announced in a solemn voice that the end was finally reached, the 'fala' was finished.

"Fuck it!" the chorus of cadets yelled. Their celebration would be heard through the entire compound.

"We've made it, we've lived through Company Zero," Roman yelled, grabbing Konrad and kissing him on the cheeks.

It was 10:00 P.M. Janek Wytwicki sat peacefully in one corner of the room, slowly strumming his guitar. Roman and Konrad were engaged in a conversation with some other cadets. They had all made plans for the holidays and Company Zero was quickly fading into their memories.

Konrad paused to listen to Janek. The cadet was playing the melody of a familiar folk tune, his eyes were closed with concentration. Konrad watched him for a few minutes and then, lighting a cigarette, he joined the conversation once again.

"The Katyń murder shall not be forgotten,"

Janek began singing. His guitar shook.

"So shudder Moscow, since revenge shall happen
You shall pay dearly for our fathers' blood
Hearing at your graves only howling dogs…"

Konrad's eyes widened with surprise. He and the rest of the soldiers listened in silence.

"... Today, lift your spirits, Poland will be free
We'll receive assistance from the great Chinese
When the Chinese Forces cross Amur in plenty
Wilno, Lwów[11], Lithuania shall be liberated...,"

Roman stared at Konrad with disbelief.

"... Dense fog covers vast areas of steppe
Winds are crying in dried river beds
Somewhere near Volga there is a Red Grave
Liberated peoples sing a song like that..."

The cadets watched Janek stand up and sing the last verse at the top of his lungs.

"Today shudder Moscow, God's on our side
And we shall demolish your red, fucking pride
You shall pay dearly for our fathers' blood
Hearing at your graves only howling dogs..."

"Janek," Wiktor cried, "you little, unpredictable bastard, you wonderful son of a bitch. Give me the words to that song."

Konrad scrambled to find a pen and he quickly jotted down the lyrics on the back of his cigarette package. Soon, the entire company was singing in a slightly uneven, but very loud chorus.

Janek looked over to Konrad and Roman and smiled triumphantly.

The song was repeated over and over again through the night - the final night of Company Zero.

---

11. Wilno, Lwów - Polish cities, from 1945 to 1991 under Soviet administration. Presently renamed Vilnius and Lviv by Lithuanians and Ukrainians.

CHAPTER 5

"Good evening, ladies and gentlemen. It's nice to see so many of you out tonight and enjoying yourself at The Arsenal Restaurant. I hope you'll stay with us," the lead singer announced. "There's a lot more coming your way. We're The Invincibles."

The patrons in the regimental restaurant clapped loudly at the figure dressed in a silver gray smoking jacket. He bowed confidently and with a smile he pulled the microphone off its stand. "Let me introduce myself and the rest of the band," he continued. "I am John Ropiel. To my left is our man on lead guitar, Tom Baran. Let's hear it from Tom, ladies and gentlemen."

The guitar player stepped forward and strummed his instrument with full and deliberate strokes.

"Next - I have the honour of introducing our bass guitar, Steve Nygusiak. How about a show of appreciation for Steve!"

Konrad and Janek sat at a table in the packed restaurant. It was Saturday evening and The Arsenal was a popular place for military and non-military customers. They were all seated around tables which encircled a small stage and dance floor. Glasses and large bottles of vodka covered the linen-clad tables. Hanging lamps saturated the room with a deep, green light.

"... Now you can't have a band without someone on percussion, and so ladies and gentlemen, here's Jim Szaflik on drums," the singer declared, his voice penetrating through the cigarette smoke-filled hall. "And last, but certainly not least, the junior member of our band, promising young Ricky Kosmala on trumpet. How about a round of applause for Ricky..."

Janek sipped his vodka and coke and chuckled. "God, it feels like we're in New York City," he said.

Konrad nodded in agreement. "Obviously their real names don't really fit their image. Ryszard Kosmala doesn't sound quite as good as 'Ricky'. I can hardly wait to hear them sing. I bet they'll pretend that they know English..."

"Ladies and gentlemen," John Ropiel announced amid clapping and repeated yells of bravo, "let's get started. The Invincibles will now play 'Waterloo', a well-known Abba hit!"

Janek waved to a waitress who was winding her way through the tables. She recognized him immediately. Konrad watched her flash a friendly smile.

"So what would Mr. Cadet like to eat this evening?" she asked Janek.

67

He and Konrad ordered white barszcz soup, along with a fried chicken with mushrooms dinner.

"All right, the soup will be ready in about 10 minutes," she said and left for another table.

They sipped their drinks and eyed the other patrons.

"There aren't too many people in uniform here, are there?" Janek remarked.

"I guess the sinks like to pretend that they're civilians."

Konrad smiled and nodded. However, three tables away he noticed an overweight colonel dressed in uniform. A handsome brunette in her early forties sat on his left. She faced a much younger woman, possibly her daughter. He pointed in the direction of their table and lamented to Janek that the colonel had two women, while they had none.

"Konrad," Janek answered. "There's nothing preventing us from asking them to dance..."

Konrad's gaze drifted around the room once more. Three couples occupied the dance floor. The brunette he had noticed before sat silently watching the dancing couples intently. A young captain approached her table and he could see her looking up at him and nodding. She left her chair and followed him outside the ring of tables. "Shit, I wasn't fast enough," he murmured.

Janek started getting out of his chair. "If you don't mind, Konrad, I'm going to grab the other one. I know you would rather dance with the older woman anyway, and besides, the blond is about my size. I'm not very tall, you know..."

Konrad gave him a small shove. "But you're great Janek," he said. "Go ahead."

Within a minute Janek was dancing. Konrad sighed and poured himself an ample glass of vodka. He gulped it down quickly and shuddered.

The band announced a 15 minute break and Janek returned to the table just as Konrad was downing a large glass of coke. He looked up at Janek and then over to the colonel's table. He sighed with relief when he saw that the officer's wife was sitting down once again.

"Her name is Ewa," Janek said, noticing his stare. "I was dancing with Mania, her daughter."

"Who are they sitting with?" Konrad asked, trying to sound as disinterested as possible.

"That's Mania's father. She's told me that he is a colonel with our regiment," Janek explained.

"What is his name?"

"I don't know, why don't you ask him yourself. If you want to dance with his wife, you'd better go now. I think the captain is moving in her direction."

They approached the table together. Konrad bowed, kissed the older woman's hand quickly and asked her for a dance. She nodded. "Do you mind, sir?" Konrad asked, turning to the colonel.

The man's head rocked back and then forward again. "What?" he mumbled.

Konrad looked down at the large bottle of vodka on the table. It was almost empty. "Do you mind if I dance with your wife?" he repeated.

"No, I don't. Go to hell," the man replied with a laugh and waved them away.

Janek took Mania by the hand and followed Konrad and Ewa to the dance floor just as the band members were picking up their instruments. Konrad turned around and looked at the solitary colonel behind him. The man was pouring himself another drink. Then, for the first time, he let his eyes rest upon her face.

Janek fanned himself and invited the two women to their table for a breather.

"Let's drink to our friendship," he announced. "Miss Basia," he said to the waitress standing nearby, "could we have two more cokes with glasses, please?"

The waitress nodded. After taking a few sips of her drink, the older woman rose from the table. "I'm sorry, but I have to get back to my husband now," she said.

Konrad decided to accompany her. When they approached the table he saw the colonel gingerly sipping a cup of steaming coffee. Another large bottle of vodka dominated the table.

"Hello," he said jovially, looking up at Konrad. "Why don't you stay and take a seat with us?"

Konrad smiled and accepted a brimful glass of vodka from the officer.

"Let's drink, Ewa," the colonel said, raising his glass. "A toast, Mr. Cadet. Pyeytye na zdaroveeye. Na zdaroveeye[12]," he added in Russian.

"Na zdrowie[13]," Konrad answered and they emptied their glasses. "Are you Russian, colonel?" he asked.

"No, he's Polish," Ewa interjected, "but we did spent many years in Moscow. My husband was serving at the Polish Embassy there..."

The colonel grinned. "Well, comrade cadet, have you been to Moscow?"

During the seventies many Poles travelled to the USSR and Konrad was no exception. By selling a few pairs of Polish made shoes or jeans for rubles, one could buy enough gold to pay for the trip and more.

"Yes. I've been there twice," he replied.

The colonel's eyes widened. "It's a great city, isn't it? Great restaurants, a great culture," he murmured.

Konrad had difficulty keeping a straight face. He tried to calm himself down by sipping slowly on his vodka, but he found the colonel's reference to the culture of Moscow hilarious. "Well, it depends on what you like," he commented. "I found the city very big and overcrowded. It was dull too. Restaurants close early and most of the bars take only American money."

"What hotels did you stay in when you were there? "

"Rossiya, facing the Red Square."

"Ah, well you should have stayed at the Belgrade Hotel. Most of the people I worked with at the embassy went there - almost every evening. It's a gorgeous place, believe me..." he said with a distinct sigh. Then he poured himself a large refill of vodka. "They take rubles there," he said with a grin. After downing his drink he excused himself from the table.

Konrad smiled alternately at Ewa and sipped his drink. She looked down at the table wistfully.

---

12. Pyeytye na zdaroveeye (Russian) - Drink to be healthy.

13. Na zdrowie (Polish) - To your health.

He tried to be cheerful. "When did you come back from Moscow?" he asked. "Last year, when he left the embassy," she answered. There was little emotion in her voice.

"Why did he leave? He seems to love Moscow."

"He was dismissed."

"Why?" he asked with genuine surprise.

"Booze," she answered sharply. "You heard him say that everyone with the embassy frequented The Belgrade Hotel. Well, that's not true. Most of them went once, maybe twice a week. But Rudolf..." she said haltingly, "Rudolf was there every single night, do you understand?" Konrad noticed that her voice was tightening with anxiety.

"How long did this last?" he murmured.

Ewa's lips pursed sharply. She turned away from him and laughed, her body racked by a mixture of bitterness and shame. "Every night," she repeated. "For three years he went there. It was almost as if my daughter and I were abandoned. We didn't know many people in Moscow so we were forced to stay in our apartment – alone. Rudolf drifted into alcoholism. Eventually... the situation got so bad that his friends at the embassy couldn't ignore it any longer. They drink a lot too, but he was just too much. That's why they sent him back here."

Konrad poured vodka into her glass without a word. He looked up at her face. It was drawn and pale and seemed to make her brown hair appear even darker.

"So how did you end up here, at this garrison?" he asked.

"Rudolf was ordered to serve here. He's going to retire in a little less than two years." She lit a cigarette and continued to stare with the same emotionless gaze.

"Are things any better for you now? He can't go to The Belgrade Hotel any longer..."

Ewa pressed her knee against his under the table. "Yes, they are," she answered slowly. "I was very lonely in Moscow. It's different here. Rudolf has lost all interest in me, but at least he's not jealous..."

The room erupted with clapping. The musicians were signing off for the night. John Ropiel smiled at the audience. "That's it, everybody. We'll be back next week."

Konrad watched the stage empty quickly. He pushed his glass away and turned to Ewa. "Would you like to join me in my hotel room?" he asked. She nodded.

"Just a minute," he said. "I have to talk to Janek."

He found him in the washroom. Janek was fastidiously adjusting his tie with the help of the small mirror on the wall. "I'm glad we bumped into each other, Konrad," he said. "I'm going to Mania's place for tea. She has promised to serve me a real Russian tea according to the recipe she learned in Moscow. If it's good," he said, winking, "I'll be tempted to write it down. That means that I might not be back for a while. Don't cry for me baby..."

Outside of the restaurant, Konrad led Ewa toward the garrison hotel. It was a warm, humid evening. He breathed deeply, inhaling the scent of freshly-cut grass. Ewa slipped her arm around his elbow.

"What will happen to your husband?" he asked, thinking of Mania and Janek. "Is he going home tonight?"

Ewa shook her head quickly. "I doubt it. He usually stays at the restaurant until 3:00 A.M. or whenever it closes. The soldiers on duty carry him to the garrison hotel after that. He sleeps it off in a small room on the ground floor," she answered with obvious disdain.

Konrad squeezed her hand and opened the side door of the garrison dormitory. They passed through a dimly lit hallway, trotting softly on the carpeted floor. The central lounge was deserted. Konrad's eyes followed the outline of armchairs and side tables, all facing a single television. An imposing palm plant sat beside the door leading to the stairwell.

He carefully separated his keys and opened the door. Ewa followed him inside. He heard her place something down on the dresser.

"I took this from the table," she explained, pointing to two bottles of coke and a half-filled bottle of vodka. She closed her purse and set it down on Janek's bed. "Rudolf certainly isn't going to need this tonight."

Lying with her in bed, Konrad was plagued by sleeplessness and anxiety. Ewa turned to look at him and placed a hand softly on his shoulder. Her voice cracked. "Don't think too much," she whispered. "There's not much to puzzle over. You don't have any obligations." She gave him a passionate kiss and then dropped her head on to the pillow.

His mind returned to The Arsenal. He imagined her husband drooping in his chair, his head nudging the edge of the table. He stroked Ewa's dark hair and listened quietly to her deep and even sleep-filled breathing. Antek Zakucki told me about the garrison women, he thought. He's right, there are no ties, no shame. When we leave, they'll forget all about us and others will come to take our place...

Konrad barely tolerated his life in the new garrison, settling into the routine of platoon commander uneasily at first, but slowly resigning himself to a few more months as a soldier of the Polish Army.

He felt less isolated at the new unit. Only a thin screen of wire mesh separated the compound from the sidewalks and shops of the town nearby. Yet, he rarely stepped outside of its bounds. The garrison was autonomous; well outfitted with a plush officers' club, canteen and meat store. There was little need to pass through the garrison gate.

He took a deep sigh and flopped down on his bed. It was a Sunday afternoon, just two months after he and Janek had received orders to report to the Zniewolice garrison. Janek was quietly reading a magazine. He lay comfortably on his bed. Konrad though, felt like talking.

"So, what do you think of this place?" he remarked suddenly. "It's not that bad - at least the officers and draftees are decent to us. I certainly don't miss Zabłocki's rhetoric. Anything is better than what we went through there."

Janek's magazine dropped onto his lap and Konrad watched his friend's eyes raise slowly up to his. "Is that really what you think?" he asked icily.

Konrad looked at him and shrugged in silence.

"If so," Janek continued, "the second stage of a carefully planned brainwashing program is succeeding."

"What are you talking about?"

"Just think about it for a moment, Konrad," Janek answered in a beseeching tone of voice. "... I have for a long time. Look back to the 17th Regiment. There, they tried to drown us in bullshit - with crap that we weren't prepared to accept, Zabłocki bullshit. But, the enlistment figures proved that the Civilian's methods didn't work. Here though, they're showing us how great life can be. We've both noticed how nice they are to us - they treat you just like one of the boys. We can buy ham, or whatever else we want, at the meat store, The Arsenal sells us liquor at subsidized prices, and to top it all off, we can have their wives and daughters whenever we want them..."

Konrad looked up to the ceiling, transfixed by Janek's astonishing narrative.

"You are, in effect, starting to like it here. And, you're starting to like them too," Janek continued, as though analyzing a patient on a psychiatrist's couch. He lit a cigarette and stretched his legs out in front of him on the bed. "The Russian stars on their billboards don't wrench your heart like they used to - you're getting used to them. I even think that you're starting to like it here. You would rather stay here in Zniewolice than go home for the weekend, right?"

Konrad turned slowly to look in Janek's direction. "Well, it is quite a way to travel, you know," he said meekly.

Janek jumped at the chance to crusade further. "Bullshit," he said, laughing triumphantly. "It's only a two hour trip by train, don't fool yourself." He paused. Konrad pursed his lips anxiously. "No," Janek continued, "no, Konrad - the distance doesn't matter. We're not bothering to go to Warsaw because we have everything we want here. I hate to admit it, but you have swallowed the bait, and so have I."

During the minutes that followed, neither of them said a word. Konrad could only hear the faint chatter of squirrels outside the window, and the regular sound of Janek's breathing. In the silence he sensed that his friend was waiting for response from him.

"I think I know what you mean, Janek," he blurted out. "Sitting here, in this garrison, we're losing touch, we're becoming more and more isolated from the rest of society." His tone of voice was lively, almost too much so. He was reluctant to reveal his shame.

Janek lit a cigarette. "I think that is what counts most, Konrad," he said. "We know what the People's Army is really like, but we don't fight it anymore. And I have a feeling that when we leave, we'll have fond memories of this place. I'll probably remember Colonel Beka's wife and daughter before I think of those stupid marches Zabłocki made me do ten months ago..." He coughed. It was a loose, ugly rasp. "You're bad, they'll crush you. If you do what you're told - be good and docile, they'll reward you. And," he paused, "the theory seems to have worked on us. We may as well opt to join the Party when we're discharged."

Konrad accused him of blowing the situation all out of proportion.

"You think so?" Janek retorted. "Well, tell me - how long has it been since your last visit to church? I don't have to remind you of our whereabouts this morning, last Sunday, and the week before that..."

Konrad drooped his head and nodded unconsciously. You call yourself a Catholic, he thought, but instead of going to church you... He turned to Janek. "You're right," he acknowledged. "And, thank you..."

Janek shrugged. "I simply like to do my duty just like I did before the oath-taking ceremony. Do you remember that night, after taps?"

Konrad's brow wrinkled with puzzlement. "Do you mean it was you that night? It couldn't have been. The voice I heard definitely wasn't yours."

Janek laughed heartily, chuckling with genuine satisfaction. "You're right. It wasn't me," he said. "It was a recording of my brother's voice."

"How the hell did you get it?"

Janek didn't attempt to camouflage his pride. "Well, I may be a slow runner, but at least I managed to do something useful during those 10 kilometre marches Zabłocki made me do. I decided to try to lift up our morale and, of course, thank the dear Civilian for the favour he did for me."

A bell jingled, signalling the beginning of seven o'clock mass.

Konrad took a last quick glance at the statue of the Virgin in front of him and walked quietly into the main nave of the church. It was almost empty, filled only by a few black-coated elderly ladies who were scattered among the numerous rows of wooden benches.

The decor of the nave was modest, almost austere, with its plain gray stone walls. The only decoration of any sort were a small number of saints sculpted in wood. They sat in sharply arched niches. A large cross with a crucified Jesus dominated the main altar and presbytery.

An elderly priest dressed in a white robe looked down on his parishioners. Father Florian was one of the few people he still knew from his first days at church. He thought back to the day when the priest reached down, caressed his hair, and said, "Welcome Konrad. Will you stay with us?"

He did. When he was young, he was one of Father Florian's altar boys. He went to summer camp organized by the parish and took religion classes.

The mass was about to end. Konrad watched some of the more mobile women get out of their seats and approach the altar for communion. He sighed as he watched Father Florian place the host in their mouths and murmur softly.

He knew he couldn't join them in the Eucharist. His seven year old romance with Klara had led him away from the temple. He smiled bitterly. Then, recalling his evenings at the army unit, he drooped his head in shame and stared at the floor.

Father Florian left the altar and began walking toward the sacristy. Konrad followed close behind and greeted him in Latin.

"Laudetur Jesus Christus," he said, pleased that he could still remember a few words from his altar boy days.

The old priest turned around and smiled. "In Saecula Saeculorum Amen," he answered with calm surprise.

Konrad knelt in front of him. "You're back, Konrad," Father Florian said. He lay a hand on the younger man's head. "I haven't seen you for years. But, you are with us now. Will you stay?" he looked down at Konrad's upturned face.

"I want to stay, Father, but..." Konrad murmured painfully, noticing the familiar scars on the priest's face and neck - grim reminders of his experiences in Auschwitz-Birkenau and five years he spent in a Communist prison. "You have been away for a long time," the priest said, lifting him up from his knees. "It will take time for you to come back, but don't be discouraged. Try to come to church as often as you can. It will help your soul and... one day you will really be back."

Konrad kissed the priest's hand as he continued to talk. "I will pray Konrad," he said slowly, choosing his words carefully. "I will pray so that this will happen soon."

Konrad kissed his hand again and left the high-ceilinged church.

It was a drizzly, miserable evening. The trees outside of the garrison dormitory drooped with a heavy burden of rain. Just two days before, Konrad and Janek had been trekking through a nearby forest, savouring the rich tones of burgundy and pumpkin yellow overhead. The forest floor mirrored the kaleidoscope of colours above and was speckled with clusters of fawn coloured mushrooms. A collection of these mushrooms had been threaded through a string and they hung to dry over the small electric heater in their room.

Sitting at his desk, Konrad stared intently at the English grammar text in front of him, trying to ignore the constant clatter of swollen raindrops hitting the window beside him.

Janek lay on his bed and fiddled with his small transistor radio. He moved the circular dial back and forth through a blanket of static and foreign voices.

Konrad heard him sit up suddenly just as the radio began to blare.

"What's going on?" he asked.

Janek looked down at the radio intently. "Shut up and listen," he said sharply.

It was an Italian station and the radio announcer spoke quickly but his message was still understandable. As they hovered over the transistor, Konrad and Janek heard that Cardinal Karol Wojtyła of Cracow had been elected to the highest post in the Catholic Church.

Janek screamed "Hurrah," and grabbed Konrad. "I can't believe it," he shouted wildly as they danced around the room. A few minutes later they flopped on to their beds.

"I still can't believe it," Janek repeated over and over again. He grinned with obvious satisfaction. "Just think, for years people have been thinking that we're just a little, crummy Communist country somewhere in the East and people like the Zabłocki's and Gapa's have been trying to wipe out whatever pride we're still able to muster."

The following day, they could see the impact of the news on people outside of their army garrison. Zniewolice was in a frenzy. Konrad hadn't seen anything like it since Poland's soccer team won a medal in the 1974 World Cup. The national anthem was shouted in the streets and Polish white and red flags were lifted high above the crowds. Churches were packed with worshippers.

The mood of triumph and joy was infectious and it soon spread through the barrack compound. Konrad issued one hour passes to his entire platoon so that they could go to church. Janek did the same thing. Just as his soldiers began trickling back into the compound, both cadets were summoned to the commander's office.

Major Zbigniew Krupniak, the head of their batallion, was a man in his mid-forties. Like many of the officers at the regiment, he was well fed and consequently he had a round and very fleshy face. This usually conveyed a jolly demeanor, but in Krupniak's case the opposite was true - he always carried a wistful expression. The major was a quiet man and rarely, if ever, raised his voice. As Konrad entered his office, he noticed that Krupniak looked more downtrodden than usual. His hands trembled as he told them to approach his desk. "Why the hell, son of a bitch, did you do that, ha?" he asked, wringing his hands nervously. "I can't, son of a bitch, understand why you would do such a, son of a bitch, thing to me. Have I ever treated you unfairly?"

Janek took a step forward. "No, citizen major," he said. "You have been very good to us."

"O.K., son of a bitch," the major answered, flailing his arms across the desk, "then why did you let those guys go to church?"

Konrad stared squarely at the seated officer. "They wanted to go," he answered with a shrug. "And besides, I don't remember receiving any orders telling me to deny passes to my platoon."

"No orders to deny passes?" the major repeated in an indignant voice. "Have I ever issued a, son of a bitch, order to send the entire platoon outside? And, what is even worse, to church?"

Janek glanced at Konrad and smiled. "Well, citizen major, you must admit that it was an extraordinary occasion. I can't remember the last time we had a Polish Pope."

"You can't remember... well I guess I can't, son of a bitch, either," Krupniak commented with stunned astonishment.

"Exactly, comrade major," Janek added. "That's why there's nothing to explain really. I hope that Karol Wojtyła will live longer than his predecessor[14] but if he doesn't and if the Vatican happens to elect another Polish Pope while I'm still in the army, I'll know not to let my soldiers go to church."

Konrad struggled to suppress a gasp of laughter while Krupniak shrugged. "Listen Wytwicki and Dymowski," he said. "It doesn't really make much difference to me whether your platoon went to church or not. But you know that the People's Armed Forces advocate the scientific point of view, and if someone from the GZP, Central Political Command finds out about your, son of a bitch, organized march to a holy temple you could be in trouble, and so could I..."

"I don't think that you have much to worry about," Janek assured him.

Krupniak sighed and dismissed the two of them with the wave of his arm.

Konrad found out that Janek's words weren't far from the truth. He sensed that the government in Warsaw had been taken by surprise. The Polish dailies he could find, carried brief announcements about the appointment, but the lack of an official response was glaringly obvious.

A telex was sent from Warsaw to Rome the following day. Gierek, Jaroszewicz and Jabłoński[15] all congratulated Pope John Paul II, and Polish television conveyed the message across the country.

---

14. John Paul I's pontificate lasted thirty days only.

15. Edward Gierek - First Secretary of the Polish United Workers' Party. Piotr Jaroszewicz - Prime Minister. Henryk Jabłoński - President of the Council of State.

The last world leader to send word to the Vatican was the Secretary General of the Soviet Communist Party, Leonid Brezhnev.

Konrad tore the second last page off the calendar in front of his desk. It was December, 1978. Only three more days in khaki, he thought to himself.

Two days later, he started to pack up his gear. He picked up his canteen. As he stuffed it into his bag, he thought back to the first trial alarm march at 17th Regiment. He chuckled silently when he remembered that he had been one of the last soldiers to assemble in the roll-call square.

The year had passed by like a wink of the eye. Too quickly for his liking. In many ways he dreaded going back to Warsaw. He would most certainly get a job as a junior engineer in a company, but there will be little hope for promotion without Party connections. And who was he after all? Just an officer of reserve who wasn't too enthused about going back home.

Company Zero was reunited on a cold winter day. A secluded garrison in the Western part of Poland was the last stop-off point before their discharge. They were joined by another S.O.R. group, Company Seven from the Military District of Silesia.

Lieutenant colonel Zygmunt Knur, the commander of the garrison, greeted them when they arrived. "Well, citizens cadets, the time has come!" he said as he began to brief them on the schedule they had to follow during their three days at his regiment. They were to be promoted on Sunday by General Gnat, but before that, they learned, more training was required. Roman yawned loudly in response.

"O.K., I'll be brief," the colonel added quickly after glancing at the drowsy-eyed soldiers in front of him. "After the promotion, you have to parade in front of the tribune, deposit your Kalashnikovs into the arsenal and then report immediately for your promotion dinner at the casino club. After that..." he said, watching Roman yawn once more, "... after that, you are civilians and you can go to hell."

To the colonel's surprise, the cadets gave him a standing ovation.

"His last sentence makes sense to me," Roman said as the cadets watched Knur leave the podium.

"That was an interesting comment," Janek murmured.

"What do you mean?" Roman asked.

Janek stopped and looked around the crowded room. "How many people, do you think, are here?"

"About three hundred or so I'd say. But why are you worrying about that?"

"Well, the local bus to Kwiatowo holds between 60 to 80 passengers. That means that the other 200 or so cadets are really going to go to hell after supper," Janek said, obviously proud of his simple but observant deduction.

"There's only one thing we can do," Konrad said as they left the assembly hall and began walking through the roll-call square.

They decided to meet with the soldiers of Company Seven and approach colonel Knur to ask for extra buses.

Witek Klepacki, a tall, red-haired cadet with Company Seven, joined Konrad and Janek in the colonel's office. He started to explain their predicament to the colonel but Knur brushed them quickly aside, insisting that he had no time to talk to them. "You see, cadets," he rapidly explained. "This promotion is an unusual event for our otherwise quiet garrison. We have spent a lot of time preparing the food for tomorrow's dinner."

"May I suggest something, citizen colonel," Wytwicki interjected. "If our dinner is going to cause you a lot of trouble, we could miss the meal. Then we could catch the earlier bus."

Konrad and Witek nodded in agreement.

"But dear fellows," said the lieutenant-colonel, "that is impossible. I am giving the promotion dinner. It is a tradition that must be obeyed. I have been given extra funds for the meal."

Janek was adamant. He struggled in vain to persuade the colonel to change his mind.

Knur shook his head. "I have already bought the ham, pork chops and Hungarian wine for you. Besides, two very important people are coming to the garrison tomorrow. Do you know who?"

"General Gnat, I guess," Janek answered dryly.

"Well yes, of course General Gnat but who else?" He paused. "Tomorrow, comrade Skupio will be here and believe me, we can't get away with anything but a very posh reception."

Janek was about to question the colonel about the expected guest when they all heard a voice coming from the hallway.

"Can I be of help?" a man said, peeking his head into the office. With a smile, he stepped inside and introduced himself. "My name is major Alfons Menda," he said. "I am a political officer here. Can I help you with anything?" he repeated.

Konrad watched the officer closely. He was tall and had a certain air of distinction about him. His hair seemed to be painted with small, even brushstrokes of gray.

"Well, I hope you can help us, comrade major," Janek answered firmly. "We need an extra bus for tomorrow so that all of us can get home."

The major looked at the cadets for a split second and then rolled his head back jovially. "Is that all?".

After Menda had assured them that the problem would be looked after, the cadets thanked him repeatedly and left the office.

Colonel Knur nervously closed the door behind them and approached Menda. The major was sitting comfortably in an armchair facing his desk. He was smoking a cigarette.

"Where the hell are you going to get a bus for tomorrow?" the colonel yelled.

Menda got out of the chair and turned away from Knur. He strode to the window, took a brief glance outside and then turned around to face the colonel.

"You Knur," he said, "you have been asking yourself for years why you haven't been promoted to full colonel status, haven't you? Well, you have an impeccable service record but you lack certain political skills..."

The colonel's mouth dropped open and his face reddened sharply. "What? What you are saying, Menda?"

"Oh, calm down, comrade colonel," the major said, tapping him on the shoulder.

"I won't," Knur screamed. "What are we doing with those cadets?"

"My dear Knur, you should have been listening more carefully."

"Didn't you say that they would go home to the city by bus?"

"I certainly did." Menda smirked and with a wink, he shoved a package of cigarettes over to his superior.

The colonel brushed them aside and took a deep breath. "I'll ask you one more time, where are you going to get the transportation? From nowhere?" Knur was becoming more and more exasperated.

Menda walked back to the armchair and sat down. "What I promised them," he answered with a smile, "was that they would leave on the bus and they will. There is no other way to leave."

"But there are three hundred of them," Knur said gloomily.

Menda burst into laughter. "I can't help that. But don't worry dear colonel Knur. They'll be happy to get out of here and they won't care how. Some are bound to be picked up by their parents and friends and the rest will figure out something."

The colonel hesitated. "But what if they come back?" he asked.

"I'll handle it, don't worry," Menda answered.

The cold weather persisted and snow began to fall as Konrad stood in line amidst countless rows of soldiers. The cold temperatures reminded him of his first day in the roll-call square of the 17th Regiment. The ceremony was short and simple. The soldiers approached the podium in neat rows and then knelt down in front of General Gnat who touched their shoulder lightly with a saber.

From there, the newly-commissioned officers returned to the back of the column and removed their simple cadet epaulets. They were replaced by two star second lieutenant insignia.

When the last row of cadets had finished adjusting their uniforms, the General reached into his pocket and took out the formal "Order of Promotion." Snow was falling rapidly by that time and he spoke quickly while trying at the same time to rub his ears. After Gnat strode off the podium, he was replaced by a slim, but warmly-dressed man in civilian clothing. Juliusz Skupio was the First Secretary of the Municipal Committee of the Polish United Workers' Party in Kwiatowo. To the cadets' dismay he spoke for over a half hour.

Konrad grumbled under his breath while Roman cursed the Party secretary out loud.

Comrade Skupio though, seemed oblivious to everything going on around him. His ears were nicely covered by a thick fur cap.

Sandwiches arranged in intricate patterns lay on white linen tablecloths. The largest room in the officers' club also smelled of ham, pork chops and hard boiled eggs. Green bottles of Hungarian Riesling filled the back tables. They were arranged in a U-shape and filled the entire room.

General Gnat stood at the front of the hall, and he raised a glass of wine to the new second lieutenants. He and the other guests then filed out of the room into adjacent suite.

The slightly-rumpled colonel Knur finished downing his third glass of wine and was eagerly looking down at a fresh plate of sandwiches when Janek approached him and inquired about the extra bus. Knur blinked erratically and dropped a ham and pickle sandwich, or what was left of it, on the tablecloth. He looked around the hall without answering.

Konrad watched his friend eye the colonel with suspicion. "Is there a problem, Mr. colonel?" he asked.

"No, not at all," Knur answered. He picked up another sandwich and pushed it into his mouth quickly. "Everything is going according to schedule," he mumbled. "Why don't you and the rest of the group go to the T.V. hall when you have finished eating and wait there? Someone will come to get you when the bus arrives."

An hour and a half passed. Roman sighed and let out a loud yawn. "Well," he said to Janek and Konrad, "I might as well visit colonel Knur with you this time."

The newly-commissioned officers peered into the officers' club. The building was completely dark except for a sliver of light coming from beneath the doorway in the far corner. They opened the door quietly and went inside. Their ears were immediately bombarded by the sound of loud laughter, a woman's laughter.

While they stood in the darkness and tried to decide what to do next, the door leading into the room opened and Juliusz Skupio stumbled out, nearly tripping over all of them. He carried a bottle of vodka in one hand and immediately offered to pour them a drink.

They looked at him with some amusement and shook their heads. Skupio smiled when they explained their predicament. "Don't worry," he said. "Just have a drink with us, comrades officers. We'll take the three of you straight to Kwiatowo. There's enough room in our Volgas for you."

"But what about the others?" Konrad asked with exasperation.

"What? There are more of you? Well, you'll have to ask Knur about that. Knur! Comrade Knur!" Skupio shouted.

Major Menda appeared at the doorway. His face had a slightly pinkish glow. "Colonel Knur has gone home, dear comrade Skupio," he explained. "He has been on duty for 24 hours. Is there anything I can do for you?"

Skupio pointed to the three soldiers. "Do you see these gentlemen, Menda? Please do something about them."

"With pleasure, comrade," Menda answered and ushered the drunken man back into the lit room. When the door opened, Konrad immediately heard the woman's laughter once more. Menda closed it abruptly and turned to them.

"Well comrades," he said in a self-satisfied tone of voice. "The bus has been waiting for you for at least an hour now."

They looked at him with complete surprise.

"They just called from the bus terminal," Menda continued. "They told me that the bus was waiting, empty."

"Bus terminal?" Janek yelled angrily. "Colonel Knur told us to wait in the T.V. hall."

"Well, Knur is an old gentleman and has been on call for 24 hours. He must have been confused. Why don't you rush over to the bus terminal right now?"

The moment they left the club building, Menda picked up a telephone. "Sergeant Kapa? Major Menda here," he said. "Listen citizen sergeant, the newly-promoted civilians... you know what most of them look like, don't you? Good. I want to make sure that once they have left the compound the gates are closed and not opened again under any circumstances. If they come back, don't let them in. Tell them you have orders not to let anybody into the barracks. Understood? Good."

Menda hung the phone receiver up quickly and sighed with satisfaction. He picked his glass of vodka off the table and swallowed what was left in one gulp. Then he walked into the next room.

The bus station was full of people waiting for the nine o'clock bus to Kwiatowo.

"What now?" Roman asked sadly.

"I don't know," Janek snapped. "Let someone else think about it for a change." He dropped on to one of the hard, wooden benches in the station. His face revealed resignation and weariness.

The soldiers looked at one another slowly. Konrad shrugged his shoulders and started to look for a spot on the floor to lay his head.

Wiktor Gran walked up to him quickly and grabbed him by both arms. "I've got it," he said. He took his fatigue cap off his head and turned it upside down. "100 Zed from you, Konrad, and everyone else," he said.

They raised about 20,000 złoty, the equivalent of a decent salary for five months. The bus driver looked at the cap weighed down with coins and bills and nodded. The soldiers crammed into the coach and left before any of the other waiting passengers could sound an alarm.

The packed bus proceeded slowly along the icy highway to Kwiatowo.

Konrad glanced at his watch. It was midnight and their train was approaching a harshly-illuminated station.

"Bieława Główna," the conductor cried. "The passenger train from Kwiatowo to Warsaw Central via Bieława, Klusków Dolny and Wonbolice will be leaving from platform number six. The train leaves at zero hours, ten minutes."

Janek stood up and handed him a tightly wrapped package. He was dressed in civilian clothing. "I want you to deliver this to the regiment stores. Will you do that for me, Konrad?"

Konrad took the package and sighed. "Sure I can, but I thought that you would be coming back to Warsaw with us?"

"I can't. The train from Bieława to my city is a lot faster."

Konrad was saddened by his friend's departure. "Well, you should get going," he said. "I'll miss you very much." Swallowing a brief tear he leant over and kissed his friend on the cheek.

"Good-bye Konrad, and don't worry. We'll see each other again." His voice was raspy and he turned his face away from the window to shield his eyes from the light of the station.

Roman stirred from his seat in their train compartment. "Who's leaving?" he asked slowly, rubbing his eyes. "Where are we?"

"Bieława Główna - and Janek is getting off here," Konrad answered impatiently.

Roman sat up quickly and grabbed his bag. "Me too," he said. "I forgot to tell you but I'm going with Janek. I still have to go back to my garrison to get my gear."

Konrad tried to muster a smile as he watched the two figures wave and disappear down a set of stairs. The sudden loss of both of his friends depressed him.

He pressed his face against the window. The train moved slowly and crossed through the glaring light of the city's core.

A large billboard came into view. It was supported by a fence bordering the train tracks. 'We shall build Second Poland,' it read. He grumbled and lit a cigarette.

As the train began picking up speed, another poster filled the window. A white background was covered in part by a gray space rocket decorated with Polish and Soviet colours. "Fraternity in space," Konrad read to himself. I am back to Second Poland already, he thought and put his cigarette out.

As he turned around and began readying himself for sleep, he realized that the compartment was fully-packed with new passengers. Beside him, a stout man with thick glasses had dozed off, his chin resting on his substantial chest. A young woman and two soldiers chatted quietly at the other end. They all faced a haggard woman with four small children.

He closed his eyes and tried in vain to fall asleep. One of the soldiers sneezed repeatedly, the children sniveled and cried, and the bright fluorescent street lamps lining the tracks were distracting.

A small amount of light filled the compartment. The train was still. Konrad woke suddenly to the faint sound of a railway worker yelling down the platform.

The heavy man with glasses was sitting across from him. The rest of the compartment was empty. "Where are we now, sir?" he asked.

"Wonbolice Główne," the man answered with a gurgled sigh. "We should be in Warsaw in about two hours."

As the train began moving forward, Konrad turned toward the window. It was five o'clock in the morning. He could see people filing behind a bus stop. He figured that most of them were trying to get to work to start the 6 A.M. shift.

A milk truck was parked beyond the stop. A man was unloading gray plastic cases full of tall bottles and carrying them to the front of the dairy store. Close by, a group of people were forming a line on the snowy sidewalk.

"What are those people doing out there?" Konrad asked, pointing out the window.

"It must be a meat line," the older man answered, "Just imagine... they open the store at ten and those people will be out there waiting for five hours." He looked at Konrad and smiled bitterly.

Konrad thought back to the farewell supper at the garrison and the steady supply of meat at the barracks. I'm not coming back to Second Poland, he thought with frustration. It isn't here. It was back at the army garrison, with its subsidized restaurants and meat stores...

The bright lights of Wonbolice faded as the train made its way out of the town. The large silhouette of a dreary factory building passed in front of Konrad. He barely caught a glimpse of a few darkly-clothed workers entering the front gate for the morning shift.

PART

Second Love

CHAPTER 1

Konrad met her for the first time that summer in Warsaw while he was on a leave of absence from the regiment. It was a hot, muggy Sunday and Tina's small living room was unbearably warm. He wore a faded yellow T-shirt and a pair of shorts. He remembered feeling ridiculous that day, looking down at the chalk-like colour of his legs. His mother wore a shapeless swimsuit in a loud shade of green.

Hanna though, was fully, if not overly dressed. She wore a tailored cream-coloured skirt and blazer over a long sleeved peach blouse. He noticed that she also had a pair of stockings on, despite the unbearable humidity. He guessed that she was in her mid-forties. Handsome certainly, with short, curly blond hair and blue eyes displaying a sense of purpose. She held her chin up slightly which at times gave her an overbearing demeanour.

Tina had told him that her acquaintance was an economics professor at one of Warsaw's universities and was involved with the United Nations in some way. There was no doubt that she impressed him. She sat, facing his mother on the couch in a modest pose, graciously thanking Tina when she was offered a drink or something to eat.

After two hours, she bid them both a courteous good-bye and promised his mother that she would come again soon. Closing the door behind her, Tina turned around and noticed the curiosity on his face. "I must admit that I feel a bit sorry for Hanna," she told him. He learned she was a divorcee and was just getting over a painful and drawn-out romance with a long-standing boyfriend. He had to leave shortly after. He was expected back at the garrison that evening and he had a fairly long trip ahead of him.

Once outside, he walked along a wide laneway which was lined on both sides by linden trees.

It was still warm despite the late hour. He passed people returning from weekend visits and took a seat on the bench beside his bus stop. A handsome woman with long, blond hair passed by the bench. For a split second he thought it was Klara and began to motion to her, but just as quickly he remembered that she was away on holidays abroad.

Klara. He could hardly believe that it had been seven years since their first meeting. We met each other on a hot summer day much like this, he thought. He could still recall how the linden trees overhead looked then, with their boughs weighed down heavily with a profusion of blossoms. He and his friend Irian had caught the downtown bus from the same bus stop. They were going out for the evening with one goal in mind - to meet some women, start up a conversation, and if possible, invite them for a drink at a coffee house.

The bus driver had let them off in front of a large construction site where a new hotel was being built. From there, they had walked through an underpass below Aleje Jerozolimskie Avenue and around a circular building which housed the PKO Popular Savings Bank. By that time, they were close to the famous 'east wall' - a block of high rise apartment buildings, restaurants, bars and department stores. They imagined that the modern urban complex was similar to those built in the United States, the country they looked up to more than any other.

Konrad wore a pair of sunglasses made in St. Louis, Missouri, and a pair of gray pants that had also been sent to him by his relatives in Chicago. He looked quite impressive - at least in his own eyes. In the breast pocket of his shirt, he sported a pack of Marlboros, an expensive touch to complete the desired image. Irian did too, though at that time neither of them smoked.

They sat down on a stone bench, adorned on both sides with red tulips, and began to closely scrutinize all of the female passers-by.

Konrad smiled when he remembered what happened next. When I saw those enormous blue eyes, I was in love, he thought. He remembered elbowing Irian and persuading him to go and talk to the two women who were standing on the other side of the sidewalk. The pair seemed to be immersed in conversation, but paused and looked at them with curiosity when they realized they were being approached. After so many years, Konrad honestly couldn't remember the other woman's face, but Klara... she was simply beautiful. They walked to the riverbank. Her hands were soft and he remembered her perfume. They kissed many times, with Konrad pausing only to look at her more closely. She was wearing a pair of black pants and a matching jacket which complemented her light-coloured hair. Her eyes were blue and her lips were delicate and moist...

His bus downtown finally arrived and Konrad, still immersed in his memories, boarded it for the long ride to the railway station. "Seven years," he murmured to himself as he took a seat on the left hand side of the bus beside a window. It quickly barrelled past the PKO bank building.

He tried to recall when Klara finally revealed to him that she had a husband and daughter. It didn't make any difference anyway, he thought, shaking his head. Klara was an integral part of his life, almost from the beginning.

As their relationship evolved, he tried to feel excited about his role - lover of a married woman. He was proud that Klara preferred him over other men. All too soon though, a set pattern emerged. He had to get used to the fact that Klara was only free to see him on weekdays. Saturdays and Sundays were reserved for her husband with no exception.

How stupid I was then, he thought. I expected her to leave him right away, without thinking twice, but what did I have to offer her? Just my love?

He often felt guilty. He could not see Klara and go to church at the same time. Somehow though, he always managed to rationalize things. He used to tell himself that their love made everything right and just. He barely convinced himself, let alone God, but he continued on, nevertheless - life was dealt with one day at a time.

Fall arrived quickly at the army compound. The tall poplars began losing their washed-out yellow leaves early, while the few maple trees on the lawn of the hotel clung on to their golden and red fingers for a few precious days longer.

Konrad continued to travel to Warsaw each weekend to visit with his mother and relatives while Klara was vacationing in Yugoslavia. Hanna often dropped in on Sunday afternoons.

On one such weekend, he sat quietly in the living room and watched his mother and Hanna chat over tea. He found himself staring in the blond-haired woman's direction. First he focused on her face. Then, slowly his eyes followed the outline of her figure.

Her eyes met his for a second when she glanced briefly past his mother. Without reacting, she lowered her head and opened her purse. She took a small mirror and lipstick out and, smiling at Tina, quickly corrected her make-up. Konrad looked at his mother's face and sighed with relief. Tina's gaze hadn't moved from the television screen.

"How is your girlfriend, Konrad?" Hanna asked suddenly. Her question startled him. It was the first time she had bothered to ask him about anything.

"She is fine, thank you," he answered, not understanding the undertone of contempt in her voice. He tried desperately to return her hard smile.

"Does your Carol work?"

"Her name is Klara," he said, emphasizing the name carefully.

Tina stepped into the conversation. "No, she doesn't," she answered sharply. "Klara's husband supports her and their daughter Ania."

His mother's response infuriated him. "I thought I was asked the question, not you," he yelled.

Tina let out an abrupt snort. She always did that when she was about to laugh. "Did I say anything wrong?" she asked, looking over to Hanna. Konrad thought he saw the woman's face wrinkle with pleasure.

"No. You were correct as always," he said, rising from his chair. He walked into his bedroom and slammed the door behind him.

That night, his thoughts dwelled on his mother's friend. Despite her superior attitude, for some reason he was still captivated by her. He tried to convince himself that nothing had happened. Klara will be back in a couple of weeks, he thought reassuringly. But he slept badly that week. When Janek tried to talk to him about something, he couldn't bother to listen, let alone respond coherently. Hanna's image continued to occupy his thoughts and dreams.

She was sitting in his mother's living room, always on the couch in front of the television set, always wearing an expensive skirt and blouse and a matching jacket. He searched for Tina but she was never there. The dream always ended when he knelt in front of Hanna and lay his head tenderly on her lap.

"Do you want a smoke?" Janek asked him one evening after dinner. He handed a package of Sport cigarettes over to him. Konrad lay down and sighed with exhaustion.

He noticed that Janek was surveying him closely. He rubbed his barely open eyes. "Do you have any problems, Konrad?" his friend asked finally. "What's wrong with you?"

Konrad whispered, "Nothing special - really," and rolled on to his bed.

Janek responded with an instant laugh. "You can tell major Krupniak that," he chuckled. "He might, son of a bitch, believe you. But I know that something is bugging you, you can't fool me. So...?"

Konrad sat up and looked at Janek's face closely. He wore a look of genuine concern. With some embarrassment he told him about Hanna.

Wytwicki stood up and opened the window to let some fresh air into their smoke-filled room. "Well," he said shrugging his shoulders, "why don't you try asking this woman if she would meet with you sometime?"

Konrad looked across the room, straight into his friends's face.

"Look Janek," he said, trying to explain his dilemma. "You don't know what kind of a woman Hanna is. She is a professional economist. She travels all over the world, she lectures at two universities in Warsaw. And, she's not bad looking either..."

Janek couldn't help letting a small chuckle escape. "Well," he said, closing his eyes in a playful grimace, "I guess that's why you like her. You wouldn't have bothered otherwise. Yet, her remarks about Klara would indicate to me that you do have a chance..."

Konrad yawned loudly. A bright light filtered through the thick curtains of his bedroom at home. He guessed it was about noon. He always took it easy on a 'Gierek's Saturday' - the one work-free Saturday per month that Poles enjoyed. First Secretary Gierek had granted the holiday back in the early 'Seventies.

He had just finished pulling on his second sock when he heard voices in the hallway. Hanna might be visiting, he thought hopefully.

After a few minutes, he heard the faint sound of the television. Polish T.V. aired a variety of feature films interspersed with political broadcasts on the holiday Saturdays. He decided to find out what was scheduled for the afternoon.

The face of Ryszard Kwapień filled the T.V. screen. "The next movie will be 'My Fair Lady with Audrey Hepburn'," the announcer said.

Konrad let out a slight groan. Tina and Hanna turned around and looked at him with disdain.

"Hello Konrad," Hanna said coolly, "What is wrong?"

"I've seen that movie at least three times already," he complained.

Tina concentrated on the television screen. "Look Hanna," she said, pointing to the well-dressed reporter. "Isn't Kwapień a gorgeous man?"

Hanna responded with a brief laugh. "I've heard that he is a homosexual..." she murmured.

Tina reacted with amazement. "That's impossible," she said with genuine disappointment. "Such a handsome man. I can't believe it - I won't." Her eyes turned once more to the television screen.

"Ladies and gentlemen," Kwapień continued, "before we see the movie, let's speak with someone who is crucial to the building of our 'Second Poland'! "

The handsome reporter turned and began to interview the director of a state-owned farm.

Tina yawned. "He might be a nice-looking man," she said, "but I don't think I can stand an hour of 'Second Poland." She switched the channel. Hanna nodded with approval.

They heard the familiar voice right away. "Dear comrade foreman, could you please tell us whether it is an easy task to build our 'Second Poland' on a day-to-day basis?" It was Ryszard Kwapień again, this time dressed in a well-cut raincoat, and standing in front of an uncomfortable figure in coveralls. The foreman of a construction crew, holding a plastic safety hat under his arm, shook his head and smiled.

Tina frowned. "I changed the channel but it looks like we're stuck with him," she said, and forcefully switched the television set off.

She sighed and looked up to the ceiling for a brief moment. "I don't think I really understand what they mean by 'Second Poland'," she revealed. "If you look at our history, the Poland established after the Second World War is really the third Polish state. And yet they brag about this 'Second Poland' from dawn until dusk."

Konrad watched Hanna put a cigarette to her mouth and light it quickly. She seemed to be listening in earnest to his mother's comments.

"But you see Tina," she said, "it's nothing more than a term used by Gierek's propagandists. It's just a good, catch-all phrase for all of the new factories, buildings and expressways built during this decade. You must have heard Kwapień say 'we'll build twice as much as we used to have... we'll build a Second Poland'. That's all the slogan means." Hanna's voice was clear and she spoke with authority, as if giving a lecture to her students. Konrad listened to her quietly, with fascination.

"I think they're only talking about their cars and villas," Tina announced angrily, not noticing his captivation with Hanna. "Everything else is going downhill. There is less and less to buy at the meat market, and Gierek and his men are the only people who can boast that they have twice or three times as much as before."

"You're right," Hanna added. "And the other important thing that is getting larger and larger is our debt."

"Five red roses, please?" Konrad stood in front of a small green kiosk around the corner from Hanna's apartment building.

The lobby was deserted. He stood impatiently, moving his weight from one foot to the other as he waited for the elevator to come down to the ground floor. In his head, he had mapped the multitude of possible ways Hanna would react to him. He knew that rejection was inevitable, but he had to see her.

A small, black poodle bounded toward him, its paws scratching the polished floor of the lobby. An elderly woman scurried after it, cooing softly "Be quiet, Bobby. This gentleman probably thinks you are a rotten little beast." She grabbed the small animal and held him up to her garishly made-up face. "Ooh, but I know you're a sweet little doggy, aren't you?" she said tenderly, kissing her pet's snout.

Konrad wrinkled his nose uncomfortably just as the elevator arrived.

"Say good-bye to the gentleman, Bobby," the old woman whispered to the dog. She grabbed one of his front paws and lifted it up and down, waving.

Konrad sighed with relief as the elevator doors closed in front of him. He pressed the small round button embossed with the number eight. As the elevator started, his heart began pounding violently. His pulse seemed to be reverberating around the small, claustrophobic enclosure.

He stood silently in the hallway in front of her door, not daring to push the button. "What if she has a guest in there right now?" he asked himself nervously. He pressed his ear to the keyhole. The only sound he could hear was the faint, uneven voice of a radio announcer.

As he held his finger just above the button, his mind continued to race with apprehension. Last chance to leave, he thought.

A loud, irritating buzz of the doorbell... He pulled back violently and began to hope that she wasn't there at all, but then he noticed the door knob turning slowly. He felt her eyes travelling from his face down to the bouquet he held in one hand. "Please come in," she said finally, opening the door just enough to allow him to squeeze through.

Once inside, he stumbled upon a large, heavily packed suitcase. Hanna apologized quickly and moved it against the door. "I'm about to leave on a four day business trip," she explained curtly.

He held the roses out to her and she accepted them with a short, "Thank you." She returned a few minutes later, carrying the deep red flowers in a cut glass vase.

Konrad looked around the room closely, searching desperately for some way to start up some kind of a conversation with the woman. The cool, freshly painted walls of her small living room were cluttered with a number of black African masks. Sculptures of elephants and turtles sat on the small table beside her sofa.

Hanna spoke first. "I'm afraid we don't even have time for a drink," she explained. "The taxi will be here any minute." He sensed a touch of annoyance in her voice.

"Well," he said lightly. "What station are you leaving from?" He struggled to hide his disappointment.

"Warsaw Eastern."

He tried to ignore the caustic tone of her voice. "Fine. I'll help you with your suitcase at the station."

She glanced over at him with indifference and then moved her gaze over to the window overlooking the road. "I don't want you to be bothered," she answered dryly.

He glanced at the wall uneasily. One of the black masks hanging in the far corner seemed to be grinning at him with ridicule.

They turned their heads in unison when they heard a car honk suddenly outside. Konrad grabbed her suitcase quickly. "It's very heavy," he said out loud, puzzled that she would take so much with her for a short trip.

Hanna sighed and turned the doorknob. "Let's go."

Inside the small car, Konrad was self-conscious of his every move. He could smell her cologne and as the cab bumped on the uneven pavement his knee touched hers lightly.

"So, how are you doing in the army?" she asked him suddenly.

He sighed heavily. It was an expression of genuine weariness and boredom about the military. "I'll be happy when I'm finished," he answered. "Only three more months..."

Hanna nodded and looked out the window. She didn't acknowledge the contact between their legs one way or another. But Konrad felt it.

A handful of people were scattered along the length of the platform. They had twenty minutes to wait before the train arrived. Hanna led him to the cafeteria at the far end of the station. They sat down at a drab steel-gray table. Konrad thought immediately of the canteen in his regiment.

He looked up at Hanna and was surprised to see a pleasant smile on her face. "Thank you for carrying my luggage," she said and then ordered two coffees.

"Thank you. I'd like to pay the bill," Konrad said. Hanna stopped his hand as he began reaching into his pocket. "I'll pay," she said firmly. "You're a poor soldier."

He couldn't argue. Instead, he offered to reciprocate as soon as she returned from her trip.

Konrad pushed the button beside her apartment door repeatedly. He paced along the hallway in frustration and then bent down to peer through her key hole. His eyes blinked briefly as they adjusted to the dim light inside. The room was deathly still. Sitting on the windowsill, was the glass vase. The roses it held were in full bloom and their stems drooped slightly, weary of the stuffy, gray apartment.

Another trip to Warsaw, the next day, was no more successful and his frustration bloomed as the words she had said to him circled through his mind, "I'll be back in four days…"

He decided to call the university and find out why she hadn't returned. "It's very simple," her secretary answered. "She is away for a two week vacation."

He couldn't help brooding over the roses rotting in her apartment.

They met five weeks later in Tina's flat.

"It's getting more and more ridiculous," his mother complained. Over a drink, the three of them were discussing the shortage of meat in the stores. "Supposedly they have rolled back the price increases," Tina continued after she swallowed the contents of her glass, "but try to find anything edible in the stores."

She walked into the kitchen and took a bottle of Wyborowa out of the refrigerator and then replenished their glasses with the frosty liquor.

Hanna looked at her with concern. "Aren't we drinking too quickly?"

Konrad's mother shrugged and her face soured. "We'd better drink this before they take booze out of our reach as well," she said. "Everything is falling apart in this country. There's little to eat, no money to buy it with…" Tina's face was strained and she was breathing rapidly.

"Things are falling apart, my toilet too," Hanna added with a laugh. Konrad sensed that she found Tina's ornery mood difficult. Hanna explained that she had called a plumber but got nowhere when he told her that it couldn't be fixed. The spare parts weren't available.

Konrad smiled. Perhaps this will give me an excuse to go to her apartment again, he thought.

Hanna declined the offer of another drink and got up to leave. At the doorway he offered to come to her apartment and fix her malfunctioning toilet. They decided that three o'clock on the following Sunday would suit them both and she left.

After a quick examination of the toilet he discovered the problem. The chain-operated lever had neatly broken in half. It was rusted and he knew that it would have to be welded back together again. At first, he considered taking it to the regiment and using the workshops there, but that would mean leaving Hanna and not returning until the following Sunday. He also knew that she wouldn't be pleased about waiting an entire week. He decided to try stretching one section of the lever and bending it into a loop right there.

Outside, in the asphalt parking lot behind her building, Konrad banged away with Hanna's small hammer. The red bricks he was using to support the piece of metal cracked, one after another, leaving scattered patches of fine, red dust. After almost two hours his hands were raw.

"Konrad, just leave it," Hanna shouted from her balcony. He grinned at her, but continued to work. He knew he was being stubborn, but he also had a feeling that she was a perfectionist and wouldn't leave anything until it was finished. Only a few more jerks of the hammer, he told himself. For a second he imagined Hanna as his. Then he shook his head and chided himself for being unrealistic. Even so, he hoped that if he could just do this one thing for her, prove to her that he wasn't completely worthless, it would be a good start.

"You must be tired," she said, when he finally entered the apartment. "It's almost dark outside."

She offered him some tea but he was anxious to test the repaired reservoir first. He mounted the lever carefully and breathed a sigh of relief when he pulled the toilet chain. The sound of a flushing toilet had never sounded so good to him.

Hanna came into the washroom. Her eyes widened with a mixture of surprise and pleasure. "Well, you are an engineer after all," she exclaimed. "Thank you very much."

They sat in her living room and sipped their tea in silence for a few minutes. It had a strong aroma. He had never tasted anything like it before.

"It's called Earl Grey," Hanna remarked, seeing the fascination in his face.

This tea is so unusual, he thought. Unusual and perfect, just like everything associated with her.

"So tell me about your business trip?" he asked. He tried to keep his voice pleasant, but a hint of fury escaped.

"Fine," she answered with a shrug and a quick smile.

"Why didn't you tell me you were going on a vacation?"

Her expression changed quickly. "I was going on a business trip, but I decided to take a holiday while I was away."

"But you can't just 'decide' to take a vacation at short notice like that. You have to fill out a form first and get approval from the personnel office where you work."

Hanna looked at him smugly. "That might be true in a regular office," she said. "But at the universities it's a bit different. We get longer vacation and there's a lot more freedom." She looked up at the ceiling and then toward the window.

He felt anger blossoming inside him. "I think you lied to me," he said sharply. "You told me repeatedly that you would be back in four days, I was at your doorstep many times after that..."

Hanna stood up without a word and approached the window. She opened the drapes and looked outside. He didn't hesitate to continue. "Your lying confused me. I don't understand. I get the impression that you look down on me, but at the same time you don't seem anxious to get rid of me either..."

He watched her approach the coffee table and pick up a package of Orient cigarettes. She lit one in silence, and sat down at the sofa. With a slight flourish she crossed her legs and then looked up at him. She smiled briefly. He had nothing more to say. Instead, he leant over and kissed her softly. Then, pushing her down gently, he kissed her again, furiously, all over her face and neck. His teeth grabbed the zipper of her dressing gown and jerked it open.

Hanna didn't move. Her face had a far away look about it, as if her thoughts had little to do with Konrad and his love-making. After a few minutes, she pushed him away abruptly.

He shook his head with confusion, and when he looked up, the zipper was neatly closed. Though they were only a half a meter away from each other, he felt totally isolated from her. She was a distant, untouchable stranger.

"Thank you for repairing my toilet, Konrad," she said coldly, "and please, don't be upset."

"Thank you for the tea," he answered quietly and walked out into the hallway.

The following day Klara returned from her vacation. She had a deep, golden suntan and Konrad thought she had never looked better. They saw each other from time to time, just as they always had.

White, violet and brown. The colours of the fall chrysanthemums crowded flower kiosks all over the city. Candles and lamps were also on display for All Saints Day.

Every year Konrad accompanied his mother to the cemeteries in Warsaw. They visited the grave of his grandfather Robert and great-uncle Wiktor when they first arrived. Konrad lit two candles and placed flowers on the two graves. Before going to the military cemetery, they passed through the gates of a small, Moslem burial site and prayed at the tomb of great-grandmother Luba.

The military cemetery in Warsaw contains a strange mixture of graves; of Polish soldiers and partisans, and those of Communist officials and other prominent non-believers. The original cemetery church had been replaced by a modern funeral hall.

"Those men were killed by the Bolsheviks in 1920," Tina told him, pointing to deep rows of concrete crosses filling the left side of the cemetery. She knew every part of it.

Across the main road, stood a large, marble grave. Wreathes and candles, lit by representatives of the government, surrounded the tomb of Bolesław Bierut, the first president of Communist Poland. Tina looked at the large grave with obvious hatred. "It's ridiculous," she said. "This man and his Jews are responsible for my father's death and here he is, lying so close to the graves of the Home Army soldiers."

Konrad gazed at the tomb quietly and thought of his grandfather Jan. He had been put in prison when Tina was still in high school and, like many other Home Army soldiers, he was never formally sentenced. For five years, the government claimed that he was still under investigation.

"I hate Jews," Tina continued. "The Poles risked their lives to help them escape the Nazis during the war and... look what they did to my father and to other men like him..."

Konrad had heard Tina talk like that many times before, but that day her remarks seemed even more repugnant then usual.

"You are not being fair," he said. "The Jews you are talking about were citizens of Poland and they're still thankful to the people who helped to save them, even today. You know that most of those UB Secret Service[1] agents, who were Jewish, came from the U.S.S.R."

Tina stopped in the middle of the cemetery road and turned abruptly to face him. "Don't defend them," she yelled angrily, stressing her last word emphatically. "They helped the Communists build the Polish People's Republic out of the ashes of our nation."

Konrad sensed that his mother was getting overly emotional but he couldn't stop arguing with her. "But you can't assume that the whole UB Secret Service was made up of Jews," he said. "Native Poles and Russians were involved too."

"How do you know?" his mother was talking in a scream. "Berman[2] ordered your grandfather's arrest and he was a Jew. The man who interrogated him for five years was Jewish too."

Konrad rubbed his eyes and forehead slowly and shrugged. It was useless trying to talk to Tina about her father. He had heard stories about her hysteria at his burial; how she had refused to let the pallbearers close the coffin. He was only three at the time and didn't go to the funeral, but he could imagine the scene. His mother had many photographs of the handsome, gray-haired man lying in an oak casket.

Jan's grave was marked by a birch cross which identified him as a Home Army soldier. Hundreds of similar crosses, some of them gray and rotten, filled one section of the cemetery.

When the cross in front of Jan's grave had been damaged so badly by the weather that it collapsed, Tina ordered an identical replacement immediately. The birch tree signified the character of the Polish 'Armia Krajowa'. Partisans of the Home Army, also known as the A.K. were often buried in forests, their main centres of defense during World War II.

Close by the monument to the Home Army, there was a small cavity. People called it the 'Katyń Hollow' and honoured it with special melancholy. The symbolic grave reminded them of the thousands of Polish officers slaughtered by the Soviets in 1940. Their bodies still lay in the Katyń forest, sheltered by delicate birch trees, but their souls, Konrad knew, gathered at the Hollow on All Saints Day.

"I'm going to go and get some water for the flowers," Tina said quietly after her silent prayer.

Konrad left his mother alone with her father's tomb.

---

1. UB Secret Service was responsible for the torturing and killing of thousands of Poles from 1945 to 1956.

2. Jakub Berman returned to Poland from the USSR following World War II. He was appointed to the politburo and became Vice-Premier in 1954. He was in charge of internal security matters in Poland from 1945 to 1956.

Along the main road, he came across the grave of one of Poland's greatest poets, Julian Tuwim. Smiling bitterly, Konrad recalled Tina's harsh condemnation of the Jews. Tuwim, who was himself a Jew, was often hailed as the man who used the Polish language like no other. He escaped the Nazis by leaving Poland for America before the war began. The poems he wrote there, expressed his homesickness and longing for his country. Konrad murmured one of the poet's phrases quietly to himself.

He lit a candle near the grave and continued silently along the road, thinking how the air was heavy with that characteristic smell of autumn – the scent of fallen leaves mixed with damp, cool air.

As a child, Konrad had been faced with two contradictory opinions about Polish Jews. In contrast to Tina's negative attitude, his grandmother Julia often praised her Jewish acquaintances. She had known many Polish Jews in pre-war Wilno, and always described them as very able shopkeepers, lawyers and doctors. She had the impression that they were often model parents and were dearly loved by their children.

Tina's mother, Xenia, didn't really care one way or another. "They're just a nation of people who have become scattered," she had told Konrad. "I really don't understand why we must always be discussing Jews. Your mother is exaggerating. I suppose she likes to forget that she has some Jewish blood in her, and you too, Konrad."

Preoccupied by his thoughts, Konrad began traversing the road. He collided abruptly into another passerby. It was Hanna, clad in a modest, black wool coat and wearing tall rubber boots.

"What are you doing here?" he asked with surprise.

"I was visiting my father's grave," she answered, pointing to the plot just to the left of the road.

"Was he a soldier?"

She nodded. "He was an A.K. fighter just like your grandfather Jan. The Gestapo murdered him in 1944."

"Tina is here, would you like to talk to her?"

Hanna's face was tight with grief. She stared at Konrad silently, her eyes intense and bright against the somber scenery of the fallen leaves. "I'm not feeling very sociable right now," she answered. There was no antagonism in her voice. She took his hand, squeezed it tightly and began walking down the cemetery lane.

He called after her. "May I see you, Hanna?"

She turned around briefly. "Come on Friday night – at six o'clock," she said and continued walking.

CHAPTER 2

Hanna's apartment had been altered slightly. When Konrad arrived, he noticed that she had pulled her sofa bed out and had arranged two pillows and a blanket on top. The coffee table and two arm-chairs had been moved forward and to the side.

She wore a pale green dressing gown which was wrapped tightly around her waist. Her hair was carefully combed; her face subtly covered with make-up. Konrad noticed a light hint of French perfume permeating his nostrils as they looked at each other without a word.

Hanna's hard, shell-like exterior had disappeared, and Konrad began to feel cautiously confident as he stared at the woman' s warm and bright eyes. Her lips were soft and inviting and he closed his eyes for a few seconds as they kissed. Feeling more confident, he quickly peeled off her gown revealing the body he had dreamed about for months. As she lay back on the bed, her breasts and thighs yielded to his lips and hands.

Joy and a sense of triumph began to swell inside him and his mind seemed to be soaring above their bodies. He felt like a man, and then like a vulnerable little boy crying and pressing his wet cheeks lovingly against her lips. They embraced closely, their privacy secure and undisturbed behind the locked door of her apartment.

In the early morning, Hanna got up and went into the kitchen. She returned a few minutes later with a tray and offered Konrad some tea and biscuits.

"I'd like you to go home now," she said in a low voice.

He put his cup down and quickly embraced her again. "I want to stay here with you."

She gently liberated herself from his arms and stood up. "I'm not twenty five anymore, Konrad." He was relieved to hear her laugh briefly. "It was marvellous but you really have to go home."

At the door, he searched for a sign from her, some indication that she wanted to see him again.

"When...?"

"Next week. Saturday," she answered absently. "Come on Saturday."

Walking along the sidewalk, he turned around and saw a dark silhouette standing near the back of her softly lit balcony. Her figure remained motionless until he disappeared behind the street corner.

He called her two days later at the university. He was eager and excited on the phone. "I can't wait until Saturday," he told her, right after they exchanged hellos.

Hanna's voice was sharp and business-like. "I can't meet you today," she explained. "I'm very busy."

He felt strangely bold with her, perhaps because of the distance between them. He insisted that he come to visit her that evening and waited impatiently for a response.

Hanna sighed. "I have to summarize an article from The Financial Times tonight. I need it for my lecture tomorrow."

"Perhaps I could help you with the translation," he suggested, thinking that any excuse to see her would do. "I don't know if you remember, but I did spend a summer in Canada..."

"You think so?" Hanna said, laughing softly. "O.K., we'll see..."

The British newspaper lay on the coffee table in her apartment. He picked it up reluctantly.

"Well, go ahead, tell me what it says," Hanna said with a mixture of impatience and amusement.

He managed to figure out that the article dealt with Poland's external debt, but he didn't have the vocabulary he needed to translate it fully. He shook his head with embarrassment and handed the paper back to her. "Sorry, I can't read this," he conceded.

Hanna glanced at him through a pair of glasses. They made her look scholarly and he was attracted to her even more. He imagined her standing behind a podium and delivering lectures to her students.

"Don't bother yourself about it, Konrad," she said, laughing somewhat contemptuously. "I have already translated it." She handed him a neatly typed sheet of paper.

As he passed the article back to her, he felt his face turning red.

"You might be able to help me in bed," she said with a smile, "but not with English."

He felt humiliated but at the same time her comment excited him. "Well, why don't I help you now?" he said and rose out of his chair.

Her apartment was overshadowed by gray. The only light managing to slip through the window blinds came from the streetlights illuminating the pavement below.

Konrad studied Hanna's face closely. She looked serene and peaceful and he sighed quietly. She opened her eyes as he touched her cheek lightly. "Do you remember the day, three months ago, when I was looking at you in Tina's apartment?"

She answered quietly, "Yes, I do."

"Did you know how much I wanted you, even back then?"

Hanna turned away from him and picked up a cigarette. "I suppose I knew what you were thinking then," she answered slowly, "but I had no idea you felt so strongly about me."

She switched on the small table lamp near the bed. It made Konrad's eyes blink and he regretted that the pleasant darkness of the room had been disturbed.

Hanna slipped her dressing gown over her shoulders and with a definite tug of one arm, she secured it around her waist. Still holding the cigarette, she sat down in one of her armchairs. Konrad was quiet while he watched her movements.

"It seems to me that most of your women tend to be older than you," she said. Her voice was terse and cutting. "I guess your Carol is in her thirties, is she too young for you now?"

His heart sank. He always thought his relationship with Klara was sacred thing. Hanna's harsh comments and her question were breaking into his private domain. He answered her in much the same tone of voice. "Her name is Klara, not Carol and I do love her if that's what you mean."

Cigarette smoke seemed to billow out of Hanna's nose. She laughed heartily. "I'm sure that your love is very, very deep," she said.

She didn't have to say anything more. Before Konrad could stop himself, he was flying into a rage.

"I don't know what you think of me," he shouted. "You don't know much about my personal life, and I don't know much about yours either. What I do know is that we seem to have a good time together and you seem to enjoy yourself very much. Why do you have to look and talk to me with such contempt?" He turned away from her and buried his head in his pillow.

Hanna didn't answer. Instead, she got out of her chair without a word and walked into the kitchen. Konrad heard the sharp whistle of her kettle a few minutes later. He got dressed and waited for her to come back into the living room.

He did not touch the tea that she put out in front of him. Instead, they both smoked in silence for a few moments. He considered leaving right then, but the thought of an angry good-bye wasn't very appealing. That would mean the end of everything, he thought.

He tried to make conversation. "You really have travelled a lot, haven't you?" he remarked after looking up to the Indian relieves on her wall. "What do you do on your trips?"

"That depends on the country. I've been to a number of them," she replied dryly.

"All right, how about India, for example," he asked, still admiring the relieves.

"Well, a group of economists from the U.N. Development Committee provides advice, quite often, to the Central and State governments in India. Our group was helping the West Bengal government in Calcutta."

Her answer puzzled him and he shook his head slightly. "It seems strange to me," he said, "that our economists leave the country and can give advice abroad while everything is falling apart at home."

Hanna's mouth tightened. "Are you blaming me for the state of the economy?" she asked harshly.

He was bewildered by her strong response and shook his head.

"At least the West Bengalese listen to us," she said, with a long sigh. "Here, economists are ignored."

Konrad nodded and picked up the translation of The Financial Times article. "You said you would be using this article for your lecture tomorrow, is that right?"

"Yes. I'm going to be speaking at the Central School of Planning and Statistics."

He looked squarely at her. "Aren't you taking a risk? You are not supposed to disseminate any information about our external debt... especially to students."

Hanna took a deep drag from her cigarette and looked at him intently. "My students will be controlling statistics and planning in Poland after they graduate," she said. "If they just went ahead and opened up one of the country's statistical digests, they'd find that per capita meat consumption in Poland rose to an all time high during the first three-quarters of 1978. Your mother and great-aunt know that this is a lie because they line up for meat in the regular stores, the ones with the empty shelves. Quite a few of my students come from families who can afford to shop at 'Commercial Stores'. They wouldn't question those statistics. I think it's my duty to tell them the truth about our economy... and I will," she said emphatically.

Konrad thought quietly about her answer. He would have liked to discuss it with her longer, but he knew it was time to catch his train to the garrison. "I'm getting fed up with the army," he said as he got out of his chair. "Too much travelling..."

"You didn't have to come here tonight."

He tried to be cheerful. "Yes I did," he said and kissed her on the cheek. Then he moved toward the door. Just as he was about to open it, she grabbed his hand. Her face looked strangely anxious.

"Konrad, I would like to just ask you one thing before you leave," she said. "Yes?"

"I don't want you to tell anybody that you are seeing me."

Her words took him by surprise. She doesn't have any confidence in me, he thought hurtfully. "Who am I going to tell?" he asked her. "No one is going to find out about our love."

Hanna burst into uncontrollable laughter. He stood by the doorway, and listened, feeling completely lost and humiliated.

"That's a strong word to use to describe our relationship, Konrad, don't you think?" she said with a small snicker. She moved toward him and tried to caress his head.

"Then what would you call it?" he asked, skillfully avoiding her hand.

"How about an adventure? Our time together is exciting, adventuresome, and it's probably going to be very short."

By this time Konrad noticed that she had reverted back to her courteous and business-like manner of speaking. "You still have your Klara, and I still remember Andrzej..." she continued.

Her off-hand manner made his temper flare once more. "You seem to be intent on downplaying the importance of our relationship," he yelled. "I would just like to know this: why would a smart, sophisticated and very handsome woman like you sleep with someone like me?"

She tried to move closer to him again, but he backed away. "Perhaps I am just a bit more realistic than you are," she explained. "We both live in different worlds and we seem to obey different moral codes. You have been the lover of a married woman for years. I have never shared a man and my lovers don't share me with anyone else either."

"What about your friend Andrzej?" he asked quickly. He hoped for a sign of disloyalty on Hanna's part – something to help him shoulder the guilt he had been trying to ignore since they first started seeing each other. "That's over," she replied with indignation. "If I was still with him, you certainly wouldn't be here."

"But I am," he reminded her.

"Yes, you are," she replied quietly, "but then again, I can't tell you how much longer I will enjoy you. You are a great lover but that doesn't mean that I let my sexual desires affect the rest of my life."

Konrad felt her words slap him violently across the face. Her sudden, acidic outbursts continued to surprise him. So did her unpredictable mood swings the other way. "I'm sorry, Konrad," she exclaimed and gently took his hand. He looked at her with amazement as she began leading him back toward the bed and started caressing his hair. "I didn't mean to hurt you. You're just a young, immature man who tends to like older women... and we," she whispered, kissing his eyes lightly, "we like to reciprocate."

The once-purple carpeting in the employment office was brown and discoloured. It was the first thing Konrad noticed when he entered the building. Luckily, the employment officer he had arranged to meet that morning didn't mirror his drab environment. Konrad found the thin, tall, man friendly and animated.

After a quick hello and a handshake, he motioned to Konrad to take the chair next to his desk. Konrad noticed that his personal folder lay in front of the man.

"O.K. Mr. Dymowski. I've got your graduation diploma, your certificate, and a copy of your student record book. Now I need three photographs – please."

Konrad laughed when he looked down at the man's hand. He was trying to terrorize him, using his index finger as a gun. He snickered mildly when he glanced at Konrad's pictures. Then he got out of his chair and walked over to a steel rack full of multicoloured binders. He selected one of them and brought it back to his desk.

"Well," he said, seating himself down again and removing some files from the binder, "as you know I am in charge of graduate engineers, and it's my job to make sure that you obtain employment in your area of expertise." He began flipping through each of the files as he continued talking. "We have a number of jobs that we can offer you, but I must add that the salaries are modest."

"What are my options?" Konrad asked with a sigh.

"O.K.," the man said, taking a deep breath. "I can offer you a job in a design office for 2400 złoty a month. The only problem with this position is that your chance for promotion is very slight. Or, you could get a job at a construction site for 3000 złoty a month. That would mean leaving Warsaw though, and staying in a staff hotel."

As the employment officer continued to open files and describe the various jobs, Konrad's attention drifted. The salaries are so bad, he thought, I might as well try to get something half decent here in Warsaw.

One file folder lay unopened on the desk. "Before you tell me about that one," Konrad told the officer, "I should tell you that I don't really want to leave Warsaw. I also want to earn as much as possible. So far nothing you've mentioned really interests me..."

The man opened the folder and smiled. "Well, I do have a job at a factory to offer you. You would be paid by the hour at the beginning, but your monthly pay would probably add up to about 3400. Are you interested?"

"I suppose so. "

"Good," the employment officer said. "Here are the particulars: United Enterprises of Industrial Apparatus in Warsaw. Products: The company manufactures a variety of industrial equipment. Address: 105 Radziecka Street. Position: Junior engineer in training. Prospects: After one year and the successful completion of professional exams, the applicant may be promoted to plant engineer with a salary of 4,000 złoty a month. As a plant engineer, further training is involved with the possibility of a promotion to departmental supervisor."

The employment officer closed the folder and looked squarely at Konrad. "Well, what do you think?"

Konrad shrugged and told him that if there was nothing else available he would take the job. "I'll be finishing my army service just before Christmas. I can start right after New Year."

"All right," the man said with a wide smile, "I'll give the company a call right now."

"There's one thing I would like to ask you before I go. Why didn't you tell me about the United Enterprises job right at the beginning?"

The man leant back in his chair. "There is a method to my madness, Mr. Dymowski. The job isn't great, but it's better than the others. You only realized that because the others I described before were so miserable."

He didn't meet her the next weekend. She had informed him that she was seeing someone else and she asked him to come by in ten days.

They met again at her apartment. He filled her in on what he had been doing since he last saw her. "How about you?" he asked. She lit a cigarette and smoked quietly for a few minutes.

"Andrzej was here," she conceded. "... But I can't make love with him anymore. I don't think we'll be seeing each other again." She turned away from him and walked quickly into the kitchen. When she returned, she held two drinks. They sipped their scotch on ice together.

"In one week I'll be a free civilian again," he told her the next morning. They were relaxing in bed, smoking Hanna's Orient cigarettes.

"I'm glad to hear that, " she answered somewhat absentmindedly. Without saying anything else she got up and went into the kitchen to prepare breakfast. A few minutes later they were enjoying a meal of scrambled eggs and sausage.

"When can I see you again?" he asked her.

Hanna kissed him lightly on the cheek. He looked up to her, expecting a response. Instead, Hanna embraced him closely.

After a few minutes she got up and switched on her turntable.

"Let's have some music," she said.

During the past few weeks, Konrad had heard many of her albums. Hanna had a varied musical taste. She liked Greek folk music, classical, and easy listening jazz. Louis Armstrong was one of her favourites.

He listened to the song without a word. Louis Armstrong's deep voice rumbled, "It was short, but it was so sweet..."

"This is the answer to your question," Hanna said. He could feel her warm tears touching his face.

"... nevertheless we may meet, some other day, some other place, some other time..."

"Are you sure that you want me to go?" he asked as she kissed him. Their tears were melding together.

Again, she didn't respond. Instead her face hardened and she calmly asked him to get dressed and leave.

While he was buttoning up his shirt, he looked carefully at her face. Her eyes were red from crying, and her mouth pursed. She stared distantly at the far wall. "When I first made love with you," she said quietly, "I thought that I could control our relationship."

"And today?" he asked her anxiously.

Hanna kissed him and began unlocking her front door.

"Today, I am positive that you must go," she said.

It was close to seven o'clock in the morning and Konrad's train was beginning to lose speed as it approached Warsaw. He clung tightly to a package wrapped in gray paper as he sat in the empty compartment.

The platform at Warsaw Central was deserted. He shivered and pulled his shirt up to his chin. His belongings were packed in a soft bag that he slung around his shoulder. The package, containing Janek's fatigues, was tucked under his arm.

A series of buses passed in front of the station's entrance. One stopped and a few passengers climbed out. It was the bus he usually took to Hanna's apartment. The driver looked down at him expectantly, holding the door open. He shrugged and climbed on slowly.

About twenty minutes later he was ringing the doorbell, dreading an angry reaction from her. Instead, she opened the door with a quiet smile, and asked him to come in.

He was grateful that he could put down his parcels and take a comfortable seat on her couch. A steaming cup of coffee sat on the small table beside him.

Hanna wore a strange, almost loving expression on her face. "Please drink it, you're shivering. It must have been a long, cold trip," she said, sitting down beside him. "Get closer to me," she whispered. "There is a lot of warmth for you right here."

CHAPTER 3

It was December 30th and Konrad was standing on the corner of Marszałkowska and Piękna streets, gripping a bunch of colourful balloons.

"New Year's Eve bargain. American balloons – great for a party, just..." he shouted through the snowy streets.

The balloons were brightly coloured and twisted together into a number of different shapes. They caught the eyes of a young couple who were passing by. The dark-haired girl wrapped in a sheepskin coat pointed at Konrad and began laughing. "I have never seen balloons like this before. They look like..." She bent over and whispered in her friend's ear. They both giggled.

"I would like two of those, please," her friend said, embracing his girlfriend around the shoulders. "Where did you get them?"

"From New York. They're genuine American balloons," he answered with a grin. He sensed that the man was skeptical of his claim. So many things sold by retailers in Poland were purported to be from the United States.

"O.K., wherever... good luck," the customer said and waved good-bye.

He couldn't complain. Business was going well and by just before 10 P.M. that night he was completely sold out. After he had watched his last balloon disappear on a bus with a little boy and his mother, Konrad walked to the phone booth around the corner, tossed in a złoty coin and picked up the receiver. The phone was dead and when he hung the receiver back up, the coin didn't move. He angrily shook the whole unit. When nothing happened, he slammed down the receiver once again and cursed, "Why the hell isn't it working?" He sighed and left the booth. There was no use looking for another telephone nearby. He had tried all of them along Marszałkowska street that day.

Snow was beginning to fall heavily and the temperature was dropping. Luckily, he had dressed for the weather. He wore long cotton underwear, two thick sweaters and his winter coat. Two pairs of gloves covered his hands; and woollen socks lined the army boots on his feet. The sidewalks were empty and he dismissed the idea of asking for another load of balloons that night. He began to shiver uncontrollably, as the cold managed to penetrate through his many layers of clothing. Feeling damp and stiff he joined a lone figure standing near the closest streetcar stop.

Soon after his discharge, Konrad was faced with severe money problems. He couldn't expect to receive anything from his new job until the end of January at the earliest, and whatever he had earned while in the army was almost gone.

Before he was drafted, Konrad had always earned extra money by tutoring high school students who were preparing for university enrollment exams in math and physics. These few hours of work provided him with quite a decent income which he usually spent on summer travelling.

At that time of the winter though, that option wasn't available to him. He couldn't have been more relieved, when one of his grandmother Julia's neighbours, Julek, offered him a job as a street vendor selling balloons.

A Polish-Canadian, who had married Konrad's friend Jolanta, the tall and blond-haired Julek, lived in Warsaw where he studied medicine at the university. He returned to Montreal every summer where he worked as a waiter to earn money to support his wife and son through the school year. During June of that year, Julek had taken a flight to New York City, hoping to hitch-hike up to Canada from there. While he was walking along a Manhattan street, he noticed some long, thin balloons on display. They were on sale for three cents a piece. He quickly borrowed a calculator from the fat salesman and added up the costs of a city vendor's license, wages and the cost of the balloons.

"Balloons can go for forty złoty a piece..." he murmured to himself in Polish, "which means that I can make a net profit of four hundred dollars. Jolanta and I can live on that for five months..."

Hundreds of inflated balloons still filled two rooms of Julek's apartment in Warsaw that New Year's Eve. On the second day of their selling push, more than 60 percent of them still had to be sold. Julek, Konrad and his other friends picked up their loads and set out through the snowbound city. A sheet of white appeared in front of Konrad's eyes as he stood along Marszałkowska street. The wind was gusting furiously and it sent whirlpools of snow streaming in all directions. City streetcar tracks were barely visible under a growing layer of newly fallen snow.

He considered walking further down the deserted street to the next corner, but he could be stopped by the police and charged for selling outside of his vending area. What seemed like swarms of 'Milicja' cruisers were out prowling through the empty downtown area. "Damned cops," Konrad shouted after a grey-painted Fiat with its blue flashing light. "I haven't seen a snow plow for 24 hours, but these SOB's are out as usual, always ready... how about picking up some shovels and doing some useful work..." Only the silent banks of snow lining the curbs were listening to his complaints.

After a full hour, he had only managed to sell three balloons. The sky began to brighten and he hoped for a few more customers. Instead, the only figure in sight was a large man, carrying a handful of balloons. Konrad laughed to himself. Instead of customers, I've got competition, he thought.

His friend Irian doggedly trudged through the snow and approached him.

"Oh, it's you," Konrad said, trying to be cheerful. Irian's face displayed frustration and he still carried his full share of balloons.

"I spoke with Julek a while ago," Irian told him. "With this weather he says he is not going to make any money at all. He'll be able to cover the cost of the balloons, but our salaries are going to ruin him."

"Well, why doesn't he just pay us less?" Konrad asked.

"I told him that but he just smiled and said, 'a contract is a contract, Irian.' That's all."

"So?"

"That means that he is going to pay us the full amount," Irian snapped impatiently. "We've got to do everything we can to keep him from losing too much."

Konrad glared at him. "Don't you think that I want to help? I can't do more than I'm doing now. There just aren't any people here."

A gust of frigid wind pushed against the two of them, and went wailing down the street.

"Right," Irian shouted. "So move your fat ass and let's find some people. There must be some milling around the downtown underpasses!"

The underground tunnel below the intersection of Marszałkowska and Aleje Jerozolimskie streets was dotted with people, but few seemed interested in Konrad and Irian's special balloons as they hurriedly lined up at the RUCH cigarette booth, made their purchases and departed. Konrad and Irian gave up after thirty minutes.

For the last five years we've been graced with warm, dry winters, Konrad thought angrily as he tried to make his way home. Not a single streetcar or bus was in sight and the few taxi drivers who were still on the road were charging heavily inflated prices. Floundering through the heavy snow, he cursed the city's non-existent snow-cleaning crews.

He and Hanna spent the first hours of 1979 together at her apartment. The coffee table was covered with a fresh linen tablecloth and two red candles burned in their wrought-iron candlesticks. Their feeble light reflected on a crystal vase holding the single sprig of white lilac that Konrad had managed to find the evening before.

Hanna got out of bed and lit a cigarette. When she sat down in one of her armchairs, her face seemed to be haloed by the flickering light of the candles which danced on the walls. She looked content and serene as he knelt in front of her and pressed his head against her lap. My dream has materialized, he thought, as he inhaled the smell of her perfume and clutched her closely. He felt joyful as she began to gently caress his hair.

It was still early – only five o'clock on that cold, January morning, but already a large crowd of people had gathered around the nearby bus stop. He overheard a woman muttering to her friend that although the streetcars were out of service, the buses were still running. She said she had seen one go by forty minutes earlier.

"It was so packed that the driver didn't even bother to stop, though," she said with a sigh, wrapping her scarf even more tightly around her neck and chin. A fine layer of tiny icicles covered her eyebrows.

The would-be passengers crowded close to the curb when they saw a bus approaching twenty minutes later. Konrad waited eagerly, clutching his ticket in his hand, and then watched with horror when it too, failed to stop.

Slowly, people began shrugging and setting out on foot. "I suppose I'd better start walking," the woman said with a sigh. "It's about five kilometres but anything is better than waiting here."

Konrad stood by the stop and watched the shadowy silhouettes struggle through the uncleared sidewalk. He had no choice. The job he was starting that morning was at a factory fifteen kilometres away. He had to get a bus.

It was 10 o'clock before he reported for work. "Could you please tell me where I could find Mr. Witold Kramer? He's an engineer here," he asked a guard when he stepped inside the office building in the factory complex.

"Down the hall, first door on your right."

He rapped on the door. An elderly man with silvery grey hair and light eyes looked up to him. With a smile he asked Konrad to come in and shook his hand.

"Sit down, sit down and relax," he said. "You must feel exhausted. I've just gone through a gruelling bus ride myself... coffee?" Without waiting for an answer, the older man approached the kettle sitting on the office window sill and plugged it into an outlet.

Konrad looked at his boss gratefully and took a chair. He watched Witold Kramer open a desk drawer and put three teaspoons of ground coffee in each of the two glasses sitting beside the kettle.

"I'm sorry, I can't offer you any sugar with your coffee," he said with a faint smile. "I'm afraid that I don't have any sugar coupons."

Konrad looked at his new employer with astonishment. Since 1976, every Polish citizen had been issued with a two kilogram sugar coupon each month. He thought it was puzzling that a man of age and position like the engineer would be deprived of his ration. "If you need some coupons, I might as well give you one of mine," he said, reaching for his wallet.

Witold Kramer burst into laughter. "No, thank you anyway," he said with a loud chuckle. "I get my coupons just like everyone else, but I have to give them all to my relatives and friends. You see, Mr. Dymowski," he explained, "my wife and I like jam. Last summer, Urszula – my wife and I, borrowed about 40 coupons so that we could make jam. We made almost a hundred kilograms of raspberry and strawberry..."

"A hundred kilograms? What do you do with it?"

"We gave about a half of it away and the rest we enjoy with tea, every night after dinner. We drink it without sugar and serve the jam on small plates..."

Konrad listened closely and he realized that the man was describing a regular ritual of his grandparents' home.

"Are you from Wilno, sir?" he asked.

"My wife is from there, yes. I am varsovian, but over the years I have learned to drink tea her way."

Konrad smiled. "I do the same," he explained. "My grandmother and great-aunt are from Wilno too." He opened his wallet and began searching for a sugar coupon. "It's funny," he continued, "since the government began rationing sugar, our cupboard has been full of it. My great-aunt insists that we buy all we're entitled to because, as she says, tomorrow there may not be anything to buy." He placed two coupons on the engineer's desk.

"No, you keep them, Mr. Dymowski," Witold Kramer said with a smile. "Your great-aunt is right. We really don't know much about tomorrow." He left his chair and silently walked over the window looking out on the factory yard. He motioned to Konrad to join him.

Outside, a handful of soldiers and workers were pushing their shovels against the frozen and unyielding snow. They were trying to clear a path from one building to another in the complex.

"You might have wondered, Mr. Dymowski," the older man remarked quietly, "why we aren't busy doing something this morning. Well, as you can see we might as well sit here for the rest of the day. God knows when it is going to get any better. Our plant has been practically shut down because of the weather and if the coal shortages get bad enough, we won't have any electricity either." Witold Kramer turned away from the window and slumped into his chair.

Konrad didn't move. He sensed that the man wanted to say more.

"I've been an engineer for forty years," he said with more than slight resignation in his voice. "I spent the war fighting the Germans as a Home Army soldier. I was involved in underground arms manufacturing." Konrad watched him reach for a package of Carmen cigarettes. "Do you smoke, Mr. Dymowski?" he asked. Konrad nodded and thanked the man as he pulled a single cigarette out. "I would like to tell you about this factory," he continued. "Before the war, it was a private company known as 'Rozenberg and Krajewski'. I was employed by the firm in 1938 and I can tell you that we made very good products back then. Our pressure gauges, flowmeters and hydraulic presses sold all over the world and they always met the best European standards..."

Konrad's boss sighed and paused for a moment. "Aren't you bored?" he asked looking at him. Konrad assured him that he was not. Witold Kramer unplugged the boiling kettle and placed two steaming glasses of coffee on the desk.

"Well, I came back here after the Americans helped to open up the P.O.W. camp in which the Nazis kept us, after they had crushed the Warsaw Uprising." He paused again. Konrad could sense that the memories were not pleasant. "We reactivated the factory as soon as we could," Kramer continued, taking a long drag from his cigarette. "We were lucky. The Nazis had been operating the plant and it wasn't destroyed..."

The engineer rose out of his chair slowly and walked over to a decrepit metal rack in the corner of his office. He pulled a swollen, black binder off one of the shelves and returned to his desk.

After he had wiped a thick layer of dust off the top, he opened a book. The first photograph showed the factory yard with some buildings in the far background. Kramer stood in the middle of a group of employees. He and the rest of the workers were smiling cheerfully into the camera.

"I think you can get a better idea of the plant through these pictures, rather than going outside," Witold Kramer said. "The building you can see on the extreme left is the machine department. We call it Department A. It's the heart of the plant. We make machine parts there and then pass them on to the building you see here behind the people in the photograph. That is Department B. From there, the semi-finished products go to Department C for final assembly and inspection. The building we are in now is known as Admin Building or Department D. It houses our technical offices and inventory."

Konrad looked down at the image of his boss in the photograph. Engineer Kramer's hair was jet black and he had a slightly mischievous look in his eyes.

"... Two months after we started up the factory, there was another shutdown," he told Konrad, slowly turning the page over. The second photograph displayed the same yard, this time full of soldiers. They were loading objects into large wooden crates. Konrad noticed stars on their military caps.

"What were the Russians doing here?" he asked.

The old engineer laughed bitterly for a moment. His voice trembled as he answered. "They took all our machines apart; our good British and German tools in Department A. The so-called Polish government told us to help the Soviets pack up everything and ship it to Russia..."

Konrad looked at his elderly boss with sympathy. At the same time though, he couldn't help wondering why the plant workers didn't do something. "I find it hard to believe that everyone agreed to this thievery," he said.

Without answering, the grey-haired man quietly turned to the next page in the album. Konrad gazed at a photograph of a military truck which was surrounded by semi-packed wooden crates. It looked as if some workers were being forced into the vehicle by Soviet soldiers wielding the butts of their submachine guns.

"There is one man who didn't put up with it," Witold Kramer said, pointing to the bottom of the photograph. Konrad saw the figure of man, struggling on the ground with two soldiers.

"That is Wiesław Stefaniak - a wonderful electrical foreman," Witold Kramer continued. "He did his apprenticeship at Siemens in Germany before the war..." He took a short puff from his cigarette and stamped it out in an ashtray on his desk. "The other men you see here by the truck, didn't submit either."

Konrad trembled. He greatly regretted his last question.

Witold Kramer sighed. "Most of those men were released after a couple of years and returned to Rozenberg & Krajewski - that is... to United Enterprises," he added. "But Stefaniak didn't. He went to Wronki Prison where they held political prisoners. I heard they beat him continually and that he died from internal bleeding."

"What happened to you?" Konrad asked quietly.

A bitter, ironic smile covered Witold Kramer's face. "I took these photographs. I wanted to make sure that I could prove what had happened," he answered. "As it turned out, I shouldn't have bothered. The Communist government confiscated the negatives and most of my prints except for the ones that I had printed twice. You just saw some of them... I urged them to keep the staff and the plant intact but they ignored me. I spent two years in prison myself..."

Konrad looked down at the floor. "I didn't know..." he said quietly, "but what happened to you after you were released? Did you get your job back?"

Kramer nodded. "I suppose the authorities decided that they needed the plant after all, so, when I returned it was already back in operation. Russian machine tools had been brought in to Department A." His voice had a hint of sarcasm. "The machines were very inefficient and our productivity was about 40 per cent less than it had been before the war. But we worked hard and... I continued to take pictures for this... chronicle."

As he flipped through the pages in the photograph album, Konrad saw how the plant looked over the years. The buildings and yard were virtually unchanged. The only differences he could spot were slight alterations in Kramer's clothing.

"... There was a lot of enthusiasm after the war," the older man continued. "But it was wasted by the government and it's never going to come back. In the 'Forties and early 'Fifties, people worked overtime without pay." His voice became suddenly distant. "Warsaw was rebuilt from shambles - industry was revitalised too. Mr. Gierek and other Communists often claim that it happened because of them," he said, his voice shedding hostility. "But Mr. Dymowski, believe me, things improved despite their interference, not thanks to their help. And now," he said, lighting another cigarette, "on January 2nd 1979, our fearless leaders are appealing once again to the nation for help and enthusiasm. Did you hear the news this morning?" he asked Konrad.

When Konrad shook his head, Witold Kramer quickly added, "They want us to shovel the snow off the streets," he gasped. "They built themselves a 'Second Poland' and they don't even have snow plows available in the dead of winter. Even the trains aren't running now..."

Konrad glanced through the office window. Outside, he saw a solitary soldier making a fruitless attempt to carve a path through an enormous wall of snow.

"And what will happen to us next?" he asked Witold Kramer quietly.

The engineer's face was deathly white. "If they can't bring coal in by train," he said slowly, "they may have to shut the generators down..."

CHAPTER 4

The temperature in Julia's flat had been dropping steadily since the New Year snowfall. Engineer Kramer's grim prophecy was rapidly being vindicated. Coal shipments from Silesia had not reached many of the country's generating stations because major rail routes across Poland had been snowed in. Due to the shortage of fuel, co-generating power plants had to reduce their heat output and radiators in many Warsaw apartments were stone cold.

Konrad worried about his grandmother's health and made plans to meet his uncle Bib after work. They both shivered as they made their way up the frigid stairwell leading to Julia and Agata's apartment.

The heavyset Bib bent over his mother's bed and kissed her on the cheek.

"How are you? Are you cold?" he asked with concern.

The bed-ridden woman feigned a weak smile. "Just a little," she answered with a small shiver.

Agata's couch was moved into Julia's room and blankets and tablecloths were used to seal the windows and doorway. Bib's wife Anka lay three thick blankets on Julia's bed. With the single electric heater that Bib had brought with him that evening, the temperature in the room hovered around 16 degrees Celsius.

Julia smiled at them with gratitude. Agata though, sat on her small couch and scowled. "I'm not going to be able to sleep here," she said grimly. "I can't take my daily bath either. There's no hot water. A disaster." She looked funny, bundled up in three woollen sweaters. They laughed when she began complaining of the heat and took one of them off.

The lights went out just as they were leaving the apartment for home. Konrad looked at his uncle with frustration. "If they have run out of coal altogether and there's no power, I don't know what we're going to do," he exclaimed.

Agata quickly fetched a candle. Its feeble light barely illuminated the cold, dreary hallway. Bib managed to find a flashlight in a small cupboard in the kitchen. "Konrad and I are going to find out what has happened," he told Anka. "Stay with Agata in Julia's room. It will be warm in there for a while."

As they walked through the building Konrad noticed that only some of the floors were affected by the power cut. "Heaters are probably buzzing in every apartment and some circuits are becoming overloaded," he remarked.

Bib nodded. "Come on," he said, leading him to the stairwell and down to

109

the basement. "I'll show you what to do. It's illegal, but we don't have any choice."

Konrad aimed the flashlight at a small metal panel and his uncle pulled its heavy hinged door open. He pointed to a fuse in the upper right corner. "This is our apartment circuit," he said. "We have to remove it first." Konrad watched as Bib loosened a screw, and re-connected a wire to a sound circuit and then replaced the fuse. "That's all there is to it," he said, placing the tools back in his suit pocket.

Winter's icy grip persisted and the government called for volunteers to help clear the streets and resurrect Warsaw's transit system. "Dear citizens," Ryszard Kwapień cried on the T.V. Daily, "this is the winter of the century. But other countries are suffering just as badly. In the United States, dozens of large cities are clogged with snow. We've heard reports from Chicago, Illinois. In that city, it was many hours before the transportation system was in operation again."

"Hours!" Agata cried as she sat in Julia's room dressed in layers of thick sweaters. "It's been a week since a streetcar moved in Warsaw. They have ruined the country and now this idiot is trying to justify things with his so-called 'Winter of the Century'. Many hours," she repeated and sighed with fury.

A joke circulated around Warsaw that winter. "No invaders have to come, minus four and we are done," people said to each other.

Cynicism was rampant. Konrad sensed this when he listened to people talking at the local bus stop or in the workshop in his factory. Their country, described as a major industrial power by Gierek's propagandists, seemed incapable of restoring even its basic services.

He watched frustrated snow plow operators working in the street and sighed with resignation. By that time, the snow had hardened so much that the plows shuddered when they hit the walls of ice which covered the city's roads.

Warsaw's streets were crowded with people trying to dig the unyielding snow. Military squads worked through the night and convicts were issued spades. In mid January, the first streetcar moved through the city, almost invisible behind the left-over towering banks of snow.

He arranged to meet Klara at his mother's apartment one evening. They hadn't seen each other for weeks, but Klara, realizing that Tina was out for the night, wasted no time slipping off her clothes and jumping into Konrad's bed. "Come to me," she whispered, covering herself hurriedly with a comforter. "I am frozen."

They lay together in silence. Konrad felt aloof and avoided her eyes.

"Do you love her?" she asked quietly. "Just tell me - do you?"

"I don't know," he revealed. He shook his head repeatedly, knowing that his words were sincere. He still had trouble trying to define his feelings for Hanna. Klara quietly asked him to pass her a cigarette.

He made no move toward the package on his night table. "You haven't smoked for months, Klara. Why do you want one now?" he asked with resentment.

"I just want a cigarette, that's all," she answered.

As he reached over to get her one, he heard the front door open. A few minutes later the telephone rang. He heard Tina's voice clearly from the other room. "Well Hanna," she said, "I don't know. Konrad has a visitor tonight and I think they need some privacy. I'll see you tomorrow. Is that all right?"

Klara took little notice of the telephone call. Instead, she seemed more concerned with his coolness towards her. "Look, don't force yourself," she said slowly. "You don't have to pretend that you love me when you don't."

He felt a painful, almost cold sensation building up in his stomach when he reached Hanna's doorway.

"So you have come to say good-bye, " she said coldly.

"No. Who told you that?" he said, mustering a nonchalant glance.

Hanna left the doorway and strode quickly into the living room. She grabbed a package of Orient cigarettes from the coffee table and frantically lit one. She inhaled deeply and gave him a hardened stare.

"I'm sorry, but you will just have to get yourself another female idiot," she said. "Did you have a good time with your date?"

"No, it was terrible," he said, moving toward her.

Hanna pushed him away abruptly when he tried to embrace her. "Don't touch me," she snarled.

He sat down in the chair across from her and pulled out one of his own cigarettes. "Will you pass me a lighter, please?" he asked meekly. Hanna threw it at him in fury.

The intensity of her anger took him by surprise. "Take it easy Hanna," he said, trying to maintain some calm. "You have always known about Klara. I didn't think you really cared."

"Up until now," she answered slowly, taking a prolonged inhalation from her cigarette. "I didn't. I do now." Then she turned away and spoke quietly. "I thought you knew that I was in love with you – but it doesn't matter. It's over."

He felt foolish because of his past uncertainty. Before today, I didn't really know if I wanted to leave Klara and be with her only, he thought. Perhaps I have lost her forever. His mind reached back to their nights together. Looking over at her, he felt that something truly important was being torn out his soul – something that he could not afford to lose. He felt his entire body shiver as he contemplated the possibility of never touching her tenderly again.

"Could I help myself to a drink?" he asked finally. His voice was trembling.

"Go ahead and have the whole bottle," she answered with a shrug.

The alcohol created a burning sensation in his throat. It also calmed him down enough that he felt he could begin to speak.

"I know I love you," he whispered. "Please, let me stay. I'll never touch another woman again." He sobbed, holding his head in his hands. Then he sat back in silence and resignation, quietly punishing himself for what had happened. He looked at Hanna with pain, then closed his eyes, trying to stem the flow of tears down his face. When he opened them, he saw Hanna kneeling in front of him. She was crying too.

Klara called him at the office the next day. Following an abrupt hello she asked him to go out with her that evening.

"I can't tonight, I'm meeting a friend," he answered quickly.

"Really?" she said with mock surprise. "What a pity. Are you that busy with this friend of yours, whoever she is? Don't worry. I was just joking. Enjoy yourself Konrad," she said, and hung up.

The next day she called again and asked him to return her photographs.

"They are my souvenirs" he protested, thinking of the pictures, framed above his bed.

"Don't be stupid, Konrad," she said. "They belong to me. We aren't together any longer and I want them back." He put all pictures in a large, brown envelope. He mailed the parcel using 'Poste Restante' service, just as she wanted.

At the beginning of his second week at work, he was issued a pair of green coveralls and safety shoes. Witold Kramer then placed a locker key in his hand.

"You will be starting your practical training in Department A," his boss said. "Mr. Bronisław Oskiernia will be your supervisor for a while. He'll tell you all the secrets of the machine department."

Konrad felt his palm completely disappear in the gigantic hand of the foreman. "Nice to meet you, Mr. Dymowski," he said jovially. Oskiernia had a bright shock of blond hair despite his age. Konrad guessed he was in his early sixties.

"I'll be showing you the various machines in this building," the foreman continued. "Engineer Kramer will introduce you to the more technical side of things with diagrams and drawings. Am I right, Mr. Kramer?"

"That's what we've done for the last forty years," Konrad's boss said with a pleasant smile. "How many young engineers, do you think, we've trained over the years, Mr. Oskiernia?"

"I really can't remember," the foreman answered, "but there have been scores of them…"

Konrad spent very little time in the administrative offices of United Enterprises after that day. Every morning he would enter a machine department, change into his coveralls and then, according to Bronek Oskiernia's instructions, he would join a team of employees. He spent two weeks with a mechanical maintenance crew and then he joined the plant's electricians.

Department A employees always ate lunch in the workshop. There was nowhere else to go. The company's management steadily refused to build them a cafeteria.

It was a favourite topic of conversation during the lunch period and breaks. Konrad heard one of the electricians, a blue-eyed man with cheeks speckled with freckles, complain about it every day.

"How long have they been promising a cafeteria?" he asked one afternoon at the end of the week.

Mietek Maliniak, a young, dark-haired mechanic, answered slowly. "I have been here for almost five years," he said, placing a tin mug on the workshop bench. "But we all know that there – in the office, there's no one we can talk to about it, except Kramer. The others are Party members and they don't give a shit about us. We've spoken to the union boss about it thousands of times, but he's not going to do anything, he doesn't need it."

His remarks puzzled Konrad. "What do you mean?" he asked Mietek. "Isn't the union supposed to represent the workers?"

Most of the men laughed loudly at his naivety. Janek Siedlak, the electrician, shook his head and smiled. "Mr. Dymowski," he cried, "this union of ours is a hoax, just like the Polish United Workers Party – a party without workers. Do you want to know what the fucking union does here?" he asked, and passed him a package of cigarettes. A number of the other men in the room put Sport cigarettes to their mouths. Janek Siedlak passed Konrad a light and flashed a broad smile.

"The Union of Metal Industry Employees does what? Well, each New Year they organize a party for our kids. They hand out some candies and one orange to each child."

"They didn't even give out oranges this year," one man yelled from the back of the room. "They gave them lemons instead."

Janek Siedlak shrugged. "O.K., It doesn't really matter." Konrad urged him to continue.

"Another union activity? – potatoes," Janek said. "They fetch them in plant trucks every fall so that we can buy them a bit cheaper. That's it."

Konrad looked at him with amazement. "Is that all? That doesn't seem to have much to do with trade unionism…"

Again, laughter rippled through the crowded workshop.

"This isn't America, Mr. Dymowski," the electrician said. "There, the workers will go on strike if they feel they need to, and they often gain something. Here, it's impossible. Our director is a union member himself."

"It's one and the same clique," Mietek Maliniak shouted angrily. "Party, union, management – they're only looking after themselves. Sroka, the Party secretary here, gets a subsidized vacation every summer, and the same goes for the union boss Mrowicki."

"I've been paying full union dues for three years now," another worker shouted, "but when I ask them about a vacation they just put me off for another year. 'Just be patient, Mr. Kowalski,' they told me."

"Zygmunt is right," Siedlak said. "Party Secretary Sroka owns a greenhouse and drives a BMW. Mrowicki has a Fiat. And yet, they go on subsidized holidays, not us."

Bronek Oskiernia appeared at the doorway and scowled. "Quit your grumbling, the break is over. You can finish tutoring our young engineer tomorrow."

With Bronek Oskiernia's help, Konrad became familiar with the workshop. One day, the foreman showed him the parts crib. It was full of rewound coils, machine spools and other spare components. Oskiernia told him that all of the parts had been made in the workshop.

"Wouldn't it be easier and cheaper to buy them?" Konrad asked.

The foreman sighed. "That makes a lot of sense, Mr. Dymowski," he said, "but not here, not with this fucking system of ours…"

"You seem to think a lot like your workers, Mr. Oskiernia, but you're a member of the Party, aren't you?"

The older man closed his eyes and breathed deeply. He sighed and pointed to a stool nearby. "Sit down, Mr. Dymowski," he said. "If you're going to

understand why I am what I am, this is going to take some time."
Konrad gratefully accepted the man's offer of a cigarette and sat down.
Bronek remained standing and began his story.
"... I was a Socialist in pre-war Poland," he said. "Mind you, life wasn't
all that bad back then. Industry was well organized and if you had a job,
everything was affordable. But, there was a lot of shit in political life back
then too, believe me."
The blond-haired man sighed and took a seat beside Konrad.
"I was with the 'Bataliony Chłopskie'[3] when I fought the Nazis. We were
an independent underground organization in the beginning but we eventually
united with the Home Army. Well, after the war - when the Polish Socialist
Party was forced to merge with the Soviet-backed Workers' Party, I decided to
stay. I thought that I could try to speak out for the workers. Ask anyone in this
plant if I have ever failed to voice their concerns... But today..." he
continued. "I realize that we, the workers can't do much. Party members have
become functionaries with better wages and fringe benefits. No, I'm not proud
to be a member of the Party, Mr. Dymowski." He looked down at Konrad
with sincerity and resignation. "It neglects us - even simple things like a
cafeteria aren't looked after. Kramer and I have told management time and
time again that we need one badly."
The shop telephone rattled on the wall. Bronek rose and took the thick
black receiver in his hand.
"I'm sorry, Mrs. Karolak, we haven't heard from Witek yet. Yes, when
we do, we'll call you right away. Please don't get too depressed, Mrs. Karolak.
God bless you, good-bye." He shook his head and sat back down on his
already warmed stool.
"Poor woman," Bronek muttered and handed another cigarette to a
concerned Konrad. "I wish I knew where I could find that boy. People are
very worried about him. If I knew, I could relieve that poor woman's mind.
She's been coming here every day since Witek disappeared. That was on New
Year's Eve."
"But she phoned today? "
"Yes, but only because our dear comrade Sroka told her that she couldn't
come in person any longer."
"Why did Sroka do that?"
"Why?" the foreman repeated, kicking an empty can across the workshop
floor. It rolled swiftly and hit a wall with a loud smash. "... Because comrade
Sroka is a son of a bitch. I told him that to his face too."
"What did he say?"
"He laughed. The bastard just laughed..."
They were startled by the sound of many pairs of heavy work boots pound
the floor of the adjacent hallway.
"Bronek! Mr. Oskiernia!" the men cried.
Although he was angered by the interruption, the foreman opened the
workshop door. "What has happened?" he asked.
Siedlak, Maliniak and two older workers rushed into the workshop. They

3. Bataliony Chłopskie [Pol.] Peasant Battalions.

were all breathing heavily. Janek Siedlak spoke first. "They just found Witek – he's dead," he screamed.

Bronek Oskiernia's eyes narrowed with disbelief. "How? When?" he gasped. "Please, say something?" The workshop was deathly quiet for a few seconds.

"They found his body when a large snow bank began melting," Janek answered gloomily. "Witek was lying just fifty metres away from his uncle's home in the outskirts of town. Snow plows don't service the area."

Bronek sat down heavily on his stool. He shook his head and covered his face with his hands. His voice cracked with pain and obvious shock.

"Do they know how he died?" he mumbled.

"During the New Year's party at his uncle's house, he must have stepped outside to get a breath of fresh air."

Bronek Oskiernia let out a small moan. "21 years old," he said, "and the best crane operator we have ever had in this plant – does his mother know? I have to call her right now..." He started to pick up the phone, when Mietek Maliniak stopped him.

"... Comrade Sroka has already called her," he said. "The police called Sroka and then he called Mrs. Karolak."

Their foreman threw the receiver against the wall. "One day I'm going to kill that son of a bitch Sroka," he screamed. "Karolak was under me, not him. I should have called his mother..."

A brief thaw descended on Warsaw, and the towering snow banks lining the streets began to recede. The discovery of Witek Karolak's body was a stinging reminder to the workers at United Enterprises of the devastation that the winter had wrought.

Janek Siedlak cupped his hand beside his mouth and whispered in Konrad's ear. The two men, along with the rest of the employees, were filing into a meeting hall. "I was listening to Radio Free Europe last night. They were estimating that dozens of people died in the New Year's Eve snowfall," he said.

Paranoid about employee unrest and militancy, the District Party Committee demanded that the factory management call a last minute meeting. Sroka, the head of the factory's Party Local summoned them to the plush room usually reserved for weekly Party meetings. They sat in neat rows of seats, facing a large portrait of Lenin.

Sroka sat with the plant director in the front row. He stayed there for more than ten minutes. The noise level in the hall was growing steadily.

Konrad ended up sitting beside Janek Siedlak. The electrician was anxious. "If we let them control us much longer," he said, "the next year thousands of people are going to die, not just dozens. Everything in this country is falling apart..."

The workers noticed that Sroka had made his way on to the podium. He had laid a number of sheets of paper side by side in front of him and repeatedly cleared his throat. His voice barely penetrated through the thick cloud of restless murmuring.

"Dear comrades and citizens," he shouted, glancing down nervously at the first page of his prepared speech. "The death of our colleague Wincenty Karolak is a heavy blow to all of the staff here. The winter has been difficult for all of us, but Wincenty is dead, he passed away in the spring of his life. We will all miss him very much..."

Sroka blinked nervously. He seemed to be dwarfed by the momentous portrait behind him. "But, dear colleagues," he squeaked, "there are other things that we must deal with now. The winter has taught us an important lesson – that is the necessity of work."

There was a rumbling growl.

"... Effective leadership of our Party," Sroka said loudly, trying to restrain himself from yelling, "could place Poland on the list of the world's economic powers. But, you can be certain that neither comrade Gierek, nor Prime Minister Jaroszewicz can operate snow plows or ship coal on their own. If the nation shirks from labour, even the best leadership is helpless..."

Janek Siedlak grit his teeth. "You son of a bitch," he gasped.

Konrad shifted in his seat and coughed repeatedly. He stared at Zdzisław Sroka. The secretary had reddish hair and the shiny, pink complexion that goes with it. His green eyes protruded rudely from his fleshy face.

"... We have to work, comrades." Sroka flashed an uneasy smile. "And, we must refrain from drinking like swine. Are any of you aware of the latest Polish statistics on alcohol consumption?"

The whites of his eyes were revealed even more as he swept the hall with a quick glance. When no one responded, he shrugged and set about concentrating on the second page in front of him. "We have the shameful honour of being at the top of the list of alcohol consumption per capita in Europe. An average Pole drinks the equivalent of 8.5 litres of pure alcohol per year, that's more than the Germans and the Swedes. They used to be ahead of us. This is the real reason behind the various disasters which have taken place this winter. If workers had not been drinking on December 31st, we wouldn't have been without snow removal services. And if Wincenty Karolak hadn't been drunk that night, he would have probably been among us today."

The men in the room reacted with loud shouts of "son of a bitch" and "bastard" but Sroka paid little attention.

"... work and don't drink comrades," he said, even more loudly. "Vodka is too cheap and those who can't resist the temptation are more like animals than human beings. Thank you for your attention, comrades," he said with a bow. He neatly folded his text and placed it carefully in his jacket pocket, seemingly unaware of the commotion he had caused.

Angry shouts were hurled across the room. They stopped a scowling Sroka from leaving the podium.

The men cried "Bronek, Bronek," and pushed their foreman to the front of the room. The heavyset man faced Sroka and then slowly mounted the podium.

"Tell him Bronek! Tell him!" his workers screamed. Oskiernia placed a hand firmly on Sroka's shoulder. He spoke loudly. "I'll be brief, dear secretary – everything you have said is pure bullshit. You look surprised. You are probably asking yourself why I'm up here doing this. Well, I don't disagree that the snow plows weren't on the streets in early January – but that wasn't because workers were drunk. They were out of order because no one had the spare parts needed to fix them."

The foreman didn't stop there. "Another thing," he said. "You're trying to tell us that vodka is cheap. It may be cheap for you, but not for us. I've been working here for 45 years and I make more than most people in this plant, but I still have to work three hours to buy a half a litre. Someone like Wincenty has to work six hours." His face whitened and Konrad noticed his grip tighten even more on Sroka's shoulder.

"You say that Poles are drinking more now than ever before. You're dead right. But why is that? Have you ever asked yourself? It's because we can't just go out and buy a car or a nice juicy steak. All we can afford is a bottle and a poor excuse for food. Before I go, just one last thing. You insinuated that Karolak died because he was drinking on New Year's Eve. Didn't you drink too? How do you know it wasn't something else? The same thing could have happened to you. You should pray for Wincenty's soul instead of trying to sell us that bullshit of yours. That's all."

Konrad looked at Bronek with admiration, but he worried about the consequences of his daring statements when he saw secretary Sroka still standing on the podium. His face was writhing with anger.

"What you're saying is false," he called after Oskiernia. His voice was highly pitched and uneven. "It contradicts the vital interests of the working class to keep someone like you among our membership. I'll be talking to someone about you."

As the plant director tried to restore some calm, Oskiernia got out of his seat again and made his way to the podium. It was evident that he was determined to have the last word.

"Before we all go, I'd like to tell you one last thing, Sroka. Don't use the term 'working class' like a napkin, OK? We're the working class not you. Our interests aren't the same as yours..."

The next morning, Konrad joined Janek Siedlak at the workshop bench. Zygmunt Kowalski and Mietek Maliniak stood nearby smoking. They were all waiting for Bronek to arrive.

"Have you seen him at all today, Zygmunt?" Janek asked.

"No, I haven't. I can't call him either. He doesn't have a phone at home."

The workshop telephone rang. Konrad was closest to it and he quickly picked it up.

"It was the director's office," he said after he had hung up. "They want a Department A union steward to go there right now."

Stefan Panek, a quiet mechanic in the shop, shrugged and left for Admin Building without a word.

When he returned, about forty minutes later, he sat down at the workshop bench and shook his head. He seemed dazed and his face was washed out.

"Would you pass me a cigarette please, Mr. Dymowski?" he asked meekly. "I left mine in the director's office."

Konrad nodded and passed him a package. "What did you find out about Mr. Oskiernia?" he asked with curiosity. "When is he coming back?"

Stefan Panek looked at him with bewilderment. Then he turned to the other men in the room. "Bronek won't be returning to the plant," he gasped. His usually calm, clear voice broke down as he tried to continue. "They have forced him to retire. They want me to take over as foreman..."

Janek Siedlak leapt up from the bench. "What? He wasn't supposed to retire until December."

"And you... what did you do? You didn't accept their offer, did you?" Maliniak asked.

Panek looked up at him. His face conveyed genuine pain. "I swear I told them I didn't want it... and I really don't, but they didn't care. They said Bronek wouldn't be returning and someone had to do it so I agreed."

"You son of a bitch," Siedlak yelled.

"How could you do that?" Mietek asked. "Haven't you ever heard of workers' solidarity?"

Stefan Panek just looked down at the floor gloomily. Then he asked: "What would you have done, Mietek?"

"I don't know," his co-worker answered stonily.

"Poor Bronek," Janek Siedlak murmured. "There will be no retirement party. You," he said, turning to his new foreman, "you betrayed him. You shouldn't have accepted their offer. After all, you are the union steward."

Stefan Panek reacted with a bitter laugh. "You have said yourself that the union is a hoax. What can a guy like me do?"

The young electrician's anger made him bold. "You should proclaim a strike," he shouted.

"Yes," Maliniak cried. "Strike."

There was silence after that as the workers contemplated the word they had just uttered.

Little work was done in Department A that day. Most of the employees would keep busy for a while and then stop to talk about the boss they had just lost.

The afternoon was interrupted by two men who came into the workshop at two o'clock. Both of them were dressed in civilian clothing and both, Konrad noticed, wore heavy black, woollen overcoats. They just stood near the doorway without a word. Most of the men eyed them nervously.

In unison, the two strangers approached Janek. "Mr. Jan Siedlak?" one of them asked.

"Yes, what do you want?" the electrician answered brusquely.

Without a response, they turned their heads and looked at the other employees. "And where is Mr. Mieczysław Maliniak?"

"I am here," Mietek answered and came out of the tool alcove.

The two men motioned towards the door. "Gentlemen, would you kindly follow us, please - Metropolitan Command," he added, flashing his ID.

Janek Siedlak didn't hesitate to protest. "Why?" he shouted rudely. "We are expected to work until three o'clock."

One of the men flashed a wide smile. "We appreciate your commitment to your job, Mr. Siedlak, but you must go with us nevertheless."

Konrad watched the electrician look down and scowl. He looked over to Mietek, and seeing his friend standing near the doorway, he grabbed a package of Sport cigarettes and strode out of the room.

Both men were back at work at their regular time the next day, but everyone in the workshop noticed that they seemed very subdued and quiet.

"If you talk with me much longer, you'll probably end up there yourself," Mietek answered bitterly when one of his co-workers asked him about his experience at the Secret Service headquarters. Nobody asked again.

At the end of the same week, Witold Kramer announced that he was going to retire, and in his usual, quiet and unassuming way, he dissuaded his workers from organizing a party in his honour.

Kramer had two days left at United Enterprises when he walked into the workshop. Konrad noticed him pace around the room slowly, running his hands along the top of the well-used machines. After talking to every single worker, he bade them goodbye. "Take care of yourselves," he said, and walked back to his office.

On the engineer's last day, Zdzisław Sroka and the union boss Mrowicki prepared speeches, brought flowers, and summoned all the workers to the meeting hall to bade one of the oldest employees farewell.

Witold Kramer didn't come to work that day. For the first time in many years he took a sick leave.

Another person left United Enterprises that month. At the end of February, comrade Zdzisław Sroka was transferred to a District Party Committee.

CHAPTER 5

His entire family was sitting around the table. Supper was almost over, and they were chatting and smiling and drinking their tea, while helping themselves to some of the strawberry jam that Julia had made. Konrad's grandfather lovingly patted his grandson's head and passed him a saucer of the sticky, sugary fruit. His dog, Lady was there too, sitting right on one of the chairs, barking eagerly, hoping also for a share of the sweets. Konrad was feeling so contented, so happy.

Lady barked again, and this time he slid out of his chair and went over to the tall, multi-coloured dog. He was so small, he was barely able to caress her soft, shiny head...

Konrad opened his eyes suddenly. He sighed and glanced over to his alarm clock. It was 4:20 A.M.

It would ring in ten minutes. He pushed a button on the top to suppress the alarm and then began searching for his cigarettes. He had recently begun to work the morning shift and that meant starting at United Enterprises at 6:00 A.M. He felt exhausted and drained. He glanced at his bedroom door. It was closed, but he decided to open the window as well before lighting up. He didn't expect Tina to be up for at least an hour, and she hated the smell of tobacco, especially in the morning.

It was just past dawn and the sun had emerged from behind the tall horse chestnut trees in the park across the street. Konrad inhaled the cool morning air deeply, and poked his head out of the window. Down below, he watched an elderly man plod along the sidewalk, leading a golden haired dog by a leash.

The sight brought back many memories, which, although pleasant, were tinged with sadness. His grandfather always took Lady for a walk in the early morning. Konrad could remember Robert's daily routine clearly. The retired lieutenant colonel would always rise at four in the morning and after quietly washing and shaving, he would take his walking stick and head down the stairs with Lady close behind. He usually picked up a bottle of milk from the dairy store and visited the local magazine booth for the morning paper.

After a modest breakfast, he would leave the apartment again and, take a bus to the outskirts of Warsaw where he worked as a payroll clerk in a factory part-time, selling transit tickets and paying the employees.

Konrad looked down to the street once more, and watched the two, now distant, silhouettes moving slowly forward, against the sunlit lilac trees which bordered the sidewalk.

Like its owner's, the old dog's steps were unsteady and arthritic. The animal could barely walk.

Lady's last days were like that, Konrad thought. When the dog had just passed her twelfth birthday, she began to limp badly. Konrad and his grandfather were told that a cancerous tumour was invading one of her shoulders. Within a few days only, the dog was suffering badly and they realized that she had to be put down.

The nearest animal hospital was almost two kilometres away from the apartment and with each step, the dog was becoming more and more exhausted. Konrad tugged gently on the leash and pleaded with her to keep going. His grandfather followed behind quietly.

Lady collapsed just as they handed her over to the orderly at the animal clinic, and they watched him drag the unconscious dog into the mortuary.

When the orderly returned and handed Lady's leash to them, Konrad began weeping uncontrollably. The man looked at him with disdain. "Why are you crying? It's only a dog." His dull, reddish face hid a smile. "We kill scores of them every day. Just get yourself another pet."

Konrad sighed and inhaled his cigarette deeply. He remembered Lady looking up at him. Even then, he couldn't help feeling badly that he hadn't carried her to the animal hospital, instead of dragging her along by a leash.

He closed the window and headed toward the bathroom.

"I wish you wouldn't smoke when you get up so early," Tina appeared at her bedroom door and scowled openly at him. "Don't you realize that you are depriving me of an hour of sleep?"

Konrad shrugged and threw the last of his cigarette into the toilet bowl and flushed it.

After he had washed and dressed, he lit another one as he headed toward the kitchen.

His mother started shouting from her room. "Smoking again! I thought I told you not to."

"If you weren't so hung over, it wouldn't bother you so much," he shouted back.

Tina flew into a rage. "Shut up," she cried. "I'm your mother. Don't you preach at me."

Although his sleeping hours were cut short when he worked the morning shift, he was consoled by the fact that the day ended very early. By 2:15 P.M. that day, he was on a bus heading toward the Mokotów district of town to see Hanna. She was supervising exams at the Central School of Planning and Statistics, one of Warsaw's universities which offered economics oriented courses.

The district was a peculiar agglomeration. From the bus stop, he faced the rather ordinary, red brick buildings which made up the university's campus. Further down the street, was the heavily fenced in and guarded compound of the Ministry of Internal Affairs. SB Secret Service was a department of this ministry.

The southern side of the campus faced an overbearing brick enclosure, a building he remembered as Warsaw's Central Prison where Eryk had served his first sentence. He climbed the wide steps leading up to the main entrance of the university.

Hanna appeared in the hall a few minutes later, following a mass of students. She carried a bundle of papers in her arms.

"Has anything happened, Konrad?" she asked anxiously.

"No, I just wanted to surprise you," he said with reassurance. "What would you like to do tonight?"

She sighed. "I have to be back at work in an hour, I won't be home until nine o'clock."

"Well, why don't we just go for a walk?" he suggested.

Hanna lifted her head and looked around. The barbed-wire covered walls close by, cast an ominous shadow over the street. Konrad could sense that she wasn't fond of the area and he suggested that they go to Zielona Gęś café. The café and a restaurant occupied a modern pavilion surrounded by ring of tall poplar trees. Inside, they found a place to sit down near a window and relaxed in comfortable armchairs.

As Konrad motioned to a waiter, Hanna grabbed his hand. "I'm paying, Konrad," she said. "This is a very expensive place."

He shook his head vigorously and smiled. "I still owe you a treat, remember? You bought me coffee at the railroad station last year."

Hanna laughed and squeezed his hand.

After two vermouths, they ordered tea and an appetizer from the café's limited food menu, fried mushrooms with bread. The small snack cost him more than a day's salary.

Konrad glanced at his watch. He was relieved that he still had a few more minutes with Hanna and lit up a cigarette.

"How do you like engineer Kramer's replacement?" she asked him.

He chuckled sarcastically. "Wiśniewski is a handsome, 32-year old engineer and a member of the Party. He's the type of person who likes to look after himself, but isn't interested in anything else. Kramer was always concerned about what I was doing at the plant. Wiśniewski just doesn't care, so, I don't care about him either."

"That's too bad," Hanna said quietly, and touched his cheek lightly with her hand. "This is your first job, I wish you were more enthused about it."

He burst into laughter. "With my wages?" he remarked loudly and shrugged. A number of customers' heads turned, and they decided to leave the café.

They paused for a few moments by some benches at the edge of the park which were shielded from the street noise beyond by a series of thick hedges. They spent more time talking about his job. Konrad's voice was tinged with bitterness as he told her that when he completed his training in Department A and moved on, his pay would be increased by a half a złoty an hour. "I'll be able to buy one extra pack of Sports a day or a lousy loaf of bread," he muttered.

"You aren't making a lot of money now, Konrad, but you are getting experience. You'll do well, I believe in you. You're ambitious."

Her words took him by surprise. "Me, ambitious?" he asked and stared at her.

"You may not realize it, but you are changing every day, Konrad," she said and kissed him on the forehead. "You are starting to think about your future more seriously now. You are going to become a good engineer - I know you will. Then, I'll help you get another job..."

He laughed and embraced her. "Maybe I can become your assistant at the university. Just imagine," he whispered in her ear. "I could make love to you right in your study. We would only have to lock the door."

"You're just spoiled," she whispered back and smiled. He could tell that the thought was a pleasant one, because she kissed him again.

Only the faint sound of distant cars and chattering squirrels could be heard in the tranquil, softly-lit park.

"Konrad," Hanna said quietly. "I enjoy you in bed, but I hope you don't think that there's not more. I appreciate your other qualities too..."

The long June day still bathed the street in full daylight as he later made his way to her apartment. As he walked, he couldn't help thinking about Hanna and the job she talked about. He didn't know what kind of work she envisaged for him. He was a graduate with a good academic record but not much more than that.

He shrugged. He had never been all that fond of his chosen profession. At school, he had always been more interested in the humanities: literature, philosophy, history. Roman was the same way.

But later, they abandoned these subjects for maths and science. Engineering seemed more practical, and as Roman maintained, it was an independent profession.

Konrad shook his head. While they were studying at university, they found out that engineering was just as politicized as anything else in the country. Edward Gierek's administration borrowed money and bought foreign licenses. Engineers were just told to implement the Party's directives, and those mavericks who refused, paid the price of a lost career.

The job Hanna had in mind, was a position with a firm which was involved in construction projects abroad. The company was called Budal and one of its directors was a friend of hers, Zygmunt Kossak-Roztworowski.

"When I was buying this at a bazaar in Nairobi the last time I was there..." Hanna explained, picking up an ebony sculpture of a turtle off one of her shelves, "I met Zygmunt. We studied together at University." She placed the small sculpture back on the shelf.

Konrad was impatient "Well, what about him?"

"Zygmunt is a director with Budal, a friend of mine, and I should add, a very handsome man," she said with a sly smile. There was no denying that he didn't like her talking about other men. "Good for him," was all he could say.

Hanna laughed. "Don't be jealous, he's just a friend. What is more important is that there are many engineers with his company who do go abroad to work - and there, they are paid in dollars."

Before Konrad could ask her how much, she continued. "You would be earning about US$400 per month. It's not as much as you could make at a sink in Montréal where, according to you, you made a small fortune one summer but still..." She looked at him expectantly.

Konrad smiled and kissed her on the cheek. "It is still fifteen times more than I am making now," he said, "and I wouldn't be washing dishes."

He lit a cigarette and thought about her suggestion. "I have a friend who works for a similar company," he remarked. "He says that most of the employees are Party members and the ones with real connections are sent abroad. He's a good specialist, but others go, he doesn't." He paused. "You have seen this for yourself, Hanna. What can I expect even if I did work for your friend Kossak-Roztworowski?"

Hanna turned around and faced him. "Don't you understand what I am trying to tell you?" she gasped. "If you are competent in your area and you know foreign language, you still might be given the opportunity to travel. They can't just send Party cronies. They need somebody to do the job and communicate with the foreigners."

"I appreciate your concern, Hanna," he replied meekly, "but you know my English is poor. I can converse but I wouldn't dare to work in the language."

"Then why don't you start studying English now, and why don't you go for an interview at Budal?"

He laughed. "OK Boss, don't yell," he said. "When would you like me to meet your friend?"

Hanna smiled with satisfaction and kissed him. "I have arranged for you to see him at the beginning of next week."

It was late Monday afternoon. Konrad stood at a streetcar stop in downtown Warsaw and smiled to himself. The interview had gone well. Director Kossak-Roztworowski was very straightforward and business-like to him, but pleasant. His message was simple. Budal seldom employed junior engineers, so he suggested that Konrad finish his job training at United Enterprises and then join his company. At the end of the interview, when he stood at the door and shook Konrad's hand goodbye, he said, "It would be a good idea for you to take a government examination in English if you want to be involved in foreign contracts."

As Konrad boarded a streetcar, he thought about the director of Budal. He had been surprised when Hanna told him that Kossak-Roztworowski was not a member of the Party because it was rare to see a man without Communist connections in a prestigious position.

He sat down at a seat beside a window. Hanna and her friend are right, he thought to himself. This is an opportunity I can' t waste. For the first time in many months, the future looked brighter.

The next week, he began working at night. His shift lasted from 10 o'clock in the evening until 6:00 A.M. He usually slept until mid-afternoon.

One day, he had dragged himself out of bed and walked into the kitchen to put a kettle on the stove. He hunted for his cigarettes, but realizing he was out of them, he quickly got dressed and ran to the RUCH booth around the corner.

On his way back, he crossed the street and walked beside the park. Children were busily playing in the sandboxes while their mothers looked on.

Tina didn't take him out much when he was young, he thought. When Eryk went to prison, she had to work, and besides, there were always his grandparents to look after him.

Still, he couldn't help resenting the little time he had spent with his mother. He saw her even less after she had divorced Eryk. Her weekends belonged to whatever man she was seeing at the time and he was shunted to his grandparents' apartment.

In the stairwell, he could hear the sharp whistle of a boiling kettle and he rushed inside the apartment and switched the gas burner off. He sat down at the small table in the kitchen and sipped his coffee. Looking down at his watch, he knew that his mother would be home soon. He wondered if she would come home alone or with her new friend Artur. He hoped not.

Until recently, his mother had been with Toniek, a middle-aged engineer whom Konrad knew very well and liked. For twelve years, he had been a regular visitor to the apartment and sometimes helped him with his homework.

I wish she had stayed with him for the rest of her life, he thought bitterly.

By the time he had returned home for good, following his year in the army, Artur had taken Toniek's place. Konrad wasn't pleased. Artur drank a lot and Tina joined him eagerly.

It had been useless trying to persuade Tina to stop seeing the man. She would tell him that it was her choice and her life. When Konrad persisted and began to point out Artur's faults, his mother always lashed back at him. "You have been the lover of a married woman for years and you have also taken a drink quite a few times yourself," she often retorted. "Why don't you just mind your own business."

He set his mug in the kitchen sink and walked back to his bedroom. I might as well concentrate on my own life now, he thought. He opened up one of his English books and sighed. It had been over seven years since he had taken English at school. Although he had tried to study a bit while he was in the army, he knew that he had a long way to go before he could pass an exam.

"I wouldn't mind this so much if this language had some kind of logic to it," he murmured to himself as he looked down at a long table of irregular verbs in his book of English grammar. "They say the past tense of 'dream' is 'dreamt', but then I have seen the word 'dreamed' used too."

He looked up some new words and tried to pronounce them. A couple of minutes later he pushed the book away. "Fucking pronunciation," he shouted out loud. "Why don't they have a general rule for all words like they do in Polish? It's just a bunch of inconsistencies..."

He lit a cigarette and stood up near the window. Down below, evidence of spring was all around. White and pink blooms on the trees lured bees and wasps, and the air felt like a gentle, warm hand caressing his face. Many people were sunbathing on the grass in the small park across the street and he looked forward to the two days he would have off when his night shift was over.

It was half past five when Konrad heard the front door open. The floor creaked slightly and he could hear Tina talking to someone.

"I still have a half a bottle in the fridge, honey."

"That's not much," another voice answered, "but I have some more with me..."

Seconds later, Konrad heard a loud crash. "You broke it, what a pity," Tina whined.

It didn't take long for Konrad to realize that his mother and her friend were drunk. He closed his bedroom door tightly and went back to his desk, determined to get some studying done, but after a minute or so he gave up and put all the books back on the shelf.

Out in the living room, Tina was sitting on their red sofa. She seemed dazed and her eyes were watery and blood shot. Artur, who looked a bit less drunk, was putting two glasses on the coffee table in front of her and pouring vodka into them. Konrad glanced again at his mother's face and sighed with disgust.

The sound must have registered with Artur, because the short, rotund man turned and smiled at him. "Hello sonny," he snickered and he and Tina downed their glasses.

Konrad's frustration and anger was barely controllable. "Look," he said calmly at first, "I don't mind you coming over here, but my mother drinks too much and too often with you." He sensed that his voice was getting louder with each word. "Why don't you just find yourself another place to haunt – this is my home after all..."

Artur turned to look up and him. His eyes were blinking rapidly from disbelief. "What do you want?" he shouted and stood up to face Konrad.

"Leave my mother alone."

Tina opened her eyes and then stumbled off the sofa. "I don't want him to leave me alone," she mumbled loudly. Konrad shrugged and went back to his room, closed the door and sat down at his desk. His hands shook as he lit a cigarette.

His mother continued to scream in the other room. "Artur! If you love me," he could hear her wail, "if you do, show him you're not leaving me..."

Just as he lay down on his bed and picked up a magazine the door opened. Artur's bloated face was pink and his eyes protruded strangely from their wrinkled sockets. He could barely, keep himself up and he clung to the doorknob for balance.

"Get up, you little bastard," he shouted. "I'm going to have a talk with you."

Konrad got up slowly and walked up to the teetering man. He smiled. "You're not much of a match for me, old man," he said. Artur nodded and led him out into the living room.

Taking a deep breath, Konrad tried to tell him to forget it and just leave.

"You're going to get out of here, not me," the man shouted back. His words were barely distinguishable. "Your mother wants it that way."

Konrad's whole body began to shake with rage. "I'm telling you one last time, get out of here, you drunk swine," he screamed.

Instead of retreating, Artur pushed him. Konrad, fought back with three furious blows to the other man's forehead and jaw. Artur, his face covered with blood, fell on the floor, knocking a large candleholder off the coffee table. Tina grabbed it and rushed towards her son. "You could have killed him with this," she screamed. "I'm calling the police."

"But I didn't touch it," he answered, more with surprise than anger. Tina glared at him and laughed hysterically. He shuddered, looking at his mother's witch-like appearance, her dark hair in complete disarray.

"You're going to go to prison, just like your father," she added as she began erratically dialling the phone.

He stalked into the front hallway of the apartment. Artur tried to stop him but Konrad shoved him away and left, slamming the front door behind him.

"Relax, Konrad. You're here, with me," Hanna's voice was soft and soothing as she tried to reassure him.

"I can't believe it," he gasped as he paced around her apartment. "She said she was going to call the police and have me arrested for assault." His hands trembled violently as he tried to light a cigarette. He inhaled the smoke deeply and sat down in the armchair beside her. "I just don't know what to do," he said. "How am I going to go to work tonight?"

Hanna kissed him and caressed his head. "Perhaps," she said quietly, "perhaps you could take a day off and stay here overnight."

Konrad shook his head. "I can't. I don't know how to get in touch with my boss. I have to go…"

"And tomorrow?" she asked in a low voice. "What will you do then?"

Konrad got up and walked over to the window overlooking the street. "Who knows," he said and shrugged. "Maybe I'll be arrested if I take a step inside her apartment."

Hanna grabbed his hand and sat him down at the sofa.

"Don't be stupid," she said calmly and smiled. "You know that your mother loves to make threats. She was drunk. By tomorrow, I'm sure everything will be different."

He took one of her cigarettes and lit it.

"Don't smoke so much. You have had five cigarettes in the last ten minutes. Try to relax."

Konrad gazed quietly at the empty television screen in front of him, barely hearing Hanna's words. "I'm not going to go home anymore," he said absentmindedly.

"But you have to," Hanna pleaded, placing her hands on his shoulders. "It's your home and she's is your mother." She knelt down and caressed his hair.

Konrad embraced her and they remained close to each other for a few quiet minutes. He felt sheltered beside the warmth of her body.

"I wish you were my mother," he whispered.

Hanna held him even tighter and passionately kissed his lips and eyes.

"You can always live with me, Konrad," she called after him as he walked down the hallway and made his way to work.

At 7:00, the following morning, Konrad unlocked the door but a bolted chain kept him from going inside. He rang the doorbell repeatedly, but when there was no response, he tried to force the door open.

After a number of loud bangs, his mother appeared at the door and let him in. Her dark hair was straggly and she had deep, purplish circles beneath her eyes. She looked at him with disdain.

Artur cowered behind her. He was dressed in a clean, blue shirt, one of Konrad's shirts. His face was dotted with bandaids. Konrad turned and looked straight at his mother.

"Can't you ask him to leave, just for a little while?" he pleaded. "I'd like to talk to you."

Tina steered Artur into her bedroom. "I don't have much to say to you before

I meet you in court," she declared. "And as far as this gentleman is concerned, he is my guest and he is going to stay here."

When he woke up, it was after noon. The park across the street was filled with crowds of people enjoying the warm spring weather. Even so, it didn't take him long to pick out the figures of Tina and Artur sitting on a blanket together. He sighed, remembering the sunbathing plans he had made for the day. Artur opened a bottle of beer and handed it to Tina. Then he pulled out another one for himself from a large, brown bag beside him. Tina was laughing as she sipped her beer.

Konrad turned away from the window and looked around his room, trying to decide what to do. His eyes rested on the empty frame which, for so long, had held Klara's photographs.

Whenever Klara became fed up with Tina's loud outbursts, she had urged Konrad to leave and move in with his grandparents. "I would never allow anybody to treat me the way your mother treats you," she often told him.

Back then though, his circumstances were different. He was still a student in university and his grandparents had Eryk to worry about. He always decided to stay with Tina, despite Klara's advice.

He thought to himself, what am I still doing here? He opened his closet and took a large travelling bag off the top shelf. He stuffed some clothing into it, tossed a few of his English books inside and closed the zipper.

Then he went down into the basement of the apartment and fetched his old bicycle. He wiped a thick layer of dust off the seat and quickly inflated the tires with his small pump. After he had secured the bag behind his seat, he set off. As he pedalled toward his grandparents' home, he felt calm, even happy.

Julia and Agata didn't ask him any questions when he threw his bag into Eryk's old room. Both of them just smiled and told him how delighted they were that he was going to stay.

Konrad took Julia's hand. "I think I could help you more, Babcia. And I know that I'll be a lot happier." His eyes surveyed the familiar shapes in his grandmother's bedroom.

"Agata and I will be a lot happier too," she answered and smiled up at him.

"Aren't you going to ask me why I've come?"

Julia just shook her head and smiled again.

"It doesn't matter," she answered. "All of the men in our family come home. Your grandfather returned from England after the war and your father came here too. Now, you have returned." She looked at him lovingly. "Agata and I brought you up, Konrad. This is your home..."

CHAPTER 6

Tina didn't go to court. A week passed and Konrad adjusted to his new circumstances. He spent most of his free time helping Agata tend to his grandmother. His great-aunt took it upon herself to do most of the shopping for the family and while she was out, he took over. He was in the midst of washing out Julia's bedpan when the doorbell rang.

"Open the door," Julia shouted. "Maybe Agata has forgotten her keys..."

It wasn't her. Instead, it was Xenia, his other grandmother.

"Come in, please," he said, after kissing her. She followed him into Julia's bedroom, placed a large bunch of red carnations down on her bed-side table and asked Julia how she was feeling.

"Oh, not bad. Konrad and Agata are taking good care of me." She smiled and looked over to the flowers. "Thank you."

They both watched Konrad put the flowers into a water-filled crystal vase. Xenia commented on it. "You have had that for many years, Julia. Did it come from Wilno?"

The bed-ridden woman shook her head. "No, this is a post-war thing, my son won it in a competition, oh, more than 25 years ago." Konrad brought the flowers over to her.

A small silver plaque was attached to the vase. It read: *To Eryk Dymowski, the fastest man on the 250 cc. motorcycle class, 1952.*

Julia sighed deeply. "He used to be such a good sportsman," she said.

Konrad turned the television on.

"Granny usually watches some TV now," he explained. He led Xenia out of the room, and sensing that she wanted to talk to him, motioned her to come into his bedroom, which had once served as a dinning room for the whole family.

A thick shroud of acacia trees filtered out most of the sunlight destined for the apartment, and the room was very dim. Konrad flicked on a switch, and the large brass chandelier lit up overhead. The room looked much the same as Xenia remembered it.

On one wall, stood an antique buffet cabinet. It faced a dark, wooden bookcase which was full of faded and well-used volumes. A little desk, covered with books, English dictionaries and a few colourful magazines sat by the window. An old clock chimed on the hour.

In a far corner of the room, a scattering of pictures of St. Mary and Jesus hung on the wall above Konrad's couch.

"Well," he said, seating his grandmother on the sofa. "It is nice to see you, Xenia. How are you doing?" He always spoke to his maternal grandmother by her first name.

The old woman smiled meekly. "I'm doing well, thanks," she replied, "but what about you? Do you like living here? It looks quite dreary compared to your new apartment."

"You mean: compared to your daughter's new apartment," he remarked, trying not to reveal his resentment. "You are right, this isn't exactly a bright flat but this is my home now. I was brought up here…"

Xenia glanced at the graying wall beside the window. It was covered with a number of framed photographs. One of them was of Wiktor, Agata's late husband, and another of Luba, Konrad's great-grandmother when she was a teenager. The last picture was taken at a gala ball, before the war. It showed Robert handsomely dressed in his best lieutenant colonel uniform. A young and beautiful Julia proudly clung to his arm.

"… You see, Xenia," Konrad said, after his grandmother turned and faced him again, "I don't feel alone here."

Xenia attempted to smile and then glanced down at the floor. "Your mother is very sorry, Konrad. I really think that she regrets what happened."

"That's very nice of her," he answered slowly, "but what has happened, has happened. There's nothing you can do about it."

Xenia grabbed his arm. "She said you can come home but…"

"But what?" he asked impatiently. He wasn't impressed by his mother's conditional apology.

His grandmother looked uncomfortable. "She wants you to tell Artur that you didn't mean it."

He broke into a fit of laughter. "She must be crazy," he exclaimed. "I think alcohol has eaten out the last of Tina's brain."

"Don't talk like that. She is your mother after all," Xenia said with resignation. She looked up at her grandson, hoping that her words were getting through to him. Konrad only shrugged. "… Please, Konrad, this is very difficult for me, I love both of you and I don't want to take sides."

Sometimes, he thought to himself, a person can't be neutral. There are moments when you have to admit that someone is right and another person is wrong. He looked at his grandmother. Her hair was almost completely gray despite her desperate attempts to dye it frequently. Numerous wrinkles lined her weary and pleading eyes.

He shook his head. "I'm not going back, Xenia," he told her decisively. "Your daughter thinks that she can torment and abuse me as much as she likes. Well, she has just gone too far. I'm sorry but there's no way I'm going back, ever."

"Xenia!, Konrad!" Julia shouted from her bedroom suddenly. "Come here, quickly."

Konrad ran past Xenia and rushed to his grandmother. "What is going on? Has anything happened to you?" he asked.

Julia smiled and shook her head. "No, just watch the TV."

A Polish Television news story showed a white-robed man, blessing crowds in St. Peter's square. A few minutes later, the image of Vatican City was replaced by Ryszard Kwapień who began to introduce the next news item.

Xenia was puzzled. "That's strange. They rarely broadcast the Pope's general audiences."

"But he is coming soon," Julia said eagerly. Konrad noticed that her face was flushed with excitement. "Before you came in, Kwapień announced that the government had agreed to a visit. John Paul will be coming here on June 2nd!"

By late May, the weather was so warm that Konrad and Agata decided to keep Julia's window open all the time. A light breeze brought the unmistakable scent of nearby lilac bushes into her room. Agata, who arrived home after an afternoon of shopping, didn't even notice. Instead, she flopped into a chair near Julia's bed and told her sister and Konrad about the news she had heard while lining up at the meat store.

"There are going to be enormous crowds when the Pope comes," she said. "Today, I saw some of the new food stands that are going to be used to sell grilled sausages. There are tables and chairs and even parasols. They're not selling anything now, though..."

"They will be when the Pope comes," Konrad added. "All of these preparations are for his two-day stay in the city."

"That's very nice," Agata snapped, "but do you know what they have done? There is nothing at the butchers, just empty hooks. Mrs. Niemirska, you know the woman with the limp who lives on the third floor, just told me that the food they're providing is going to cost four times the usual price. I have also heard that they received permission from the Episcopate to raise prices for two days..."

Julia shook her finger at Agata. "Sister, sister," she said. "Don't be like Judas who rebuked Mary Magdalene for washing Jesus's feet with perfume. Our meat stores are always empty anyway. If they have to hoard food for the Papal visit, let them. The people who are coming to see him have to eat." Before Agata could counter with an equally acid remark, Konrad quickly turned the television on.

They all sighed when they heard Ryszard Kwapień's voice. "The preparations for the Papal visit are moving ahead on schedule," he announced. "Many schools are being converted into dormitories. Warsaw will host over two million visitors for two days and nights. The government of the Polish People's Republic will be cooperating with the Episcopate over the next few weeks. These harmonious relations between the Polish State and the Polish Church are an example to the rest of the world. We can say, with pride, to those Western nations which continually search for signs of East European religious intolerance, that Socialist Poland has built more churches than any other country on the continent."[4]

"You son of a bitch," Konrad yelled. "How many years did it take for them to approve the construction of Roman's neighbourhood church? Twenty, maybe."

Agata walked up to the television and turned it off. "I can't listen to that man," she explained. "Even when he talks about the Pope, he manages to

---

4. Kwapień's statement was technically correct since many of the churches, destroyed during the war, had to be rebuilt. Edward Gierek's administration eagerly took credit for that.

spout propaganda." She picked up her small bag of groceries and disappeared into the kitchen.

Agata's initial impressions were right. The city quickly began to bustle with activity. Crews of workers started erecting billboards covered with enthusiastic greeting to Pope John Paul II. The Vatican coat of arms, white and yellow flags with two crossed keys, dotted the city's lawns and trees.

On the Sunday, just two weeks before the Pope's visit, Konrad made a special trip to his parish church. He approached Father Florian after the mass. "This time for good?" the priest remarked with a smile. Konrad knelt down and kissed the old pastor's hand. "I heard that the parishes need volunteers to control the crowds during the two days."

"I'm glad that you are here," the priest answered and motioned to him to get up from his knees. "Do you remember your friend Witold from our parish summer camp?"

Konrad nodded. He couldn't have forgotten his favourite vacation companion. When he and Witold were away, they often visited the local bars and drank some wine and beer together. Father Florian didn't allow his flock to drink but that just made their small adventures more exciting.

"What about Witold, Father? I haven't seen him for years."

"I haven't either," the priest answered with a chuckle, "until today. He came in this morning to enlist as a 'Papal Guard' just like you." Two teenage altar boys entered the sacristy and approached the priest. Father Florian briefly touched Konrad's head and then asked him to come back on the Sunday before the Pope's arrival.

All of the parish volunteers were told to assemble together in the large room at the rear of the church where Konrad had once taken religion classes. A black crucifix hung on the wall behind the large podium. By the time Konrad arrived, the benches were filled with men.

Witold was sitting in the front row. He hadn't changed much, except for a bit of graying around his temples.

"I wish I could give you a seat," he said apologetically, "but there's no room on the bench."

Konrad stood beside him for the next hour as Father Florian explained their duties and entered their names officially in the parish register.

They walked out of the dim church into the glaring sunshine of a busy Warsaw street.

Then they decided to walk to the intersection where their parish was going to be standing to welcome the Pope and his entourage.

"I guess, this is the place," Witold said when they reached the spot. "We'll be in front of the roadblocks, along with the choirs and the local clergy. We can't miss him."

They sat down on the gray-painted benches which were set back on the sidewalks and bordered by thick hedges. Konrad looked down the road which led to Warsaw's airport. The wide highway was decorated with Polish and Vatican flags and people displayed large images of St. Mary, Pope John Paul II and Cardinal Stefan Wyszyński on balconies along the route.

"I've never actually seen the Pope," Konrad told his friend with regret.

"Cardinal Wojtyła was very active in pastoral work all over Poland but I haven't attended church for years."

As the day approached, Warsaw became schizophrenic. Flags seemed to be flying everywhere, booths lined the streets, and even the old, once abandoned public washrooms had been opened up and repainted. The mood throughout the country was joyous.

Gossip about all aspects of the visit was rampant. One rumour indicated that the government agreed to the visit only because the Vatican supported further credits to the Polish government. Another claimed that the Victoria Intercontinental Hotel had raised its rates from US $150 to $300 and was virtually empty.

Mietek Maliniak eventually found the subject tiresome. "There are other things happening here which are equally important," he told his colleagues during lunch one day. "We should be rejoicing the greatest news of the decade."

"Yes, we're happy about the Pope's visit..." Konrad said.

"I wasn't talking about that," Maliniak retorted, flinging his arms around with enthusiasm. "The Pope's visit is probably the most important event since the war, but I'm talking about some other good news. Haven't you heard about it, Mr. Dymowski?"

Konrad looked at him with puzzlement. The young mechanic burst into laughter. "Jarocha has fucked into the calendar," he yelled triumphantly.

It didn't take Konrad long to figure out what Mietek was talking about. He was alleging that the Prime Minister of the country, Piotr Jaroszewicz, had died. The Premier had been out of the public eye for over two weeks, but government spokesmen maintained that he was getting over an illness. Poles were always skeptical about the news they were fed each day by the state media.

"He might have died," Konrad surmised, "or maybe he's in hiding so that he won't have to meet the Pope. I have heard that he's one of Moscow's closest men."

"All of those fucking bastards are Moscow's men," Janek Siedlak added, "but I agree with Mr. Dymowski. If Jaroszewicz had died there would have been a state funeral. You shouldn't rejoice, Mietek, until you've cried at his grave."

"I'm telling you," Mietek persisted, "they're just keeping his corpse in the refrigerator because now is not the time for sorrow. We're all so happy these days. You'll see for yourself. As soon as the Pope goes back to Rome, there will be a big, posh state funeral. It is going to happen..."

The Pope's itinerary was set. Following his arrival, the Holy Father was scheduled to hold talks with Polish authorities represented by the Chairman of the State Council Henryk Jabłoński, and the First Secretary of the Party, Edward Gierek. An open-air mass for hundreds of thousands of participants was also set for Victory Square.

Konrad stood proudly along the Papal route, waiting for John Paul II to pass by. Behind the barricaded portion of the street, thousands of people joined him from all parts of the country. It was easy to spot the pilgrims who had travelled to Warsaw. Colourful folk dresses of Cracovian women, were mixed with white woollen capes of mountaineers, and striped, multi-coloured skirts of Łowiczians. Every province seemed to be represented and Konrad was fascinated by the different traditions that had been cultivated through the centuries and were vividly displayed that day. He felt plainly dressed in comparison, but looked down at his yellow and white armband with satisfaction.

A small girl dressed in white, with a flower wreath around her head, tugged on his pant leg and asked him if she could see too. He smiled and lifted her up onto a large can beside him. She immediately began clapping. "Now I'm taller than you," she said. "Now I will see the Holy Father."

Konrad saw Witold waving to him from the opposite corner of the intersection. "His plane has landed," he shouted.

Welcome, Konrad thought to himself. The loudspeakers echoed that message just seconds later.

The crowd stirred but quickly quieted again as everyone strained to hear the Pope being greeted at the airport. People cheered when they heard their Primate, Cardinal Wyszyński, welcome the Pope. As Konrad listened, he felt strangely calm and solemn. The Pope is our pride and our triumph, he murmured to himself, but the Catholic Church might have disappeared if it hadn't been for Wyszyński's efforts.

The Cardinal had led the Church through its most difficult period, the Stalinist era. He spent many years in jail and under strict house arrest. When obstacles were imposed, Cardinal Wyszyński fought them tooth and nail. He was the country's strongest advocate of human dignity and rights and, for years, the Catholic Church was the only force willing to denounce the government.

The student protests of 1968 - who could forget the beatings, the dismissals, the cessation of classes, and the calls by Party members to do away with enemies of Socialism and foes of the state. People had thronged to the Cathedral to hear the Cardinal's words.

"Don't be afraid... don't fear," the Cardinal cried. "They think that they can control everything but they are only temporary, like a pestilence. They will perish. You Poles, you Christians, remember the truth will last. Don't fear, ever."

The Cardinal's dream-like image faded quickly from Konrad's mind as he looked up and realized that everyone surrounding him was waving and cheering. As the white vehicle drew closer, people sang, chanted and applauded wildly. A white-robed John Paul spread his arms out to the crowd as if he was embracing the thousands of people out to greet him. Standing beside him, the Cardinal smiled proudly and also blessed the crowd.

When the Pope's motorcade had disappeared, the crowds dispersed and Witold and Konrad left their post. They decided to meet an hour later and walk to the mass site together.

Konrad was anxious to see Julia and Agata. When he arrived at their apartment, he found the two ladies in front of their TV set.

"Hello Konrad," they both remarked quickly, their eyes never leaving the screen.

After filming the Pope's vehicle and the applauding crowds, the television cameras focused in on the Papal Coat of Arms, adorning the hundreds of banners decorating Warsaw's streets. The letter *M*, which had been chosen by John Paul II himself, was clearly distinguishable on the banner's design. An "M" for Mary...

Konrad looked up to the two framed pictures of the Virgin which hung on the wall over his grandmother's bed. One was a woeful image of St. Mary of Ostra Brama, the other the Black Madonna of Częstochowa, with the infant Jesus resting in her arms. "The day belongs to John Paul and through him... to her," he murmured.

Saint Mary was recognized as the spiritual queen of the country. She was often accepted as the universal figurehead by Poles of various religious denomination. Even Julia and Agata, who were Augsburg Lutheran, and Konrad's Moslem great-grandmother, worshipped her faithfully. The two holiest shrines in the country were devoted to St. Mary. The shrine of St. Mary of Ostra Brama had a special significance for Konrad's paternal family. It was in Wilno, the city they lived in before the war. When Wilno was taken over by the Russians in 1944, the family brought the effigies of St. Mary of Ostra Brama with them to Warsaw.

The other shrine, the Monastery of Częstochowa, boasted the holy icon known to most people as the Black Madonna. Millions of pilgrims came each year to see the miraculous painting.

"The Pontiff will arrive in Czestochowa in two days time," the TV commentator announced to the spectators, and signed off.

Konrad and Witold walked briskly along the traffic-free Marszałkowska street, one of the few streets in the city which had been reserved for the millions of pilgrims, crossing through Warsaw on foot. Square gray apartment buildings lining the route were covered with Polish and Vatican flags.

They passed the large Parade Square in front of what many varsovians thought was the ugliest building in the city. It was the Soviet-built Palace of Science and Culture, a forty-storey high, pyramid-like skyscraper. It housed a complex of theaters, museums, libraries, and the congress hall, where Party conventions were usually held. It was surrounded by fast food stands that day, offering canned soft drinks and grilled sausages at exorbitant prices.

At the entrance to Saski Garden, they were asked to show their passes. Then the 'papal guard' in charge of the district led them into Victory Square.

Saski Garden and the square were built in the 1700's by Saxon Kings, called Sas's in Polish. Over the years, the monumental square, right in the heart of the city, went through a number of transformations and titles, but most varsovians preferred to call it Saski Square. At one point it was named after Marshal Piłsudski, the founder of the resurrected Polish state. The new name, though, was never very popular despite Piłsudski's own fame.

After the war, the Communist government carefully removed every reference to Piłsudski in the streets, plazas and the history books. New plaques were erected with the inscription, 'Victory Square'.

"I'm glad we decided to come so early," Witold remarked. "It's still two hours before the mass and 'Saski' is already packed."

People were sitting underneath the tall horse chestnut trees trying to escape the heat. Many of them had transistor radios and followed continual coverage of the Pope's movements. There were nuns of all orders, boy scouts in green uniforms and others with sleeping bags. Elderly people had come well prepared, bringing chairs and canvas stools to sit on. Most of the police were busy trying to yank children out of the trees. They had climbed up the thick trunks, hoping for a better view.

A gigantic wooden cross dominated the square. It had been incorporated into a large podium. Interestingly enough, Konrad thought, the cross, and the altar below it, faced the tomb of the 'Unknown Soldier', a memorial to the millions of Polish fighters killed over the war years. It was strategically placed below a stone archway, the last surviving remnant of the once imposing Saski Palace. The home of Polish General Staff before the war, the palace was heavily bombarded by the Nazis in September of 1939 and, finally, levelled to the ground five years later, during the Warsaw Uprising.

An eternal flame marked the memorial tomb which was surrounded by numerous plaques listing the battlefields of Narvik, Tobruk, Monte Cassino, Warsaw, and Berlin. Two soldiers armed with obsolete, ceremonial rifles, guarded the tomb around the clock.

Witold nudged him. "Konrad, are you sleeping? Look..." The crowds began waving and clapping their hands. The Pope's vehicle entered the square and immediately headed in the direction of the guarded tomb. John Paul II got out of his car. After laying a wreath, he knelt and silently prayed.

Konrad watched the Pope's every move and gesture as he approached the altar. Silence filled the square. As the service began, thousands repeated the text of the mass in a powerful chorus.

"May the Lord accept the sacrifice at your hands, for the praise and glory of his name, for our good, and the good of all his Church..."

They knelt on the grass and almost shouted out the prayer. Konrad was elated. There, in the very centre of a Communist capital, the people ruled by a government who professed no faith and opposed all religion, spoke to God in a powerful voice.

They awaited Pope's Homily. The square was so quiet that Konrad could hear the distant sound of bees, sampling the flowers in the chestnut trees overhead.

John Paul II mounted the pulpit. He spoke first about the difficult times they had all faced before their meeting, before God allowed them to gather in Victory Square. The Pope's opening statement was carefully worded but the emphasis he put on the word 'victory' was unmistakable.

Karol Wojtyła went on to talk about his responsibilities - his duty to serve all the nations in the world, to help the needy and the persecuted everywhere. Even so, Konrad could sense that he was grateful for the opportunity to address his fellow Poles.

The atmosphere in the square became tense as the Pontiff started to talk about national issues. As Konrad listened to his words, his ears strained with concentration and expectation. Everyone in the square at that moment was waiting for something.

"Without Christ," John Paul II said loudly, "a man cannot understand who he is. He cannot be aware of his dignity as a human being, of his vocation or what his final destiny must be. That is why," he cried, "that is why the Christ must not be excluded from the history of mankind in any place on this Earth." His voice seemed to soar over the crowd.

The square erupted in a torrent of clapping and the crowd began waving like a sea of wheat being blown by the wind. Konrad was enveloped by the sound and movement, and the Pope' s words echoed through his mind. He joined thousands of others who pushed small, white crucifixes into the air. The applause lasted for about twenty minutes.

John Paul raised his hands to bless the crosses. Slowly, the clapping subsided. Only when the square had become completely quiet, did he begin speaking again.

"Without Christ, no one could ever understand this nation with its grandiose and difficult past," he said. "We are standing here, at the Tomb of the Unknown Soldier. Polish blood has been spilt in the defense of many other nations but yet, there can be no justice on this continent without an independent Poland." A rush of applause filled the square once more, but it quickly subsided as the Pontiff raised his right hand, gesturing people to listen carefully. "I am crying," he shouted, "I, the son of Polish soil, and I, John Paul II the Pope, I am crying from the very depth of the Polish millennium, today, on the eve of Pentecost – may the Holy Spirit descend, may your spirit descend and change the face of this earth, the face of this soil. Amen."

Strong gusts of wind began blowing above the heads of the spectators as they responded to the Pope's words with a mass of applause. The ovation triggered by the final message of his Homily lasted over half an hour.

As Konrad waved his white cross he looked at the people around him. He felt a tremendous sense of unity with them. They had been joined together by the white-robed man standing before them. With him and their creator. Everyone was smiling triumphantly as if an important battle had just been won.

"From now on, it will be a 'Victory Square'," Witold commented.

To Konrad, his friends and relatives, the Pope's pilgrimage to Poland seemed like an eight-day celebration. Every evening he took a seat beside Julia and Agata and watched the TV broadcasts from across the country. John Paul visited Gniezno, Poland's first capital. He prayed in Częstochowa and then headed for Cracow and Wadowice, where he was born. In a somber mood he spoke in Auschwitz-Birkenau. In the town of Nowy Targ, the Pontiff celebrated a mass for mountaineers in a rustic, wooden chapel which had been built by the parishioners especially for the occasion.

At each of his stops, the Pope's message was the same: "Live according to your faith, defend human dignity and do have hope."

John Paul II's image was all over Warsaw. Everyone wore the special lapel pins that were distributed by the parishes during the visit. Konrad even pinned one to the front of Julia's nightgown.

At the airport in Cracow, the Pontiff knelt down on the ground and kissed his native soil good-bye. Then Konrad, Julia and Agata watched his white jet slowly ascend and head south, towards Rome. They sat in silence for a few minutes; the eight days had passed so quickly.

The next day, Prime Minister Piotr Jaroszewicz appeared in public.

"Well... Mr. Maliniak, your prophecies were wrong. Comrade Prime Minister seems to be doing fine," Konrad told his friend at work.

Janek Siedlak and a few other workers burst into laughter. Mietek spit on the floor and sighed.

"What can you expect from a man like that? What a swine. Everyone was gearing up for his funeral and... he recovers, the son of a bitch."

It was obvious that the government was concerned about the effect of the Pope's message. Media coverage of domestic political issues and the country's economic development increased.

A Soviet-made movie about Lenin's life was shown on Polish TV two days after the Pope's departure.

CHAPTER 7

The autumn weather was unusually mild and lasted long that year. It was the end of October and most of the trees in Saski Garden - the maples, oaks, and stout beeches, were stubbornly clinging to their sun-drenched leaves.

Gray, faded benches on the edge of the park were empty, except for a few elderly people - and Hanna. She had been sitting at the bench for more than an hour, quietly observing the comings and going of people through the park. One was an elderly gentleman who was happily feeding a flock of multi-coloured pigeons directly in front of her. He leant heavily on a bamboo walking stick, tossing chunks of bread on the pavement. When it was all gone, he walked slowly to one of the benches and sat down. Most of the pigeons followed behind like ducklings after their mother.

He has probably been coming here for years, she thought. That must be 'his own' park bench.

Hanna liked old people. She felt compassion for them, somehow understanding the frustration they experienced when even small tasks became difficult and yesterday's events became dim.

I'm glad that I came here, she thought to herself as she got up from her bench. It is quiet and tranquil, something that I needed badly.

She glanced to her right and saw a group of soldiers changing guard near the tomb of the Unknown Soldier. The men were young and energetic and, though they were over a hundred meters away, she could hear their commanding officer barking orders and the pounding steps of the squad.

She turned away and headed further into the park.

She had seen her doctor earlier that day, for a regular medical examination, and had left his office feeling rather puzzled about some of his comments.

"You realize, Hanna," he had said, "that even though you had tuberculosis many years ago, it can flare up again if you don't take care of yourself. You have to limit your smoking, and," he emphasized, "to slow down."

Hanna didn't know what he was getting at, and looked at him with bewilderment.

"I mean exactly what I said," the physician emphasized, "slow down, don't rush. Try to make your life less intense. I understand that there's stress involved with your job and the daily queues but please, take care of yourself."

Before she left his office, he advised her to spend four days away from work. "There's nothing wrong with you. You just seem worn out," he said. "Spend those four days alone and... relax."

Hanna let out a long sigh and sat down on another bench, this time one which faced a small, reedy pond. She reached into her purse and took out a package of cigarettes. She lit one of them and inhaled deeply.

Ahead of her, two pairs of swans basked in the reddish sun as they swam back and forth in the middle of the pond. Yellowed weeping willows rustled softly and created a dappled effect of shadow and sun around the edge of the water.

As she flicked away her cigarette ash, she remembered her doctor's advice. "Limit smoking and don't live such an intense life..."

He's right, she realized – if he only knew what kind of a life I have been living this past year.

When she first met Konrad at Tina's apartment, she had never dreamed that the young, then overweight, military cadet would become so important to her. At first, Konrad only interested her because he was seeing Klara, a woman that Hanna knew could have her pick of men. She used to wonder what the attraction was between these two people.

She uncovered the younger woman's secret the first night she spent with Konrad.

She had been with many men over the years following her short marriage, but Konrad was different. With him, all her subconscious desires came into the realm of reality. She was amazed by the tender, but at the same time uninhibited way the young man made love to her.

But she had to admit to herself that her sexual intimacy with Konrad was only the beginning of their relationship. Intense love, and sympathy, increasingly played a larger part.

She often thought back to the night when Konrad sought refuge in her apartment after the quarrel with Tina and Artur. "I wish you were my mother," he had said to her.

I wish you were my son, she often thought to herself when they were in bed together.

This yearning grew stronger as the months passed. I would have liked to have had a son like him, she reflected. I am old enough to be his mother. Unfulfilled maternal instincts mixed with sympathy and physical desire to create what, she knew, was the greatest love of her life. Her feelings were so intense that at times she felt mentally and physically exhausted.

Hanna pulled her coat from under her arm and slipped it over her shoulders. Taking on last look at the dark and quiet pool in front of her, she started walking slowly towards Victory Square. An empty bus was parked nearby and she rested by a tree and waited for its driver to return.

I have had so many different emotions within such a short time, she thought to herself and sighed. Then she thought of her chronic weariness and the gray hair and wrinkles that she saw in the mirror every day. A dry cough, from smoking probably, she thought, wracked through her chest.

A group of young people headed toward the Europejski Hotel, across the square from the tomb of the Unknown Soldier. They were laughing and joking in English.

Hanna watched them disappear into the hotel. She smiled sadly, thinking how lucky they were to be young. To be young, and to be able to plan your future, to know you can get married and have children. She began coughing again.

The driver honked his horn and she rose from the bench. She felt very weak and it was a struggle to climb the three steps up into the bus.

The greatest love of my life is going to be my last, she thought when the driver started the engine.

A light dusting of snow floated down on Hanna's street, but it melted quickly, making the cement and asphalt of the city's surfaces glisten with moisture and reflect upon the illuminated windows of her high-rise apartment building.

Inside, she waited for him in an apartment which was gray with cigarette smoke, butts spilling out of the two ashtrays in the living room. After pouring them both some tea, she hurriedly lit a fresh cigarette. Her face appeared strained and Konrad noticed that her hands were trembling badly.

"I phoned your friend Kossak-Roztworowski last week," he remarked enthusiastically, trying to bolster her spirits. "He wants me to join Budal right after my English exam. But," he hesitated, "that is only a few months away. I'm going to have to study very hard."

Hanna smiled briefly and then looked down gloomily at her tea cup. "You should study hard, yes," she said quietly. "We are seeing each other less often now but you must keep working. It's your future, if we have a future at all," she said in a hoarse voice. "Look at what is going on today – Afghanistan is in blood, the Americans are blindfolded and perhaps tortured in Teheran and here, in Poland things don't look very good either..."

Konrad watched her sink into a state of near despair. It was painful for him to see Hanna so tense and he worried about her health. She seemed to be smoking even more than usual and there were times when she couldn't keep from coughing. When he stayed over on Saturday nights, he noticed that she would wake up in the morning at about six A.M. and a dry, hard cough would keep her awake for a good half hour. They had become a daily occurrence.

He decided to try to change the subject. "Fortunately the winter hasn't been too bad so far," he remarked. "You remember last year. What a disaster."

Hanna barely acknowledged his comment. She just stood by the window and looked out into the illuminated street below. "Do you see that butcher shop down there?" she asked. "The meat lines are twice as long this year..." She drew the living room curtains across with disgust.

He sighed. It seemed that Hanna was determined to be depressed that night. "What's even worse," he said with a mischievous pout, "we have been together for more than a year now. Does that upset you too?"

Hanna leant over and squeezed his hand. "It is the most important thing to me," she answered, kissing him softly. "I have never loved anybody more than I love you. But," she said quietly, "our love is changing."

Konrad was taken aback by her comment. "What do you mean, Hanna?"

"Don't you realize that our relationship isn't normal? We live like caged animals," she answered quietly. "We can't go out to meet other people and I feel strange when I talk to your mother. We are condemned to stay inside this tiny apartment." Her eyes swept quickly around the four small walls of her living room.

He got out of his chair and walked over to her. "We can go anywhere together, Hanna. It doesn't matter to me," he pleaded.

She laughed bitterly. "We belong to different generations, Konrad. We would never be accepted by other people," she said in a matter-of-fact tone of voice. Then she leant over and kissed him.

"I love you," she said. "I don't feel any shame about that. It's just that I would like to open up the door of this apartment and tell everyone about it because our love is true and has been beautiful."

He stepped back and looked at her. "What do you mean, has been beautiful?" he asked quietly. "Isn't it anymore?"

Hanna peered behind the drapes, and looked down at the street once more. "A year ago you were coming to see me every day whether I wanted you to or not. You were so spontaneous. Now you come only once a week. I know you are working and you are busy studying, but the fact remains that we're only seeing each other on weekends..." She turned and looked straight into his eyes.

"I love you," he said.

Hanna put her head on his shoulder. He could feel her tears flowing down his chest. "Soon you'll realize that I am old. You won't overlook my wrinkles and I won't be able to accept the secrecy any longer..."

Following the completion of his training at United Enterprises, Konrad was given the title of plant engineer. He shared an office with engineer Wiśniewski.

"There's a call for you, Mr. Dymowski," his supervisor said and handed him the receiver.

"Dymowski speaking."

He heard the voice of Zygmunt Kossak-Roztworowski. "I was out of town when you phoned me last week," be said. "I am returning your call."

"Thank you, sir. I just wanted to tell you that I passed the English exam and I was given an A grade."

"Congratulations, well done," the director of Budal exclaimed. "When would you like to join our company then?"

"As soon as possible?"

"All right. We'll see you in two months time then. Good-bye."

The telephone started ringing just a few seconds after. Konrad sighed and picked it up. It was Hanna.

"I got a call from the man who looks after the apartment building my mother and I used to live in," she said. "The apartment has been empty for a few years now..." Her voice was barely audible. "He wants me to go over there tomorrow and clean everything out. I... I was hoping that you could help me..."

The one room apartment was located in a tall, dreary group of old row houses. Hanna lived there during her adolescence with her mother, following her father's arrest by the Nazis. It had been their home until Hanna's mother had a fall, broke her hip and died. The apartment hadn't been lived in since.

Hanna stood in the middle of the dim, box-like room. Konrad watched her eyes move from bare corner to bare corner and then down to the dusty cardboard boxes on the floor. She asked him to help her sort through them. He threw out four enormous bags of various kinds of rubbish into the garbage.

One last piece of furniture remained. It was her mother's heavy wooden bookcase.

"This was her favourite collection," Hanna said, pointing to the bookshelves. She grabbed one of the yellowed volumes and handed it to him.

"You should read this one. It's a pre-war study of international Jewry." She sat down on a pile of tattered magazines and started scanning through the book herself.

She must be joking, Konrad thought to himself with surprise, but when he looked at her face closely, he realized that Hanna was leafing through the book with intense interest.

He lit a cigarette, leant against the only windowsill in the apartment and reflected on what she had just said. It reminded him of Tina's negative attitudes towards the Jews in Poland. She had always maintained that they were staunch Communists. For a long time, Konrad was heavily influenced by her opinions.

Back in 1965, he remembered that the principal of his grammar school summoned Tina to his office. "Your son has been telling Jewish jokes which make fun of some of the most respected members of our Party," he told her. "He has been slandering the governments of the Polish People's Republic and the Soviet Union. What are you going to do about it, Mrs. Dymowska?"

"Not much," Tina answered sharply. "The boy knows who tortured my father during the 1950's, that's all."

"But this must stop," the principal yelled and slammed his desk with his fist. "Unless you improve Konrad's mouth, I'll have to notify the authorities..."

Two years later, when the Six Day War erupted, the Soviets supported Israel's Arab adversaries and began carrying out anti-Semitic purges at home. Concussion grenades and tear gas filled the streets of Warsaw in March, 1968. University students and intellectuals demanded freedom of expression and free development of the Polish culture. Within a week, many university faculties were dissolved and students expelled. Konrad's cousin Ryś, who was himself a university student, also had to file a new enrollment application. He told Konrad in detail about massive protests which were supported by the vast majority of students. From die-hard Catholics, such as Antoni Macierewicz, to Trotskyists, Polish students tried to defend their campuses against the police and their voluntary reserves, ORMO.

The government censured small group of Catholic Members of Parliament, headed by Tadeusz Mazowiecki, for voicing an official protest against brutal pacification of universities in the House.

When the smoke settled, the government condemned the Jews for the unrest. "This act of war against Socialism and the Polish State, the unprecedented riots by the students who owe everything to the Socialist motherland were obviously a plot by the Zionists," the government propagandists screamed.

"Zionists out," The TV Daily blared. Konrad had never heard the word before.

For a number of years after 1968, the government continued to blame the economic woes of the country on the Jews, although none of them occupied prominent positions in the government at that point.

Hanna called him. With her head still buried in the book, she asked him to fetch her cigarettes. "I'll be right with you," she said. "I just have to complete this chapter; it's so exciting."

He handed her a cigarette and she lit it quickly without lifting her head. "Unbelievable," she murmured. "The Jewish Mafia was formidable..."

Having opened the small window looking out on the backyard, he sat on the sill and gazed at the children playing soccer outside.

Hanna startled him when she dropped the book suddenly into one of the boxes. "I am sorry," she apologized. "I was reading a very interesting story about Rozenkrantz, the man who caused the financial ruin of about fifty Polish shopkeepers in 1931."

Konrad shrugged. He knew that there were many bankruptcies during the Depression. "Yes, it must have been a very difficult time," he conceded, "but it happens everywhere. When I was in America, I watched a number of small owners struggle against large grocery chains. Maybe Rozenkrantz was just a better businessman."

Hanna's face soured. "But the fifty were Poles. Don't you understand that, Konrad?"

"Rozenkrantz was a Polish citizen too, wasn't he?" he asked her.

"Rozenkrantz was a greedy Jewish swine," she shouted and glared at him.

Konrad shrugged and said boldly, "Believe me Hanna, there are worse swine in the Party these days, and they're 100 percent Aryan and Polish!"

His face burned when Hanna's palm sliced against his cheek. She didn't stop there either. "How dare you say that? Those Poles became beggars because of Rozenkranz," she gasped.

Holding his hand to his cheek, his head was filled with perplexing questions. He had just told her about his feelings for the Communists. He knew that she didn't like them herself. And what about Rozenkrantz anyway? he asked himself. The man has probably been dead for years...

He watched her hands shake as she gingerly lit a cigarette. She didn't look up at him.

He was filled with disgust and disappointment. Hanna had always appeared so clearheaded and wise to him. Now she seemed to be totally enveloped in an uncontrollable racial fever.

She deserves a good lesson, he thought to himself.

"I'm partly Jewish myself, Hanna," he said suddenly. "Didn't Tina ever tell you?"

Her eyes widened with disbelief. "What are you talking about? Why are you telling me this now?"

"I am partly Jewish," he repeated in a voice void of emotion. "One of my ancestors was called Rozenfeld. I didn't tell you earlier because I didn't think it would make much difference."

She slumped on to the dusty linoleum and wept. "Why are you telling me this?" she wailed.

His voice was business-like when he answered her. "I only told you this because it is true." As he looked down at her, he knew that there were no feelings of sympathy and understanding to express.

"Do you want to hit me again?" he asked, and started toward the door.

Hanna shouted after him. "Forgive me Konrad, please. I love you. It doesn't matter who you are."

"You hit me in the face."

That was not the end of their relationship. They still continued to meet once or twice a week, and as usual, Konrad spent his Saturday nights at her apartment.

Hanna made things difficult. She often asked him to stop coming, but he would show up anyway. When she repeated her request, he didn't bother calling her for three days, after which she phoned him.

They were uncomfortable when they talked to each other and Hanna cried often. A barrier separated their psyches, once so in tune with each other.

And, as Hanna had feared, the physical attraction that had been so strong between them, began to fade.

There was no use trying to ignore his feelings. He knew that his second love was over.

PART

3

Candlelight

CHAPTER 1

Sister Maria appeared at Julia's door quite unexpectedly one day. Maria was a Sister of Charity and she, along with other nuns from the nearby parish, spent hours tending invalids in the neighbourhood, helping them to wash, doing their shopping and cleaning their rooms. She was a rather short woman, in her fifties with a pleasant manner which was infectious.

The nun marvelled at the number of St. Mary effigies in their home. "I come to an apartment inhabited by two Lutheran ladies and I find more pictures of the God Mother than I have ever seen in any Catholic home," she often joked.

The gray habits of Sister Maria and her fellow sisters began appearing at Julia's bedside on a regular basis, but Julia still felt guilty about taking up so much of her family's time and attention. She was well aware of the time Agata spent in the kitchen preparing meals, or lining up for meat in the ever lengthening queues.

When Anka and Bib invited Konrad to their wedding anniversary celebration, Julia suggested that Agata go too. "Your great-aunt really needs a break, Konrad. I'll be fine on my own for a few hours," she insisted.

Konrad felt anxious when they returned to the apartment from the party. He quietly opened his grandmother's bedroom door and peered inside. Julia was lying quite still in her bed, her eyes wide open. She didn't respond to his greeting.

"Would you like to watch TV, Babcia?" he asked cheerfully, as he turned the television set on.

"No - I - don't - think - so," she answered feebly.

He remembered that voice. Looking more closely at his grandmother's face, he noticed that her eyes were glassy and that she seemed dazed. His mind raced. The image of cots lining the dim corridor of the overcrowded neurological ward appeared before his eyes. He rushed to the window and opened it completely to let some fresh air into the room. The apartment was stifling.

Running to the bathroom, he grabbed a washcloth, soaked it in cool water, and placed it on her head. He felt instinctively that it was the best thing to do. It was after midnight and he dreaded the thought of calling an ambulance. It could take hours for one to arrive.

He decided to call a doctor anyway and began looking for some spare change for the pay telephone. Julia shook her head. "Konrad, I'm feeling much better now, please don't call anybody..."

He looked at her eyes closely and sighed with relief when he saw that they were clear and bright once again. Even the gray pallor in her cheeks had disappeared. She fell into a deep, comfortable sleep soon after. As he stood over her bed, Konrad felt strangely weak. He sat down at her bedside and stayed there through the night.

Sister Maria confronted him the next afternoon. "Why didn't you tell me that you were leaving your grandmother alone last night? I would have looked after her."

He didn't answer at first, but instead looked down at the floor and shook his head. "We didn't think that anything would happen, sister. She said she felt perfectly fine before we left," he replied sheepishly.

The nun led him into the kitchen and they sat down at the table. She spoke quietly, almost at a whisper.

"Listen Konrad, I know you love your grandmother very much. We all do, she is a lovely person. I don't think I have ever cared for someone like her before. But," she said, placing her hand on his shoulder, "you mustn't forget that she is very ill, and she is not going to get much better. Count your blessings that she is coherent, that the almighty God has left her brain intact. With that, she is a participating member of your family."

"I know, sister," Konrad said quietly. "We are thankful to God for her."

Konrad watched as Sister Maria turned and looked out through the window into the narrow and dim backyard. Her voice became very quiet and solemn. "Her life is a feeble candlelight, Konrad. God has embraced it in his loving palms so that the wind can't reach it and put it out. But it is a feeble candlelight."

Julia's wheelchair sat in a corner of her bedroom, barely used. She had been wheeled around the apartment a couple of times, but Konrad longed to take her outside to get some fresh air.

"We're going for a walk, Babcia," he declared one warm afternoon.

"No, we are not," she replied stubbornly.

"Why not?" he asked her playfully.

She seemed aggravated by his persistence. "I am not supposed to leave my bed."

Julia hesitated. Konrad sensed that she was apprehensive, and perhaps even a bit ashamed. She had walked around her neighbourhood for over thirty years, shopping, chatting and visiting.

"My hair is dirty, Konrad," she finally argued. "I can't go outside looking like this."

"All right. I'll wash your hair," he answered, and quickly went into the washroom before she changed her mind. He brought back a large bowl and a bottle of shampoo.

He handed her a mirror when it was finished. Although her face was very thin, traces of beauty were still visible. Julia's fine, strong features were highlighted by her softly waving hair. "We can go now, Babcia. You look fine," he said, trying to reassure her.

149

He sat her down into the chair and wheeled it towards the back door of the apartment building. Four steps barred their way, so he left the wheelchair momentarily, and went to ask a passer-by to help him.

The yard was infused with a bright, warm sunlight. Lavender coloured lilac bushes gave off a delicate scent and overshadowed an oval-shaped lawn dotted with acacia trees.

Carefully, he took the handles of the chair and pushed it around the garden. His grandmother stared at the grass and the trees and then up towards the sun. The glare made her eyes blink and she shielded them with her one good hand.

She sighed. "My God. How long has it been? Two years? It can't be true."

Konrad then wheeled her past an effigy of St. Mary which was encircled by small bushes. Freshly cut flowers lay in front. She asked him to wheel her closer to the shrine and he edged the wheelchair between the bushes.

The statue of Mary was painted in a soft blue and white. She wore a white veil which draped over her head. Above, a wire halo punctuated with small stars crowned her head.

"I brought you here often when you were an infant," his grandmother murmured. "I would sit on the little bench here and you would fall asleep under the shadow of the trees."

Konrad looked closely at the statue. A short prayer was engraved on its granite pedestal. *"At your feet we put our prayers asking for your help, Mother. The tenants, 1943."*

He took hold of the wheelchair handles and pushed the chair into the street. The sidewalks were cracked and uneven and the wheelchair creaked and rattled on the hard cement. As the quiet side street was relatively free of traffic, he steered Julia on to the asphalt roadway.

His grandmother gazed at the local stores she had frequented almost every day before her illness.

They passed a small confectionery and bakeshop. Pushing the wheelchair along, he stared at the pavement below. He knew every stone embedded in the asphalt, every tree overhead. He was born there. All his childhood memories flooded back.

Carefully, he pushed the chair across the street and steered it into a narrow sidewalk which led to The Gardens. They were small plots of land bought by varsovians after the war, when land was cheap. Once located in the outskirts of town, over the years The Gardens were slowly embraced by the expanding city. Fruits, vegetables, and flowers were grown by the plot owners, but many others just liked to walk through the area and enjoy the quiet of the compound. The tranquillity was refreshing.

Julia was bewitched by the spring landscape. "Oh, how beautiful," she repeated as she looked at the roses, carnations and tulips enveloping one garden. Her eyes slowly passed over every flower and tree.

"You can't imagine how beautiful it is in The Gardens, Agata," she exclaimed when they returned home. "Everything is in bloom - the flowers, the apple trees, everything." She spoke of nothing else the entire evening.

The following weekend, they ventured out again. When Konrad wheeled her toward a streetcar stop, Julia looked up at him. "Where are we going?" she demanded.

"I'm taking you to the cemetery to visit Dziadek's[1] grave."

After purchasing two bunches of white and red carnations and some wax lamps, they entered the park-like cemetery, where trees and bushes were in great profusion, and flowers lay like blankets upon the burial sites.

He knelt down at the gray stone frame which embraced his grandfather's burial plot. Julia watched him place the flowers on Robert's tomb and light the lamp. She remained silent, but Konrad watched her eyes close tightly and her lips move quietly in prayer. After a few minutes, she placed her hand on his arm and thanked him for bringing her to the cemetery. "If you hadn't taken me here, I would never have visited Robert's grave. This may be the first, and possibly the last time," she said, and smiled sadly.

He began wheeling the chair away from the grave. He couldn't imagine life without her. He knew only that he loved her and wanted desperately for her to live. If she wants to survive she will, he told himself. He felt a strong determination inside – a hope that he, through his will and love alone, would keep her from dying.

He pushed the wheelchair across the street towards the Moslem cemetery where Julia's mother Luba was buried. Some Turkish and Arab graves dotted the area, but most of the tombs belonged to the Polish Tatars. They had a long history in Poland. In the 14th Century, their ancestors, the last remnants of the once powerful Gold Horde established by Genghis Khan[2], were defeated by Tamerlane[3].

The leader of the Horde, Tochtamish, sought refuge in the Lithuanian court. During the next century, many Tatars were given gentry status and large estates. This was largely in recognition of their successful combat against Poland's German enemies, the Teutonic Knights, at Grunwald in 1410.

Although they were free to practice their Moslem faith in Poland, many had embraced some Catholic traditions. The most important was the cult of St. Mary.

Konrad had been told the history of the Tatars many times. His great grandmother always stressed her ancestors' participation in the Battle of Grunwald.

Konrad strained as he lifted the wheelchair on to the elevated lawn near Luba's grave. He looked at the crescent and star engraved in her tombstone.

After he and Julia had silently prayed together, he pushed the wheelchair along a pathway. They gazed at the rows of graves on either side.

"Many of these people were my cousins or friends," she said. "Here is the grave of Captain Sulejman Kryczyński of the Thirteenth Regiment of Wilnian Lancers. He served with the Tatar Cavalry Squadron. I knew that gentleman very well," she said sadly.

---

1. Dziadek (Polish) - Grandpa.

2. Genhis Khan [1162? - 1227] - Mongol - Tatar conqueror of Asia and today's Russia.

3. Tamerlane (Timur Lenk) [1336? - 1405] - Mongol conqueror of Asia.

Konrad blew out the candles with one long breath and supper began. The birthday cake didn't last long, and when it was finished, he and the rest of the guests began eating 'nic po nim' pudding. The party was a real surprise to him, having been secretly organized by Agata and Julia.

After drinking some tea and clearing away the dishes, he was handed a few presents. Agata smiled proudly as she brought out her gift. "Julia and I bought this for you. It is a cosmic T-shirt. Take a look."

Konrad unwrapped the present, a white shirt spotted with light blue clouds and space rockets.

"Agata was shopping and she found this beautiful shirt," Julia said. "We decided to buy it for you. It's pure cotton."

All of the guests smiled and laughed, murmuring quickly about how much they liked the garment. Konrad looked carefully at the tag. "Cosmic-shirt commemorating the first Polish cosmonaut. 100% cotton, machine-washable. Fits children 7 through 13."

"Do you like it?" Agata asked him eagerly.

"I like it very much," he said, and kissed them both.

It was April, 1980. Konrad had been living with his grandmother and great-aunt for almost a year.

With some reluctance, he started working at Budal. Although he had not found his work at United Enterprises very challenging, he appreciated his co-workers for their straightforwardness and down-to-earth manner.

At Budal, he was employed in the Foreign Customer Service department, The department occupied two rooms, which faced each other, in a dim and narrow corridor. The smaller of the two, was the office of the department head, Wiesław Smrodziński, and his secretary.

Konrad was given a desk in the other office, along with a number of engineers and technicians. An attractive blond woman, Małgosia Karska, occupied the desk closest to the window. Konrad found himself facing Waldek Marciniuk, a forty year old technician. His right-hand neighbour was a handsome engineer in his mid-thirties, by the name of Maksymilian Wysmukłowski, who smoked cigarettes constantly and had a chronic smoker's cough.

Unlike at United Enterprises, employees rarely discussed politics during company hours. Konrad quickly got the impression that most of his new colleagues were simply reluctant to voice their opinions. They concentrated on sports, the weather, or the various foreign projects that the company was undertaking.

Konrad seldom took part in their discussions. He was inexperienced, and he sensed that he was being treated like an intruder by his fellow workers. At the beginning of his second week there though, his boss, engineer Smrodziński, surprised him with a question. "What about you, Mr. Dymowski? Have you ever been abroad?"

"Yes, I have," he stammered. He could feel his face getting hot rapidly.

"And where have you been, may I ask?" his boss inquired further.

Konrad glanced at his supervisor. The man had a round, pinkish face. He was very overweight and had an ego to match. He was also a member of the Party Committee at Budal.

"Well, I have been to the USSR," Konrad said quietly, trying to feign a modest demeanour.

"Ah there. Anywhere else?"

"Yes. I have also been to the US and Canada."

"You have?" Smrodziński remarked with astonishment. Konrad savoured his obvious surprise and smiled proudly. "Well," his boss said after clearing his throat a few times, "I suppose you must know some English then..."

Konrad nodded. "Oh yes. I passed a government English exam before I started here."

"Well, well," Smrodziński murmured and got out of his chair. "We need skilled people at Budal. Now let's get back to work." He set his mug down on the window sill and left for his office.

When the door closed after him, the entire room filled with laughter. Konrad could tell that the other employees were beginning to look at him more favourably.

His knowledge of English was a noticeable boost at work. His boss often asked him to translate business letters and was full of praise. But Konrad wanted to go even further with the language. He spent most of his spare time going to English classes, studying grammar books, or reading any American magazines that he could lay his hands on. During breakfast, and later in the evening, he listened to the Voice of America radio broadcasts.

CHAPTER 2

"So sad a face at the sight of an old friend? Mr. Dymowski, I expected more from you?"

Konrad squinted in the dim light of the train compartment. A tall man with a head of lavish blond hair and a few freckles, smiled and winked at him.

Konrad returned the smile and rose from his seat. "Mr. Siedlak, Janek," he exclaimed, "I didn't expect to see you here. Sit down, please. A cigarette?"

Janek Siedlak nodded and Konrad handed him a package of Marlboro's. His friend turned the package over and grinned at him. "Well," he commented. "Luxury cigarettes. When you worked in Department A, you smoked Sports just like the rest of us. Quite a change."

Konrad burst into laughter. "It's only because I am starting my holidays," he explained. "Believe me, I don't make much more at Budal than I did at United Enterprises. How are things there, by the way?"

Janek lit his cigarette and sat back in his seat. "You might be interested to know about some recent changes," he remarked. "Our chief union steward, you remember Mrowicki? Well, he has moved on to the CRZZ, Central Council of Trade Unions." Konrad looked at his friend with interest. "And who got his job?" he asked.

"Stefan Panek, the son of a bitch."

"Do you mean the guy who took over Bronek Oskiernia's position?"

Janek nodded. "Fortunately, he's not our foreman anymore. He was nominated for the union job and now Zygmunt Kowalski is our boss."

Konrad smiled. It appeared that life at United Enterprises hadn't really changed.

"What a mockery," Janek Siedlak muttered. "You should have been there for the 'election' of our new union steward. Gdzieś, the director of the company, chaired the meeting himself. He got up on the podium and said to us: 'Dear colleagues, because of comrade Mrowicki's transfer to the CRZZ, we have to elect a new Chief Steward. The management, the Factory Party Committee and the Union of Metal Workers Executive has established a candidate list. The candidate to be considered is the union steward of Department A, comrade Stefan Panek'. After he said that, he began clapping, so did Chlewnik, Sroka's replacement. The rest of us just sat there. Gdzieś looked around and asked if any of us wanted to comment on the candidate. No one said anything for about a minute, and then Mietek Maliniak stood up and started shouting. We all applauded. He said, 'Janek Siedlak and I spent ten hours at Pałac Mostowskich[4], being interrogated by the SB-Secret Service. I don't think a man who is an informer would make a good union leader.' Well, Panek jumped out of his seat and began denying everything. After he and Mietek exchanged a few insults, Gdzieś tried to get the meeting going again. He asked Mietek if he had anything else to say. Mietek nodded and nominated another candidate - Maryla Kozłowska.

Konrad shook his head. "Unbelievable, I wish I had been there," he murmured.

"You did miss a lot," Janek acknowledged. "There was a vote. About 60 percent of us voted for Maryla."

"Well, then why isn't she the new chief steward?"

Janek Siedlak sighed. "After the vote, Gdzieś started screaming like hell, saying that the vote didn't count because Maryla's nomination hadn't been approved by the Party Committee."

"Unbelievable," Konrad repeated, "and what happened next?"

"Well, Maryla wasn't at the meeting so we decided to wait until she came back from vacation and then ask her if she really did want to run against Panek. She happens to live in my building and two days after the meeting she knocked on my door. She was hysterical. She said that Mrowicki had called, and had asked to see her in his office. I told her that I would go with her to the CRZZ. The next day, we got off the bus around the corner from the union council building and I stopped to get a package of cigarettes. When I looked around for Maryla, she wasn't there. Then I saw her sitting in a car, Mrowicki's brand new Polonez to be exact. The next day, Maryla refused to accept the chief steward's position and Panek got the job. What is worse, that S.O.B. Mrowicki received a talon[5] for another Polonez."

Konrad nodded with understanding. High-ranking officials with the Central Council of Trade Unions were known to enjoy a number of benefits. They had access to a well-stocked cafeteria and special internal meat stores, but most importantly, they received 'talony' - small slips of paper, issued by the government, that allowed the lucky holder to purchase a car at the regular price in Polish currency. When the system was first introduced, 'talony' were to be distributed evenly, as a way of balancing the huge demand for cars which were in short supply. In practice though, the 'talony' were an institutionalized form of corruption among the Communist hierarchy.

"With a 'talon', Mrowicki bought that car for about 300,000 złoty," Janek muttered. "Now he'll probably turn around and sell it for twice as much in the free market, get another 'talon' and..."

Janek laughed bitterly and continued talking. "That's how our privileged comrades have made their fortunes," he said. "The rest of us sit back and gnash our teeth - who the hell invented trade unions in Socialist countries anyway? They don't do a thing..." He sat forward in his chair. "We need something else," he

---

4. Pałac Mostowskich - Mostowski (family) Palace, the headquarters of SB Secret Service Metropolitan Command in Warsaw.

5. Talon (plural: talony) - a car coupon.

said, lowering his voice, and glancing uneasily at the compartment door. "Some people I know are already working in free, underground trade unions. Have you heard of them?"

At that moment, their compartment door slid open, and the train conductor asked them to present their tickets. The train began to slow down. Out of the fog, the outskirts of a large town became visible through the window. Janek started to get out of his seat, explaining that he was getting off at the station. They shook hands. "My wife and kids are vacationing near here. It was nice to see you again. Call me sometime if you have a moment. I'll be back in Warsaw by the beginning of August. Bye now."

Konrad watched the figure of his tall, blond-haired friend walking along the platform. I wonder what kind of 'free trade unions' he was talking about, he thought to himself.

Konrad put his suitcase down and surveyed the room he had been allotted for his vacation. It was sparsely furnished with only two narrow beds, night tables and a washbasin. A bathroom to be used by all the occupants on the floor, was at the far end of the hall. The former staff hotel for construction workers, had recently been converted into a vacation place open to the general public. Its nondescript dormitories, dining hall, and discotheque overlooked a narrow, reedy lake. It couldn't have been more different than the small, remote cottage that he and Hanna had talked about just months before. We had planned to spend our holidays together, he thought bitterly, but our love didn't survive the spring.

"We'll go to the country and stay in a little house," she had said to him. *"A friend of mine gave me the address of some farmers who rent out cottages in the summer to visitors. They're not expensive because they're in the middle of nowhere, perhaps close to a river and a forest with rarely traveled road and calm... We'll eat home baked bread and farmer cheese and on Sundays, I'll buy a chicken from the local people and cook a good dinner for my son because that's what I'll be calling you."*

It is amazing how two people's feelings for each other can change so quickly, he thought. Inexplicably though, he was still relieved that they had parted for good.

Swollen, murky-coloured clouds cast a dark shadow over the lake, turning it into an ominous, rolling gray mass. Feeling a raindrop on his face as he looked out the window, Konrad was grateful that he wouldn't be alone for long. His friend Albert was expected to arrive in two days.

They met many years before when he, Irian and Roman had gone to Albert's apartment to play bridge one afternoon. Albert only knew Irian well, but he greeted them all enthusiastically at the door. "Come in, come in," he had exclaimed. "I'll get you some snacks and something to drink."

He remembered looking over to Roman when Albert set a huge plate of ham sandwiches down on the table and poured them some Cinzano vermouth. The two of them were lucky to get ham twice a year, at Christmas and Easter.

"This is a great treat, Albert," Roman told him. "Thanks a lot."

Albert shrugged. "Go ahead and eat," he said with a laugh. "My mother will buy more tomorrow."

For a long time, Konrad was reluctant to meet Albert again. After their first meeting, he found out that Albert's mother Eleonora was an important official with a powerful government ministry. When Irian suggested another game of bridge, he declined. "His mother is a Communist and she is rich," he told him. "My family is poor, but it's certainly not red."

Irian often argued with him about Albert and his mother. "But you have never met her. She is very nice."

"But, she's one of them," was always his final answer.

He finally met Eleonora quite unexpectedly, a year later. It was the summer of 1968 and Russian tanks, assisted by other Warsaw Pact armies, had just rolled into Prague. Photographs in the Polish dailies showed Russian and Polish tanks parked in the city's old town. "The Czechs have warmly greeted the allied forces. Our troops have spared their freedom and prevented fraternal Czechoslovakia from being overrun by the vicious imperialists," the headlines screamed.

Konrad was furious about the Polish Army's involvement in the invasion but when he looked around Warsaw, he found that most of the people walking around were laughing and talking as though nothing had happened.

Armed with a handful of newspapers with coverage on the invasion, he sought out his friend Irian. He found him in the amusement park near the Warsaw Central railway station. Irian, who looked much older than his age, was standing near an amusement kiosk, talking to a girl.

When he approached the couple, Irian started to frown and then quickly flashed a friendly smile at him. "What's up my friend?" he asked with false enthusiasm. "You haven't met Teresa. Teresa, this is my younger friend Konrad."

"We're the same age, you bastard," Konrad growled under his breath. "Could I talk to you for a moment?"

When they were safely out of view behind the carousel ride, Irian grabbed his arm. "What do you want and why the hell are you bothering me now?" he yelled.

Konrad sighed. "Look Irian," he said, spreading one of the newspapers out in front of them. "The Soviets and our puppet army are in Czechoslovakia. And what are we, brave Poles, doing about it? Nothing. Look at you, you're trying to make it with a woman... you don't give a shit," he shouted.

Irian began shaking his head. "Of course I'm against the invasion," he said, "but the government sent the troops in, not us. We can't do anything about it."

"But we can and we must," Konrad answered with determination. "Somebody has to show them which side the Poles are really on. Will you help me?"

Irian looked around the corner of the carousel to make sure that Teresa was still waiting for him, and then turned and faced Konrad again. "What do you mean?" he asked quietly.

Konrad briefly explained his project and Irian nodded.

That evening, Konrad shut himself in his bedroom and prepared the posters. He took the front pages of the Polish newspapers he had collected, and painted them with red stars and black Nazi swastikas. Then he wrote in large letters across the front, "Poland supports Czechoslovakia, we're ashamed of our troops - Capital, awake!"

The next evening, he slung a large bag over his shoulder and joined Irian, who had stowed a bottle of glue in his pant pocket. He grinned widely as they pasted about ten of the posters in the busiest areas of the city - the heavily traveled intersections and popular movie theaters and restaurants.

Irian seemed to be pleased with the job. "We've done well here. Why don't we put some in my neighbourhood?"

They had just finished affixing the last poster on the wall of an apartment building when Konrad noticed bright headlights in the distance. "Run Irian, run," he shouted, realizing that it was a police van.

They raced along the sidewalk. The van was getting closer. Irian grabbed Konrad's arm. "Let's go to Albert's flat," he shouted and they ran into the lobby of his building.

Albert lived on the 14th floor and Konrad pushed the elevator button repeatedly.

"Shit, it's going to take ages," Irian murmured as they watched the elevator's light start slowly descending. Heavy footsteps and blaring flashlights greeted them seconds later.

"So, here you are," one of the police officers said. "Well, it's nice to meet you two. Put out your hands." With a chuckle, he handcuffed their wrists.

"Those were very nice posters that you were pasting..." he said as he led them out to the van. "We need more guys like you - in the reformatory of course. Get moving!"

The sergeant opened the back door of the van, and started pushing them inside when they heard a strange voice behind them. "What are you doing with these boys, officer?"

"It's none of your business really, madam," the sergeant said, and began closing the van door.

"You're wrong there. I happen to know them," the woman answered.

"That's Albert's mother," Irian whispered. Konrad poked his head outside and saw a short, handsomely dressed woman standing in front of the officer. She opened her purse and flashed her ID card.

The sergeant retreated quickly. "I'm sorry, madam. How was I to know?"

"That's all right, officer," Eleonora answered with a smile. "Just take the handcuffs off and I'll make sure that they behave properly. There won't be anymore problems in the future. You can just forget that you ever saw any trouble, all right?"

"Yes, madam," the officer answered quietly.

Konrad smiled when he recalled that evening. Soon after that, he began visiting Albert from time to time. In the mid seventies, they spent a lot of time in beer bars. He reluctantly had to spend the money he earned through tutoring, while Albert doled out the allowance he received from his mother.

In many ways, Konrad thought, Albert was like a troublesome, spoiled child. He took whatever he could from his mother without thinking twice. But he was her only child and she devoted most of her life to him.

He smiled bitterly, thinking how Tina had often made the same claim. He shook his head. No, he thought, I was never very important to Tina. Her men came first. Now, after more than a year living away from her, his negative feelings hadn't diminished. "We have always been so far apart," he murmured quietly.

The following day, the weather at the resort changed dramatically. In the morning, the sun burned its way through the thick veil of fog and dappling waves on the small lake let shine, distinct but very transient, flickers of silver. But after lunch, when Konrad looked down at the lake from a cafeteria window, he noticed that the sky again had begun to darken and to swell with rain clouds. As he looked around the busy cafeteria full of strangers, he felt depressed and solitary. He was relieved when Albert finally pulled up in his car.

The routine of getting up and going to work each day was replaced by yet another strict schedule which revolved around meals at the resort. Three meals were included in the cost of the vacation. One hour was allowed for breakfast and dinner, and two for lunch.

Albert sighed and laid his fork down on the table.

"What's wrong with you?" Konrad asked him.

"This isn't a decent breakfast. I'm going to buy something at the take-out canteen."

He slapped down a sausage and three beers. Konrad glanced at them and decided to do the same.

They sat in the eating hall and drank while the rain pounded on the glass panes.

"This place isn't bad, but the weather here is fucking awful. So was the breakfast," Albert groaned. "Are they going to feed us like that all the time?"

Konrad shook his head and laughed. "Ask them yourself, how am I supposed to know?"

"My mother and I went to the seacoast last year," Albert said, and took a gulp from his beer. "We stayed at a holiday spot there. The food was great and the beer was much cheaper," he added with obvious boredom and yawned loudly.

"I'm sorry Albert, but I don't work in the Ministry like your mother. This is just an ordinary vacation. While we're here though, we might as well try to enjoy ourselves. What would you like to do tonight?"

Albert swallowed the last of his sausage. "Well, there is that disco down the road. I suppose we could go there, drink some beer and pick up two nice babes. What do you say?"

Konrad feigned astonishment at Albert's remarks. "You, girls? I thought you were planning to see Henia tonight?"

"No, I spoke to her on the phone. She's meeting me tomorrow."

Konrad had never met Albert's fiancée, but he felt as though he did because Albert talked about her almost constantly. They had met during a New Year's Eve party when Albert was vacationing in the mountains.

"You don't seem to be very faithful to your future bride," he joked.

Albert began laughing hysterically. "You're a bloody hypocrite, Konrad. You dare say that to me? I still remember - I'll never' forget it - the time you ran out of my apartment with one shoe on. You were still dating Klara then, weren't you?"

"All right, all right, " Konrad agreed. He could feel his face turning red. "I suppose I knew I was just about to go into the army and that I wouldn't be seeing any women for a long time. Anyway, the whole thing was your fault. You told me that your mother wasn't going to be coming home from her business trip for two days and it was your idea to invite those two girls in." He playfully scowled at Albert for a second and then opened another bottle of beer.

"It's not a matter of blame, Konrad, it's a matter of principle. There you were, screwing the girl you had just met in a beer bar and at the same time you were proclaiming your endless love to Klara. She was your sweetheart for almost eight years, wasn't she?"

"Yes, she was," Konrad conceded, swallowing the last few drops of his beer.

Albert took a good gulp of beer and continued. "Konrad, my dear friend, it was a picture. I don't think I'll ever forget it. Just think back: there you were with that girl in my mother's room and then we heard Eleonora trying to unlock the door of the apartment. Both of you grabbed everything and started running into my room. I saw you hopping along with only one shoe on. I'll never forget it," Albert said, choking with laughter.

"Well, I won't forget it either. It's the only time I've tried to make love to a girl and didn't finish. Your mother arrived twenty seconds too early."

"You wanted to leave but you needed your shoe. Do you remember?" Albert asked, pointing a finger at Konrad. "I asked my mother if she had seen your shoe. What did she say? Do you remember?"

"Yes, she said, 'I can't see any shoes but I found your friend's underwear on my bed.' And then she said, 'and it's not very clean!' I was so ashamed. I wanted to disappear."

"Well, it was pretty funny but there weren't any hard feeling after you sent mother some roses the next day." Albert got up, unsteadily, and went to the bar. He ordered four more beers.

Konrad sat at the empty table and thought about the Konrad of three years before. He had changed. Hanna's face appeared before his eyes. Her image was painful.

Henia isn't expecting me so early, Albert thought to himself as his tiny car sped along a narrow mountain highway the next morning. I'll call her at the factory and we'll have lunch together. She'll take the afternoon off and I'll invite her to an expensive restaurant for supper. We'll see what happens after.

He felt content as he drove along the lonely roads. He had just finished his final exams and Eleonora was pleased. She was always urging him to complete his degree but he didn't know why. He thought of Konrad's situation. His friend had been working for a year and a half and he still had to do extra tutoring to make ends meet. Albert extended his time in school as long as he could. I'm not going to be that stupid, he often thought to himself. Eleonora loves me and if she's willing to support me through university, fine.

He wasn't in a hurry to do anything. By Polish standards, his mother earned excellent salary. He grew up expecting life to continue the way it always had - in comfort.

When he first met Henia, he knew that she fit his image of an ideal wife. He thought she was very attractive, with her delicate features and slight, but shapely frame. She was also modest, which he liked.

Her family lived in a small house outside of Nowy Targ. They all worked in a nearby factory. Henia had a degree in economics from one of the country's most prestigious institutions, the Uniwersytet Jagielloński in Cracow. As he passed small mountain chalets along the road, he wondered how she could live in such a remote area after spending so many years in Cracow. He didn't know that Henia's memories of Cracow weren't completely happy. At one time she had been engaged, but her fiancé had died. It was only after his death that she decided to return home to her family. She did miss the city. During her four years at university, she had enjoyed Cracow's museums, cinemas and theaters. Memories of her childhood in Nowy Targ were pleasant, but when she returned home, she found things very different than she remembered. She felt like an outsider in the all too small town. It was as if she had returned to a vacuum. Most of her friends were married and had their own lives to live. Those who left for Cracow or Warsaw seldom came back.

When she met Albert at a party one evening, she really wasn't all that impressed. He seemed shallow and had an undeserved air of self-confidence about him. He was nothing to look at either. His only nice feature was a pair of warm, brown eyes. Despite all of that, they began dancing together and she eventually ended up spending the night with him. She still had trouble figuring out why. It didn't matter if he had a car and money to blow, she supposed. She needed him. Her body longed to be loved.

"I'll come back to see you," he had whispered in her ear the morning after the party. "Whenever I have time, I'll come," and he drove off in his car.

She tried in vain to forget him. During the first month after their encounter, she spent many hours in church, praying, and in open confession to her priest. She even went as far as joining the village Women's Circle, but she quickly realized that she didn't belong with the older women who spent most of their time chattering in the local dialect that she never used and poking their needles in and out of the fine linen spread on a hoop.

Her days were always the same. She would return home from work in the dark, during the short days of February, and would know that nothing was going to happen, that she would end up watching a dull television program with her parents and go to bed too early.

Albert pressed the accelerator to the floor. The rolling hills of the rural landscape gave way to large, commanding ridges on either side of the road, which were dotted with solitary spruce trees. Forest covered mountains in the distance were enveloped in clouds.

He smiled. She must remember the letters I sent her. I'm sure she cherishes them, he thought.

"My exceptional girl. Although I have had many other women in the past I think that you are the one for me," he had written in his first letter. *"Did you count the number of times we made love during our first night together? I did. I haven't had a night like that since I was eighteen. I want to come and do the same again with you. Don't worry that you don't have much money. I can afford the best hotels so that we can have all the privacy that we want. I'll make love to you many mores times as soon as I pass my mid-term exams. Love, Albert."*

After reading his letter, Henia was furious. She tore it into little pieces and stuffed it into the coal stove in the kitchen. What a boor he is, she thought angrily. The words "don't worry that you don't have much money," continually circled through her mind. Then she laughed at his macho literary display. He's not as rich as he thinks he is, she thought with satisfaction. The small Fiat that he drove, was the cheapest car available in the country. Very few Poles could afford one at all, but a Polonez car, not a Fiat, signalled greater wealth. Henia smiled when she remembered one cold winter morning when Albert struggled for fifteen minutes to start his car. Poor Albert, he was just trying to impress me. That was what the letter was for, she thought. It was mostly about love, she conceded.

Love. That was a feeling that she had known in Cracow but not in Nowy Targ. In Cracow, she loved and was loved.

Her boyfriend Marek had been a poet and a painter, a person who was always so cheerful and giving, and who knew how to make the best out of everything. She remembered one evening they spent in his small studio, in the old part of Cracow near St. Mary's Church. He asked her if she felt like having some wine. "Yes, but we can't," she answered. Her scholarship hadn't come in yet, and she knew that he was always short of money unless he managed to sell some of his paintings to foreign tourists.

"How much do you have?" he asked with a short laugh. She put a 10 złoty coin down on the table. Marek added 13 złoty and disappeared. He returned ten minutes later carrying a bottle of the cheapest apple cider known as Alpaga.

"Marek," she wailed. "We can't drink that. I can't stand it."

He kissed her, rushed into the kitchen and poured the contents into a pot. Then he added a little cinnamon and some other spices and heated it up.

"Did you like it?" he asked eagerly when they had both finished emptying their mugs.

"Even Alpaga is good with you," she whispered.

She spent hours in his studio posing and watching him paint. When she was at her own hostel room studying, he would slip poems underneath her door. They became engaged quickly and enjoyed two years of happiness together in Cracow – then the cancer came.

Marek seemed to disappear before her eyes. During his last few weeks in hospital, she watched him deteriorate into a meager pile of skin and bones. He struggled to remain conscious.

"Remember, Henia," he told her one day in his hospital room. "I am leaving soon, but you are still going to continue living. Pray for my soul, but please, try to be happy. Get married. I don't want you to cry for the rest of your life." The doctor asked her to leave soon after.

The next day, she walked into the hospital determined to tell him that no, she would not 'get married' and 'be happy'. He was dead. She ran out of the hospital into the bright afternoon sun and started to walk, wandering without purpose. A few minutes later she realized that she was standing in front of the stairwell leading to his studio. From the entrance hall, she could see the sign in front of the locked door: *Marek Wysocki – artist*. She turned away quickly and stepped out of the dim hall into a sun-drenched street in Cracow's old town. I'll go to the Mariacki Church, she thought. The church was right across from the market area where Marek used to sell his paintings. It was always a popular spot for tourists. There, she could hear the clicking of Japanese cameras. She remembered how the two of them had joked, pretending that they were Americans. "My goodness. Unbelievable!" Marek would mimic in English. "Such a beautiful place in a small, obscure Communist country."

For the next two years she remained quite alone. Her days were filled with studying and crying. She returned home after her graduation.

Henia hadn't forgotten Marek, but Albert's letters excited her. It was a strange feeling. Her life in the town was so monotonous that she had almost forgotten that she was a woman.

She lay one of his letters down on her bed and got up quietly. The floors in the house squeaked and she didn't want to wake the rest of the family. She pulled her nightgown up over her head and stared at the full length mirror beside her dresser. She looked down at her body and then glanced up at her breasts. They were well-shaped and soft and her nipples were prominent. She started to massage them with her left hand and sighed deeply. The door opened suddenly and she heard her mother scream from behind. "You whore, get out of this house." She slapped Henia across the face.

Henia stayed at the town motel for the next five days. Her room was small and dreary and at night she shivered under a single, thin blanket. She picked up the telephone receiver many times to phone her parents, but always put it down in shame. She hid in her hotel room and worried. Her money was running out and she didn't know what to do next. Her mother called her the next day at the factory.

"Come home, Henia, but don't ever do that again, do you understand?"

She came home but made no promises. She had felt something and she knew it wasn't a feeling she could repress. When Albert came to visit her, they would go to a motel together. She found herself succumbing to his caresses so easily but she couldn't understand why. Unlike Marek, he hardly spoke of love. Their relationship seemed to be strictly physical.

Albert's car passed through the outskirts of Nowy Targ. He smiled as he approached the red brick wall of the factory compound. Once inside the guard's booth at the entrance gate, he dialed Henia's extension.

"Hi, it's me," he said when he heard her voice. "Can you take the afternoon off?" He smiled confidently at the guard.

"No, I can't. We'll have to meet at three o'clock."

"Why? What am I supposed to do for the rest of the afternoon? Tell your boss I'll pay him twice as much as he pays you if he will let you meet me now, will you?"

"Don't be stupid, Albert," she replied angrily. "I'll see you at the gate when I finish work. Good-bye."

"Wait!" he cried, but the line had been severed. "Shit," he cursed as he hung up the phone. The tall guard in a navy blue uniform glanced at him and burst into laughter. In a fury, Albert slammed the guardhouse door and hopped into his car. His anger subsided slowly as he drove away from the factory and headed into Nowy Targ. He recalled that Henia had mentioned something about a new supervisor in her last letter. Perhaps she really couldn't leave work early, he concluded.

The town's main street was crowded with cars and numerous horse-driven carts. He bought gas at a local station and looked around for a place to eat. The modest vacation meal he had eaten for breakfast, satisfied him for only an hour or two. He decided to buy a piece of sausage at the fast food stand down the street. The cashier handed him a sausage on a paper plate and he paid fifteen złoty. He sighed, flopped down on a nearby bench and looked at his sausage. It appeared a bit brown, but otherwise all right. He happily bit off a large piece and started chewing. The sausage seemed hard and stringy. "Ugh. It's just a bunch of bones and tendons." He spit it out into a garbage can beside him and marched back to the cashier.

"What did you sell me? It's not edible. I thought I was buying a sausage, not a piece of sole."

The bald-headed man behind the cashier shrugged and peered angrily at Albert.

"Well," Albert shouted, seeing that the man's hands were not moving towards the cash register.

"You, whoever you are, you sound like you've just returned from a trip to the United States. I suggest you go back to the town limits and figure out just where you are right now. Then look at the sign at the top of this stand. It reads 'Grilled Sausage', not 'McDonald's hamburgers'."

"Are you trying to be funny?" Albert was getting angrier by the minute. "I just came from Warsaw. We have grilled sausages there and they are edible." As he glared at the cashier, he couldn't help thinking that the man reminded him of a small, gray rat.

"Good for you," the sausage seller said with a loud chuckle. "Someone has to pay the price and it's not the people in Warsaw. If they put more meat and less shit in the sausages that go to the cities than the rest has to go somewhere. That's exactly what we get here, in the country. It's as simple as that."

Albert put his hands up in exasperation and walked down the street. He shook his head. That guy doesn't know what he's talking about, he murmured to himself. He spotted a butcher store at the end of the block and smiled. He had it all worked out. He would buy a sausage at the store and if it proved to be better than the one at the stand, the owner would hear about it.

The store was full of large hunks of pink meat trimmed with orange. It was called 'ground pork' and contained a lot of fat and artificial substitutes. He had only tried it once, and hated its unpleasant scent. He looked around the deserted store. Its many rows of tiled shelves were completely empty.

"Do you have any sausages or other smoked meat articles?" he asked the middle-aged woman behind the counter.

The saleswoman attempted to smile graciously and answered, "Yes, we do. We receive a good deal of pork, smoked ham and sausages but today, unfortunately, we have only ground pork. Would you like some?"

"No, thank you. I know what it tastes like. Will you be getting the other things that you just mentioned later today?"

164

The saleswoman looked at him with some puzzlement. "We only get that sort of things twice a year," she answered. "The next supply is coming at Christmas. That's too bad. You should have come three months earlier. We had a huge supply at Easter. Some fifty hams and a half-a-ton of regular sausage." With that, she burst into laughter. Albert left the store without saying a word. As he began walking down the street in search of a florist, he felt grateful that he lived in Warsaw, and that his mother could shop at the internal Ministry store.

After stopping a passer-by and asking for directions, he turned off the main avenue and began walking down a muddy, cobblestone street lined with steeply-roofed wooden houses. The pungent scent of farm animals reached his nose and he squirmed. I hate the countryside, he thought, cursing loudly at a pile of fresh horse manure just centimetres from his feet.

Outside of the florist, he pressed his nose into the freshly cut roses and breathed deeply. Henia should be pleased with these, he thought proudly. He smiled, glad that he could afford to buy her such an expensive bouquet.

"Thank you, Albert. They're very nice," Henia said as she kissed him hello.

As they headed towards the outskirts of Nowy Targ, Henia clutched the roses in her hand and tried to ignore Albert's outright condemnation of her home town. "Where are we going?" she asked, cursing him furiously under her breath. Albert wheeled on to the main highway. "The only decent place that I've been able to find around here, is the Hotel Ambasador," he said. "Everyone who is rich eats there." In a harsh voice, Henia pointed out that she wasn't rich.

"You will be when you become my wife," Albert answered and flashed a confident smile.

Henia's face soured. "Are you rich? I thought you were only a graduate from university, just like me?" She turned her face away from him and gazed intently out the car window.

"Eleonora just got a raise," he announced with obvious pride. "She'll be getting a new talon in the fall. She's probably going to buy a Polonez."

"But that's your mother's salary and her car," Henia screamed furiously, almost grabbing the steering wheel away from him. "I thought I was marrying you, not your mother?"

Albert was surprised by her hostile reaction. "Calm down. Eleonora loves me," he answered innocently. "She likes giving me money. And you know that I am getting an apartment of my own next year." He smiled at Henia and grabbed her hand. "Just wait. I will work and we'll have children. I won't be driving a little Fiat in a few months, but a Polonez. Why don't you take it easy now and enjoy our little private happiness and luck?"

Henia sighed when she saw a large sign with 'Ambasador' on the left hand side of the road ahead.

After crossing the hotel's plush lobby, they entered a dimly illuminated dining room, its furniture and decor resembling a comfortable mountain lodge. Albert chose a table in the far corner. While he surveyed the menu, Henia gazed closely at a small vase of flowers in front of her. A candle, set in the middle of the table, flickered erratically.

"What do you want to eat?" he asked her.

165

She shrugged. "Whatever. I'm not really hungry."

Albert ordered two filet mignons, and a bottle of red wine. Taking a long sip from his glass, he sat back in his chair. "Why were you so busy today?" he asked her. "I was hoping that you could have left work a bit earlier."

"If you know you want to take a day off, you have to apply to the personnel office a week in advance. It's not possible to simply take a few hours off."

The waiter brought their order, steak with French fries and green peas. Albert ate it hungrily and poured another generous portion of wine into his glass. Then he looked up into Henia's large, gray eyes. "I thought we might stay here overnight," he said, leaning over and kissing her lightly on the lips. Henia sat stiffly in her chair and didn't move. Albert looked at her impatiently and demanded to know what was wrong.

"I am working tomorrow, Albert. They refused to grant me a leave," she said flatly.

"Are you kidding?" he shouted. "We've been planning this little holiday for a long time."

"There's nothing that I can do. I can't even put the blame on my boss. We've been working overtime for the last two weeks..."

Albert sighed and lit a cigarette. "Why are you so busy?" he asked gloomily.

"I told you about the new American assembly line that was just installed..." she answered. "Well, it doesn't work. About a half of the finished product is faulty. They're shutting it down today and there is going to be an investigation."

Albert was surprised. "I don't understand? American technology not working?" he asked her. "Someone must have approved the project."

"Yes, somebody did. The line worked well in the States, I heard, but our representatives decided not to purchase the on-line quality control apparatus. It saved them three million dollars in licensing costs. Our former director got an award from the government because of the saving." She paused and took a sip of her wine. "But," she said, shaking her head with regret, "when they installed it, they realized that without the quality control equipment, it was useless. Nobody seems to know how to adjust the machines properly."

"Nobody seems to know...?" Albert repeated, his eyes wide open with disbelief. "What about the workers who were trained in the US? They must know how to operate the equipment. I read about it in the press. Those bastards were trained for six months in Alabama. They were paid a lot too - in dollars. And now they can't even operate the machines? It's criminal. They should go to prison. No wonder nothing works."

Henia looked at Albert in surprise and burst into laughter.

"What are you doing that for? It's not funny," he told her angrily.

"I'm laughing because you are so naive, Albert."

"Me, naive?" he exclaimed, jumping out of his seat.

"Yes, you. You said you would put the workers in jail. Don't you know who spent the six months in Alabama?"

Albert shrugged. "Workers, technicians and engineers I guess," he answered reluctantly.

Henia stared at him intently. "That would sound reasonable, but you're wrong. Only one engineer was sent and he insisted that the government buy the entire system. They ended up sending him back here after just a month."

"And the rest?" Albert asked expectantly.

"Well, the first secretary of our factory Party Committee was sent there, along with the chairman of the trade union and our former director. None of them have any technical training, really. Three men from the District Party Committee also went along, while technicians and blue collar workers stayed behind."

"Unbelievable. What is going to happen to the people who were in Alabama? Are they going to be punished?"

Henia broke out into laughter. "Who is going to do anything to them? Our former director is now with the Central Committee. He will cover up the whole thing. If he didn't, he would endanger himself."

Henia looked at Albert closely from across the table. His eyes were wide open with surprise. That's good, she thought to herself.

"Well, in the Central Committee, he is safe," Albert conceded and began scratching his head in puzzlement. "I don't understand why they're conducting an investigation at your factory, though."

"I guess I used the word 'investigation' incorrectly, Albert," she said. "It's not really that. It's just a mammoth amount of paper work to write-off the losses. The management has already figured that the old production lines manufacture enough to cover our losses at the factory level. We have to enter all the particulars in the books."

"Shit," Albert yelled. "I don't believe it. It may be okay at the factory level but that doesn't account for the millions of dollars spent on the license and the equipment. It was purchased using foreign credits."

Henia was pleased with his statements. "There is a multi-million dollar loss at the central level, you're right, Albert," she conceded. "But who is going to do something about it? Gierek?"

After a minute, Albert shrugged and touched her hand. "Look Henia, let's forget about all of this. What difference does it really make? It's only a matter of a few million dollars here or there. Let's concentrate on us, Henia. Why don't we just try to enjoy our life as much as we can. That's the only thing to do. We're not going to change the system. Why don't we just try to live with it?"

"Who can live with it? Not me," Henia answered defiantly.

"Everybody," Albert countered, "including you and me. You shouldn't bother thinking about it so much. We are young, and we have our whole future ahead of us. We'll get married, you'll leave that job of yours and you'll come to Warsaw with me. Everything will be different there. There's more food and the entertainment is better. You'll be happy there, believe me."

Henia stared at him. "It will be a long time before I'd be happy with you..." she muttered under her breath.

CHAPTER 3

He pushed Julia's wheelchair along the avenue in front of their apartment. They were heading for Łazienki Park.

"Łazienki Park?" his grandmother asked anxiously. "I haven't been there for ages." She seemed happy about the plan, but the distance worried her.

Łazienki or 'The Baths', was one of the most beautiful park complexes in Europe. It once belonged to the Lubomirski family but during the 18th Century it was taken over by the Royal Court. Its palaces, orangeries and open air theater were painstakingly renovated after the war, and foreign tourists flooded to see it every year. Many varsovians enjoyed going too. The estate was a reminder of the country's past glory.

To get into the park, Konrad had to wheel the chair down a steep, ramp-like sidewalk beside a cement stairway. At first he thought he was going to manage all right. He slowly started down the walkway, but the downward angle was so extreme that the wheelchair handles slipped out of his hand. Julia let out a small scream. The chair sped down the sidewalk, and before he could catch up to it, she was lying on the ground with the wheelchair on top of her. He screamed and rushed over to pick her up gently in his arms. Concerned passers-by brought the wheelchair to them. Julia's face was pale and ashen. "My whole body is sore, Konrad. Please take me home now," she whispered. He lifted her back into the chair, as quickly as he could, and without a word he started pushing the wheelchair along. She was trembling badly by the time he got her home. Her face was a colourless shade of gray. Agata was distraught. "She doesn't look good. She looks as if she's going to..."

He rushed to the neighbour's and called an ambulance. Forty minutes later, he was at her side and they were heading towards a hospital. The trip seemed very long, and he became more and more anxious.

"Where are we going?" he asked the ambulance driver after they had passed a nearby hospital.

"We have to go to the other side of town," the man explained. "That hospital isn't designated for emergency service today."

The ambulance attendant decided to administer oxygen, to help Julia breath more easily, but the oxygen tent wouldn't function properly. The breathing lines were clogged with water.

He sat in a crowded emergency ward for two hours before a doctor approached him. "Are you looking after the paralyzed woman who fell out of the wheelchair?"

Konrad felt his heart pound as he stood up and asked the physician about his grandmother's condition.

"Well, she is bruised and shaken but fortunately her hip is not fractured. I suggest you take her home immediately. Her pulse is very weak and irregular. She needs rest." He went over to his grandmother who lay on a stretcher. She was vomiting. Konrad held her head up to keep her from choking.

It was late evening. Julia lay in bed and Konrad sat nearby and watched her closely. She was very pale and her breathing was shallow and raspy.

Agata whispered to him to come into the kitchen. He noticed that she was holding a candle. "Julia might not live through the night, Konrad. But before she dies, we should light this," she said solemnly. Konrad shook his head repeatedly. "No, she can't."

"Noo[6]... Konrad, she wants to live. She wants to live to see Eryk out of prison. Pray for her." They parted in the hallway and he headed back to his grandmother's bedroom.

Only a single, bare bulb illuminated the tunnel passage outside. He drew the drapes and sat down in the old armchair near her bed. He watched as her chest fell and lay still for many seconds before it rose again with another inhalation.

"Will God answer me?" he asked out loud. The breathing became more rapid. "Lord," he whispered. "I know that I have lived an unworthy life. I know that I have sinned and that I have breached many of your commandments." Konrad stayed on his knees, and raised his eyes to the picture of Jesus on the wall.

"Lord Jesus," he continued. "Please punish me. I deserve it. Please save my grandmother. She is good and so helpless. Please." He started to murmur, "Our Father who art in heaven..." His eyes moved along the wall to the painting of the Madonna of Ostra Brama that Julia loved so much. "Hail Mary, full of grace. The Lord is with thee..." Hours passed and he remained on his knees.

"Lord. Let her survive and be well. I will confess all of my past sins. I will go and take the Holy Communion this week and never will I be so far from you and the Church as I used to be. God, I know my prayer might be strange; I realize that I am trying to bargain with you like the prophets of the Old Testament did. Forgive me, Lord. Oh Mary, who art our Mother, please hear my prayer. You know, Mary, how imperfect I am, but you also know, Mother, that I love Granny Julia. You know she is everything to me. Please, have mercy. Lord have mercy on us."

Right after her stroke when the crucial forty eight hours began, he had promised God that he would repent for his sinful life, confess, and live differently if only her life was spared. Julia did survive but he didn't live up to the pledges he had made. He felt strangely alone now, as he asked God for another miracle. He knelt on the rug beside her bed and continued praying.

---

6. Noo (actually: nu, but spelled phonetically throughout the book): an equivalent of English "well...". The word is of Russian origin and was used by old Polish people who had once lived under the Russian rule.

Although the curtains were drawn, he could sense that dawn was approaching. As the weak light started to stream into the room, he began to feel calmer. Hope was filling his heart and it felt joyful and warm. "Mother of God, pray for us sinners," he whispered again. The feeling penetrating his heart and brain grew stronger. He was happy, for he knew instinctively that his prayer had been heard. He was positive about it.

He remained on his knees for a few minutes more. Then he rushed to his grandmother's bedside and looked down on her. Julia's breathing was deep and regular. Her forehead felt cool and she was sleeping soundly. He knelt again, and repeated "Hail Mary" over and over again. "Thank you, Lord Jesus and Holy Mother of God. You heard my supplication. Thank you for your blessing."

He sat quietly and gazed at her sleeping frame. "Thank you, God," he whispered, crossing himself. Dawn arrived outside.

"You almost killed your old, disabled grandmother, Konrad," she said when she awoke and found him beside her. "It's all right. The walk was very pleasant. Just a bit too long," she said smiling.

Agata was ecstatic about Julia's condition. "I can't understand it," she told him in the kitchen later that morning. "Yesterday, I was sure that she was dying and today? Just look at her."

The family doctor and sister Maria visited the next day and were surprised at how fast she had recovered from her accident. Her hip was bruised but the doctor was confident that it would heal quickly.

"Agata, did you pray last night?" Konrad asked her.

"We both did," she answered quietly.

The fever came on a week after the accident. Agata waited for him in the hallway when he returned home from work. "Noo... Granny sick," she told him in her characteristic, Wilnian way. She was very depressed, and her stooped silhouette seemed smaller than usual as she walked with him back towards her sister's bedroom.

Julia's temperature was high, and he decided to contact the local polyclinic. Doctor Kamińska, who had been looking after the family for years, sighed when he told her that his grandmother was ill once more. She agreed to come over to the apartment as soon as possible.

"This fever is related to her kidneys," she concluded after a brief examination. Blood test results confirmed her suspicions. They revealed that there was an alarming amount of urea in Julia's blood and that her red blood cell count was very low. Another hospital stay was inevitable and his grandmother reluctantly resigned herself to the fact.

Konrad decided to visit the hospital ward before she was admitted and talk to the physician who would be looking after her.

Dr. Milewska was an attractive brunette in her mid-thirties. He handed her a piece of paper their family doctor had given him, and introduced himself. The woman asked him to sit down and began reading the form. "I was wondering, doctor," he interjected sheepishly, "whether there is some way my grandmother could receive intensive treatment so that we could bring her home more quickly."

Dr. Milewska turned away from the medical form and looked at him with amazement. "We don't try to keep people here who don't require hospitalization, Mr. Dymowski. You are lucky that we have some spare beds now and that your grandmother is going to be admitted at all. Usually people are overflowing into the corridors. Besides," she added. "how can I say anything without even seeing your grandmother?"

He apologized. "She has spent so much time in hospitals during the past three years that she's very apprehensive about going back." He was thinking about the first neurological ward that Julia had stayed in. The doctor smiled. "Well, I might have a bit of good news for you and your grandmother. We recently opened a special geriatric ward. It's modern and has received a fair amount of attention and publicity. Our standards are much higher. The meals are better and most importantly, there are more nurses."

Konrad looked at her with delight. "That is marvellous," he said. "But I can't believe that they are allotting money for seniors."

"It is not a gift from the government, believe me," Dr. Milewska said firmly. "Our medical society has been fighting for this forty five bed ward for more than ten years. We have sent a number of petitions to the Ministry of Health and to Sejm[7]."

Julia received careful attention and her fever disappeared the day after her arrival. Glucose was given to her intravenously and it helped to decrease the level of urea in her blood.

The sunlight streaming into the hospital room danced as it hit the large spot of shiny linoleum floor between Julia's bed and the one adjacent to it, which was occupied by a shy, overweight woman. On each of their night tables, there were white plastic mugs with spouts, and paper cups. Urine collecting bags dangled from the bed frames. Konrad sat by his grandmother's bedside on a small aluminum stool.

"You can take *'Night Work'* with you, Konrad," his grandmother told him. "I just finished it."

He took the book from her. "What do you think of Irwin Shaw's writing, Babcia?" he asked.

"Oh, I liked the story, it was amusing. I only wish we too could make a quick fortune like the hero in that tale did."

He put the paperback in his bag. "Agata wants to know if you would like her to bring you some soup?"

"No, it's all right. I'm really surprised about the food here. We have ham for breakfast at least four times a week and dinners are good too. No, let Agata have a rest from cooking. She deserves it."

Konrad looked over to the patient in the neighbouring bed, and noticed that she was trying, without success to reach for her mug. She smiled broadly and thanked him as he handed it to her.

"O.K.," he said, sitting down again beside Julia. "Is there anything else you would like?"

"Actually," she said sheepishly. "There is, but I don't know how to ask

---

7. Sejm[read: saym] - Polish Parliament, the equivalent of the House of Commons.

you... You are so busy." Her face became flushed. He laughed. "Go ahead, Babcia."

"Noo, you know that Eryk is coming back in a month, don't you?"

Konrad nodded. "Yes, of course I know. Unfortunately, I'm not looking forward to seeing him again and you are."

"Konrad. Please don't be so hard on him. He is my son and your father. He will behave, I'm sure." Her eyes expressed an immense feeling of sadness and pain. He decided against any further comments, and instead, asked her what she wanted him to do.

"I know he will be coming back to the apartment when he gets out," she said in a steady voice. "He will probably stay in the small room off the kitchen."

The room off the kitchen had not been touched since the death of Julia's mother Luba, and she asked him if he would be willing to paint it. Somehow, she believed that a newly painted room would help Eryk start a new life, that it would help him change. "Would you do that for me?"

Konrad hesitated for only a few seconds. "The answer is - yes, Babcia - provided I can buy paint someplace. I've heard that there is a real shortage."

"I knew you wouldn't let me down," she said, grasping his hand.

"It's all right," he said, kissing her on the cheek. They sat quietly in the room together.

As he walked down the hospital corridor, Konrad thought back to the first time Eryk returned home from prison. He was very young but he could remember the countless fights and arguments between his parents. Eryk was unhappy and disenchanted with life, while Tina always seemed to be restless and she drank heavily. One day, she even tried to jump out of the window of their third floor apartment following a quarrel. His father managed to hold her by the waist and pull her back into the room.

The next day, Eryk took him out for a drive. They went to a small restaurant out of town, the Berentowicz restaurant, he thought. There, Konrad had his favourite green pea and potato salad. Eryk watched him eat, smiled warmly and took his hand. "I know that what I am about to say is going to be hard to understand, Konrad," he said quietly. "You love Tina and I do too, but I've decided I have to leave her. It doesn't matter whether I love her or not. She doesn't want me anymore."

"But you are her husband and she is your wife and I'm your child," Konrad cried.

Eryk stared at him silently for a few minutes. "You are my only son," he said in a low voice. "She is your mother and you have to love her just as I do. You are probably too young to understand what I mean when I say 'divorced', but your mother and I aren't together any longer. She has a legal right to stay with someone else. No, don't cry..." Eryk turned his gaze away from him. "Unless I move out, unless I leave her alone, she may one day succeed in killing herself. Then you wouldn't have a mother at all."

Empty aluminum shelves lined the walls of the neighbourhood paint store.

"We don't have white, or any other colour, sir," the paint salesman said, shaking his head at Konrad. Sitting down in a rickety, old stool behind the

172

empty counter, the elderly man sighed. "I'm told that the stuff has all gone to Moscow," he said, with a scowl. "Our brothers have painted their city for the Olympics, but why the hell did they have to use up all Polish paint? All that, to impress a few stupid tourists who will choose to ignore Carter's Olympic Boycott..."

The two men discussed politics for another ten minutes, and then Konrad started to bid the paint man good-bye. The talkative gentleman stopped him and scurried into the back of the store. He returned seconds later, lugging a single can of paint. Seeing Konrad's surprise, he smiled gleefully. "This really is my last one," he said. "You may have it... although the colour is a bit strange."

"The room is painted, madam, as per your instructions," Konrad told his grandmother two days later. He made a courteous bow before her bed. "Is there anything else your grace wants?"

"No, Konrad. How does it look?"

"It is painted in canary yellow. That was the only colour I could get, but it looks O.K. You'll see for yourself soon."

"Yellow," she murmured. "Yes, I think it will look nice."

Konrad knew he had gained weight. The sports jacket that he was wearing felt tight around his shoulders. As he stood there on the crowded bus, heading downtown, people pushed and pulled against him, and he felt the fabric of the jacket tighten even more.

Outside, at Victory Square, he carefully scrutinized his appearance in a darkened café window.

Across the square, rows of cars lined the brightly illuminated driveway and entrance of the Victoria Intercontinental Hotel. As he walked past a maze of Polonezes and Mercedez–Benzes, he puzzled over the strange dinner invitation he had received from Julek and Jolanta for that evening. Porters dressed in quiet, beige uniforms with gold buttons, carried dozens of large suitcases by hand, and pulled others on small carts across the lobby's marble floor. A well-stocked Pewex dollar store to the right was crowded with tourists.

He began cursing himself for putting on his tight suit jacket when he saw Julek, who was wearing only a pair of jeans and a wool sweater. Jolanta, and Julek's sister were also dressed casually. Only five-year old Marek looked smart, dressed in an elegant gray suede suit.

There were three restaurants in the hotel. They started walking towards the one with a large sign 'Boryna' across the front. Jolanta firmly held Marek's hand as they crossed the lobby.

A well-dressed man, not more than eighteen, casually stood in front of the restaurant entrance, blocking their way. "Dollars, francs, marks – good price," he said in English confidently, at the same time flashing a captivating smile.

Julek stopped to think for a moment. "I may need some more Polish money for the dinner," he whispered to Jolanta.

"What sort of exchange are you offering?" he asked the man in English.

"Ninety for a buck." Julek countered with 110.

The stranger's red striped tie coordinated nicely with his expensive, dark blue wool suit. He cocked his head, smiled and quietly began adjusting the tie.

"One hundred is my last offer," Julek said with an equally pleasant smile and handed the man two ten dollar bills. They disappeared instantly into the nicely tailored pocket, and the man slowly handed Julek 2,000 złoty. Almost with automatic precision, another smile appeared on his face.

Jolanta gave her husband a stern look as they walked into the restaurant. "What are you doing, selling dollars to a cinkciarz[8] in a hotel?" she asked hastily in Polish. "What if a policeman or SB-ek was watching?"

"Don't worry, madam," the younger man said in equally perfect Polish. "I know the SB agent on duty tonight. This country's economy would collapse without us," he added, looking with pleasure at the amazement on her face.

They were seated around a heavy, dark wooden table. Only a reddish-orange light from the lamp above them illuminated their section of the restaurant. Konrad faced Jolanta, with Marek between her and her brother's wife, Hala, who was six months pregnant. Hala's husband had just been drafted.

He gazed at Julek's wife. She had generous lips and well-defined, dark eyebrows. The long, blond hair gently caressed her shoulders. Although it was barely noticeable, she seemed more quiet than usual.

A well mannered waiter arrived at their table. "Welcome to the Boryna Restaurant," he said. "What can I do for you?"

"We'll decide on our food in a moment," Julek answered. "I think my friend and I will have a beer."

Jolanta ordered a gin and tonic for herself, while Hala quietly asked for a glass of white wine.

"Is there anything else that Boryna can offer you before the meal? Perhaps a fruit salad for your son?"

Marek eagerly tugged at his mother's shirt. "What is Boryna, Mama," he asked.

Jolanta sighed. "We should have left you at home with your younger brother. You promised you would keep quiet, remember?" Marek sat back in his seat and began to pout.

"O.K., but this is the very last one," his mother said, looking at the other guests around the table. "Agreed?"

"Yes, yes, Mama, agree..." Marek yelled, jumping up and down in his seat.

"Well, Boryna is important," Jolanta began. "There was a Polish writer by the name of Władysław Reymont who wrote a novel called 'The Peasants'. One of the main characters was called Boryna. In 1924, Reymont was awarded the Nobel Prize and I guess that's why they named the restaurant after one of the people in the book. I suppose, the idea was to advertise our natural culture to visitors. If you look around, you can see that everything is furnished in a rustic style. Everything is in wood. It's like we're sitting right inside an old inn in the middle of the country... And now, my son," she said, passing the fruit salad to Marek. "My son won't be asking anything more for the next two hours, right?" Marek could only nod. His mouth was stuffed with fruit.

They sipped their drinks and chatted. Konrad polished off the first half of his beer and looked around the room, as Julek and Hala talked. The table just

---

8. Cinkciarz [Polish slang] - someone who illegally exchanges foreign currency for profit.

beside them was occupied by a group of smartly dressed men and women. They were laughing and giggling loudly and from small bits of their conversation, he concluded that they must be greenhouse owners.

Another large group pored over their plates of food and drinks. It looked as if an American relative was treating his family to a night out. "Na zdrowie, Wituś," they cried, and sang, 'Sto Lat'.

The second half of the huge restaurant was virtually empty, except for a single table in the far corner which was occupied by a middle-aged Arab and young woman, who wore an expensive, and very low cut, silk dress.

"Well," Konrad remarked, turning his attention back to the table. "We seem to be joined by an aristocratic clientele tonight. Tomato magnates, a boozing compatriot from Chicago, an Arab and a hooker..." Julek and the others laughed. A woman from the adjacent table glared at him.

Julek urged them to choose whatever entrée they wanted. Konrad looked at the exorbitant prices and jokingly threatened to order filet mignon. "You'll spend more here tonight than you'll earn next New Year when we sell the rest of your balloons," he added.

"Don't worry about that," Julek remarked. "I don't think we'll be doing that again."

Konrad looked down hungrily at his plate of thick, medium-rare steak, fried potatoes and mushrooms, and tried to remember the last time he had eaten anything like it. It was after the Party Deed while I was in the 17th Regiment, he thought. Klara made it for me.

"What about dessert?" Julek asked.

"I scream, you scream, we all scream for ice cream," Konrad chanted in English. He explained to Julek that he had heard the saying in Montréal and the two reminisced about the city. Konrad soon realized that his friend's annual vacation in Canada was approaching, and that Jolanta and the children would be going as well. The thought depressed him.

Julek stood up. "Hala and Konrad," he said, taking a brief bow. "I would like to thank you for accepting my invitation to dinner tonight. Jolanta and I appreciate it. " His face was filled with a jubilant smile as he talked. In contrast, his wife looked down at the table, as if she was trying to ignore his words. "In a week's time, we will be in Montréal."

"When are you coming back?" Konrad asked.

Jolanta sighed and answered quietly, "We aren't coming back this time."

Her words caused surprise and then confusion. Konrad quickly asked Julek about his upcoming graduation from medical school. His friend still needed one more year to finish.

"Julek has arranged for a transfer to the University of Montréal," Jolanta explained, trying to remain calm. Then her voice started to break, "...and I am going with him."

Everyone at the table was quiet, even Marek, who had dozed off, resting his head on his aunt's stomach.

Julek managed a smile and started to explain the reasons behind his decision. "Actually," he said, "I was offered a transfer a year ago, but I just couldn't take it. They repeated the offer this year, but at first I had the same problem, not enough money. Then, just two days ago, I received a letter from

Toronto. My uncle Wojciech has just retired and sold his business. He sent me a $5,000 gift plus the promise of more interest free loans if I decided to move to Montréal. I telexed the university that night." He was the only person at the table who was smiling.

"You seem quite happy about leaving, " Konrad said with a bitter scowl. "But, why shouldn't you. We've always been so close that I just forgot that you aren't really one of us…"

Julek's face quickly hardened, and he began shouting, "I have lived in Poland for a number of years, I have queued up at the same damned meat stores, worked hard in Canada every summer, tried to make ends meet, and put up with the bullshit they give us on the TV Daily. Now you're telling me that I'm not a Pole." Then he lowered his voice. "I am a Pole – a Polish Canadian. Is there anything wrong with looking forward to seeing my parents and being there?"

"Wrong? No, not at all. I'm just losing good friends, that's all."

"Stop it, please," Jolanta cried. "Has anyone thought about my feelings?" she said caustically. "You stay among your people Konrad, Julek goes back home, and me?"

For a moment, Marek was the only one making any noise at all. His breathing was deep and regular as he continued to sleep.

"It won't be that bad," Julek said, kissing his wife's cheek. "You'll make friends in Montréal."

As the airport van, sped past a row of tall birch trees, the brown, modern-looking Warsaw Okęcie International Airport loomed ahead. Konrad helped Julek get his family's luggage into the crowded departure hall of the terminal. Without saying a word, he put the bags on the scale at the ticket counter. Jolanta and the boys started to check in.

"Good-bye uncle Konrad, " Marek yelled. "Don't forget to come and visit us in Montréal."

An hour later, he was still standing on the airport observation deck. Their plane slowly wheeled toward the runway, with red signal lights on its tail and wings flashing. It turned around and paused momentarily as it awaited the go ahead from the control tower.

Konrad watched the aircraft accelerate and finally take off. It circled over the airfield and he had to shield his eyes from the glare as the plane crossed the path of the sun.

Konrad sat in Julia's bedroom, watching TV. The room had never looked more dreary to him. Not only was she not there, but for the duration of her hospital stay, the bed had been stripped of its sheets so that it could air out. Three tired brown chairs and Robert's canvas seat from the army, were arranged around the bedroom television set which stood upon a small round table in one corner of the room. Agata peeked her head inside the doorway. She waved a white envelope in her hand and told him that she had just found it in the mailbox. "It's for you," she said, looked at him expectantly. He laughed at her insatiable curiosity. "All right," he said, taking the letter from her. "Let's see what this is…"

He tore the edge of the fine envelope carefully. Inside, there was a thick, white card, lettered in gold. It was an invitation to a wedding.

"Roman? Getting married?" Agata asked with surprise. Roman had often visited the apartment while he and Konrad were going to school together and she knew him well. "But he is still so young," she murmured.

"Not any more, " Konrad answered dryly. "The two bachelors will be one by the end of next week." The news did little to improve his mood.

Roman's and Krystyna's close friends and relatives were invited to the reception at Mr. and Mrs. Cybulski's flat following the wedding ceremony. Their balcony was overflowing with the bouquets of flowers which the young couple had received at the church. Tables had been carefully arranged in the family's brightly-painted livingroom. Bottles of wine and vodka, plates and cutlery, as well as an impressive selection of food had been set on the white linen covered table in the middle of the room.

"What is your name?" the young, dark-haired girl beside Konrad asked him. "Are you one of Roman's cousins?" He shook his head and explained that he was Roman's best friend.

She smiled pleasantly and told him that she was Krystyna's sister Basia. "It is funny that I have never met you before," she remarked.

"We haven't seen much of each other since we left the army," he explained. "We now live in different parts of the city and I only bump into him occasionally."

Konrad was concentrating more closely on the woman's appearance, than on her words. There was no doubt that Basia was the prettiest girl at the party. Her sea-green coloured eyes were intelligent, yet playful looking.

"They are leaving Warsaw," she said, casually lighting a cigarette. "Roman has decided to take a job in Kępno. They're starting a new electrical plant there and they need engineers. They'll get an apartment right away..." At first Basia just laughed at his surprise, though her smile disappeared once she realized that the news wasn't as funny to him, as it was to her.

"Who would leave the capital for that place," he murmured.

"It is called Kępno," she repeated and then leant over and whispered in his ear, "I must admit, I would never leave Warsaw; certainly not for a little town like that. But don't say anything. My sister isn't too fond of the idea either," she explained. "Roman decided on his own. I think he likes small towns. His last girlfriend lived in a village."

She's an intelligent girl, Konrad thought to himself. It was true, Roman's last love had been serious, but after he left the army, the relationship collapsed. Probably the result of the small number of passes we were issued at the 17th Regiment, Konrad thought.

He had only met Roman's wife once before the wedding, Krystyna came with Roman to his nameday[9]. He looked up at the couple sitting across the table from him. The blond-headed Krystyna didn't share her sister's natural

---

9. Nameday - in the Polish calendar, each day is assigned a name, and is celebrated much like a birthday, although it is more important. St. Valentine's or St. George's day proves that the above tradition used to exist in the West too.

beauty. Her eyes were also green, but they were smaller, and her chin was overly round. Yet, she had a jolly smile that seemed to envelope her whole face, and a good sense of humour.

Konrad filled his glass with vodka and swallowed it quickly, in one gulp. He refilled his glass immediately. Among the crowd of cheerful guests, he felt lonely, the same feeling that he had experienced when he stood in the airport terminal and bade Jolanta and Julek good-bye just one week before. He sensed a feeling of emptiness inside. His love affairs and joyful days seemed far in the past, and he began doubting whether he would ever have a wedding party of his own. He decided to get drunk, and gulped down another full glass of vodka.

Basia touched his arm, and he realized that it was time for him to get up and say a word to his friends. He rose from his chair and looked down at the smiling faces around the table.

"I would like to offer my best wishes to Krystyna and Roman on their great day," he said after taking a deep breath. "I am convinced that he will be a wonderful husband and father." A few of the young people listening began laughing, and he realized that his words sounded like empty slogans. "Ladies and gentlemen," he continued, "you may think that I'm a bit of a buffoon standing up here and heaping unnecessary praise on my friend, but I am not."

He coughed and took a deep sip of the drink in front of him. "I have known Roman's parents for years. I think Mrs. and Mr. Cybulski are the happiest married couple that I have ever encountered. They are also wonderful parents and Roman has been brought up in an atmosphere of warmth, love and marital loyalty." His voice began to shake. "Over the years, I have always looked forward to visiting the Cybulski family... I have never felt as comfortable in my own home as I do in theirs." His own childhood, the time spent in the communal apartment flashed before his eyes. He could hear Tina screaming that she would jump out of the window if Eryk stayed with her.

"I know that love and trust will continue in Roman and with Krystyna too," he continued, "and will form the basis for what I hope will be the second luckiest married couple I know." He thanked everyone and sat down. Mrs. Cybulska began drying her eyes with a handkerchief.

"That was beautiful," Basia murmured to him. "I wish someone would say something like that at my wedding party..."

After another hour of chatting around the table, Roman got up and walked over to Konrad. "What about a private talk over a bottle of well frozen Żytnia?" he asked. "The rest will probably dance up a storm without our help."

He, Roman and Krystyna sat down at the small table in the corner of the kitchen and Roman took a bottle of chilled vodka out of the refrigerator. Krystyna took one sip and let out a big yawn. She confessed that she wanted to take her overly tight, silk dress off and lie down for an hour. She kissed her husband on the cheek and promised to return awhile later. An evening breeze drifted through the kitchen window, gently lifting the fabric of the flowered curtains.

"So Konrad," Roman began, "what is going on in your life these days?"

What is my life like? Konrad murmured to himself. He didn't have a woman to share his life with any longer. He spent most of his time with two old ladies. Though he loved them very much, it was almost as if they were slowly eking out their last days, waiting for the end to come. Julia's health was declining, and Agata found the daily hardships and the queues difficult. In a month his father would be getting out of prison and returning to the apartment...

Roman looked at him with sympathy and understanding. "I realize that you have a lot of problems, many that I have never had to face," he said quietly. "But... your love life. You always get involved in relationships which have no future. Why don't you think of finding yourself a young woman, someone like Basia, for example?"

Konrad smirked at him. "Are you trying to arrange another marriage in the family?" he asked.

After a few more glasses of vodka, he became more reflective. "I appreciate your concern, Roman, but you know me. I did love Klara and I did love Hanna... but I have never loved a woman younger than I. Perhaps this has always been a form of convenience for me. I haven't had to assume responsibility for anybody else. Besides," he continued, glancing at his silent friend, "I don't think I will ever love another woman the way I loved Hanna. That was the apex of my emotional capabilities. I wouldn't have much to offer anyone now..." Without adding anything more, he lit a cigarette and sat in his chair, grimly trying to force a smile.

"But what are you going to do with the rest of your life?"

Konrad shook his head. "I am needed now," he said. "Babcia requires a lot of care. But if one day she... dies... I won't be important to anyone else – at least not the way I am to her."

He heard the sound of liquid trickling out of the bottle and looked down at the clear vodka in his small glass. The orange kitchen light overhead gave it a warm, golden hue, as it reflected off the surface of the liquid. Roman's face was as solemn as his. "But when she dies," he said quietly, "What are you going to do? Do you have any plans?"

He didn't respond at first. He didn't even know if he had an answer to Roman's question. Lately, he had had a tendency to just take each day as it came. He knew though, that he was fed up with the propaganda and the Party control, and it sickened him to think that he would have to live with the system for the rest of his life. The leadership of Edward Gierek meant the rule of thieves, demagogues and sycophants to him. People like Ryszard Kwapień or captain Zabłocki of the 17th Regiment.

"Do you remember sitting in the Company Zero's TV hall, watching the news every night?" he asked Roman. "Do you remember the broadcast about Huta Katowice?"

"Yes, and the TV Daily is even worse now," Roman added with a long sigh. "It's just a pile of propaganda."

"I have had enough," Konrad said abruptly in disgust.

Roman motioned him to pick up his glass. "Everyone has had enough, not only you," he said. "but 'a Pole can' surely drink still. What else can we do?" There was a tremendous sense of resignation in his voice. Konrad glanced at Roman's face. As he looked at his friend's serious expression, he tried to picture the Roman that he remembered in the army. He couldn't. They swallowed their vodka in one gulp. Roman smiled.

"So what are you going to do? Leave for the States?"

Roman has already pointed out the inevitable conclusion of this exercise, Konrad thought. A conclusion that he had been reluctant to face up to by himself. "For the States, for Canada; maybe Australia, I don't quite know yet. But the farther the better. I want to get away from the lies, the corruption…"

"But Poland is more than that," Roman told him. "Poland is more than the Reds and the land… it is our history, our faith. It is us."

The two men sat in silence for a few minutes, each thinking of the days, even the years to come. Konrad noticed Roman smiling to himself and looked at him with curiosity. "What is so funny?" he asked.

"Do you remember," Roman said, "what we used to talk about in high school, on our way home through the park?"

"It's hard to forget about something you talked about almost every day," Konrad answered. He looked at his friend again. The last few years had caused him to age considerably. But, as they reminisced, the wrinkles around his eyes and the touch of gray hair at his temples seemed to disappear.

"We were fanatics," Roman said. "Followers of Hoene-Wroński and Andrzej Towiański, and their 19th century philosophy, and we really believed in the ideas they professed: the merging of intelligence, the mind and the will, into the Absolute. We always hoped that the theory about universal wisdom would materialize. But now…" He paused and looked at Konrad sternly. "I am not so naive. How can we, here in 'Second Poland'!" he screeched, "believe that it will still happen? Will Poland's messianic destiny bring about the 'worldly wisdom' that they predicted, like Christ's Passion brought salvation to humanity? No, Konrad, I find it hard to believe…" He coughed and filled their glasses. They were emptied quickly. As Konrad listened to Roman's discourse, he looked down at his empty glass in wonderment. Instead of blurring his concentration, the vodka seemed to be setting Roman's words in front of him, much like a producer's script.

"… But you are still hoping to attain even a minute portion of that vision, aren't you, Konrad? Fulfilling the dream we had during our days in high school. Am I right?"

Konrad nodded. "Time hasn't lessened my determination," he said, "even though life is so prosaic and senseless with its meat queues and everyday lies, even though I have done so many stupid things. I have to try…"

"You still want to perform a 'deed' don't you?" Roman asked him. "A task that will be yours only, independent of circumstances and constraints, authorities and cliché…"

Konrad nodded repeatedly. "And what about you?" he asked. "Have you come to terms with yourself, with your deed?"

Without answering, Roman got up and opened the kitchen window. Fresh air immediately rushed into the room. He smiled at Konrad, but it wasn't an expression of happiness or contentment. "You know, Konrad," he began, "that I have always been carefree and at times flamboyant. Well," he said with a shrug, "I asked myself a question: why pretend any longer? Why sneer? Then I met Krystyna. She was straightforward and honest. I decided to marry her. You must remember Konrad that Hoene-Wroński taught us that everything is subject to the mind and wisdom. We use our mind and wisdom to act. I suppose my 'deed' is my marriage. I have willed it," he said, his jaw set with determination.

He sat down at the table and drained the rest of the bottle of Żytnia into their glasses. It was enough to fill them to the halfway point and, again, they drank.

"Yes, I am a married man, yet, I know that wouldn't be a solution or 'deed' for you, Konrad," he continued, "so what are you thinking of? What beyond the situation here, may force you to leave?"

Konrad contemplated the question for a few minutes, seeing that Roman's assertions were, as always, right on the mark - linking his plans to leave with the desires that they had always talked about.

"I'm thinking about writing a book," he said. "In English. A book which would convey everything - the country, the people I have loved and still love... whatever I feel inside. I would like to publish the book in North America some day..."

"A book about us?" Roman repeated. "But do you think that Americans or Canadians would care about Poland and about what we love? They have their own problems: recession, unemployment... If it doesn't attract any attention you might as well just write it here and put it in your drawer. To North Americans, Poland is just an obscure spot on the map."

Konrad persisted. He sensed that Roman was missing the true essence of the task he had envisaged. "If I don't try, I will never know whether or not the book will succeed, Roman. I want to write this book. You say that Canadians and Americans don't care, but they have hearts and minds just like you and I. Why wouldn't they understand?"

The day before Julia was to be discharged from hospital, Konrad paid his grandmother one last visit. Although her blood count was still below normal, she appeared less pale and certainly much more energetic. He handed a bunch of flowers to the head nurse as well as a box of tarts and pączki[10] and a package of coffee beans. "This is for your night duty," he said. The nurse thanked him profusely for the rest of the staff. "You really shouldn't have," she said with a smile and walked off with her gifts.

Dr. Milewska had arranged to meet him in her office.

He thought she was a striking woman. The white lab coat that she wore contrasted with her dark hair which was pinned in an elegant twist above her tall forehead. He also admired her large, brown eyes, with their warm look of compassion.

"Why are you looking at me like that?" she asked.

Trying not to blush, he held a huge bunch of red carnations and a small parcel out in front of her. "Thank you so much, doctor, " he said, and kissed her hand. "My grandmother came to the hospital in very bad shape and now she is much better. You did a wonderful job. She's going home after only two weeks."

"Oh, thank you," she replied and gently placed the flowers down on her desk. "Your grandmother is a nice, pleasant person and an ideal patient." She opened the small package and held up a bottle of Nina Ricci cologne. "No, I can't accept this," she said.

---

10. Pączki [read: pontshki] - Polish donuts (without a hole).

"It's not from me," he answered. "It was your patient who told me to buy it for you. Please, this is just a little expression of her gratitude. We owe you so much…"

Dr. Milewska smiled and opened the bottle. "L'Air de Temps," she marvelled. "I wonder how she knew that this was my favourite. Thank you. Tell your grandmother that I will enjoy this."

She asked him to sit down on the extra chair in front of her desk. "Now," she said, taking a deep breath, "why don't we talk about our patient's condition." She handed him a patient information card.

Konrad puzzled briefly over the medical terms, most of them were in Latin.

"I'll summarize it for you," she interjected. "The level of urea had dropped significantly and is now satisfactory. The iron shots have also helped her blood count quite a bit. Further recommendations: a low protein diet, more injections at home, and I have prescribed some drugs that she can take orally as well."

"Can I take her out for a walk occasionally?"

"Yes, as long as you don't go too far, and stay away from underpasses," she commented, laughing briefly. Konrad nodded. The doctor gazed at him quietly for several seconds and sighed. He wondered if there was anything more that she wanted to discuss with him.

"There is more," she blurted out finally. "I wish I could stop right here, say good-bye and let you go off happily, but unfortunately I cannot. Just this morning I conducted an abdominal examination on your grandmother. It revealed a hard, round formation in her upper abdomen." The word 'cancer' flashed in Konrad's mind immediately.

As if she predicted his question, the doctor shook her head. "I don't know," she explained. "The examination I made was only preliminary. To be sure, we would have to take a tissue sample and I don't think that she is up to that. If it is cancer, we can treat it with chemotherapy. That sometimes stops the growth of the tumour for a while, but it is very hard on the patient. It can have devastating effects on people who are much younger and stronger than your grandmother."

"Does that mean that you're not going to do anything?" he asked desperately. He sensed that the doctor already knew that Julia was going to die.

"Mr. Dymowski. A doctor cannot refrain from using a cure that he or she feels is appropriate for a particular patient. I am no exception." She spoke in a calm, matter-of-fact, voice. "I have prescribed some mild testosterone injections. They may postpone the development of the tumour. But, I don't think that we can subject your grandmother to a biopsy and chemotherapy."

"How long…?"

"I don't think that it's a question of weeks. With the shots I have prescribed, maybe five, six months." She looked at him with sympathy. "I know you love your grandmother very much and that you would do anything for her. She is in good condition and as far as we know, she will stay that way, at least for a little while. Take her for walks in the park. Let her see the trees, the birds, the people in the street. She deserves to be happy."

"Is there nothing else that we could do?" he asked quietly.

"Yes. Pray. Don't think that I'm trying to shirk from my responsibilities. Sometimes physicians like myself are helpless. God knows no limits. Pray to Him and thank Him for the blessing of her life so far and in the future. Don't blame anyone, least of all yourself. Just continue on, helping her, making her happy. She loves you very much. I know that you will be at her side when the candlelight fades and she joins Him forever."

CHAPTER 4

His grandmother's illness had made Konrad oblivious to a number of unusual developments that were going on around him. One day, when he and the rest of his colleagues were eating lunch in the office room, Waldek Marciniuk motioned to him to come over. "I want to show you something," he said.

Ever since Konrad's amusing confrontation with their boss, engineer Smrodziński, Waldek had taken a liking to him. "I'll never forget his face when you told him that you had passed the government English exam," he would often remark. "That is something that Smrodziński would love to do himself but there is no way. His English is terrible!"

Konrad took a bite of his sandwich and went over to Waldek's desk. It was covered entirely by a large newspaper, 'Polityka'.

"Look," Waldek said and pointed toward editorial signed by Mieczysław Rakowski,

"What about it?" Konrad asked. Rakowski, Polityka's Editor in Chief, had been a supporter of Bierut during the Stalinist era, then Gomułka and finally of Edward Gierek[11]. Konrad seldom read his weekly.

"I suggest you read this article," Waldek said. "It makes me think that the winds might be changing…"

"What changes are you referring to, Mr. Marciniuk?" their boss asked from the doorway.

Waldek turned around and looked at him with distaste. Not many people in the office liked Smrodziński, but Waldek was the only one who didn't bother to conceal his feelings. Konrad sighed and looked at his supervisor's jowly face. He had a peculiarly disturbing habit of showing up unexpectedly and taking part in conversations uninvited.

"I'm talking about changing winds, Mr. Smrodziński," Waldek explained sarcastically. "You know – hot masses of air rise and cold ones drop. This creates a horizontal thrust which we call 'wind'. These winds tend to change direction from time to time."

"You are speaking in riddles," Smrodziński declared, and left the room in a huff. When the office door closed behind him, Konrad picked up the

---

11. Bolesław Bierut, Władysław Gomułka and Edward Gierek - successive Party bosses in Poland; from the 'Fifties to the 'Seventies respectively.

newspaper and read the editorial through quickly. After just a few lines, he understood Waldek's comment. There was little mention of the country's ambitious industrialization strategy or Gierek's successful building of the Second Poland. Instead, Rakowski suggested that the government try to curb overspending, halt further economic expansion and just try to keep what the country had acquired through the decade. Without actually coming right out and saying it, Rakowski suggested that the country's external debt was high. The general public should know the full amount, he wrote.

"Well, what do you think, Konrad?" Waldek asked.

"I don't know really. His remarks do sound reasonable."

"A bit too reasonable for this man, wouldn't you say? Something really must be happening..."

Konrad still wasn't convinced. The way he saw it, the article was just a small, albeit surprising aberration. The next day, he saw a preview of an upcoming series to be shown on the 'TV Daily'. It was entitled 'The Anatomy of Success'. The series, which was expected to air in December, was a tribute to the tenth anniversary of Edward Gierek in the position of First Secretary of the Polish United Workers' Party. 'It was during this decade that Poland was judged to be one of the nine major economic powers in the world,' Ryszard Kwapień had announced. 'The Anatomy of Success will be a true-to-life chronicle of Second Poland.'

"No, I simply can't listen to him anymore," Agata gasped and sat back in her chair. "If he stood in a meatline for just one day, he would see his major economic power."

Kwapień was deaf to her curses. He continued to smile and started reading his next item. As Agata, Julia and Konrad listened, he announced the end of beef, poultry and bacon sales in the regular meat stores. "In order to overcome the temporary difficulties in the market, the government has decided to place the articles I just mentioned in the commercial stores permanently."

"What?" Agata and Julia cried. "What is going to be left in the regular stores then?"

"Probably 'ground pork'," Konrad said sheepishly. Then, trying to make Agata feel better, he remarked, "It won't make any difference, Agata. There hasn't been much available anyway."

His great-aunt shook her head with determination. "You're wrong, Konrad. I still managed to buy some beef at least once a week, and chicken too, so that I could make Babcia some soup. Now it's going to cost three times as much. Take our neighbour, Jacek Malinowski," Agata continued. "You remember, the railroad worker from the third floor?" Konrad shook his head.

"He has five children and an attractive wife," Julia added. "You once told me you were sorry that she was married."

Konrad coughed to clear his throat and then looked at his great-aunt and grandmother. "Yes, I do remember now," he said. "What about them?"

"Noo, they have been taking shifts at the meat store," Agata explained. "Mrs. Malinowska would stay for a few hours, and then one child, and then another would keep their place in the line. Jacek would line up himself when he got back from the station and, they always managed to get some meat. Now that's gone."

A few days after Waldek Marciniuk had showed him Rakowski's article in Polityka, they discussed the effects of the government's decision. "There is no way the workers are going to put up with this," Waldek said. "I've already heard rumours of unrest amongst Marceli Nowotko factory employees. Something is going to happen, no doubt about it."

"But what?" Konrad asked with a shrug. "I saw the unrest at United Enterprises in the spring of 1979 and what happened? The two men who were stirring up trouble for the union were taken to the Security Headquarters in Pałac Mostowskich, the workers got scared and calmed down. One of the ringleaders made a very brave speech at a union meeting recently, but the response was poor. Don't worry, Gierek's machine controls everything very well..."

Konrad stopped when he noticed engineer Smrodziński at the door. Their boss glanced at Waldek and left without saying a word.

"We've just seen one of the small cogs in the machine," Waldek said and laughed, "but its backbone might be weaker than you think. Have you seen this?" He handed Konrad a neatly printed leaflet entitled 'What Bloody Maciek Has'.

Konrad read the text quickly. It was a list of possessions belonging to the country's Radio Committee head, Maciej Szczepański. According to the pamphlet, he owned many private villas in Poland, a collection of foreign porno movies, a mountain resort, a hunter's cabin in Kenya, two helicopters, an executive plane and four Mercedes Benzes. It also alleged that 'Maciek' was employing five women on a continual basis to entertain his friends. The list also included an expensive apartment he rented in London for his mistress.

Konrad gnashed his teeth. "Son of a bitch," he said. "And all of this is financed from the Radio Committee's budget – that's public money!"

Waldek burst into laughter. "That's not the point," he said. "All funds the Party and the government have mishandled is public money. We pay for their wealth with our empty stomachs, don't we? Maciek, no matter how spectacular his adventures, probably hasn't been any worse than the rest of them. This leaflet is important not because it lists his possessions. People have known about them for years."

Konrad handed the leaflet back to him and lit a cigarette. "So what is so different about it then?" he asked quizzically. Waldek also took a cigarette out of his package and smiled.

"Didn't you notice the quality of the printing job?" he asked. "It doesn't look like an underground publication from K.O.R.[12]

Konrad was puzzled by his co-worker's riddles. "You're not trying to say that Gierek ordered these leaflets himself, are you?"

Waldek burst into laughter. "Of course not, but listen to me, Konrad. Don't you think that it's a bit of a coincidence that someone like Rakowski suddenly publishes a 'freedom-minded' article and now we got these leaflets... I've seen thousands of them littering the stairwells in our neighbourhood. They are slandering the man who is regarded as the closest crony to Gierek."

---

12. KOR (Polish Acronym) - The Committee for Workers' Defense. An organization of Polish intellectuals which was established in 1976 to raise money for workers who were fired for involvement in strike activity in Radom and Ursus (Warsaw).

Konrad looked closely at Waldek. Only the two of them were in the room. He didn't know him very well, but he sensed that he could trust him. Waldek was straightforward and seemed honest. "O.K., from what you're saying I assume that there's some factional fighting going on within the Party. Is that what you mean?" Waldek nodded.

The office door opened and engineer Smrodziński came into the room. "I have the impression, gentlemen, that you don't work much," he said and stared blatantly at Waldek's neat desk.

Konrad looked down at his work, as if expecting that Smrodziński would leave again. Instead his boss said: "Mr. Dymowski, it was you that I wanted to speak with, as a matter of fact. You're going on a business trip next month. It is scheduled for the middle of August. We have foreign customers coming and you and I will be taking them to Gdańsk for two or three days. They want to do a quality check on the machinery they're about to purchase. Because of your good grasp of English, you may be helpful during the contract talks." Engineer Smrodziński smiled at Konrad and then turned to Waldek and frowned. He closed the door and started down the hall. Waldek and Konrad began to snicker. "Unbelievable!" Waldek exclaimed. "He's admitted that your English is better than his."

Rumours of strikes started circulating through Warsaw. One day, when Konrad returned home from work, his great-aunt told him an incredible story. "In Lublin, the railway workers welded a locomotive right to its track."

He was skeptical. Action like that seemed a bit beyond the realm of reality. "Who told you that? Why would they want to do that?"

Agata smiled with self-satisfaction. "It's true. Mrs. Malinowska told me today when we were queuing together at the butcher's. The train was packed with hams and was heading for Moscow. They were hidden in kegs which usually carry tar. When the workers found out about it, they welded the locomotive and the train didn't leave for three days." Konrad turned to Julia. "Do you believe it?"

"People are always spreading gossip these days," she answered quietly. "Why don't we tune in to Radio Wolna Europa[13]. They must know what is going on."

"I wish we could," he answered with disappointment, "but unfortunately my radio is broken. I won't get it back from the repair shop for two weeks..."

Agata scratched her head and stood there, deep in thought. "What about that American magazine that you get sometimes... what is it called? Ah, yes Noosick?" she asked. "What does it say?"

Konrad burst into laughter after hearing his great-aunt's comic pronunciation. "Newsweek can't help us much either, I'm afraid. There is at least a seven day time lag. The last issue was devoted almost exclusively to the Moscow Olympics."

They didn't have to wait for the next edition of the magazine. Before it arrived, the Polish media began reporting 'work-stoppages' affecting many

---

13. Radio Wolna Europa - Radio Free Europe, Polish Radio broadcasting from Munich, West Germany. It was financed by the U.S. Congress.

factories across the country. The word 'strike' was skillfully avoided and replaced with descriptions of 'idle periods' and 'work activity slowdowns'.

"The situation is difficult," Ryszard Kwapień declared one evening. "What our nation needs the most, is calm."

"What we need the most is meat, Mr. Kwapień," Agata screamed at the TV screen.

Konrad told her to be quiet as they watched the producer of the program, Jerzy Ambroziewicz take Kwapień's place. "In the midst of this difficult social and economic situation," he said, "work-stoppages just add to the problem. I, Jerzy Ambroziewicz appeal to you, not as the producer of the TV Daily but as a citizen of this country, please, let's see an end to these work-stoppages."

"This is amazing," Julia exclaimed. "Yesterday Kwapień was going on as usual about Poland's economic successes and now his boss is saying our situation leaves a lot to be desired. Have things changed overnight?"

The roses out in the back lawn were in full bloom and birds were singing in the tall acacia trees overhead. Konrad and Agata opened all the apartment windows as wide as possible to let some of the pleasant summer air inside. Julia shook her head, when Konrad suggested that they go outside for a walk. She complained about the injections she was receiving, saying that they were very painful, and she wanted to wait until the treatment was over. There wasn't a hint of disappointment in her voice. Instead, she answered him almost joyfully and smiled incessantly.

"You look quite contented today, Babcia?" he remarked. "Why?"

She smiled again. "Don't you remember, Konrad? Eryk is coming home tonight."

Agata, who was sitting in Robert's old canvas chair, sighed. "I wish he would stay right where he is," she remarked resentfully.

Julia glared at her sister. "Very nice. That's a nice thing to say about your nephew and my son, Agata. The man is coming home after three years..." she said bitterly.

Agata remained steadfast. "I've had enough of his drinking, stealing and lazy dependence on all of us. We all have to feel ashamed for the offences he has committed, and all of those people after him for the money he owes? No, I am not looking forward to seeing him."

"Stop it please," Konrad pleaded. In many ways he shared Agata's opinions but he didn't want his grandmother's happiness to be spoiled. "It doesn't matter what any of us thinks," he added. "The fact remains that he is coming home tonight."

Agata persisted. "We won't be able to survive on our pensions even if you help us out, Konrad. We simply cannot afford to support a drunkard. We are getting older and prices are going up all the time."

"He will get a job," Julia replied.

"You still believe that?" Agata asked with cynicism. "He's been looking for a job for fifteen years now. I don't think he has changed, Julia. He will drink away our money because I know you'll give it to him. We're going to become beggars."

Konrad told them both to stop quarreling. He knew his words lacked conviction. "Eryk is Babcia's son. She has been saving the money he earned in prison. She loves him."

Agata scowled. "Well, I know Julia. She'll give it all to him and within a week it will be gone. Then he will come and ask for more."

"You are awful, both of you," Julia yelled from her bed. "You hate him, I know you do. But you're wrong, Agata. His money is with Konrad. He's going to be looking after it."

"Yes, the money is with me," he confirmed.

"You'll both see," Julia added. "He has changed. He'll be a different person from now on."

"I hope you are right," Agata said. She sighed and went into the kitchen to start dinner.

Eryk stood at the apartment doorway, an old canvas bag dangling at his side. His face was a bright pink, and he smelled of alcohol. "You could have come home sober," Konrad said with resignation and let him in. Eryk looked at him without a word and then dropped his bag on a chair. He headed down the hall to Julia's bedroom, carrying a bunch of daisies and a small parcel.

"Mother, I am back," he said. "here are some flowers for you and a cake for auntie." He handed the small, wrapped package to Agata.

"My son. My son is back home," Julia exclaimed, trying in vain to sit up. "Come here. I have been waiting for you for such a long time." Eryk knelt beside her bed and kissed her hand. Then he kissed her moist cheeks. "I am home, Mom," he said, "and from now on, I'll be helping you. You won't be alone any longer."

As Konrad watched in silence, the memories of the hours, days and nights he had spent at his grandmother's bedside came back to him. "Where have you been all these months, you good, loving son?" he thought to himself. Julia seemed oblivious to the smell of liquor on Eryk's breath. He was her son and he had come home. That was all she cared about. Is it right for her to forgive him again and again? Konrad wondered. How many times can she just forget what he has done and continue on as though nothing had happened? And then, even though he continued to feel resentment toward his father, Konrad's face started to turn red and he looked down at the floor in shame. He remembered the night he had knelt down beside Julia's bed and prayed for her survival. How many times have I gone astray? But still God hears my prayers...

In the kitchen, Agata sat at the table and sipped a mug of tea, savouring a piece of Eryk's cake at the same time.

"You don't seem to be doing too badly," Konrad remarked with a wry smile.

"I might as well enjoy myself while I can," she replied and swallowed the last sliver of icing on her plate.

"Did you see Babcia? She's so happy."

Agata nodded without smiling. "Yes, Julia is happy that he is back," she said, taking another sip of her tea. She looked up at him and patted the seat beside her. "I want to tell you a little story, Konrad., " she said, and he sat down. "Julia, Fryderyk and I grew up with it. Noo... we didn't like it very much but we had to listen to it. Whenever we were bad, Luba wouldn't spank us. Instead, she would look down at us with a sad expression on her face and then tell us this tale."

"Go on."

"Noo, a young man asked his mother for some money one day, and because she loved him very much, she gave it to him. It was gone within days. Then he met a girl and decided that he needed more. He went back to his mother and she gave him whatever she had without leaving any for herself.

Next, the son decided to marry the girl, but she wouldn't go to church with him. She demanded that he bring her his mother's heart first. So, he killed his mother and carved her heart out. Then, taking the heart with him, he rushed to his bride-to-be. He was so happy and excited that he had fulfilled her request. But along the way, he tripped and the heart fell on to the ground. As he was getting up, the bleeding heart cried out to him with concern: 'Did you hurt yourself, my son?'"

Konrad and his father sat in the kitchen in silence. They had just finished the breakfast meal and were drinking tea. Eryk clung to his mug without moving. Before he got up to leave for work, Konrad decided to confront him. "So what are you going to do with yourself now?" he asked.

Eryk shrugged. "I still have to think about it. I just got out yesterday."

"Well, what are you going to do for money while you are making your big decision?"

Most of Eryk's prison earnings went directly to the government, but a portion had been sent to Julia, in the form of a support payment. Konrad knew that his father looked upon that money as his, and he wasn't surprised when Eryk remarked, "Well, there is the small amount that Babcia has been keeping for me. That should last me for a while."

"I have all that money, Eryk, " Konrad blurted out. He braced himself for his father's reaction.

"What do you mean: you have the money? It's mine."

He was determined to show Eryk who was boss. "Not while I have it. Julia and Agata need it more than you. You want money? Go out and get a job!"

His father jumped out of his chair. "Well, you lousy..." he shouted, "give me my money back!" His face was red and his eyes were wide open in an expression of disbelief. Konrad just smiled and shook his head.

Eryk slumped back into his chair, his arms dangling by his sides. "We've been through a lot together, Konrad," he said in a raspy voice a few minutes later. "I thought that we could be friends."

Konrad eyed his father with his usual skepticism. "Well, why not?" he said in a business-like tone of voice. "But it depends on you. I'm ready."

Eryk looked hopeful again. "All right, let's start right now. First you give me the money and second..."

"There won't be any second, father," Konrad answered coolly. "The money is in my account and it's going to stay there."

Eryk carefully studied his son's face. His tea remained untouched. He picked a package of Sport cigarettes off the table and lit one.

"I mean business," Konrad told him. "You just have to get out and work."

190

Eryk puffed on his cigarette in silence. "All right," he said with a deep sigh a minute later. "What do you want me to do?"

Konrad had to struggle to keep a triumphant smile from forming on his face. "We'll go down to the employment agency together and find you a placement."

"Are you crazy?" Eryk yelled. "I could go out right now and get a job anywhere I want. I'm not going to an agency like a convict."

"But that's what you are. You have to face up to that. Today I'm going to Gdańsk on business. I'll be away for three days. When I am back, we'll go to the agency together."

Konrad and his boss met their clients at the airport and escorted them to Gdańsk by plane. The two businessmen were from Kenya. Engineer Smrodziński sat beside the senior executive and Konrad sat with another man, across the aisle.

The executive turned to engineer Smrodziński. "My colleague and I are of course concerned about the quality of the product we will be getting from you, sir," he said, "but we also want to make sure that our order arrives on time. A predetermined arrival date must be spelled out in the contract."

Smrodziński blinked his eyes and appeared puzzled. "Could you repeat what you just said, please? This time a bit more slowly."

The foreigner smiled. "How - can - we - be - assured - that - our - order - will - arrive - on - time?" he asked.

After a minute, Smrodziński nodded. "There won't be any problem," he answered, "Once we have signed the contract, you will get the equipment without delay. I guarantee it."

The other man, who up until that point had been content to sit quietly, also turned to Smrodziński from across the aisle. "That equipment must get to us on time. I hope that everything will go as smoothly as you say. However, suppose you have a strike? Last year, labour walkouts in our country stalled all construction sites for two months."

Konrad's boss began to chuckle. He seemed to radiate self-confidence. "We don't have problems like that here," he explained. "You see Mr. Mwamba, in a Socialist state there is no such thing as a strike..."

John Mwamba sat quietly for a moment while he thought over the engineer's words. "But you have workers and employers just like everyone else," he said. "Why should things be any different in Poland than in Kenya, for example?"

Wiesław Smrodziński and his colleagues with Budal's Party Committee had all been trained extensively on the proper way to converse with foreigners. Smrodziński grinned proudly and answered without hesitation. "Now, Mr. Mwamba, you have to understand the basic difference between our two political and social systems. You are a developing nation, but you organize your economy on capitalist principles. As a result, your working class struggles against those who exploit it, i.e. capitalists or employers if you wish. In Poland, a struggle like that would not make any sense because the working class is the ruling class. In other words, all the factories and businesses are owned by the workers themselves. Our government and the Party represent the workers. The employers are also members of the Party and are considered part of the working class. A strike by the working class against the working class wouldn't make sense, would it?"

Konrad and the customers listened intently to Smrodziński's smooth and well-rehearsed rhetoric.

"So," he continued. "There is no danger of strikes here. They just simply wouldn't happen."

Kamau Nyoka, the man sitting beside Smrodziński, seemed visibly aggravated by the engineer's answer. "Despite all that you have just said, I'm afraid that I have heard of serious labour unrest here. Explain that if you will?"

"You might have heard of sporadic work-stoppages, but I can tell you that they were very small and short-lived."

"So you do have strikes then?" John Mwamba asked with a smile.

"No, of course not," Smrodziński exclaimed. "A strike is a legal protest by the working class against the capitalist owners of a company." He went on to finish the answer he had prepared for that question. "You see," he explained. "These work-stoppages you've heard of are illegal, and they are organized by anti-Socialist elements. We know as well that they lack public support and are isolated events. Once they are dealt with by the Party and the government, we'll have complete social peace again. Besides, these lapses in work are not strikes."

John Mwamba smiled sarcastically at Konrad's boss. "Whether you call it 'a strike' or 'work lapse' or whatever," he said, "it's just a matter of semantics."

Smrodziński's eyes narrowed and he turned in Konrad's direction. "What does that mean?" he asked him in Polish.

"Semantics is a branch of knowledge dealing with words and their meaning," Konrad explained.

Konrad had always liked Gdańsk. He had visited the city many times when he was a child. He and Tina stayed at a tourist camp in Gdańsk-Stogi, on the outskirts of the city. It boasted one of the widest and most beautiful beaches on the Baltic coast.

Gdańsk had a long and tumultuous history. At one time, it was a part of pre-partition Poland and served as an important harbour for grain shipments to Western Europe and America. There, rich Polish noblemen would sell the wheat they had grown on their estates in Polish - Lithuanian Commonwealth.

Colourful burgher houses, dating back to the 16th and 17th Centuries, which lined Długa street, were reminders of that era. Many old churches and harbour buildings were still standing as well. Newer sections of Gdańsk showed influences of German architectural styles. Throughout the 19th and early 20th centuries, Gdańsk was called Danzig and belonged to Prussia and later Germany along with other territories in the northeast. After the First World War and the Peace Conference in Versailles, Gdańsk became a free city under Poland's protection.

The two businessmen listened attentively as Konrad told them the history of the town.

"This is fascinating, Mr. Dymowski," John Mwamba remarked. "But following the treaty, wasn't Gdańsk to be shared by the Germans and the Poles? I understand that it was the source of a lot of trouble. Did World War Two start because of Gdańsk?"

Konrad smiled. "Not exactly," he explained. "That was just the excuse Adolf Hitler needed. You see, Germany controlled territories to the east and west of the city. The Führer demanded permission to build a highway across the 'Gdańsk corridor' but our government refused. After that, the Nazis invaded Poland. It's true that the first salvoes of the Second World War were shot near the entrance of the harbour, but I don't think there's much doubt that Hitler was determined to destroy Poland no matter what. Germany and the Soviet Union signed a treaty known as the Ribbentrop-Mołotov Pact. It wiped out the Polish state and divided our territory in half."

Wiesław Smrodziński glared at Konrad. "What bullshit are you telling the two Negroes?" he exclaimed in Polish.

"I was just acquainting them with Polish history," Konrad explained innocently. "It's all true."

"Yes, but you don't have to mention the Ribbentrop-Mołotov Treaty," his boss said angrily. "I'm going to tell them the rest. You just be quiet."

The two men from Kenya seemed perturbed and they looked at Smrodziński with puzzlement. He smiled at them sheepishly. "Now, as Mr. Dymowski was saying, the city was always threatened by the Germans. That is no longer the case. Thanks to our allies, especially the Soviet Union, nobody is going to challenge Poland's sovereignty over Gdańsk. In 1945, the invincible Red Army and the Polish troops allied with it, put an end to any German presence in the area."

Konrad signed. He knew that in 1945, the Soviet Army deliberatly destroyed parts of the city, long after all military objectives had been achieved. Large sections of Gdańsk had to be rebuilt.

The two clients gazed up at the tall burgher houses and admired the hand-made jewellery for sale at the market stands lining Długa Street. Mr. Nyoka looked down at the silver earrings and amber necklace and sighed. "I wish I had more Polish currency with me," he muttered. "If we have time, I'd like to come back here tomorrow, after I have changed some money. My wife would love this jewellery. This is beautiful amber."

Engineer Smrodziński coughed and motioned to Kamau Nyoka. "I think I could help you out," he offered. "What foreign currency do you have?"

"American dollars."

"How much do you get for one dollar at the exchange cashier?" Smrodziński asked, trying to stem his enthusiasm.

Nyoka burst into laughter. "I don't really know. What is it Mr. Mwamba?"

"After all the deductions and additions we get about forty złoty to a dollar," John Mwamba answered.

"I guess I could give you fifty złoty," Smrodziński murmured quietly. "Then you could buy the necklace right now. I have a lot of Polish money with me."

Kamau Nyoka shook his head and turned to his colleague. "Mr. Smrodziński told us that his country was free of capitalist flaws," he said with a chuckle, "but he is a very enterprising man."

Konrad glanced over to his boss whose face had reddened with embarrassment. "I was only trying to give you a hand," he muttered, "so that you could buy the necklace..."

Smrodziński's answer sent the two businessmen into hysterics. They clapped their hands and began dancing around the red-eared engineer. "Yesterday, we went to the bar in the Forum Hotel," John Mwamba explained, once he had caught his breath. "A fellow there, offered us 100 złoty and you want to give us half of that? You are a good, capitalist businessman! Mr. Nyoka and I have to be careful about signing the contract. What a businessman you are," he exclaimed sarcastically.

Engineer Smrodziński persisted. "The man you met was a criminal. I don't deal with foreign money very often. I just mentioned 50 złoty because you were in need. If you want a better exchange I could give you 110. How does that sound?"

Konrad was so ashamed of his boss' actions that he wanted to disappear. The black market price for a US dollar was 140 złoty.

Kamau Nyoka turned to his colleague. "What do you think?" Mwamba sighed and nodded and within a minute, engineer Smrodziński had pocketed their American currency. Then Konrad watched him take a pile of 1000 złoty notes from his wallet.

"I liked Gdynia quite a bit," John Mwamba told Konrad on their way back to Gdańsk by train the next day. "It is a beautiful, although very modern harbour city." He commented on the architecture of Gdynia and Konrad explained the history behind the city's expansion before the Second World War.

"Wasn't Gdynia the scene of bloody riots about ten years ago?" Kamau Nyoka asked. "I don't know any of the details, but I do remember hearing something on the BBC World Service news. About 100 shipyard workers were killed. Can you tell us something about that?" he asked Konrad.

Konrad nodded and was about to begin the story, when his boss elbowed him. "Shut up," he said in Polish. "I'm going to explain everything."

Konrad shrugged and apologized to the two visitors. He then took a copy of Newsweek out of his travel bag and began leafing through it. Smrodziński started his diatribe.

"Yes gentlemen, there were serious riots in Gdynia, Gdańsk and Szczecin in December, 1970," he said in an assured tone of voice, "but do you know who was behind it?" He smiled when the two men began shaking their heads. "The BBC will tell you that something happened but they will never explain the reason behind it. Anyway, I must admit that our Socialist motherland in 1970 was not perfect. Our former leader Władysław Gomułka was senile and not aware of what was really going on... a few Zionists still occupied positions in the Party and the government," he explained emphatically. "There were riot ringleaders, counter-revolutionaries who took orders directly from the CIA - people without morality or feeling for their country. They created the unrest and a few workers were stupid enough to follow them." Smrodziński nodded and sat back, looking very satisfied with himself.

Kamau Nyoka was somewhat annoyed by Smrodziński explanation. "OK, Mr. Smrodziński," he said. "The workers were exploiting the circumstances... but could you tell us how they were killed?"

Konrad sighed and, taking his magazine, he left for another train compartment. He couldn't bear to hear his boss' answers. He sat down at an empty bench and opened his Newsweek again to an article on the Moscow Olympics. One large photo displayed Polish pole-vaulter Władysław Kozakiewicz just after he had broken the world record. Konrad read the text beside it closely. "After Kozakiewicz had beaten the record," it read, "the Soviet spectators started whistling with disapproval. The Polish athlete bowed and then with a proud smile he made a rude gesture in the audience's direction." Konrad examined the photograph and immediately began laughing. Kozakiewicz had placed his right arm across his left elbow and jerked it upwards. It was a well-known Polish gesture, and not a complimentary one.

Wiesław Smrodziński was jubilant. The two Kenyan clients seemed quite satisfied with the quality assurance service provided by the Gdańsk branch of Polcargo, the company which inspected all the equipment that Budal supplied to foreign customers. They still had some doubts about the delivery of the equipment, but were confident that small delays would not cause them a lot of difficulty. They arranged to sign the contract at Budal's head office the next day.

It was 1:00 P.M. They still had two hours to get to the airport to catch their plane back to Warsaw. When they walked out into the Polcargo yard, they found the company's driver bent over a car engine. "I don't think there's much I can do about this right now, Mr. Smrodziński," he explained.

Konrad followed his boss back into the office. "We need a car to get our clients to the airport," Smrodziński told Polcargo's manager. "They can't miss their flight."

The man smiled sheepishly and shrugged. "I'm sorry but we don't have any other vehicles available."

"What about the other cars in the yard?"

"We've been waiting for imported spare parts for our two Toyotas for six months," the man answered with a nervous laugh.

Konrad asked him how they could find an airport bus and the manager directed them to the Targ Węglowy Square. They walked along the muddy cobblestone street. On the left, beyond an imposing fence, was the large compound of the Lenin Shipyard. "That's where we build our ships, gentlemen," engineer Smrodziński said, pointing at the cranes dominating the factory yard. "It is a very busy area..." Konrad's eyes followed Smrodziński's finger and he looked up at silhouettes of steel cranes overhead. They were completely still; their shadows crisscrossed the almost deserted street below.

Not a single streetcar had passed them in over twenty minutes, which was unusual for the busy downtown area. Targ Węglowy Square was empty and the four of them were the only people waiting at the bus stop. No coach was in sight.

Wiesław Smrodziński glanced at his watch and sighed. "I think we had better take a cab," he said in Polish. "We don't have much time left."

A long line of people, stretching all the way down the road, waited behind the nearest taxi stand. "Is it always this difficult to get a taxi?" Kamau Nyoka asked.

"I don't know. I don't live here," Konrad explained, "but I'll go and ask a local about the situation." He stopped a man who was making his way down the street at a brisk pace and inquired about the cab service. "Are the line-ups always this long?" he asked.

"No, only when the shipyards go on strike," the man answered. He flashed a mysterious smile and continued walking.

"Wait!" Konrad yelled, eager to hear more. His eyes followed the man's bobbing head disappear down the street. The two African visitors seemed to understand the significance of the exchange. They gave Wiesław Smrodziński a sarcastic stare.

Once inside the cab, John Mwamba cornered Smrodziński. "Well, sir, how do you explain this?" he asked. "A break in work activity? A work stoppage? How about a nice, short word like 'strike'?"

When he arrived home, he noticed that his father's jacket was missing from the coat rack in the hall. The small bedroom off the kitchen was dark and deserted. He greeted his grandmother with a kiss on the cheek and asked her about Eryk's whereabouts.

"He left yesterday, in the morning. He didn't say where he was going or when he would be back," she answered sadly.

Konrad felt his body tighten with anxiety. "But we have to go to the agency on Monday," he complained. "It was all arranged."

"Maybe he'll come back tomorrow," Agata said. "Granny only gave him 100 złoty. That won't last him long."

Waldek Marciniuk and Maksymilian Wysmukłowski grabbed him when he walked into the office the following Monday. "Did you witness the strike? A governmental commission may be on its way to Gdańsk right now," they burst out. "Do you know who they'll be talking to?"

He shook his head and explained that he hadn't had a chance to get into the shipyard area. "The streets were quite empty and there was no transit service. And the shipyard cranes? They weren't moving at all. I'm telling you... when I saw them just sitting there, jutting into the sky, I had a feeling that something was going on. That was before I found out about the strike."

The image of the motionless cranes haunted him continuously. It was almost as if his mind had unconsciously acted like a film and photographed them.

Małgosia Karska rushed into the room. "I ran all the way from the bus stop," she exclaimed. "Was Smrodziński wondering where I was?"

"No, he's still busy with his two clients. You are lucky, Małgosia," Maks remarked. "Did you have a good sleep?"

Małgosia slumped into her chair. Her long hair was in complete disarray and mascara streamed down her face. "Don't be sarcastic, Maks," she pleaded. "I didn't sleep in. I was up all night trying to call my sister in Gdańsk."

"What is going on there?"

"I wish I knew," Małgosia answered with a long sigh. "I keep thinking about what happened there in December 1970 and I'm worried. I dialed her number for two hours. The lines were busy at first and then they went dead. I tried again early this morning and still no luck. When I finally got in touch with an operator, do you know what she told me?"

Konrad and Maks looked at each other and shrugged.

"She said that Gdańsk and Gdynia have been cut off from the rest of the country. Nobody can put a call through. Can you imagine?"

When he got home that evening, Julia also asked him about the strikes in Gdańsk.

"Anka told us that she tried to tune in Radio Wolna Europa yesterday but couldn't get anything but interference," Agata remarked and turned the television on. They saw Ryszard Kwapień collecting up his papers and signing off for the TV Daily.

"Well, I guess we're a bit late," Julia said.

"Noo, we didn't miss much," Agata said. "Kwapień wouldn't tell us the truth anyway." Since the latest price increases, her attitude toward the journalist had become even more antagonistic.

"Agata would kill Kwapień if she could," Julia remarked with a chuckle.

The television began to blare as the TV Daily narrator announced a special programming feature: a speech to the people by the Party First Secretary, Edward Gierek. They all stared at the screen in silence.

Gierek was seated behind a desk. He looked as well-dressed as ever, but his hands fiddled nervously with the sheets of paper he had in front of him. The First Secretary cleared his throat and began reading prepared address in a shaky voice. He urged the workers to return to their jobs and assured them that there would be no reprisals. Konrad, Julia and Agata's eyes widened and their necks strained closer to the set as they heard Gierek admit that his industrialization program was facing some difficulties. He was skillful about avoiding his own slogan, 'Second Poland'.

"Why didn't you talk like that a year ago?" Agata yelled.

Julia and Konrad responded with a chorus of: "Be quiet". Their eyes never left the television screen as they watched the anxious First Secretary suggest that workers might be granted the right to strike in the future. By the end of the fifteen minute broadcast, Gierek appeared troubled and, for the first time, Konrad thought, vulnerable. "We are ready to discuss everything," he said, "but not under pressure. We must have social peace. This is the most important thing. If this is not achieved, everything else may cease to have any significance…"

1968 in Prague, 1970 in Gdańsk… despite the hot August afternoon, Konrad felt a shiver creep up his spine as Gierek's words echoed inside his head. His grandmother and great-aunt did not seem to share his feelings. "But what are the workers in Gdańsk asking for?" Agata yelled at the television set. "That fat idiot Gierek talked for almost twenty minutes and all he said was that the workers were asking for too much. Why didn't he just come out and say what their demands were?"

Konrad and his grandmother looked at each other and burst into laughter.

"Sister," Julia exclaimed, "were you born yesterday? Don't you understand that he didn't just forget to mention the workers' demands? They're afraid that we would think that it's a great idea."

Konrad nodded in agreement, and got up to fix the pillow behind Julia's head. "My office friend Małgosia Karska has a sister in Gdańsk," he said. "She went there today after work. After I talk to her, I'll be able to tell you what's really going on."

"You can't imagine what it is like in Gdańsk," Małgosia exclaimed when she walked into their office the next Monday. Everyone in the room gathered around her desk and listened eagerly as she told of strikes in all of the Gdańsk factories and enterprises. "I think hospitals, ambulances and trains are the only exceptions," she said. "The shipyard rules the whole Gdańsk-Gdynia area. 'Prohibition' is being enforced. The Inter-Factory Strike Committee, the MKS, is making sure that no alcohol is bought or sold in the region and local authorities are complying. The streets are virtually empty. Most of the vehicles still moving through the city serve the MKS. It's very easy to pick them out. They carry Polish flags. White and red banners have also been put up on the front of enterprises which have joined the strike."

"What about the police? What are they doing?" Waldek asked her.

"I don't know. I didn't see any. They certainly weren't in sight around the shipyard. The MKS has a list of demands. There are twenty one in all. Lawyers and other intellectuals, who serve as experts for the workers, helped with formulating the demands. A full-length document was given to the government commission."

Konrad noticed engineer Smrodziński's ears perk up at the word 'government'. He stood in the far corner of the room and waited for his kettle to boil. Since his return from Gdańsk he had avoided any casual discussion with his employees beyond business matters.

"So there is a governmental commission in Gdańsk?" Smrodziński asked cautiously.

"Yes, of course," Małgosia answered proudly. "It is headed by Vice Premier Mieczysław Jagielski."

"Very strange, very strange," their boss muttered and left the office.

Konrad looked around at the crowd of people encircling Małgosia and thought how much their attitude had changed in just a few weeks. The weather and sports events were not the main topics of conversation any more and their voices revealed genuine excitement and enthusiasm.

Despite the upheaval of August, 1980, the executives at Budal seemed to be playing a waiting game amidst the frenzy of enthusiasm in the office. The company's director, Kossak-Roztworowski was away on a four month long business trip in Africa. His temporary replacement, vice-director Józef Ubiak remained cool and didn't say much. Engineer Smrodziński was the same.

The entertainment of foreign clients continued unhampered. A farewell dinner for Kamau Nyoka, John Mwamba and some of their Kenyan colleagues was scheduled to take place at a restaurant in Warsaw. Engineer Smrodziński informed Konrad and Maksymilian Wysmukłowski that they were expected to attend because, apparently, the interim director knew little English and Smrodziński wasn't confident in the role of interpreter. The situation changed quickly though, once the chilled glasses of Żytnia and Wyborowa vodka started to take effect. The alcohol armed Smrodziński with self-confidence and Konrad and Maks were virtually ignored during the meal.

"Down the hat, Mr. Noyka," Smrodziński shouted.

"It is down the hatch," Konrad added, trying desperately to remain serious.

"Who cares…" his boss answered in Polish. "I don't know what 'the hatch' is, but I do know the word 'hat' and see," he said, pointing to John Mwamba emptying his glass, "they seem to understand…" The entire table shook with laughter.

To one side of the restaurant, lights suddenly illuminated a small stage. Minutes later, two couples dressed in Cracovian clothing appeared and began to sing. Their chorus was slightly out of key and too loud, but their performance elicited a standing ovation from the table of Budal employees and customers. Konrad shrugged and turned toward Maks, the only person at the table who he considered to be 'right-minded', besides himself. "Don't you think that we're bastards for sitting here like this?" he whispered.

"Why?" Maks whispered back.

Before answering, Konrad looked around the table, to make sure that the other guests were still caught up in their vodka and conversation. "Well..." he continued, "here we are, drinking with people like our boss, while so much is going on in Gdańsk. Don't you think that we're betraying the workers by fraternizing with this trash," he asked, glancing over to Smrodziński and Ubiak.

"Maybe you're right," Maks agreed. "But it could be the last time we have to attend a reception with Party characters like these two men." His face soured. "This system isn't going to survive the strikes," he said firmly. "I'm positive it won't!"

"And I think that it will," Wiesław Smrodziński declared. With a wide grin, he sat down, somewhat unsteadily, in the chair beside Konrad and remarked, "You don't mind if I sit here, do you gentlemen?"

"No, not at all," Maks answered grimly. He filled his boss' glass with vodka and hoped that he would quickly get completely drunk. Indeed, Smrodziński emptied the glass within a couple of seconds and quickly refilled it. He turned to Maks and smiled again. "So... Mr. Wysmukłowski, you think that we are in for a lot of changes?"

"That is my impression," Maks answered in a caustic tone of voice. "Even the media are talking about change now."

Their boss sighed and knocked back the contents of his glass. His eyes closed and he leant heavily against the table. "Changes, changes," he muttered. "Everyone is so scared of fucking changes. Have you noticed Ubiak? He is afraid... everyone is." His eyes narrowed into slits. "But I don't think that it is going to be as bad as everyone thinks..."

Konrad was just about to say that he wasn't afraid of change; quite the contrary but Maks kicked him.

"Keep quiet," he warned in a deep whisper.

Smrodziński started to mutter to himself. "They say that Gierek is going. Well, too bad for him. Gomułka went and what happened? - nothing. They say there will be a new trade union, but who gives a fuck for trade unions? The Party is going to get through this unscathed." Smrodziński's eyes were red and swollen and his hands trembled with anxiety, a sure sign that his own words weren't doing much to convince even him. "Changes," he murmured again, "Nothing is going to change..."

"And what are you going to do if you're wrong?" Konrad countered. "What if the demand about promotions is accepted? What if one's abilities, not Party connections were to count?".

Smrodziński looked up at him, but only semi-consciously. He seemed to have lost all sense of time and place and started to thunder out his answer.

"The Party won't allow that to happen," he yelled. "That would mean a whole life of service, for what? In the 'Fifties, when I joined the Party, I stopped going to church. I was once an altar boy, you know. My mother cried. But ever since then, I have never opposed the Party. I was faithful to all of them: Bierut, Gomułka and Gierek. And now what? Give up my position, my trips abroad, just because someone else is a bit smarter, or knows English better than I do?"

He grabbed the vodka bottle and drained the rest of its contents into his glass. The alcohol seemed to strengthen his will, because when he started to speak once more, his voice was more decisive. "Nothing will change. Nothing," he cried. "We still have the police. Gierek has to go. Too bad for him... but the Party will survive. It has the real power."

"It used to," Maks said, but Smrodziński scarcely heard him. His forehead was balancing on the edge of the table and he snored loudly.

The next day, Konrad stopped by the newsstand at the Grand Hotel. The woman behind the counter smiled and handed him two issues of Newsweek. He glanced at the covers. The first one showed the cranes and the entrance to the Lenin shipyard in Gdańsk. The headline read, "Showdown in Poland." He placed that issue in his briefcase and looked at the second. It's cover read, "Polish Resistance." Beneath it, was a photograph of a man that Konrad had never seen before. A short, unassuming looking fellow with a long, brown mustache.

During the ride home he was very impatient. He wanted to scan the magazines but there was no way he could even open his briefcase in the congested bus.

"What does it say, Konrad?" his grandmother asked anxiously.

He opened the magazine and slowly read the printed English.

"It says that an Inter-Factory Strike Committee has been formed and that it is headed by a shipyard electrician called Lech Wałęsa. It says that the Lenin shipyard in Gdansk is on strike and that hundreds of other enterprises have joined as well." He paused for a bit, trying to translate the text accurately. "It goes on to say that the coastal cities of Szczecin, Gdynia and Gdańsk are completely paralyzed by the general sit-in, that the nearby city of Elbląg is also affected. It's not on the coast but it has a large steam turbine factory. Its representatives have joined the MKS, the Inter-Factory Strike Committee."

"Brave workers," Agata declared, "and here, on television Kwapień interviews 'common Polish mothers and wives.' Do you know what they are saying? They are pleading for their sons and husbands to get back to work and stop ruining the country." Julia picked up the remote microswitch near her bed and switched the television on. Konrad saw a row of women in front of a factory gate.

"Who will unload the oranges from the ships?" a large, blond-haired woman screamed into the camera. "Our kids will go hungry while you are on strike..."

Agata called the woman an idiot, saying that people needed meat, not oranges. Julia switched the TV off quickly.

"Please go on, Konrad. Show us the rest."

The moving images on television contradicted the slick colour photos in Konrad's Newsweek. He opened the pages slowly and showed the two ladies pictures of thousands of strike sympathizers standing outside the shipyard fence with food and cigarettes for the men and women inside. Bunches of white and red flowers were placed right at the gate. Other photographs showed open-air masses and priests hearing confession behind the shipyard enclosure. A portrait of the Pope and a holy cross were fixed to the strikers podium. There, Wałęsa and the other leaders addressed the crowds of strikers and the people who stood beyond the fence.

"And the demands?" Julia asked him.

He handed her the white and red leaflet that Małgosia had given him earlier that day.

"What does it say?" Agata asked with excitement. Julia put her glasses on and quickly read through the text. "First, they want free trade unions independent of the Party. They quote a labour convention here. I don't really understand. You'll tell us about it later, Konrad, won't you?" He nodded.

"They also want the right to strike and guarantees of personal safety for the strikers and strike supporters."

"Go on," Agata urged.

"Noo, they want freedom of speech without censorship. Let's see, and, access to the media for all churches and religious groups. They want wages to be indexed. They also ask for the freeing of political prisoners, government compliance with the constitution, all Saturdays off and, listen to this: they want pensions revised to reflect the inflation rate."

She and Agata looked at each other and shook their heads.

"My God," Agata exclaimed. "It isn't possible. It's like a dream. I don't think they have left anything out. They even thought about pensioners. But do you think the Communists will agree?"

Konrad pursed his lips and looked at his great-aunt. His face was very solemn. "You probably know the answer to that question better than I do," he replied quietly. "If they did, they would have to accept a sharing of power and wealth with the people."

"What was the Convention #87, that the workers referred to?" Julia asked.

Konrad then explained that Poland was a member of the International Labour Organization. During the 'Seventies, Gierek's administration signed a number of international treaties and agreements, hoping that it would improve Poland's image in the West and open up new lines of credit. One of the treaties the government signed was Convention #87. "It calls for 'free trade unions independent of employers and government interference'. I'm sure that the people who signed it never dreamed that the workers would ask them to honour it," he added.

Julia was full of questions. "But how did the workers find out about it?"

"It is not just the workers, Babcia," he explained. The MKS is supported by experts – university professors, lawyers, many of whom belong to K.O.R., the Committee for Self-Defense of the Society[14]. They're standing by the workers in the shipyard. They won't be fooled by the government…"

Strike fever became infectious. Not only did the workers on the seacoast stay on strike, but other factories and enterprises decided to walk out as well.

---

14. K.O.R. - The Committee for Worker's Defense was, by 1980, renamed to KSS KOR; the Committee for Self-Defense of the Society, KOR.

The Silesian coal mines joined the movement and established an Inter-Factory Strike Committee of their own. It began communicating with Gdańsk and Szczecin.

"I'm going to find out what's going on at United Enterprises," Konrad told his friend Waldek Marciniuk. He picked up the phone and started the dialing.

"Is that where you worked before you came here?" Waldek asked.

Konrad nodded as the switchboard operator answered the call. "I'm sorry, Mr. Siedlak is not available right now and I can't connect you with anybody else either," she said. "We have been on strike since yesterday," she revealed in a proud voice.

Konrad shook his head with surprise and put the receiver down. Waldek looked at him and nodded.

The First Secretary's television address was repeated even more strongly by Ryszard Wojna, a journalist closely associated with Gierek's clique. Wojna seemed determined to throw the country back into the past by predicting a grave future. He told the Poles that he envisaged the end of the Polish state and a partition much like the one which occurred in the 18th Century. He warned that this would happen unless the workers terminated their sit-ins.

"Do you think that the Soviets will invade?" Konrad asked Maks the next day.

His friend shrugged. "I think that if they were going to come, they would have done it long ago. As the strikes drag on, it's becoming more and more inconvenient for them to act that way."

Waldek then yawned loudly. "There won't be anything like that," he commented. "Gierek is just finished, that's all."

Their boss, had just entered the room. "What did you say, Mr. Marciniuk?" he asked quickly.

"I said that our fearless leader, the First Secretary of the Polish United Workers' Party is finished. F-I-N-I-S-H-E-D. Do you follow me?"

The engineer's eyes narrowed. "I haven't heard anything about it," he murmured.

Waldek jumped out of his chair and approached his superior. "I don't think your Party knows what is going on," he said loudly. "Here, take a look at this!"

He took a copy of 'The Banner of Youth' out of his desk drawer. The paper was the official organ of the Socialist Union of Polish Youth.

"Look," he repeated, and tossed the paper on the desk.

Konrad and Smrodziński read the front cover carefully. The twenty one demands of the MKS in Gdańsk were printed verbatim.

"Do you remember what I said about changing winds?" Waldek continued. "Well, this is Edward Gierek The First's epitaph," he said triumphantly.

In a last ditch effort to solve the crisis, the Communist officials approached the Polish Primate, Cardinal Stefan Wyszyński. Konrad watched a television broadcast and saw the Cardinal speaking from the monastery in Częstochowa. The elderly man admitted the right of the workers to resort to strike action, but stressed that such a way of solving labour disputes was a very costly method, which adversely affected the country's economy.

Konrad was disappointed and depressed after watching the broadcast. "I can't understand it," he told Sister Maria the following day. "It appears that the Primate is supporting the government, not the workers."

The nun pursed her lips and her face became grave. "Perhaps the worst sin of all, Konrad, is to be ungrateful," she said to him. "I have brought you a copy of the Cardinal's sermon," she added handing him a small booklet which bore the insignia of the Warsaw Curia. Konrad read it quickly while Sister Maria was brushing Julia's hair.

"All right, sister. I see now that the government did censor many of the Cardinal's comments, especially his references to human rights. But he doesn't seem to be encouraging the workers to stick to their demands. On the whole, the speech is conciliatory."

"Don't feel hurt, sister," Julia said. "Konrad doesn't mean any harm. He is just a young and overly zealous boy. He doesn't want to criticize Cardinal Wyszyński."

After giving Julia's hair one last stroke, Sister Maria put the brush away and sat down in a chair beside her bed. "I'm not hurt," she said with a mild smile, "I'm just trying to decide how I am going to explain the whole issue to him."

"Konrad," she asked, "who, do you think, knows the Communists better. You or the Primate?"

He shrugged. "Well, to be honest, I think we both know them pretty well."

"Ah. You think that you know them as well as the older generation. I think the people in the shipyards would probably agree with you but," she said, staring at him squarely, "you tend to forget that in the 'Fifties when you and most of them were just crawling, the Cardinal was imprisoned by the Communists. And in 1970, when you were a schoolboy, the Communists slaughtered several hundred workers in Gdańsk, Gdynia and Szczecin. I'm sure you know that one of the current demands is the construction of a monument to commemorate the people who were killed ten years ago?" Konrad nodded. "But what the workers don't know," she continued, "is whether or not the army and the police will come, today, tomorrow or the day after and shoot them. Can you guarantee that this won't happen? You are here in Warsaw and they are there, on strike."

She stopped to clear her throat and then continued, "You said earlier that he doesn't seem to support the workers. But Konrad, who do you think sent the priests into the shipyard? And do you know why?"

Konrad looked at her sheepishly. "I have no idea... they wanted to confess?"

"All right, then I will tell you," the nun said firmly. "It is very inconvenient for the government to kill priests at the altars. And they are everywhere in the shipyard, mixed up with the strikers. The Primate supports them and prays for them just like you and I, but he bears a good deal more responsibility for this country and its people than any of us."

" My God, my God," Agata murmured to him later in the kitchen. "When is it all going to end?"

"It's them or us," Konrad answered, pouring some tea into a glass. "But it looks as though we're in the lead."

"But what is stalling the agreement?" Julia yelled from her bedroom.

"The first demand," he yelled back, "the free trade unions would challenge their monopoly on power."

"We'll see," Agata murmured. "We'll see if Wałęsa has enough strength to withstand their pressure."

But Wałęsa stood firm. He told Vice Premier Jagielski that without an agreement on the first point, any further discussion would be useless. The workers' experts once again pointed out that the Polish government itself had signed Convention #87 of the I.L.O. Its text was simply copied verbatim in the first demand.

More and more factories joined the strike across the country. One after another shut down and started to display the Polish flag at their gates. The government had no choice. It signed the agreements – first in Szczecin, then in Gdańsk and the last at Jastrzębie in Silesia. The agreements were similar because the three strike centers were in constant contact. The majority of the Poles turned to the Gdańsk agreement because it was the clearest and most universal.

It was 31st of August, 1980. The signing of the Gdańsk Agreement was televised across the country.

Konrad sat in his grandmother's bedroom and watched the broadcast with Agata and Julia. They were thrilled. "Look Agata," Julia said, trying to sit up to get a closer view, "that is Wałęsa, the man with the drooping mustache."

"Noo, Julia. Don't you think that I know who he is? Of course I recognize Wałęsa," Agata answered in an annoyed tone of voice.

Konrad could see two figures leaning over a table. Sheets of paper lay upon it. Lech Wałęsa initialled the document with a huge plastic ball point pen. He held it up so that everyone could see that the historical act had been completed.

"I'm off to work," he told the cheering crowd.

Konrad glanced at his bed-ridden grandmother's face as she clung to the sheet of her bed with excitement. Her eyes were wet.

"Why are you crying, Granny?" he asked her. "You should be happy. It's all over."

"I know, Konrad. We have won."

CHAPTER 5

In the factories and offices, people discussed the possibility of forming new unions using the framework provided by the Gdańsk Agreement. In Budal, an employee meeting was scheduled for September 22nd. Some people thought that it was not soon enough.

When the steward for the existing union, Zygmunt Król, made the announcement, Maksymilian Wysmukłowski protested. "Why do we have to wait that long?"

"The decision was made by the management and the executive of the Export Industry Workers' Union," Zygmunt Król answered.

"But we don't want our old union anymore," Maks exclaimed. "Your decisions don't mean a thing to me."

The union head burst into laughter. "But you are still a member," he said. "You still belong to the existing union."

Waldek Marciniuk tapped Maks on the shoulder. "Take it easy," he said. "We might as well wait a few days. What union would you establish right now anyway? We don't know anything about it. Someone has got to go to Gdańsk and see what Wałęsa and the others are doing."

"I'm going to Gdańsk next week for five days," Małgosia Karska said. "When I'm there, I'll go and talk to the people at the shipyard."

Maks shrugged and they all returned to their desks.

Konrad looked out of his office window. In the small park across the street, he saw an old woman leading a small black dog by a leash. Other people were sitting on benches and tilting their heads up toward the autumn sun.

Waldek joined him at the window. "It looks as though everyone were taking a deep breath - like a short break before the real action begins."

Konrad turned and looked at him with confusion. Waldek smiled. "Haven't you been thinking that everything is just a bit too quiet now? It's as if nothing had really happened. You see, Konrad," Waldek said, glancing outside, "the workers in Gdańsk have only initiated the process. The next few months are going to be long and very tough."

Julia's health had stabilized and while the weather was still warm, Konrad decided to take her for a walk in a community park close by. He carefully pushed her wheelchair up the main asphalt path into the open area of the park and wheeled it into a sunny spot beside a park bench. They overlooked a grove of linden trees and a large pond, the result of a once-thriving brick factory excavation. Some chips of red brick rubble were scattered on the shore. The skeletal remains of the factory walls were barely standing.

He looked down at the water below and then glanced over to his grandmother. She was looking ahead but he could sense that her mind was far away.

"Konrad, do you realize that we haven't seen Eryk for almost four weeks?" she asked suddenly.

He nodded. "It proves that he doesn't care about you and can't be bothered to change at all."

"Please Konrad, don't hate him. I can't accept hatred."

His mouth opened with disbelief. "Can you honestly say that I have ever hated him?" he asked with resentment. "When he left his last job, which only lasted three weeks, to go on a drinking spree, who begged his boss on his hands and knees to keep him on? And it didn't do any good, remember?"

"That's true, Konrad, but he was an alcoholic. He didn't have any will power." She paused. "I've heard that we can get special pills that could help someone like him. We could…"

Konrad tried to remain calm. He had given up on Eryk long ago, and his grandmother's persistent optimism aggravated him. "Yes, we could, Babcia, but where is he now? He promised to go to the employment agency with me and then he ran off. Please don't tell me that you still maintain any illusions about him."

He heard some shouting behind them. A group of schoolboys were kicking a ball on the small soccer field fifty meters away.

"Here Bogdan! Here! Oh, you lost it," one of them groaned. The ball hit a tree and went flying into Julia's wheelchair. Konrad scowled and kicked the ball as far as he could.

"Get out of here," he yelled.

His grandmother chided him. "Don't yell at the children. They're just playing."

"But they shouldn't be playing soccer around here."

Julia patted him on the hand. "They're just children," she said. "You were just like that when you were their age. You don't remember, but you weren't an angel. Many a pane was broken by your balls in our backyard."

"I remember," he answered and smiled at her. They sat quietly for the next few minutes.

Julia was the first to break the silence. "Konrad, I waited for three years for Eryk to come home. I want to see him change before I die. I can't take him to the agency myself. I can't take him to a doctor either. I was hoping that you would do it for me."

Konrad sighed. "Haven't I wanted to? Everything was arranged but he took off."

"He'll come back," she answered with determination.

"I'm sorry, Babcia, but I'm just being realistic. I don't believe in miracles."

The old woman glanced at him with surprise. "Are you sure?" she asked. "No, Konrad, you are not speaking the truth. Who went to confess for the first time in eight years after my accident? Didn't you thank God for the miracle that occurred that night?"

Konrad closed his eyes, and remembered kneeling beside her bed, listening to her sporadic, sickly breathing.

"Haven't we all," Julia continued, "been witnessing something else lately? Isn't it a miracle?"

Konrad felt a tap on his shoulder. "So here you are, taking sun, noo..." Agata said. She was all smiles, dressed in her best suit with her walking stick resting on her elbow.

"Here is another miracle, Konrad. Agata is out for a walk," Julia commented. They all laughed.

Agata sat beside Konrad on the bench and they spent at least an hour chatting and enjoying the freshness of the afternoon.

"Noo, I'd better be going back now. I have to cook dinner." Agata sighed and rose from the bench.

She took her walking stick and marched home. Konrad looked at her and chuckled. "I've always wondered about that walking stick of Agata's. Both of her legs are in perfect shape. She doesn't even know how to use it."

"It does help her a lot in the meat store, though," Julia explained. "The manager lets her stand in the crippled citizen line which is much shorter than the other."

Konrad began pushing the wheelchair along the path which led back to the street. Just as the chair started down the smooth lane, Julia raised her hand. "Konrad!" she exclaimed. "I just heard Eryk's voice." He turned the chair around and they both saw him crossing the leaf-covered lawn. He was wearing the same pair of coveralls as the night he returned from prison. Walking beside him, was a shabbily dressed man of about the same age.

"Don't force him into anything, Konrad. Just tell him that I want him to come and see me at once."

He nodded, made sure that the chair wouldn't move, and followed the two men, who by that time had disappeared behind the grove of linden trees.

"Eryk," he shouted.

His father turned around and was about to say something harsh when he noticed Julia watching from a distance. Instead he smiled and asked his friend to wait. The pink-faced man nodded awkwardly.

"What do you want this time?" Eryk asked. "I haven't been bothering you. Why are you after me?"

"Listen, you old S.O.B.," Konrad said angrily. "I couldn't care less if I ever saw you again, but someone else does."

Eryk reacted, not so much with anger, but with sad resignation. "You don't have to talk to me like that. I am your father after all."

"Unfortunately that is true."

Eryk just sighed and glanced anxiously at his watch. "Look, is that all you wanted to say to me? I'm in a hurry."

"No. Your mother wants you to come home, get a job and stop drinking. She wants to talk to you right now," Konrad answered firmly and pointed in Julia's direction.

Eryk agreed and as they walked across the park lawn toward her, Konrad inquired about the other drunkard.

"Him? Oh, he's a friend of mine. His name is Tadeusz Kohut and he used to be a swimming champion."

"That must have been ages ago," Konrad commented, looking back to the unsteady man behind them.

"No," Eryk disagreed, "Just in the mid-'Sixties."

He faced his mother. "How are you feeling, Mummy?" he asked and flashed a bright smile.

The old lady didn't answer her son immediately. Instead, she stared at him closely for a long time. She then raised her one good hand and shook it at him furiously. "Come home at once. You're not going to be roaming through the streets with hooligans any longer."

"My friend isn't a hooligan, Mummy," Eryk protested. "Right now I'm collecting money from people who owe it to me. When that's done, I'll come home for good."

Julia looked at him and sighed. Her eyes expressed disappointment and sadness. "Eryk, you are the one who owes money, not the other way around."

Eryk nodded unconsciously and looked back at his friend. Tadeusz was signalling to him to leave. "Look, Mummy, I will be back as soon as I can." He kissed her quickly on the cheek and scurried off.

The next day after breakfast, Konrad peered into his father's room. The blanket was still folded up at the end of the bed. He thought of Julia and walked into her room. She was staring sadly out the window. Outside, the rain, which had begun around midnight, was still pounding on the pavement.

"I'm glad that we decided to go for a walk yesterday," he remarked, trying to be cheerful. "It was a beautiful day." He was determined to get Julia's mind off Eryk.

Julia looked up at him and smiled. "Yes, the park was very nice, Konrad," she said quietly. "It might seem strange, but when I was there yesterday, I started to think of Wilno. The lake, the green grass on the hill, it all reminded me of countryside around Wilno. Your great-grandfather owned a summer house in Nowa Wilejka which faced a large pond. I almost drowned in it one summer," she said and laughed.

"You told me about that but I thought it happened to Agata, not to you?"

"We both almost drowned," she said. Konrad watched her short-lived cheerfulness disappear quickly from her face. "I wish I could go back there now."

"We can still go," he answered.

She shook her head. "You know we can't. It would have been difficult even before my stroke. There are too many obstacles – the border, a formal invitation from someone who lives there, a visa, and of course, money."

Konrad looked at her face. Her eyes were closed. He knew that her soul was somewhere in the northeastern city which he had never seen himself but loved, because of her. He bent his head down and looked at the bedroom rug.

"I wish I had taken you back there. I should have done it," he said quietly.

"Don't blame yourself, Konrad." Julia looked at him with kindness and smiled. "You must realize that my Wilno is quite different from today's Vilnius. Even the river's name has been changed from Wilia to Neris...

Besides, I have one consolation – the name on my mug." She pointed to the souvenir that Konrad had brought her from Canada. He had bought it in the church in Wilno, Ontario, the country's first Polish settlement.

He smiled. "But there still must be a number of places that you would have loved to see."

"I suppose, but a lot has changed too. The cathedral has been converted into a museum and there is a monument to Lenin at Łukiski Square. The second oldest Polish university there, is named after Kapsukas, the Lithuanian Communist. It used to be the King Stefan Batory University of Wilno."

Konrad looked down at the thin woman on the bed by his side, with her completely gray hair, and faded, weary green eyes. He recalled his vacation near Poland's eastern border – gazing at the railroad tracks that had once linked Wilno with Warsaw. They were divided by a threatening wire fence. Only a small belt of plowed soil separated it from elevated guard posts, armed with machine guns. He remembered seeing a small village in the distance beyond the barricade, inhabited, he knew, by people who spoke his language but were now citizens of the USSR.

"The union is called 'Unity' and it is completely free and independent," Konrad's co-worker Edward Ulizański said, and shoved a registration card into his hand.

Konrad eyed the man with suspicion and handed it back to him. "I don't want it, Mr. Ulizański. We are all going to discuss a new union together, next Monday." He knew that Ulizański wasn't a Party member, but something about him was irritating. He was a senior clerk in the personnel office and was well known for the way he annoyed the director of the company, Kossak-Roztworowski. Ulizański would bow and smile incessantly whenever he met his boss in the hall and it drove everyone crazy, especially Kossak-Roztworowski.

Another Budal employee approached them. "So what are you peddling here, Mr. Ulizański?" Adam Babinicz asked as he looked down at the leaflets in the clerk's hand.

"We want to form a new union, comrade Babinicz," Edward Ulizański explained cheerfully.

Babinicz looked at him with disgust. "I am certainly not your comrade, Mr. Ulizański and I would prefer it if you didn't address me like that. I am a Party member but I have often wondered why you are not," he said and burst into laughter. He turned one of Ulizański's brochures over. "Well, an independent labour union under the name of 'Unity.' Very interesting. How many members are there in the union?"

The clerk stared at the man with confusion. "Well, we are just forming it now," he answered.

"'We'? Who do you mean by 'we'?"

"I don't have to answer any of your questions, comrade Babinicz..."

"Mr. Babinicz, please," Adam told him decisively.

"Union pluralism is guaranteed, Mr. Babinicz," Ulizański said and grabbed his pamphlets back.

They watched him scurry down the stairwell. Then Konrad glanced up at the tall, blond-haired Adam. He liked the man's straightforward manner but thought that Ulizański was right. As if he had read his thoughts, Adam Babinicz suggested that they have a smoke together. They sat down in two armchairs in the Budal lobby. Konrad pulled a package of Sports out of his pocket and offered one to his co-worker.

"No thanks," he answered and pushed the pack away. "Let's smoke some better stuff." He passed Konrad a Marlboro and waited for his reaction. "I know what you are thinking, I'm just another fat cat in the Party, right?" With that he chuckled loudly.

Adam Babinicz lit his cigarette, took a puff and then set it down on the ashtray between them. He turned toward Konrad. "Listen," he said. "We both know that there are basically two major forces that have a hold over the people in this country: the Party and the Secret Service. Mr. Ulizański is not a member of the Party and yet he spent four years in Algeria. That's longer than any other employee in the firm. Don't you find that interesting?"

"You have been abroad too, Adam."

"Yes, but only for a year even though I am a competent engineer. I speak three languages too. Ulizański doesn't."

Konrad shrugged. Other engineers in the office, like Maks, were just as competent but had never had the opportunity to earn a dollar on a Budal foreign contract. Maks didn't belong to the Party.

"Whether we like Ulizański or not, it really doesn't matter," he said, puffing on his cigarette, "but perhaps 'Unity' isn't a bad idea..."

Adam Babinicz shook his head and laughed again. "I don't want you to take anything for granted," he explained. "Just think – what kind of manpower is there in this company? We are a bunch of engineers, some accountants, a lot of clerical staff and five blue collar workers. If we created our own union, what sort of strength would it have?"

Konrad asked him to continue.

"If we want to have any say at all, we have to unite with the working class," Adam said. "We have to join up with large factories like United Enterprises, Żerań F.S.O., Huta Warszawa. If we go on strike all by ourselves, who will give a shit? But if a metallurgical factory like Huta Warszawa walked out and we went with them, it would make a big difference to the government and the Party, wouldn't it?"

Konrad nodded. All of the engineer's arguments had been very reasonable. He started to tell Adam he agreed with him, but stopped himself. Adam stretched his legs and offered Konrad another cigarette. "What you are wondering," he said as he passed him a lighter, "is why I joined the Party? Isn't that right?"

"Yes. Why the hell did a nice guy like you do that?"

The older man laughed. "It's a long story, like most stories are," he said and set his cigarette down. "I joined almost ten years ago, right after Gomułka was dismissed and Gierek was promising changes, renewal. You must remember how it was back then, don't you?"

Konrad nodded and listened attentively.

"I realized that there were a lot of SOB's in the Party, but I thought I could do something to improve things. My father used to say 'Join Adam.

Maybe if there are more people like you, it will be a big help to Poland.' So I did. Since then, my father has died and I have seen all the shit there is. I have also realized that no one can change the organization. It's just a bunch of sycophants who applaud whatever leader happens to be in power at the time. They just make sure that the Poles don't rebel against the Reds. That's it." He sighed and took up his cigarette again.

"Why haven't you left then?" Konrad asked.

"They don't force anybody to become a Party member," Adam answered bitterly, "but once you join, you can't leave all that easily. They would treat you like a traitor and do all they could to hurt you. Take Kuroń, for example, one of the founders of K.O.R. He used to be a Party member, but he chose to leave and accept the consequences." He took a drag from his cigarette. "But... when you have a wife and kids, things don't look that straightforward." He took a deep breath and lowered his eyes. "I wish I had never..."

To get home from work, Konrad had to make one transfer. He got off the streetcar near Warsaw Central. As he walked across the street to catch the bus to his apartment, he spotted a flower stand bursting with bunches of roses. A small elderly woman was selling nicely wrapped flowers outside the train station.

"They're twenty a bunch," she said, anticipating his question. He handed forty złoty to the saleswoman and picked out two small bouquets.

"Well, buying for two ladies at one time. You haven't changed, Konrad," he heard a cheerful voice say from behind.

He turned around quickly. "Janek!" he yelled and grabbed his friend.

"Don't break my ribs," Janek Wytwicki cried as he was lifted right off the ground.

Konrad shook his head and smiled joyfully at him. Janek seemed calm and relaxed and he boasted a dark suntan. His hair had started graying around the temples. "You little S.O.B.," Konrad murmured. "You didn't come to visit me after we left the army. You promised."

"Well, I did write you two letters but you only answered the first one."

Konrad felt his face turning red. He had received a second letter from Janek, but it had come when he was spending all his spare moments with Hanna. He suggested they go for a beer, but Janek declined.

"I wish I could, but my train for Rzeszów leaves in twenty minutes."

Konrad offered to put Janek up for the night.

"Thanks Konrad, but I really can't. I was away in Gdańsk for three days. My wife is waiting for me and, apart from that, I have a meeting at work tomorrow morning." He paused and then his eyes brightened. "Why don't you come with me to the station? We can talk there for a while."

They walked into the building and Janek led him to a stairwell down to the lower level. He retrieved a small bag out of a locker and then they made their way to his platform.

"So... you're married," Konrad remarked, after they had sat down on an empty bench alongside the platform. "Who is she?"

"She is Mrs. Daniela Wytwicka, maiden name Hurewicz. 158 centimetres tall, just three centimetres shorter than me," he answered with a laugh. "Other than that, she has blue eyes, brown hair, a nice curvaceous figure, has her masters in pharmacy, and is the mother of young Mr. Lech Wytwicki. He's less than two weeks old and hasn't even been baptized yet, but he will be soon and I swear that he'll be christened after the most important man of postwar Poland – Lech Wałęsa. He'll even have the same initials."

Konrad shook Janek's hand. "Congratulations."

After they had lit up cigarettes, Konrad asked Janek about his trip to Gdańsk.

"I will start at the beginning. I have been working for Mechanical Works-Rzeszów for a year and a half. Last summer, the word 'strike' was being uttered everywhere except in our plant," he said, flicking his cigarette. "On August 25th, I got up from my desk and I told the other people in the office that they should think about joining the nation-wide sit-in. You should have seen my boss. The good, old Party member just scowled at me and said: 'Are you, fuck-your-mother, crazy?' in just the same way that Major Krupniak used to say, 'son of a bitch', do you remember?"

Konrad nodded but he glanced uneasily at the clock. "What happened next?"

"Well, I said to him. 'My mother is dead, but I'm 'fuck your mother' not crazy, sir."

Konrad looked at Janek with admiration and laughed.

"Anyway, the old guy picked up the phone and called the Secret Service. He was going to show me who was boss."

"And then?"

"A black Volga pulled up the driveway and the agents called him from the guard house. They suggested that I be escorted out of the building and my boss agreed. They didn't want the rest of the workers to know what was going on. So, I got up, grabbed my cigarettes and engineer Świniak rushed me out the door into the hall. We started down the corridor and then, all of a sudden, five workers from the fitting department blocked our way. I only knew one of them well, a young guy, Franek Rybicki. 'Where are you going, Mr. Wytwicki?' he asked me. I told him that I was being arrested for suggesting that the factory should go on strike. Rybicki then turned to my boss and told him that they had other plans for me. They took me back to the workshop and they kicked Świniak out of the gate. The agents were told to 'fuck off or else'."

Konrad looked at him with disbelief. "What did they do after that?"

"Not much," Janek said with a chuckle. "They didn't have the manpower or the will to fight the whole staff. By that time, everyone had assembled in front of the building. They just told Świniak that he was an idiot, jumped into their Volga and drove away. I found out, a few minutes later, that our workers had already decided to walk out when they met me in the corridor. Rybicki was just on his way to our office to get some engineers for the strike committee. He had me in mind right from the start."

The station loudspeaker announced that the train for Rzeszów was delayed for a quarter of an hour. Konrad sighed with relief and tapped Janek on the shoulder. "Tell me quickly," he said anxiously, "What was it like at the plant when you were on strike?"

"It was fine. Why not? We slept on the floor covered with styrofoam sheets and our wives and other supporters brought us food and cigarettes. I had my guitar too. You'll never guess what our favourite song was..."

"Shudder Moscow? Janek, you haven't changed a bit."

"We watched the signing of the Gdańsk Agreement on television in our conference hall. After that, we ended our strike. But before we went home..." he said, grinning at Konrad, "the guys at our factory... do you know what they did?"

Konrad shrugged. "Did they blow up the plant?"

Janek chuckled. "No, a lot worse than that. They made me, your friend, chairman of the committee to establish a new trade union. That's why I was sent to Gdańsk."

Konrad grabbed him by the shoulder and kissed him on the cheeks. "Congratulations again," he said warmly.

Janek looked down at his watch "I don't have much more time, Konrad. Have you formed a committee at your office yet?"

"We have a meeting next week," he answered and then went on to tell Janek about his conversation with Ulizański and Babinicz at Budal and his apprehension about the Party member's advice.

Janek thought for a moment about his concerns.

"Not everyone in the Party is inherently bad, Konrad. Engineer Świniak with our company is a member but our fitter, Rybicki is too. Those two men couldn't be more different. Generally, I think Party members are bastards, but there are exceptions. You yourself told me in your letter about a foreman you admired. I think Oskiernia was his name."

"O.K., but you haven't answered my question yet. Can I believe someone like Adam Babinicz?"

Janek shook his head and smiled. "Do what your intuition tells you. Don't be fooled by names like 'Unity' or 'Independence' or 'Power'. We're all going to be united under a powerful federation of free trade unions, organized geographically. It will be called 'Solidarność - Solidarity'. " He opened his travelling bag and took out a heavily-printed bulletin. "Here. Give this to your friend Babinicz."

The pamphlet was white with red lettering. An inscription read like a banner across the top, "SOLIDARNOŚĆ with a small Polish flag flying from the top of the letter N. "Solidarność," he murmured. "That's a good name for the union. Who thought of it? Wałęsa?"

Janek shook his head. "No, it was Karol Modzelewski, the journalist and historian from Wrocław, a member of K.O.R."

Finally, the loudspeaker overhead announced the arrival of Janek's train bound for Rzeszów. As he picked up his bag, Janek invited Konrad to his son's baptism, scheduled for Christmas time. They walked over to the train. Janek pulled down the window in his compartment.

"Remember, this country will be ours from now on, not theirs." Konrad thought that his friend's voice sounded unusually solemn. "This past August has changed everything. 'Party member', 'non-Party member'... things don't work like that anymore. The true test is still to come, though. Then we'll see just who is who. Today, we're just starting from the beginning," he yelled, as the train began to move away from the platform. "Everyone has to be given a chance..."

Since Julia's accident, Konrad had been spending his Sunday mornings at Father Florian's church.

On a particularly mild Sunday he went to mass as usual and prayed for his grandmother's health. When he returned home, he sensed that the spirit of prayer was still within him. Taking out the old, battered prayerbook that he had inherited from his grandfather, he knelt down in front of his bed.

"Oh Lord of the purest love, the giver of all happiness," he whispered.

"Here I am, coming to thee filled with a feeling of gratitude for the sweetness of friendship and love. I would like to beg thee for the blessing for her, whom my soul loves.

Spare her, oh Lord, from danger to her life and from all accidents and disasters.

Remove all sorrow and oppression. Let her enjoy every daybreak which will encourage her to joyfully fulfill the duties of her vocation...

Spare her, oh Lord, from the enemies, illness and suffering. Be her defender if anything might endanger her life. Let her become an example of piousness and virtue for all the poor and sad...

And when she is eventually called before thy Majesty to receive the eternal reward, please allow my soul to join hers in this land of happiness where love and peace rule, for ever and ever. Amen."

As he repeated the prayer, he began to feel more confident about Julia's continuing health. Instead of feeling anxious and fearful, as he had when he first knelt down, he was brimming with confidence and a sense of serenity and warmth. God, he thought, was reassuring him.

His grandmother was reading a book when he walked into her bedroom.

Both of them turned their heads when they heard Agata greeting someone at the door.

"Noo... Eryk. You have returned at last. Come in."

Eryk murmured a hello and walked directly into his mother's room. The pungent scent of alcohol followed him and Konrad opened the window. He stood by and watched his father without a word. He was determined to control his anger.

"Good day, Mummy. How are you today?" Eryk asked.

Julia smiled and replied that she was well. Then she looked Eryk squarely in the eye, in much the same way as when they had talked in the park and asked, "what have you been doing since you left home?"

Eryk's head lowered and he slumped into the armchair beside her. He didn't look up at his mother, nor did he answer her. His hands moved from his side and clutched his face violently.

Konrad's lips pursed with bitterness. "Your mother asked you a question, Eryk. Aren't you going to answer it?" he asked icily.

Again, Eryk failed to respond. While Konrad, Agata and Julia watched, he trembled and the torment of guilt swept through his body in waves. Julia tried to sit up in her bed and Konrad noticed that she was looking at his father with wide open eyes.

"Stop it, Eryk. What has happened to you?" Konrad asked. Eryk clutched his face even more tightly. Julia looked down at him in pity.

"Don't cry son," she murmured quietly. "You can still change. Konrad will help you. Won't you, Konrad?" she asked, glancing up at him expectantly.

"I will, Babcia."

Eryk sighed and without lifting his head, he bent over and kissed Julia. Then he got up and left for his room. Slowly, he emptied his pockets and the bag he had brought from prison, on to the small cabinet in his bright, yellow room. He painstakingly arranged all of his things in an orderly way – his twenty-year-old Tissot watch, a worn wallet, a nickel-plated lighter and an old American sweater. He went through the pockets of his jacket and pulled out his ID card. A slip of paper fell on the floor and he stooped to pick it up. He found Konrad in the kitchen making tea, and he handed the wrinkled note to him.

"This is my prison certificate," he explained. "We may need this when we go to the agency. Take it, but make sure that you don't lose it. It certifies that I am a free man..."

Konrad examined the paper slowly and then folded it up. "O.K. Eryk, we'll go in tomorrow as soon as you are sober."

"I'm not drunk now."

"Well, you smell like it," Konrad said sarcastically. "Why don't you take a bath and go to bed early."

His father sighed and then started to walk away. At the door he turned around and paused. "May I ask you a favour, Konrad?"

"It depends what you want?"

"I'm just wondering if I could have something to eat. I haven't had anything for two days."

Konrad nodded and opened the refrigerator. After a few minutes he brought Eryk a fried hamburger steak, some potatoes and a tomato.

"Thank you," Eryk said gratefully and gulped down the plateful of food. "May I have another tomato?"

"They are expensive, you know," Konrad answered. "Agata and I have only one a day each. There is only one more left and Babcia will be having it if she feels up to it."

"I see," Eryk said. "I'm sorry, I shouldn't have asked, but that tomato was the first one I've had in three years. We didn't see a single fresh vegetable in prison."

Konrad looked down at his gray-haired father and kicked himself for his selfishness. Why can't I be more like Julia? he asked over and over again. He walked back into the kitchen quickly and looked inside the vegetable bin of the refrigerator. There were two small tomatoes. He took one of them out, washed it, and sliced it. Then he added some onion, salted it and poured sour cream on top.

"Thank you, Konrad," Eryk said and ate the food eagerly.

The next morning, after he was assured that Eryk was still willing to go to the employment agency, Konrad went over to his neighbours to call engineer Smrodziński, He told him he had to take the day off. When he returned, he noticed that Eryk was neatly shaved and fully dressed in a lightweight gray suit. It was out of style and too large for the now slim Eryk, but he looked respectable.

Even at that early hour, the waiting room at the agency was full of men. Most of them, like Eryk, had made an attempt to dress nicely and they looked uncomfortable. Eryk sat down beside Konrad on a gray painted bench in the corner. They lit cigarettes and Konrad suggested that he look at the ads posted on the bulletin board.

"Do you see anything that you think you could and would like to do?"

Eryk nodded. "There are three jobs for maintenance technicians working on municipal sewer systems. I studied some of this at college, and I got some experience when I was in prison. I think I could apply..."

"But for which one?"

"Well, all of them have been issued by the same company, the only difference is the location. This one," he said, pointing to the bulletin board, "offers a job in our district of the city. The others are farther away."

"You are going to take the first one, aren't you?"

Eryk didn't answer right away. Instead, he seemed to be in the process of deep deliberation. He shook his head after a minute or two. "No, I'm not going to take the job close to home. I think I'd better take the one across the river."

"Why would you want to commute that far?" Konrad eyed him with skepticism.

"I wouldn't know anyone there," his father answered matter-of-factly. "If I took the job close by, I would be only three blocks from home. You know what would happen. I might meet one of my buddies, then another, and they'd say, 'Come on Eryk, have a drink with us,' and that would be it. That's why I left my last job seven years ago."

As Eryk disappeared into one of the counsellor's office, Konrad thought of Julia, and the faith she put on miracles. Maybe this time... he murmured to himself.

Two days later, Eryk did start working. The next few weeks weren't smooth or easy for him. They weren't easy for Konrad either. After only two days, without telling anyone, his father took a sick leave and started drinking again. But Konrad made sure that he called his boss every day and found out about his absence soon enough. He decided to register Eryk with an out-patient rehabilitation program for alcoholics.

"Forget it," Eryk said stubbornly. "I'm not going there every day and taking those dammed pills they give you."

Konrad stared squarely at his father. He was determined to be just as hard-nosed. "Listen Eryk," he said. "Either you agree to stop drinking completely or you might as well forget about your job, despite your good intentions."

Eryk turned away from him and lit a cigarette. He seemed bolder than he had been when he first returned home. "I can stop drinking without taking those anti-booze pills," he declared.

"I wish you could too, but so far that hasn't happened," Konrad answered with resignation.

With Julia and Agata's support, he finally managed to get Eryk to agree to the pills. He decided to administer them himself under a doctor's advice. The physician in charge of the rehabilitation program gave him a bottle of anti-alcohol pills and prescribed some mild tranquilizers to aid in the treatment.

Konrad got up early each morning and forced Eryk to swallow the medicine and eat breakfast. Then he took him to the bus stop. After that, he returned home, had a coffee, and listened to the Voice of America breakfast show. He made sure that he called Eryk at least twice during the day.

The late afternoon worried him. He never knew if Eryk would come home from work. Although he was forcing him to take the pills, he knew that his father was still trying to drink. During his second week on the treatment, Eryk came home and slumped on to the small couch in his bedroom.

"You can't cheat when you take the pills," Konrad warned. The next morning, he escorted his father right to his desk at the office.

This happened twice more until eventually Eryk started to get used to the idea that he couldn't have booze.

Julia was ecstatic about his progress. Every morning, he would come in to say good-bye to her after bathing and shaving. "Have a good day son," she invariably told him as he left for the day.

In the evenings, Eryk was also given the job of preparing supper for the family. Julia always smiled proudly when Eryk brought sandwiches nicely arranged on a plate in to her. Even Agata seemed to be happier. She was pleased that her initial fears about Eryk didn't materialize. "He's doing so well," she would exclaim. "He's just like a new man."

Just like a new man, Konrad thought to himself. More than anyone else in the family, he knew that his father's good performance was being maintained by a number of artificial factors, namely: his close supervision and the anti-alcohol pills he forced Eryk to take.

The next obstacle was his father's first paycheque. On the last day of the month, he confronted Eryk. "Before I decide that your alcoholism is cured, I'm going to ask you to give me your pay," he said with determination. "Part of it has to go toward the household, another part I'll put in the bank on your behalf and you will get a small allowance for cigarettes and other things."

Eryk could hardly wait until Konrad had finished speaking. "I am not in prison any longer. I am a free man and I can manage my money by myself. I am not an alcoholic anymore either..."

Konrad paused and lit a cigarette. "Think about it," he said.

"Well, there is nothing to think about," his father said with a nervous laugh. "A man works to get money. And why do we have money? So that we can spend it, right? Without that, we wouldn't work..."

With a determined flip of the wrist, Eryk then pulled a cigarette out of his pack and flicked his old lighter. It didn't work and he tossed it away angrily. He used Konrad's matches to light up. Konrad sat there, and quietly watched as Eryk picked up a copy of Newsweek and began browsing through it. Minutes later his eyes brightened. "Here is something for me," he said cheerfully.

Konrad figured that he was looking at a car advertisement. His father had been crazy about them at one time. Eryk smiled and held up a two-page ad for Heineken beer. When he saw Konrad's reaction, he dropped the magazine. His cheerful smile had disappeared.

"I'm asking you again," Konrad said flatly. "Are you willing to accept my terms?"

Eryk looked at him much the same way as he had done when they went to the employment agency together. "Perhaps I will," he said after a few minutes, "but you must promise that one day, I will get back my money and my freedom."

Konrad looked straight into his eyes. "Believe me," he said. "I don't want to prolong this any longer than you do. Do you think that I enjoy being your warden?"

"It feels like ants are crawling up my left hand," his grandmother complained to him one night. "The whole left side of my body feels numb and cold."

Konrad tried to massage her hand and leg, but it didn't do any good. Doctor Kamińska came in a few days later and she was very concerned about his grandmother's condition. He spent every evening at her bedside. Despite the pills that the doctor had prescribed, her condition worsened. Soon, she was too weak to use a bedpan on her own which made her very depressed.

One evening, they sat together watching a movie on television. Julia sighed when it was over and switched the television off.

"My time has come Konrad," she told him.

"No," he answered, trying his best not to burst into tears. "You are going to be okay, Babcia."

The thin woman shook her head. "I know that you want me to recover. You would do anything to keep me from dying. We love each other very much, don't we?" Not waiting long enough to hear his 'yes', she continued. "You cannot change my destiny, Konrad. I feel it in my bones, the time is coming. I don't want you to stop helping Eryk. Take care of him when I am gone..."

He did not answer. Instead he ran into his room and cried. And he prayed. He prayed every day. But there was something missing. He didn't get the feeling of confidence and hope. It was as if everything had already been decided.

Relatives started visiting more often. Anka and Bib came every day and Julia's brother Fryderyk, his wife and daughter came three times a week. Soon, Julia started experiencing a tremendous pain throughout her whole body.

Konrad counted the months since she had left the hospital. Four – Dr. Milewska had said five, six. He flung himself on to his bed and pushed the pillow into his face. "They can't know," he wept. "They can't."

"Babcia is going to die soon," Agata told him in the kitchen that evening.

"Perhaps she will recover," Konrad said. He knew his words weren't convincing.

Anka came in later that night and urged them to take Julia to the hospital but Konrad protested. Let her die at home, he cried inside.

"Anka doesn't want Bib to see his mother's agony," his great-aunt said in a low voice. "Bib has been coming twice a day lately and he is suffering very much."

Bib and Anka returned later that night. By that time, Julia was crying out in pain. Her younger son stood by her bed and watched silently.

"I can't stand it," Anka said. "Let's call an ambulance."

They reached the hospital around midnight. All the available beds were taken and the orderlies placed a cot in the already crowded corridor for her.

Konrad informed Budal that he might be away from work for an undetermined amount of time. He was his grandmother's first visitor at the hospital the next morning. The hospital staff was on strike. 'Solidarity' posters were everywhere, demanding working conditions and salary changes according to the Gdańsk Agreement.

All of the doctors and other employees performed their usual duties. The only signs of the strike beyond the posters, were large white and red banners over the entrance gate of the hospital and similar bands on the strikers' arms. And then, there were the badges. For the first time Konrad saw 'Solidarity' buttons.

He approached a female orderly. She, like most of the others in the hospital, was wearing a white and red armband. He tried to put some money into her hand but she refused.

"There's no need for that," she answered. "I'm doing it anyway. I have been attending your grandmother since she arrived yesterday."

"But please, take the money. It's just normal practice."

"It may have been normal in the past," the woman answered with a smile, "but you don't have to do it anymore. I am a member of the Union and we are fighting for our rights. It is our duty to serve our patients the best we can. When you have time, just read the Solidarity posters near the gate."

Bib and Anka visited in the afternoon and Eryk joined them at five o'clock when he finished work. Julia complained of severe pain but doctors wouldn't give the family any specifics.

On their way out of the hospital, they stopped at the gate and read the union posters. The hand-painted placards bore the familiar 'Solidarity' logo.

> We have been serving you the best we know how.
> But we cannot help it if we are paid poorly.
>
> The salaries of the orderlies, nurses and even doctors
> in our hospitals are well below the national average.
>
> That is why we don't have enough personnel.
>
> That is why there is only one nurse and orderly
> for every fifty patients.
>
> We are not responsible for the insufficient number
> of hospital beds or the lack of drugs.
>
> We demand that the government implement the
> provisions of the Gdańsk Agreement.
>
> We will not abandon our patients but should the
> government fail to act quickly, our union colleagues
> with a number of key industries will go on a Solidarity strike.

His grandmother asked to see the pastor and Konrad called the Augsburg-Lutheran Parish.

The pastor was sick and could not come. Sister Maria suggested a Catholic priest but Konrad still hoped that the pastor would recover and make it to his grandmother's bedside.

Their farewell took place later that evening. Julia was hallucinating. She recalled Sulejman Kryczyński, the captain of the Tatar Cavalry. She revealed that he was the man she had loved in her youth, before she married Robert; something that she had never mentioned before. Konrad and Bib stood over the hospital bed.

"Monte Cassino, pain, pain," the dying woman shrieked. "I want to go there," she whispered.

Bib leant over the bed. "Why?" he asked her in a gentle tone of voice.

"So many soldiers died at Monte Cassino," she gasped, clutching the sheet over her. "I want to be there."

Tears flew down Konrad's cheeks as he watched the last glimpses of Julia's consciousness slip away. She was pale and her breathing was rapid and irregular. "Monte Cassino, pain, pain," she cried.

Later on, she screamed but no words were uttered. Konrad rushed to the nurses station. "Please give her some morphine to kill the pain, please," he cried. "She is suffering so much."

"Eryk, Eryk," his grandmother started crying when he returned to her bed. "Is that you?"

"No, it's me, Konrad, Eryk's son," he gasped, trying to control his weeping. "Don't you recognize me, Babcia?" She did not respond.

The next day, Eryk, Bib and Konrad watched the unconscious woman from beside her bed. Her complexion was gray and her left hand waved erratically.

Konrad took out his Bible and started to read some verses out loud. He knelt in the hospital corridor.

Anka put a small cup of liquid tranquilizer into his hand. "Drink it. The nurse says it will only be minutes," she said.

By 9 P.M. Julia's breathing was shallow and erratic. Bib, Eryk and Konrad stood over her bed and watched her gasping suddenly stop.

The next morning, Konrad was with her again - just the two of them in the cold hospital mortuary. She lay in the coffin, dressed in her best black dress, one that she hadn't worn since her stroke. The large, brown crucifix hung on the wall above her head.

He began placing a few items in her coffin. Eryk had said that she would have wanted them with her: her husband's prayer book, a small picture of the Pope, and Konrad's own photograph. He also threaded a St. Mary of Ostra Brama medallion through the chain around her neck.

He kissed her cold forehead and looking down at her, he took a small bottle out of his bag and sprinkled some of her favourite cologne on her hair. Then he prayed and kissed her again.

Eventually, he closed the casket and nailed it with the copper nails he had brought.

He put the hammer back in his bag and heard a clinking sound. I forgot Robert's Virtuti Military Cross, he thought painfully. She wanted it with her too. He sighed and nailed the medal to the top of the coffin.

A chapel inside the Augsburg-Lutheran cemetery was gently lit with white candles. The pastor, dressed much like a Catholic priest, began the service in front of the coffin, which was showered with wreathes and bunches of cut flowers.

Konrad listened to him talk about Julia's life. He spoke well, but Konrad's mind wandered. Pre-war Poland in Wilno filled his mind. She had been only a teenager when her Poland became a free nation, and Julia's love for the country remained with her through the war, the occupation of the Soviets and the Nazis and the signing of the Gdańsk Agreement. He remembered her joyful reaction, 'We have won', and her tears.

His emotions were so intense that it seemed like all of his shared experiences with Julia rushed down upon him, like a storm descending. The pastor's words became barely audible and his head began swimming, drowning in memories.

He thought he heard the pastor praising his grandmother for her desire to die in the faith she was brought up in. There was also an expression of thanks to Sister Maria and the other nuns who had helped care for her through her illness.

Then he talked about her participation in the church choir before the war. "Let's listen to 'Ave Maria' now," he said in conclusion. "This is a song that Julia used to sing."

Agata had arranged for a woman to sing the aria at the funeral. When she finished, the organ sounded and the funeral march filled the chapel. Only then did he cry. He realized that his duty to her was the one thing in his life which he took some pride from, and that it was ending then, at the simple oak coffin.

The pallbearers knelt on both sides of the catafalque, in front of the statue of Jesus Christ. The effigy's arms were spread out, as if he was welcoming a child into his Kingdom.

The dark-suited men rose, picked up the coffin, and carried it to the graveyard.

WITOLD UŁAN

P A R T

4

Hope

CHAPTER 1

Konrad set his hot coffee mug down on the desk in his bedroom. It was cluttered with a few copies of Newsweek magazine, English dictionaries and a Solidarity bulletin, the one Janek had given him just the day before. It was only 6:00 in the morning and Eryk was safely on the bus.· He had almost an hour to just sit, relax and read.

The pamphlet bore the now familiar red 'Solidarność' title. Below a summary of the 21 points of the Gdańsk Agreement, he noticed the words, *'Independent Self-Governed Labour Union Solidarity – guidelines for the establishment of committees'*. The pamphlet acknowledged that blue collar workers negotiated the three agreements signed by the government, but that everyone: teachers, doctors, nurses, engineers, pensioners... would be welcomed into the union. "The new union has to have a national character to reflect this."

The next paragraph explained the basic tenets of the union program, the crucial elements of the future Solidarity Union Charter. *'As you read this, your colleagues - the workers and intellectuals who advise the KKP Country's Commission[1] are working on the Charter. When it is completed, it will be filed in the District Court of Warsaw so that our trade union will be officially registered.'* The title, 'Country's Commission,' attracted his attention. The words 'committee' and 'national', had been skillfully avoided. They were words, which had been flaunted all too often by the Party and the government.

Konrad glanced at his watch. He still had another twenty minutes. He opened the red and white brochure and continued reading about the proposed structure of the union. 'Solidarity' was in essence a federation of free trade unions, organized along regional lines. Regional Chapter offices would be located in major cities and in areas where there had been a significant amount of strike activity in August 1980. They would be autonomous organizations with the authority to proclaim a strike on their own. As he read further, Konrad learned that chapter chairmen, who were democratically elected by the regional membership, would automatically become participants in Solidarity's highest body – the Country's Commission for Consensus or KKP. The head of

---

1. KKP - Polish acronym - Krajowa Komisja Porozumiewawcza - word for word: Country's Commission for [achieving] Consensus. It was the official name of Solidarity's National Council. It was to maintain liaison between Solidarity Chapters all over the country.

the executive committee of the KKP, was its chairman, Lech Wałęsa.

He began skimming through the text. The second last paragraph explained that major trades and professions like miners, teachers and health service employees, would be allowed to form their own union within the Solidarity federation. He set the leaflet down for a moment and pondered its contents, marvelling at the way everything, down to the last detail, had been worked out logically and coherently. This realization was encouraging.

"Konrad... you have to go now," Agata said. Still dressed in her nightgown, his great-aunt stood at the doorway and yawned.

"I know, go back to bed," he told her and glanced at his watch. It was 6:55 and there was still the last paragraph to read. *"Solidarity was born out of the protest of the Polish workers against injustices, totalitarianism and inefficiency. Our day-to-day duty is the protection of all employees to ensure that everyone has a decent standard of living and personal freedom. Our ultimate goal is the transformation of the Polish People's Republic into a self-governed Republic – a free and democratic society which will help in the building of a just and self-supporting nation.*

Join 'Solidarity' today. By democratically electing our leaders, we hope to resurrect Poland's grandiose tradition of tolerance and democracy. 'Solidarity' is an organization for every Pole of good will. Everybody will be given a chance in a self-governed society."

Konrad walked slowly through the park across from his office, stepping over hundreds of gold and red leaves littering the ground. He almost bumped into a couple rushing to catch a streetcar. The two were laughing and frolicking. He smiled as they ran past him. Seeing jubilation of that kind was common during the autumn of 1980. It was as if a great weight had been lifted off peoples' shoulders. They talked openly in the streets about politics; there was constant laughter, and, for the first time in many years, expectations about the future were optimistic.

Everyone waited for more news from the north of the country. The Solidarity Charter was rumoured to be completed. Varsovians anxiously awaited Lech Wałęsa, Bogdan Lis, Andrzej Gwiazda and other Solidarity officials to bring it to the city for registration at the district court.

Sometimes, the extent of the recent changes overwhelmed Konrad. In June, and even July, 'Gierek's machine' still appeared to be in control, but by September, Edward Gierek no longer held the position of First Secretary. Six days after the agreement in Gdańsk, the media reported that he had resigned from that post, and from the Politburo, claiming deteriorating health. Gomułka had tried to save face the same way, back in 1970.

If Gierek's departure from the Central Committee was relatively painless, the same couldn't be said for Poland's Sejm. M.P.'s: Gierek, Prime Minister Babiuch and their other cronies were literally expelled from the parliament.

Konrad sat beside Adam Babinicz's desk. The two men were sipping their coffee, smoking, and pursuing their favourite topic of conversation - politics. Konrad was curious if Adam knew anything about the newly-appointed First Secretary, Stanisław Kania, and the Premier, Józef Pińkowski.

"I don't know much about Pińkowski," Adam replied, "but Kania might not be a bad choice. He doesn't have a villa or a Mercedes, like Gierek's men. He is also a close friend of Wojciech Fiszbach. Have you heard of him?"

Fiszbach was the First Secretary of the Party's Committee in Gdańsk. He lived in an ordinary apartment and drove the cheapest car available in the country – the Fiat 126. Even more intriguing was the man's behaviour at the time of the August strikes in Gdańsk. During the worker sit-ins, he urged negotiation, not force.

"Fiszbach might be all right," Konrad said, with a careless shrug, "but Kania? He's a terrible speaker." With a smile, he forcefully extinguished his cigarette and jumped out of his chair. "Humpph, comrades and citizens," he said sternly, imitating Kania's well-known stuttering manner. "... Poland's economic and social situation has deteriorated during the last decade. But," he said, shaking his forefinger in Adam's face, "it was not, let us stress, because of Socialism... humpph... on the contrary, it occurred because our former leaders abandoned their Socialist principles. The Party has recognized this, and is now at the helm of the Socialist renewal. We will work to regain our credibility and maintain our contact with the masses... Poland's renewal is a Socialist renewal, comrades." Konrad sat down, quite pleased with his performance. Roman couldn't have done better, he thought to himself.

Adam laughed loudly during the entire performance, but as Konrad sat down, he noticed his friend's smile transform into a grimace. "Things haven't changed much, have they?" Adam remarked bitterly. "The workers go through the ordeal and the Party takes credit for it. Two months ago, the word renewal was never mentioned. Now they're at the 'helm' and they call the changes. Socialist."

Konrad gripped the edge of Adam's desk. "They talk about liaison with the people. Well, Wałęsa and his guys don't need that... they are the people, they are us," he said excitedly. "Why do we need the Party at all?" He sat back in his chair and waited, confident that Adam would reaffirm his anti-Party sentiments. Instead, his co-worker remained mysteriously silent, and stared vacantly at the bare wall in front of him.

"The enthusiasm for Socialist renewal in Poland might not be as stupid as you think," he said finally, in a grave tone of voice. "Do you know that Polish tourists have been banned from all Socialist countries except Hungary, or that sixty Soviet divisions are surrounding us from the east, west and south?" He paused, giving Konrad an anxious glance. "Don't you see," he continued, "that we do need the Party? We must use it to continue the revolution – as a screen. Just think what happened to Hungary and Czechoslovakia. The Soviets came only after the Party itself went astray. Yes, we need the Polish United Workers' Party, Konrad. Nice and strong on the outside, but weak compared to Solidarity. We need a union which is strong enough to force the government to implement the reforms we want." His eyes gleamed. "The truth will surface whether the Party wants it or not. The process is irreversible..."

The eighty percent of Budal employees who had joined the newly-formed Solidarity Local, voted for their representatives by secret ballot. Four people were selected for the positions of Chairman, Vice-Chairmen and Treasurer.

Konrad hoped that the Chairman's position would be filled by a non-partisan person, his own age. Someone who was too young to remember the dreary days of Stalin's terror, and not burdened with the weight of fear felt by his parents. That breed was the driving force behind the walk-outs in mid-August.

He smiled when it was announced that Wojtek Buliński, a man just three years older than himself, would be the new chairman. He fit the image of the new union with his tall, determined stance, straightforward blue eyes, and aggressive manner.

Adam Babinicz collected thirty fewer votes and he, along with Małgosia Karska were named Vice-Chairmen. Surprisingly enough, Zyzio Król, the former head of the old union, joined and was elected Treasurer. The twenty percent of the staff who refused to vote for Solidarity were astounded. They had assumed that Zyzio would stay on, and head their union. "What do you mean, you have registered with Solidarity?" Wiesław Smrodziński asked. His eyes revealed genuine stupefaction. Zyzio laughed right at him.

"Well, you seem to be in a good mood, Konrad," Adam remarked after he tapped him on the shoulder. "You're daydreaming with a big smile on your face."

"I was just thinking about our union meeting..."

Adam smiled and dumped a bundle of newspapers on his desk. "There's no time for dreaming, Konrad."

"What's this?"

"I just came from Szpitalna Street. That's where the Solidarność-Mazowsze[2] regional office is located. These," he said, pointing at the desk, "are the local newspapers of Mazowsze Region – The Daily News[3] and The Independence[4]. The newspapers are edited and printed by the union staff right there and immediately distributed to enterprises and factories. They are legal and completely free of censorship. And you should see the Union members working at the office. Most of them are fairly young people; you would be considered old, Konrad. They're marvelous, young workers, students..."

Konrad shared Adam's excitement about the Mazowsze papers but he was still anxious to see the national Solidarity newspaper that was promised after the Gdańsk Agreement. Adam shook his head.

"These aren't going to supersede our national Solidarity journal. But remember, the national Solidarity paper will still be subject to censorship, which, let's hope, won't be too harsh. These papers are the beginning of the truth. We have all waited much too long for this..."

Hundreds of people gathered in front of the dreary building complex housing Warsaw's courts. Konrad looked up at the inscription engraved above

2. Mazowsze - a geographical region of Poland which includes Warsaw and surroundings.

3. "The Daily News" was the first, censorship free, official publication in Poland. It was edited by Antoni Macierewicz, a Catholic activist, later an Advisor to Lech Wałęsa. In 1991 - 1992 he was a Minister of Internal Affairs.

4. "The Independence" was the second, censorship free, official publication in Poland. It was edited by Adam Michnik, an opposition leader since 1968, a member of KOR. Michnik was Macierewicz's opponent. Since 1989 he has been an Editor in Chief of "Gazeta Wyborcza", the first free daily in Poland.

the entrance: *'Justice is the foundation of a Republic'*. A young man beside him pointed at the quotation: "We'll soon see if that tenet means anything," he said. "So far, the judge has acted like a paid attorney for the Party... he has to be impartial."

Many people in the crowd, including Konrad, nodded in agreement. The Union had filed all the necessary documents for registration but the court was proceeding cautiously. The government was concerned that 'Solidarity' might become a 'political organization' and cease to recognize the leading role of the Communist Party. During the negotiations in August, the striking workers pledged that they would not violate either of the two conditions, but the court insisted that they be included in the Charter.

The local union newspapers responded quickly with an outburst of angry editorials. "The Gdańsk Agreement provides for all the guarantees that are required and it is an inherent part of the Union constitution. The court is seeking something other than a formalization of the commitment. We cannot agree to be legally subject to the Party's control. If we do that, we will become just another pseudo-union in a pseudo-republic..."

After weeks of demonstrating and waiting, some of the protesters began to doubt Lech Wałęsa's ability to stand up to the court officials. Konrad heard one of them expressing those fears. "Lechu is being too lenient with those bastards. There they are, sitting in the courtroom. Why bother? We should walk out first and then talk to the S.O.B.'s."

It was an unsmiling group of Solidarity representatives who finally emerged from the courthouse. Wałęsa, wearing a button with a picture of the Black Madonna pinned to his lapel, looked down at the crowd, with an expression of quiet defiance on his face. "Ladies and gentlemen," he cried, "Solidarity is registered but the Charter has been reworded. Our Union cannot accept this..."

"Lechu, Lechu!" the thousands of supporters chanted. "Let's go on strike... let's show them once more." Wałęsa climbed up on to an improvised podium and faced them. "Ladies and Gentlemen," he shouted. "We do not accept the modification of our Charter. We think it is illegal. But that doesn't mean that we have to go on strike. My friends and I have always fought for law and justice. The legal system of our country does recognize the process of appeal to a higher court. We will appeal this ruling in the Supreme Court of Poland."

Soon after, downtown buildings were plastered with union posters. Every wall, even the city streetcars, bore the white and red slogans, "We demand registration, not edition."

Two days later, in an official government communiqué, it was announced over national television that the Supreme Court of the country had registered the Charter in its original form.

A very agitated Agata greeted Konrad when he returned home from work the next day. "I am so glad that you are back, Konrad," she said, wringing her hands together. She closed the front door tightly and motioned to him to follow her into the kitchen.

"I am worried about you and Eryk," she said, lowering her voice to barely a whisper. "They are going to come..."

Konrad managed to get her to sit down at the kitchen table with him. "Now, who is going to come?" he asked.

Eryk, who overheard their conversation from his bedroom, walked into the kitchen and patted his aunt on the shoulder. "Agata is worried that the Soviets will invade and kill everyone in Solidarity," he explained with a chuckle.

"You laugh like an idiot," Agata shouted at him, "but you listen to this. Mr. Klepka, here in the building, told me that Solidarity had stolen a secret government document. He says the Soviets won't stand for it."

Konrad gently chastized his great-aunt for talking to Klepka who served with ZOMO riot police, and then he turned to his father. Eryk told him that the Union had managed to get a copy of a ministerial document issued by the Attorney General to district prosecutors. "At a union meeting today, we were told that the thing reads like an instruction bulletin," he said. "It tells them how to put people in jail when there are no legal grounds for their imprisonment." He then went on to tell Konrad and Agata how the document was obtained. A Solidarity member employed in the Attorney General's office had managed to xerox the document and deliver it to another Union member in the Solidarity printing department who had it copied in bulk. Both men had been arrested and were being charged with treason.

"The regional Solidarity chapter in Mazowsze has proclaimed a strike at the Ursus tractor factory. It may eventually turn into a regional strike," Eryk added excitedly.

Konrad glanced at his father. Eryk hadn't had a drink for over three months and the effects were obvious. He had put on some weight, his eyes were clear and perceptive, and his complexion looked healthy.

Eryk urged Konrad to turn the television on. The Ursus sit-in turned out to be the major news of the day.

"The TV Daily is now going to interview the head of the strike committee, the chairman of Mazowsze's Solidarity chapter, Zbigniew Bujak..." a tall, clean-cut reporter announced.

The strike leader emerged from the factory building wearing a dark, unassuming sports jacket, white shirt and a tie liberally loosened around the neck. The reporter pushed a microphone into the strike leader's face. Bujak, a former electrical technician with Ursus, quickly got down to business. He proved to be an eloquent representative for the workers.

"Mr. Bujak... could you tell me why the employees here are refusing to go back to work?" the newsman asked.

"Ursus workers put down their tools at our request, and they will remain on strike until both men are released," Bujak answered resolutely. "Solidarity means all for one and one for all," he added with a flourish.

The reporter persisted. "But do you realize that Sapeło and Narożniak have broken the law by stealing and trying to publish a classified document?"

Bujak smiled. "Have you read the document yet, sir?"

"Well - no, I haven't," the reporter replied with frustration.

"Then I advise you to read it. It will be available at your Solidarity Local by tomorrow. After that, everything will be seen in a more appropriate light."

The journalist sighed. "Do you deny, Mr. Bujak, that the Union has stolen a secret government document?"

Bujak's response was cool and calculated. "We are in possession of a document which was at one time classified 'secret', but after tomorrow, it will not be secret any longer. We hope that such 'secrets' will cease to exist in the future. The very fact that such a document was issued is a crime, not the attempt to make it public."

Wojtek Buliński and Adam Babinicz handed out copies of the xeroxed document to all of Budal's employees the next day. "*It is important to know the correct approach when dealing with a dissident who has done nothing to justify charge and arrest. First of all, it is crucial to differentiate right at the start, whether the person is an inexperienced or an experienced dissident. The former can be threatened very easily. One could tell him/her that any printed material he possesses constitutes a criminal offence and he could be arrested and held for some time without any fear of repercussions.*

The latter, however, is likely to know his/her rights. The preferred way to deal with this person is harassment. Anyone can be jailed for up to 48 hours without charge. It is recommended, therefore, that such an individual be detained for two days and then released. He will of course be trailed and then jailed shortly after. One more important note. It is not necessary to rush with your dissident. Let him or her relax, have a coffee and something to eat, then re-arrest him. This practice has been used successfully in the past..."

Konrad burst into laughter and threw the document across the room.

On December 16th, 1980, ten years after the pavement in Gdańsk, Gdynia and Szczecin was splashed with workers' blood, Solidarity unveiled the commemorative monument which had been promised during negotiations which preceeded the Gdańsk Agreement.

December, 1970. Gdańsk was smothered with tear gas and smoke; machine guns rattled in the harbour city. Its sister town, Gdynia, was still relatively calm, though workers from its main shipyard were on strike. The First Secretary of the District Party Committee, Stanisław Kociołek, pleaded with the workers, asking them to return to the shipyard and initiate discussion together, peacefully.

Many workers agreed to comply, and although armoured cars surrounded the shipyard gate, they walked toward the complex undaunted, the words of Kociołek still ringing in their ears. But then, they were replaced by the sound of approaching helicopters, and then of rifles shooting at them from above.

A lunchbag fell on the bloodied pavement, just a meter from the body of its owner, a young shipyard apprentice. The workers dispersed, two returning minutes later to fetch the boy's body. Others joined them as they wrapped the corpse in a Polish flag and raised it above their heads and began marching toward the City Hall, singing the national anthem.

In Gdańsk, demonstrators retaliated for the bullets by burning the District Party Committee building. Curfew was enforced by tanks and armoured personnel carriers stationed at each major intersection.

Konrad knew that he had to come to Gdańsk on the tenth anniversary of those events. Two tears began rolling down his cheeks as he looked up at the towering monument, in front of the shipyard – three solid concrete crosses aimed toward the darkening sky, bare except for the representations of anchors which hung from each of them, as if crucified.

Thousands of candles flickered in the evening breeze as the mourners listened to the chanting of Wałęsa. "The Lord shall give power to his people The Lord will grant his people the blessing of peace."

Czesław Miłosz's[5] poetry was engraved on a plaque on the front of the monument.

> 'You who did wrong to a simple man
> Burst into laughter at his injury
> Do not feel safe, the Poet remembers
> [Yes] you can kill him, a new will be born
> The talks and deeds [of yours] he'll record.'

December, 1980...

---

5. Czesław Miłosz - a Nobel Prize winner for literature in 1980. Miłosz left Poland in the 'Fifties and now lives in the United States.

CHAPTER 2

With the first snow of the winter, Konrad always thought of Christmas. It didn't matter if the snow melted and disappeared without a trace. The sudden contrast between the seasons calmed his soul. Carols started to go through his head and he thought of his family gathered around the dinner table on Christmas Eve. It would be their first Christmas without Julia. Agata talked about it all the time. "The holidays without her... they won't be holidays," she repeated. Often, she would stand at the doorway of Julia's old room, looking sadly at the small sofa which had taken the place of her sister's bed.

Konrad felt satisfied about one thing that year. As the end of 1980 approached, Eryk was still getting up every morning and going to work. Konrad continued to call him every day at the office and his father was always there.

He felt a bond developing between them. It was fragile and couldn't be well defined, yet it existed. Despite his loud protestations, Eryk willingly submitted to Konrad's care, even if it was initially just a policing of his movements.

Before his last prison term, the only people who took any interest in his welfare were his parents and Agata, but they were elderly and not strong enough to shield Eryk from his own weaknesses. With Konrad's help, he had become a contributing member of the family again. He had a job and he didn't have to worry when someone rang the doorbell. All of his creditors were satisfied.

When he returned home after his monthly Solidarity meeting, he was in a very talkative mood. "Our Local just tabled a resolution to have our director fired," he told his family with satisfaction.

"Why?" Agata asked. Her eyes blinked with amazement and Eryk laughed.

"... Because of the summer cottages," he explained. The union that had been in place before Solidarity came along, owned a summer resort, a number of small cabins in a picturesque spot beside the upper Vistula river. Most of the company's employees spent their vacation at the resort, and their union dues were supposed to be used for its purchase and upkeep. During the past year, it was discovered that the company director and the head of the old union had built themselves weekend cottages near Warsaw with some of the money.

According to Eryk, the summer resort was still under the control of the defunct union. "We want them dismissed, tried and the cottages along with the resort turned over to Solidarity."

Meat was being rationed by the government, and was hard to get despite a food coupon system. 'Solidarity' itself had proposed rationing to put an end to the enormous queues in the stores. Many people thought that the idea would have worked fine if only the government had supplied enough food. Instead, people holding meat coupons in addition to money, formed lines in the streets waiting for supplies to arrive while Wałęsa and other Union leaders threatened strike action if the food situation didn't improve.

Just before Christmas, some meat and fish were delivered to the stores and Agata, with Konrad's help, was able to prepare carp in jelly for a traditional Christmas Eve dinner. It took hours to complete the recipe. Wrapped in an overly large, blue apron, and wielding an enormous butcher knife, the stooped, gray-haired woman moved swiftly between the kitchen sink and table, which was scattered with peeled onions, carrots and morsels of fish. When the entire meal was prepared, Eryk brought in a tall, natural spruce tree and set it up in one corner of the living room.

Seated at the round dining table, which was covered with the well starched, white tablecloth, the family divided up the wafer[6] and wished each other happiness. From time to time as they made their way through the meal, they would glance at the stately evergreen adorned with silvery tinsel and a collection of colourful Christmas globes and Santa decorations, all made by Julia. Two miniature Polish soldiers, dressed in uniforms lined with rows of brass buttons, presented their sabers and rifles, standing on guard at the paper Christmas stable at the foot of the tree.

Following dessert, which consisted of fruit stew and poppy seed cake, they exchanged gifts. Konrad had sweets and cologne for Agata and Anka, and a neck-tie for Bib. Eryk was delighted by a wool sweater, a black Ronson lighter and a carton of Pall Mall cigarettes, his favourites.

As he watched his father proudly displaying his new sweater for the rest of the family, Konrad was reminded of their afternoon together at the Berentowicz restaurant, years before. He had trouble believing that it had been twenty years since Eryk and Tina divorced. He remembered jumping out of his father's car and following him into the restaurant. Eryk was wearing expensive sunglasses and a tailor-made suit from Germany. The waitress at the restaurant greeted them with a cheerful smile and had complemented his father. "...Always in a beautiful car and always so elegantly dressed..." he recalled her saying.

Konrad looked over to his now gray-haired father holding his new, black lighter. He was fingering its smooth finish. "Thank you, Konrad." He bent over and kissed him. "This is really what I needed." Eryk tossed his old, unreliable nickel lighter into the garbage can.

---

6. Wafer - according to Polish tradition, sheets of wafer blessed by a priest, are shared by the participants of Christmas Eve dinner before the meal begins. This is not, however, a sacramental communion.

Three hundred thousand Soviet troops sat alongside the Polish borders that winter and the people were anxious. "Will they come?" everyone asked. The optimists said no. "We have two Poles in the American Administration[7]. The Russians wouldn't dare," they contended.

"But Carter is a lame duck, the new Administration is coming and the Soviets may try to benefit from the transition in the White House," others argued.

Some young workers and students reacted with boldness. "Let them come. We have enough bottles for Mołotov cocktails."

More food items were being rationed, and queues in the streets lengthened daily.

Małgosia Karska sighed. "I am so exhausted... I wish we could get our Saturdays off," she complained to Konrad. He nodded in agreement and looked at the young woman with sympathy. She had dark, purplish circles under her eyes and her hair was beginning to turn gray. He knew Małgosia had two children and that her husband Mietek, an electrician, had to moonlight every day after work to feed his family.

"What is our life like?" Małgosia added, as she plugged an electric kettle into the wall outlet near his desk. "I queue until seven o'clock every night... then I take Beata and Józio from the kindergarten. We eat supper at 9:00 when Mietek comes home. On Sundays, the most we can do is go to church..." The kettle began rumbling loudly and Małgosia poured steaming water over the tea leaves in their mugs. Then she smiled briefly and opened the cabinet beside her desk. Konrad looked at her with surprise as she passed him a piece of delicious-looking cake.

"I baked it yesterday, after my medical appointment," she explained with a whisper.

A five-day work week was one of the points agreed upon in Gdańsk, but it did not materialize. The government seemed content to talk a lot about the Socialist renewal and do little.

"They're trying to handle the current situation just as they did in 1971..." Konrad complained to his father.

Eryk nodded. "I remember too," he said. "When Gierek became First Secretary, there were many words... many promises... and then, all of a sudden, the Party regained full control and discussion with the people ceased."

Wałęsa and other Solidarity leaders had assumed that the Gdańsk Agreement would be implemented gradually, point by point. The government, however, insisted on further discussions between the Union leaders and the government Commission for Trade Unions.

"In two days time, Vice-Premier Rakowski will be meeting with the leaders of the Independent Self-governed Labour Union Solidarity," TV Daily reported. "The issue of work-free Saturdays will be on the agenda."

Konrad, Agata and Eryk sat in the living room and watched a journalist interview varsovians along the busy Marszałkowska street about the meeting.

---

7. Edmund Muskie was a Secretary of State in Jimmy Carter's Administration in 1980. Zbigniew Brzeziński was a National Security Adviser.

It was a bitter, cold day and banks of shovelled snow crowded the sidewalks. The reporter stepped in front of a short man in his early fifties and introduced himself. "Excuse me, sir... what do you think of the planned discussion between Rakowski and Wałęsa?" The camera focused in on the man's expensive sheepskin coat and round face. He hesitated and then began yelling into the microphone, "I think that the government should rule and stop Solidarity from meddling in politics. Their place is in the factories urging employees to work and not just demand..."

Agata uttered an abrupt snort, lifted her arms up in exasperation and left the room. Konrad also reacted with a groan. "Did you hear that, Eryk?"

He was about to switch the television off but his father asked him to wait. They watched as puffs of white steam trailed from the reporter's mouth as he approached a young, thin woman who was leading two children down the street. "... And what do you think about the Rakowski - Wałęsa meeting, madam?" he asked. Her children smiled mischievously and immediately began making faces into the camera. Telling them to behave, she turned to the microphone. "We were supposed to get all of our Saturdays off when the government signed the Gdańsk Agreement," she snapped. "But the Party and the government in this country tell you one thing and then do another. I don't think Lechu should even bother talking to Mr. Rakowski. We should go on strike or they won't give us anything..."

Eryk chuckled. "You see, Konrad... that woman knows what she's talking about."

Konrad nodded. There was no doubt that the TV Daily and other shows on Polish television were beginning to reflect the situation in the country. The government was shaky, the new Premier not very convincing, and the First Secretary was essentially dovish and he seemed determined to allow some limited reforms.

When the discussion on the five-day work week began, millions of Poles watched the events on television. There was an obvious bias of the government media to discredit Solidarity's representatives and favour Rakowski. The Vice-Premier was portrayed as a decent, deeply humanitarian intellectual, who was sincerely concerned about the country and its future. His broad face, lined with wrinkles, appeared solemn and very calm as he greeted Lech Wałęsa in his office.

"Now, Mr. Chairman," Rakowski said with a smile, "let's be realistic about this issue."

The television camera moved on to the familiar face with the long, drooping mustache. "I would be delighted, Mr. Vice-Premier," the Union leader answered. "I have been a realist all my life."

"Well, I am pleased to hear that, Mr. Wałęsa. That will facilitate an agreement," Rakowski said, and encouraged the Solidarity leader to sit down.

The two men faced each other at the Vice-Premier's conference table. Wałęsa placed his hands flat on the table in front of him. "As far as I know, an agreement between us exists already. It was signed in Gdańsk four months ago," he commented.

"Yes," Rakowski answered quietly, "but we have to agree on the particulars, don't we?"

"You are forgetting that the agreement the government signed went into great detail," Wałęsa responded. "Let me refresh your memory." He reached inside his briefcase and put a copy of the Gdańsk Agreement down on the table.

"Point Number 21: To make Saturday a holiday. In those factories where there is round-the-clock production, Saturday labour must be compensated for by a commensurate increase in the number of holidays, or through the establishment of another day off in the week. It has been agreed that the principle of all Saturdays off is to be put into effect, or another method of providing time off should be worked out by the government by December 31, 1980. The measures should include an increase in the number of work-free Saturdays from the start of 1981, unquote." Wałęsa paused momentarily. "We have reached 1981, Mr. Vice-Premier, and you were supposed to have this plan ready by now. What is your proposal?"

Rakowski looked at Wałęsa with reluctance. "You have promised to be reasonable, Mr. Chairman," he said.

"Yes."

"We propose a postponement of the implementation of the five-day work week until the economy recovers. However, we do recognize the need for granting every other Saturday off. What do you say to that, Mr. Chairman?"

Eryk whistled at Rakowski's remark. "With him at the helm, the economy isn't likely to pick up until after my retirement..." he commented. The TV screen showed Wałęsa picking up his briefcase in readiness to leave the room. He indicated that he had to consult with other members of the KKP executive before responding to Rakowski's proposal. The television camera then focused in on the bearded face of Andrzej Gwiazda, as he and other Solidarity leaders accompanied Wałęsa into an adjacent room. They returned ten minutes later and an unsmiling Lech Wałęsa approached Rakowski and sat down.

"Our decision is unanimous," he announced in a matter-of-fact manner. "Your proposal contravenes the Gdańsk Agreement. You have not tabled a plan to implement a five-day work week. Instead, you have proposed that we wait until the economy recovers. However, there is no such provision included in the document your government signed with us in Gdańsk. Let me remind you that we are not responsible for this country's disastrous economic state. Rather, you or the government you have served, Mr. Vice-Premier." Wałęsa paused to clear his throat. "You have also neglected to specify a time frame for a full guarantee of four Saturdays off per month. As such, your proposal has been rejected by the Union represented here by the Presidium of the KKP. Thank you, Mr. Vice-Premier." Wałęsa collected his papers and stood up, ready to leave the room once again.

"Mr. Chairman," Rakowski said calmly, attempting to restrain a hint of a grimace on his face. "Why are you not willing to discuss the proposal in realistic terms? This is a fair proposal..."

Wałęsa shrugged in response. "It is not fair. If it had been, we would have accepted it."

"But we should discuss it, Mr. Chairman. For the benefit of our countrymen, let us discuss it," Rakowski said, as he leant across the table and pushed his face closer to Wałęsa.

"If I stay, will you modify your proposal?" Wałęsa asked.

"The proposal is fair, Mr. Chairman. We will discuss its implementation. Are you willing to talk?"

Wałęsa, who up until that point had managed to control his temper, glared at the Vice-Premier. "Yes," he answered firmly, "but it will be a very short talk as far as I am concerned. Yes, no, end of discussion. Thank you, gentlemen."

A propaganda blitz on Polish Television and in the hard-line Communist newspapers, portrayed Solidarity's leaders as a bunch of militant extremists. They were blamed for the breakdown in 'meaningful negotiations'. This coverage was countered in the Solidarity press across the country.

The Union informed its membership that until the government was willing to offer a fair proposal, all Saturdays were to be treated as holidays, starting the following weekend.

Engineer Smrodziński assembled his employees at Budal on Friday. "I hope everybody is going to be in tomorrow," he remarked eyeing them closely.

"You can come in, sir, you're not a member of Solidarity," Konrad said. The images of Lech Wałęsa confronting Rakowski were still fresh in his mind, and seemed to lessen his usual apprehensiveness.

His boss' sparrow-like eyes widened in disbelief. "Does that mean that you aren't coming?"

"I don't think there will be many people here tomorrow," Konrad replied.

Smrodziński looked around the room nervously. "Is Mr. Dymowski speaking for all of you when he says this?"

Waldek Marciniuk reacted to his boss' question by bursting into laughter and leaving the room.

"There's no question as far as I am concerned," Maks answered, looking squarely at his superior. "Tomorrow is Saturday and all Saturdays are deemed to be holidays. All members of Solidarity are going to follow their Union's directive."

Smrodziński's hands trembled as he turned to Konrad. "Do you realize that the government pays you, not the union?" he shouted.

Konrad responded to his boss' challenge with equal vigour, his confidence bolstered up by his co-worker's support. "Do you have any idea, Mr. Smrodziński, what a trade union is all about? It is an organization to help an employee in his quest for fair treatment by his employer. In this struggle, union members might be asked to defy their employers, which in our case is the government."

"And you want to work abroad...?" Smrodziński shrieked. "After what you just said... unbelievable."

"You should watch what you are saying, Mr. Smrodziński," Maks warned. "I think you are still living in a different world than the rest of us. The Gdańsk Agreement states that promotion should depend on an individual's abilities not his Party or union affiliation. Konrad is a good worker, his English is excellent, why shouldn't he be sent abroad?"

The following day, engineer Smrodziński was the only person to show up in their department.

After a few weeks, the government tabled a modified proposal. Three Saturdays off per month were granted, along with a provision for year round five-day work weeks in the future.

"So what now?" Konrad asked Adam Babinicz a few days after the issue was resolved.

Adam smiled and patted him on the shoulder. "Let's go into the lobby and talk," he said. The two men sat down in the same armchairs they had used during their first conversation four months before. As they lit their cigarettes, Konrad recalled how he had doubted the other man's sincerity. During a recent visit with Janek and his family, he had learned that Budal-Solidarity's vice-chairman was not only well known, but highly respected in Gdańsk.

"Now, tell me how you feel about the economy?" Adam asked.

"The food rationing system isn't working at all. There seems to be less and less food in the stores."

Adam nodded and puffed on his cigarette. Then he sat forward in his chair and looked straight into Konrad's face.

"We have many important things to achieve still," he said firmly. "First, production planning must be decentralized and the Party's monopoly on the appointment of directors and managers has to be stopped. If not, the lines will only get longer..."

"There are so many ifs, aren't there?" Konrad said with a sigh. "What is the solution? Capitalism, right here beside the Soviet border?"

"No, something much simpler," Adam answered laughing.

"But what precisely?"

"A pluralistic society," Adam answered decisively. "We need a well managed economy with publicly-owned enterprises which would be subject to market forces, and the goods would be distributed in stores, not kept for those privileged through a quota system... We want political pluralism as well," he continued. "Take the trade unions, for example. We have Solidarity but that doesn't mean there isn't room for the old branch unions and the autonomous unions for special-interest trades. This creates competition and we have multiple viewpoints. Do you know what that would mean?"

"Well..."

"It would be democracy," Babinicz said. "Even some Party members are becoming attracted to the idea. Take me, for example," he said with a wink. They both laughed.

Adam was right. Hundreds of thousands of Party rank and file joined Solidarity. Initially, the government hoped that these people would help to control the Union but as it turned out, most of them joined in good faith. Instead of trying to influence Solidarity with Communist dogma, they wanted the Party changed, reshaped in the democratic mode. Demands for the democratic election of the Party's Central Committee grew stronger.

Even the police (milicja), traditionally pillars of the Party's power, joined the drive toward reform. One group of policemen vowed to become the protectors of the people, not a blindfolded tool in the hands of the government, and they established their own union. Its certification was refused in court and its members fired, but Solidarity pledged to support the Union of Police Officers.

Shortly after 8:00 A.M. one morning, Konrad's office telephone rang. It was Adam Babinicz. "Do you want to join me at the Regional Union meeting today?" he asked. "I'll make sure that I talk to your boss about it. I think you should come with me..."

Adam's car travelled along the highway connecting downtown Warsaw with the district of Ursus, a western suburb of the city. Ursus Tractor Factory was one of the first enterprises to respond to Solidarity's appeal for work on Saturdays. The tractors they assembled during the weekends were being sold directly to private farmers. "We're managing to by-pass the whole state distribution system. A member of Rural Solidarity's founding committee will be at the meeting. He is going to tell us about the farmers' problems..." Adam said.

Konrad sat back and then turned to Adam again. "I don't understand why we are not working on Saturdays. It isn't fair to the workers at Ursus."

Adam smiled. "You don't have to feel badly, Konrad. I have already spoken to Bujak about it."

"And what did he say?"

"He is a marvelous fellow, our Mazowsze leader," Adam said with admiration. "... He just tapped me on the shoulder and said, 'Adam... we appreciate your readiness, but it is not required. What do you manufacture in Budal? Papers, drawings? Solidarity is appealing to businesses which can produce goods to beef up our depleted market, especially agricultural articles. Why not let your people rest on Saturdays, and you can be sure that the workers won't feel bitter about it!"

They left the main highway and crossed over a set of snowy railroad tracks. Three story houses lined the road. The car pulled up in front of a movie theater. The building was covered with Polish and Solidarity banners. Adam and Konrad climbed up a flight of stairs and squeezed through the crowded entrance to the meeting hall.

A young worker in green coveralls greeted them at the entrance of the hall. "Your passes please." A large Solidarity badge was pinned to his lapel.

Konrad looked down at his own lapel pin. "Why passes?" he murmured. "I feel like I am in the army."

The young man chuckled. "I am sorry, but we must have security. We don't want any Secret Service agents in here."

Adam produced two passes stamped with the Solidarity seal.

"Well, Mr. Adam Babinicz and Mr. Konrad Dymowski – Budal, Solidarity Local 806. May I see your I.D.'s? Thank you."

The hall was jammed with people. Zbigniew Bujak mounted the stage. He was accompanied by a stout man in white shirt. Konrad guessed he was in his mid fifties.

The dark-haired Bujak picked up the microphone. "Good morning everyone. Why don't we start right away. I would like to introduce our friend, Stanisław Helski, a private farmer from Wałbrzych Region. He is just one of the people struggling to have Rural Solidarity registered. He is also a close friend of the Bartoszcze brothers, well known leaders of the farmers' union." Zbigniew Bujak handed the microphone over to Stanisław.

The farmer bowed and coughed to clear his throat, and then began to talk clearly and very quickly. "Who are we?... We are the Independent Self-Governed

Union of Individual Farmers 'Solidarity'. We are called 'Rural Solidarity' for short... Who do we represent? Three million private farmers who own about 80 percent of farmland in this country and produce almost all of the food... What do we want? First, we want our union to be certified. We also want fertilizers, seeds, building supplies and other implements of cultivation and husbandry that we need. We want them in sufficient quantities and we would like them to be priced in Polish złoty, not American dollars... We protest against the provision of the goods I just mentioned to state farms before private farmers. State farms account for only twenty percent of farmland and supply a negligible amount of all foodstuffs produced in the country, but they have been receiving preferential treatment by the Polish government at our expense..." The farmer paused and looked down at the crowd of Solidarity members. "What is our ultimate goal?" he asked. "To feed the nation adequately. Poland can be self-sufficient. Don't let anyone tell you otherwise."

Everyone in the room applauded and cheered. Stanisław Helski smiled openly. When the ovation subsided he approached the microphone again. "I would like to thank you for the three tractors that you supplied us with last week. I have brought letters from the farmers who bought them. They are very grateful and so am I - your work is not in vain."

Adam stood up. "I would like to know how the certification process is progressing?"

The farmer nodded. "Well... so far the court has refused to register our union on the grounds that private farmers are self-employed, and therefore not able to form unions. We have responded with hunger strikes and sit-ins throughout the country. There's not much they can do about us. You can't fire a farmer like they fired the police officers who were trying to unionize."

The audience responded with a loud ovation. Someone from the back of the room shouted, "How long are you going to maintain the sit-ins?"

"As long as it is required," Stanisław Helski answered gravely. "We are very stubborn Polish peasants, as you can see."

March arrived and with it the first important anniversary of 1981. There was a special session of parliament to commemorate the events which had happened thirteen years before. Then, students and intellectuals had demanded freedom of expression. Students Adam Michnik and Henryk Szlajfer were condemned as ringleaders, expelled from the university and imprisoned. Squads of police and ORMO volunteers had charged the demonstrators. Then newspapers reported that 'some workers had been forced to use batons on the students' who were allegedly being led by a handful of 'Zionist agitators'.

Konrad thought back to his own recollections of those days in March, 1968. Although he had only been in grammar school, he remembered being puzzled by the media coverage of the beatings. He still was. Sitting at his desk at Budal, he murmured, "Thirteen years ago, the press reported that the workers had used truncheons to beat the students. Don't policemen use clubs, not workers?"

"The students weren't beaten by the police at the beginning," Waldek Marciniuk remarked from the other side of the room. Puzzled by Waldek's comment, Konrad turned to him.

"What do you mean?" he asked.

"Just what I said," Waldek answered with a shrug. "I was a member of the Party back then. I joined three months before the protests began. My company director promised to send me to university part-time if I did. I was stupid and ambitious and I signed up."

Konrad shook his head again, and without saying a word, he pulled his chair closer to Waldek's desk.

"... On March 8th, in the morning, three SB-eks came to the office where I worked. They told us that the Jewish instigators took over the University of Warsaw. Then, all of the Party members were taken to a restaurant close to the university. We were all handed two large glasses of vodka and then one of the Secret Service guys asked us, 'What do you want, a nightstick or a belt?'

I didn't care. I just took a belt and followed the group as they walked over to the campus. The students were shouting, 'don't beat us, join us'. They also tried to give us some of their leaflets which explained why they had gathered there.

I didn't have any idea what I was doing, but before I knew it, the guys from my Party cell were shouting, 'beat the Jew' and charging at the protesters. The first blows those students received were from the drunk Party members from my office. It was later that the police and ORMO volunteers joined us.

A short, obese man I knew, began kicking a young pregnant woman furiously in the stomach. I just watched, I couldn't move. The woman was screaming, 'Why? Why?' and the man just laughed and shouted, 'That's your gift for International Women's Day, you bitch.'

I felt sick and ran away, throwing the belt into some bushes. The next day, I told my Party cell that I was quitting."

Waldek took a deep breath and sighed. His face had a slightly greenish tinge to it, as if he was reliving that feeling of revulsion and nausea all over again.

"At first they didn't accept my resignation," he added slowly. "but, after a month, I sent my membership card into the District Committee. They left me alone after that..."

Konrad remembered that even young, grammar school students weren't immune to the government's raving back then. He and his school friends had to attend a 'Citizens' Education' class given by the school principal. Zionism was the subject of instruction.

To Konrad, it seemed strange that the principal was involved with the anti-Jewish action. He was the same man who had summoned Tina to school about her son's anti-Semitic jokes three years earlier.

In March 1981, during a special session of the Polish Sejm, MP Gustaw Holoubek, a respected actor and theater director remarked, "Over 36 years of witch-hunting have marked the history of the Polish People's Republic. Beat the workers! Beat the students! Beat the Jews!..."

After work, Konrad made his way to the University of Warsaw campus, searching for the commemorative plaque erected on the 13th anniversary of the riots. The bronze tablet was shaped to resemble one of the folded student leaflets which had been handed out in March, 1968...

The resurrection of Jesus was celebrated with an unusual amount of enthusiasm that Easter, while fears of Soviet intervention became paranoid.

Konrad was terrified by an article he read in Newsweek which included a detailed attack scenario.

"Have you seen this?" he asked Eryk, pointing to a coloured map which depicted a series of red arrows pointed at major airports and garrisons in all three Polish military districts. He sat down and crossed his arms. "I tell you," he remarked, "I'm pissed off with the Americans. The article says they're just trying to figure out which division is going to attack first, instead of doing something…"

"What do you expect them to do?"

"President Reagan seems to mean business," Konrad said sternly. "Surely, he could, say, blockade Cuba and tell the Soviets to keep their fucking hands off Poland or else. After all, it's their duty to protect our freedom."

Eryk just laughed. "Who says so?" he asked.

"Don't you know what America stands for?" Konrad retorted. "America supports freedom and justice for all people, including our nation."

Eryk smiled sadly and shook his head.

"You are too much of an idealist. Nobody is going to go to war for Poland…"

CHAPTER 3

He was swimming through a black, slimy liquid. It felt cold and abominable. Captain Zabłocki cringed. His fatigues were constraining his motions but he didn't even consider taking them off. His uniform was the only thing protecting him from the sticky, icy fluid. He was about five metres from the shore, a steep muddy bank. He could see Colonel Gapa watching him from a jeep parked just by the edge of the ridge. Zabłocki sighed. I am lucky he's here, he thought. He can help me out... Just two more strokes and I'll be there.

"Włodek," Gapa yelled, jumping out of the jeep. "Hurry up."

He felt the muddy bottom of the lake in his hands. Its piercing cold shook his fingers. He stretched his hand up for Gapa... but nothing. The colonel was back in his jeep and two men were driving him away.

"Gapa, Gapa," he cried. "Don't leave me here... come back!"

"Pochyemoo krichish, Vołodya? Shto s toboy?"[8] his wife Emma asked. "Why are you crying? What has happened?" She lit the night lamp beside her and bent over her husband.

"Are you sick?"

Włodzimierz Zabłocki shook his head.

"No, I'm all right," he answered and reached for his cigarettes. "I just had a bad dream, that's all."

"Well, you should sleep," his wife said with a yawn. She turned over and pulled their comforter over her head.

He listened to her breathing deepen as she fell back to sleep. He sighed, put out the cigarette and flicked the light off. He lay on his back. The room was completely dark. For a second he thought he was back in the river once more. He put his hand up to his forehead. It was dripping with sweat.

Colonel Marek Gapa had been transferred to a secluded garrison in western Poland just two days earlier. The abrupt transfer was suspicious. Colonel Gapa had been the commander of the 17th Regiment for almost ten years. Zabłocki didn't say anything about it, but he sensed that it was just the beginning of something much more ominous. Their quiet garrison would not be immune. Marek Gapa was known to have had important connections with

---

8. These questions in Russian are explained further in the same sentence.

the former government and he had orchestrated Edward Gierek's triumphant visit to the garrison in the mid 'Seventies.

During the last days of February, 1981, the media attacked former First Secretary Gierek and his clique even more harshly. Zabłocki cringed when he heard of demands that they all go on trial.

Back in 1980, little had changed at the Regiment even after the resignation of Edward Gierek. Tight control over the garrison was maintained by regimental staff. Zabłocki remembered the day Gapa had summoned all of his officers together. It was a month after the signing of the Gdańsk Agreement. The colonel talked in his usual relaxed and self-confident manner, yet his face appeared strained and he sighed often. "Although the TV Daily has been watched by every draftee who has come into this regiment, this practice is being temporarily suspended," he said. "The television broadcasts contain too many references to Solidarity and other anti-Socialist phenomena. The TV Daily is no longer a proper tool for the political education of the soldiers of the People's Armed Forces. Any questions, comrades?"

Zabłocki smiled when he recalled captain Gugawa's reaction. The officer stood up and opened his mouth but not a word was uttered. He was so surprised that he remained in that position for over a minute. "What are we going to do... I mean what... with the soldiers... without the TV Daily?"

"We will all be conducting additional battlefield exercises every night," the colonel explained in a matter-of-fact tone of voice. "Starting today, we have trial alarms, long marches..."

Captain Gugawa's head dropped.

"Don't worry, comrade Captain," Marek Gapa said in an effort to reassure him. "This might cost us some extra effort now... but we have to keep the boys from hearing that shit. Ever since the 'renewal', the TV Daily has gone haywire. But, it won't last long. Remember 1956 and 1970... things will be normal again soon. Then you'll be able to turn your television set on again, Captain."

Zabłocki wasn't too pleased with the idea of jogging through a training field with the cadets. His domain was political training, not battlefield education. Soon, it became clear that even that would be curtailed. The same day, Gapa informed him that his classes would be replaced with shooting range practice and sports activities in the gym.

Zabłocki was aghast. "But why?" he asked the colonel.

"My dear Włodek," Marek Gapa said and tapped him on the shoulder. "Soldiers are stupid but not that stupid. What have you been telling them for the last month... that the Party must resist anti-Socialist elements... that Wałęsa is on the CIA's payroll? Well, just a month ago you were praising Edward Gierek. Now he's gone. They've seen the new Premier and the First Secretary almost kiss Wałęsa's feet on TV. No, we must wait..." The colonel lit a cigarette and walked over to his office window. Outside, a platoon of S.O.R. cadets were circling around the rollcall square carrying their rucksacks and Kalashnikovs. "Let Suka and Gugawa keep them busy for now," he said quietly. "I'm still waiting for guidelines from the Central Political Command in Warsaw. Lt. Colonel Kliski has promised to send them to me next week."

The guidelines turned out to be disappointing for Zabłocki. They advised the colonel to censor all material coming into the regiment. Only the military's own newspaper, Żolnierz Wolności[9] was allowed. He decided to draw up his own schedule of lectures, concentrating on the importance of the Warsaw Pact, the role of the USSR in the struggle for world peace and the vicious attempts by the Americans to destroy the country's system of social justice. The agenda had been sent on to Lt. Colonel Kliski in Warsaw and the officer was full of praise for it. "It is consistent and ideologically correct," he told him over the phone. "I think we may use it as a model agenda for our other units in the future."

Zabłocki smiled to himself and reached for his alarm clock. He wanted to make sure that it was set properly. Instead of putting his hand of the clock though, he pushed his glass ashtray on the floor.

"Shto s toboy...?" Emma asked sleepily. "What is going on with you? " She pulled the comforter even more tightly over her head. The captain threw his comforter aside and bent down to pick up the smelly cigarette butts covering the floor.

He woke up and yawned. A second later he realized that the phone was ringing. He forced himself out of the bed and stumbled into the hallway.

"Captain Zabłocki," he muttered sleepily.

The voice at the other end of the line was clear, and obviously quite awake. "I am waiting for you in the Command Building. Please report as soon as possible for your transfer order, comrade Captain." The phone clicked off before Zabłocki had time to even utter a word.

He glanced at the clock. It was 3:00 A.M. Who would be calling me in the middle of the night, he wondered. And why didn't he identify himself?

Still yawning, he picked up the phone and dialed the Command Building.

"Duty reporting officer, corporal Wątróbka...

"Captain Zabłocki here... Did anyone just call me through your lines?"

"Yes, citizen Captain," the soldier answered promptly. "A Lt. Colonel from Warsaw is waiting for you in room 101."

"Thank you, Wątróbka." Zabłocki hung up the receiver and walked back into his bedroom.

The piercing cold of the dry, clear winter morning chilled his bones as he walked toward the Command Building. He trembled and his stomach churned, but he knew it was not just because of the cold. It is happening, he told himself. Gapa's transfer was just the beginning.

That tearing, wrenching feeling in his gut wasn't unfamiliar. There he was, standing outside the Dean's Office, clasping his student record book to his body, knowing deep down that his marks would do little to help him. That dreaded feeling had returned so swiftly, he thought, despite his impressive captain's uniform, and the many years that separated that life from the one he led at the garrison.

The stars shone silently overhead. Zabłocki quickened his pace. His boots pounded on the frozen surface of the pavement.

As he entered the regiment compound, he glanced at the casino club to his right. Seven years... he thought, and now a transfer... to where? And why the

---

9. Żolnierz Wolności (Polish) - The Soldier of Freedom, an orthodox Communist newspaper of the military.

hell couldn't they wait until a decent hour of the morning. Then he remembered that Gapa had been forced to leave in the middle of the night. They didn't even have a chance to say good-bye to each other.

At the entrance of the Command Building he rubbed his hands together and blew his warm breath on them, his gut still unsteady. In a few minutes it will be over, he told himself.

Inside room 101, he faced the back of a gray-haired officer. The man, who was leaning against the window sill and looking out on the garrison roll call square, turned around when he heard the door open. His light blue, almost watery eyes stared directly at Zabłocki.

The captain swallowed and addressed the officer. "Comrade Colonel," he said, according to the rules, "Captain Zabłocki reports as ordered."

"Let's not be so formal, comrade Captain," the Lt. Colonel answered. "My name is Błażej Kliski. Sit down, please." Kliski picked a package of Marlboros up off the table and pushed them in Zabłocki's direction. "Do you smoke, Captain?"

Zabłocki nodded and the two men sat down and smoked their cigarettes quietly for a few minutes. The fluorescent illumination from a light outside in the square flickered erratically.

"I would like to apologize for this," the higher-ranking officer said. "I imagine it must have been difficult to get up in the middle of the night?"

Zabłocki nodded silently.

Kliski opened up his briefcase. "I'm afraid this couldn't wait until tomorrow. The issue is urgent and we have to act quickly." He handed the captain his transfer orders.

Zabłocki's hands shook. After scanning the text he sat back in his chair and sighed. "GZP, Warsaw," he murmured.

Kliski burst into laughter and grinned. "Yes, you are right," he confirmed. "You are being transferred to the Central Political Command of the People's Armed Forces in Warsaw. Congratulations, comrade Captain." He stood up and shook Zabłocki's hand. Then he sat down and crossed his legs. "I'm sure you were convinced that you would be going somewhere else," he said coolly. "You must have been quite disoriented after Colonel Gapa's dismissal..."

Zabłocki's head reeled. "What do you mean... dismissal?" He was so stunned that he forgot to address Kliski using his full title. "I thought that he was transferred!"

Kliski's face was stone-like. "That is only the official version, comrade Captain," he said slowly, "the one which the cadre and soldiers here must believe; Gapa has indeed been dismissed. He is no longer with the army and he may have to stand trial."

"Trial?"

Lt. Colonel Kliski got out of his chair and walked toward the window. "Don't look so surprised, comrade Captain," he said sternly. "Ex-colonel Marek Gapa was simply too greedy. A recent investigation revealed that he owned a private villa worth roughly five million złoty containing more than $10,000 in imported furniture. Don't you think that is a bit much for a colonel?" Kliski asked, turning and staring at him once again.

Without moving his head, Zabłocki lowered his eyes toward the floor. He had nothing to say. He was not surprised about the estimate of Gapa's home. He had spent many weekends there. Gapa was a widower but he loved to have lavish parties and his house was always full of young women.

The Lt. Colonel must have read his thoughts. "Well, Captain Zabłocki... we have all done strange things in our lifetime, especially during the last decade." he said. "As I think back," he continued, walking around the room, "the most interesting period of my career was the early 'Fifties when I was with the U.B. Secret Service. We had power and we fought the class enemies. Everything was ideologically clear then." The colonel's lofty, nostalgic voice hardened. "Unfortunately, this is all in the past. October 1956 arrived, the U.B. was dissolved and then all the shit about détente and borrowing foreign money emerged... Yes, we have all done something."

Kliski lit a cigarette and continued to talk. His voice was harsh and cutting. "The Party is in shambles now... the population is going crazy and... this is important, the only group of Polish Communists with any credibility is the army. We must maintain our credibility, Captain. Luckily, cases like Gapa's are rare among our ranks, but they must be dealt with ruthlessly."

Zabłocki pondered the officer's words. The status and privileges of the military were never questioned. Moscow made sure that its budget was set at the Politburo level and the general population had no influence on the army at all.

"Excuse me, comrade Colonel," he asked sheepishly. "We don't depend on the support of the people. As far as I am aware, we have always been quite independent of them."

Kliski began to laugh. "You are only partly right, comrade Captain," he answered with a cool smile. "The situation in the country is damn serious and the Russians cannot provide the medicine for every ailment. Yes..." he added quietly, turning back toward the window, "we must maintain our credibility at home."

Zabłocki eyed him with some skepticism. He sensed that he was being drawn into a bizarre game, with secret rules. He was suspicious of the motive behind his transfer to the GZP.

"Excuse me, comrade Colonel," he said boldly. "But why am I here? Who would need me in Warsaw?"

Kliski didn't respond at first. Instead, he puffed on his cigarette and simply stared at Zabłocki.

"Questions, questions, comrade Captain," he remarked a few minutes later. "Well," he said with a grin. "You have been doing a lot of good work. You are intelligent and flexible and that is important. You were praising Gierek when it was required but you never forgot about the Party and the USSR. After last August you adjusted to the new political climate with ingenuity..."

Zabłocki still wasn't satisfied with the officer's answer but he was reluctant to ask any more questions. The former U.B agent's cool, blue eyes intimidated him. He was smart and tough, just like other military officers who had once worked for the U.B.

Kliski grinned again. "I appreciate your patience, comrade Zabłocki," he said. "But you do deserve some answers. Why is the issue so urgent? Simply, dear comrade, if we don't man the GZP with our people now, somebody else will do it."

247

Zabłocki shook his head with puzzlement. "You keep saying 'we' and somebody else. Who are you talking about?"

Kliski glared at him. "At this stage I can only tell you that 'we' denotes a group of realistically minded Communists who are determined to gain full control of all this mess. Look at our civilian comrades," he continued scornfully. "They're all shitting their pants and shuddering at the thought of that mustached monkey and his union bastards. To counter this, we need intelligent people... like you." He looked at his watch. "I would like you to come with me right now," he said. "Orders have been issued to transfer your belongings to a new apartment."

Zabłocki nodded with agreement and got out of his chair. "If you don't mind, I would just like to call my wife before we go..."

"I did that for you while you were walking over here," Kliski said.

Zabłocki looked out the window. A black Volga sedan was just pulling up the driveway in front of the building.

He was dropped off in downtown Warsaw. Kliski said he wanted him to walk around and survey the situation in the streets. "It's a lot different than in the barracks," he said. "It would be a good idea to orient yourself." He promised to send a driver to pick the captain up at the same location at 8:30 A.M. "You will report to your new boss according to your transfer order. Have a nice day."

Zabłocki thanked him and got out of the car at the intersection of Marszałkowska and Hoża streets. He glanced down at his watch. It was only 7:00 A.M. He was pleased that he had an hour and a half to spare. He noticed a phone booth closeby and entered it. He sighed with relief when he heard a dial tone. It was working. Holding the receiver by his chin, the captain searched through his pockets for his notebook. He then dialed the number for Military Counterintelligence.

"Hello, is major Krupa in?" he asked. "Hi, Stefan." He was pleased to hear his friend's voice.

After leaving the phone booth, he realized that he was quite hungry and started to hunt for a restaurant. At that hour of the morning, the only place he could find open was a small milk bar with its skimpy selection printed on a menu board on the wall. He ordered a serving of macaroni and cheese and a mug of hot cocoa. It was all the place would offer. The macaroni turned out to be lukewarm and he burned his tongue on the cocoa. He set the mug down quickly to wait for it to cool and looked around the milk bar. The girl at the cash register was sporting a large Solidarity button and the few customers inside wore the same thing.

"... We can't agree to superficial changes of the system," the man closest to him said loudly. Zabłocki figured he was about thirty years old. "... If Poland is to remain Socialist, we have to have Socialism with a human face. That won't happen in a system which controls its media and doesn't allow people to respond. Radio, television, and the press are the property of society, not just private domain of the Party..."

Zabłocki almost choked on his macaroni. The man's statement was overtly counterrevolutionary, but what really drove him crazy was the Union member's boldness. He couldn't believe that the man dared to make such a statement in the presence of an officer of the People's Armed Forces. Zabłocki abandoned the rest of his meal and left the milk bar. In the underpass close by, he could see Solidarity posters demanding registration of the farmers' union. They were stuck to virtually every store display and available wall. As rush hour picked up, he saw more and more Solidarity buttons on the streets. He joined some people lining up at a RUCH booth to buy cigarettes.

"What makes me so mad," the woman in front of him said to her friend, "is the fact that they distribute more copies of Żołnierz Wolności than Życie Warszawy[10]." Her companion nodded. "Życie is readable now but who reads Żołnierz Wolności? They do it deliberately... the red swine..."

The captain spat on the ground and left the queue. This was just too much for him. The old deal still existed in the barracks, but there was no doubt that it had disappeared from Warsaw's streets. As he stood at the street corner, he imagined people grinning at him impudently as they passed by.

He sighed with relief when he saw a Volga sedan approaching him in the white, snow-filled street. The driver took him directly to the GZP headquarters.

He was content to just sit in a comfortable chair in the waiting room and smoke one of his last cigarettes. It was much more pleasant than the noisy street he had left behind. The plush, dark red carpeting in the building dampened any sharp noises and the secretaries who shared the outer offices spoke in hushed tones. He stretched out his legs and relaxed.

He started, when a young, disagreeable-looking woman opened the door beside him.

"Comrade Captain Zabłocki?" she asked.

He stood up and nodded.

"Comrade Colonel is waiting for you," the girl said without the slightest hint of a smile.

The woman's stern demeanour pleased him. It was more to his liking than the brash expressions that he had seen in the streets. He pushed against the colonel's door. It was heavily padded and difficult to open.

A steel-gray haired man looked up at him without a word. He had deep set eyes and a hawk-like, prominent nose. On the whole, his features were refined and he had a well polished appearance. Zabłocki guessed his age to be about fifty five. He stood at attention and raised two fingers up to the visor of his cap.

"Comrade Colonel, captain Zabłocki reports his arrival."

"Thank you Captain, at ease," the colonel answered and started to browse through some of the papers on his desk.

Zabłocki remained standing, unsure about what to do next. It was quite a few minutes before the colonel noticed what he was doing and asked him to take a seat. The captain sat down and faced him at his desk.

"I'm sorry..." the colonel said. "You have to excuse me for a minute. I have to answer this memo right away." With that, he turned his attention to his

10. Życie Warszawy (Warsaw's Life) - a non-partisan daily newspaper which achieved a relatively high level of journalistic excellence during the period of Solidarity.

papers once again. After finding the letter he was looking for and placing it carefully in an envelope, he turned to Zabłocki. "Well," he said, smiling for the first time. "I imagine you didn't get much sleep last night. Would you like a coffee?"

Before the officer could answer, his superior had pressed a button beneath his front desk drawer.

Zabłocki could hear the secretary's voice coming from a speaker behind the desk. "Yes, comrade Colonel?"

"Miss Kowalewa, would you please bring us two coffees?"

"The coffee will be ready in a minute, comrade," the woman answered quickly.

The colonel rubbed his hands together and sat back in his chair. His secretary entered the room promptly and placed two steaming glasses of coffee on the desk.

"Is there anything else, comrade Colonel?"

"No, thank you... just leave us alone now."

They sipped their coffees for a minute or so and the colonel offered the captain a cigarette. He nodded and accepted a Marlboro.

"Well... let's start talking business, comrade Captain."

Zabłocki sat up and looked at the man eagerly. The colonel stood up abruptly and began to walk around Zabłocki and the desk one, two, three times...

"I know quite a bit about you, Captain Zabłocki," he said slowly, "but how much do you know about me?"

The captain wasn't rattled by the man's odd manner. His telephone call earlier in the day had been a wise move on his part. He smiled confidently.

"Well, I don't know too much, I'm afraid," he said. "I know you are Colonel Alfons Menda and that you served with the U.B. Secret Service, starting in 1952. Your first assignment involved interrogations of junior officers of the Home Army and you performed that job very well." Zabłocki made sure that he emphasized his last two words. "... You advanced quickly and you reached the status of captain. After the agency was dissolved, you joined the People's Armed Forces and you completed your training at the General Staff Academy with good results. That graduation led to a promotion to major, in 1970. You served as a political officer in various outfits across the country... and in January 1979 you became a Lt. Colonel." He paused and looked up at Menda.

"That is very interesting, comrade Captain," the colonel said. "Please continue."

"Well... a year ago you were transferred to the GZP, Central Political Command and you were promoted to full colonel status earlier this year. That is all I know about you, comrade Colonel..."

Colonel Menda smiled proudly. "Bravo, bravo. Very impressive. I have heard a lot about your abilities and intelligence, Captain, but now I know that you are an exceptional man. Kliski didn't exaggerate. I'm sure you and I will work together very well."

Zabłocki was relieved. He had gathered from his phone conversation with his friend at Counterintelligence that Menda was a person to be reckoned with, but now he wasn't so sure. *It looks as if he'll be as easy to handle as Marek Gapa was*, he thought.

He smiled confidently at the officer and asked him to explain the sudden transfer.

Menda stared down at him. "Kliski told you, didn't he? I asked him to explain everything to you."

Zabłocki tried to be nonchalant.

"Well, colonel Kliski did tell me a little, but I'm not really very clear on a number of things." He shrugged and waved his hands in the air. Menda nodded.

"You will understand everything by mid afternoon. I have prepared an orientation package for you," he said calmly and pushed a button beneath his desk.

The substantial window drapery slid shut, immediately dimming the room. Just as quickly, other curtains which covered the far wall separated, and a screen descended. A gray projector emerged from a cupboard on the other side of the room. Menda pushed another button and the first slide filled the screen. It was made up of a number of blocks of varying sizes. They were all connected by thick, red lines. Menda waited for him to survey the image and then began talking.

"Here Captain, we have a pictorial representation of all the important political forces in the country." He took a pointer and approached the screen. He touched the large box on the top first.

"This is Solidarity, " he explained. "I don't think I have to elaborate about it. I would just like to mention at this point that despite a lot of effort on the part of the S.B. Secret Service, we still have very few people sitting on the KKP National Council. It is the same story with the Union's Regional Chapters. We have some people but not enough to take control..."

"Why hasn't the S.B. managed to penetrate the Union?" Zabłocki asked.

The issue was obviously a point of irritation to Menda. He sighed with exasperation.

"The S.B. decided to act too late," he explained. "Although they ordered some of their agents to work as strike leaders, most of the sit-ins were already well underway and the strikers had selected their representatives. Following the Gdańsk Agreement, many agents were engaged in strike actions and they have managed to gain some credibility because they screamed louder than anybody else. They're more Catholic than the Pope," Menda said and started to laugh loudly. He stopped just as abruptly and pointed to the screen again.

"We hope that quite a few of our people can be elected to sit on Regional Executive and even to central bodies at the first national congress of the Union sometime in the fall. Any questions?"

"No."

"All right, let's continue." Menda moved his pointer down to the next block.

"This is Rural Solidarity. This union has not been certified yet, but registration is imminent. However, the farmers aren't much of a worry to us. They are more scattered then their blue collar brothers. Next, we have the Confederation of Autonomous Unions. We have managed to install a few people inside, because these organizations were formed much later than Solidarity. However, a majority of the Confederation's leaders are closely linked to Wałęsa's union. They provide support for similar projects under a different name which leads one to believe that more organizations want the same as Solidarity. Fortunately, its membership is not very large. However, we will have to keep a close eye on them."

Menda looked at Zabłocki and seeing that the captain had no questions, he moved his pointer to the fourth box on the diagram. "Now, here we have the Industry Branch Unions[11]," he said. "They account for almost two million people. Its leadership basically consists of former trade union officials who moved up after their senior colleagues were swept out by the August strikes."

"What about the Unions' membership?" Zabłocki asked.

"It is comprised of white collar employees and the working class, mainly unqualified construction workers. Branch Unions enjoy strong support from them. Its leadership formally advocates renewal in an attempt to hold on to as many members as possible. They negotiate with Vice-Premier Rakowski much like Solidarity, but just about wages... We don't foresee too many problems with these unions. Most of its members are long-standing Party members and they are quite docile. We might be able to use one of their leaders in the future. Have you heard of Albin Siwak?"

Zabłocki nodded.

"Well," Menda continued, "a complete idiot but he is a member of the Party's Central Committee and he might be useful."

Menda pushed a button and a second slide appeared on the screen.

Zabłocki read the letters PZPR[12] on the top. To Zabłocki's surprise, the Party was depicted in many different sections, not like the monolithic organization that he had been lecturing about for years.

Menda waited patiently for Zabłocki to look up from the slide.

"Yes, Captain," he said quietly. "Here is our battered Party. I think it will be useful to cover every faction, group and individual who is pursuing a specific political line." He lifted his pointer up to the top box. "Here we have comrade First Secretary Stanisław Kania. He is the most nondescript leader we have ever had but the Poles seem to like him the best. Neither a thief nor a murderer, they say. He is a transitional figure but we cannot ignore him. He seems to be willing to cooperate with the Unions. From the outside, he doesn't appear to be very smart but he has been purging local Party committees and manning them with his own people. Any questions?"

Zabłocki nodded.

"What is the source of Kania's support?"

Menda thought for a moment before answering.

"Mainly the Party's rank and file," he answered. "The former hierarchy opposes him and he has no support in the army whatsoever. He even lacks popularity within the Secret Service although he supervised its operations in the 'Seventies. We will be trying to remove him from the scene at the next

---

11. The Industry Branch Unions were organized for particular branches of industry. They did not have regional structure or a provision for a solidarity strike in their constitution.

12. PZPR - (P.U.W.P.) - Polish United Workers' Party.

Party Congress which will be convening later this year but one never knows. Revisionist fever is strong among the Party rank and file and he may well pull through. We can't underestimate this man. He is dangerous..."

The second block on the diagram was labeled with the name of the country's Vice-Premier, Mieczysław Rakowski. Zabłocki looked at the name and smiled. The politician was his idol. He had been a staunch Stalinist and then a Gomułka supporter. In the 'Seventies, he was able to do well under Gierek and still managed to get promoted during Solidarity era. The trick was to be flexible but remain in a position of control. That was what Zabłocki had been trying to do in the army.

"That man will ally with anyone who is in power," he commented.

The colonel nodded.

"He is very smart. His goal now is to keep his reputation as a liberal until he gets past the Party Congress this summer."

Menda began circling the room and swinging his pointer from side to side.

"I don't know if you have heard, Captain Zabłocki, but the next convention is being called the 'Extraordinary Party Congress' because it is going to be held one year ahead of schedule. And yet," he paused and looked at the screen, "by all odds it is going to be extraordinary. Do you know what will be different?" he asked and leaned forward directing his gaze right at Zabłocki. The captain moved his eyes to the side.

"No, I don't," he answered.

"There will be a number of possible candidates to choose from for the top job, and secret balloting is most probably going to be used. What we have to do is influence the people who are voting to vote the right way. That is the real challenge isn't it?" Without answering his own question the colonel started pacing around the office once more.

"The next block," he said, not bothering to point at the screen, "represents the bulk of the Party."

Zabłocki looked at a large rectangle with a black triangle in the middle.

"What is that supposed to represent?" he asked.

Menda smiled. "That small, dark area is us," he answered. "But we will talk about that after lunch. The white area you can see on the outside, represents about ninety percent of the Polish United Workers Party, a shattered, demoralized bunch of former sycophants. I suppose you have heard about the horizontal Party structures devised by comrade Iwanow, haven't you Captain?"

Zabłocki nodded. A low-ranking Party member, incidently bearing a Russian last name Iwanov, had devised a scheme to create a horizontal Party structure. His plan ran counter to the Soviet model. Party members would be assembled together from various factories and they would directly elect delegates to the Party Congress. Zabłocki realized that the proposal would lead to the demise of the stratified system of selection that had been operating successfully within the PUWP for 32 years.

Without looking up at him, Menda pointed to a brown circle to the right of the box representing the party membership.

"This, comrade Captain," he began, "is the only self-governed association we included on this slide - the Association of Polish Journalists. Its Chairman,

Stefan Bratkowski is dangerous. He, and a sizable minority of journalists, went completely crazy after 1980. Led by Bratkowski, a Party member by the way, they are writing things that shouldn't be printed but because of the mess we're in, they are being published. This has had a great effect on the Party's membership. Bratkowski and his reformist followers might cause a lot of problems during the next Party Congress. And, as in the case of Solidarity, we don't know how to neutralize Bratkowski and the journalists who follow him... not now, anyway."

A number of names and groups that weren't present on Menda's diagram popped into Zabłocki's mind but he was reluctant to ask too many questions.

Menda cocked his head and eyed Zabłocki.

"A somewhat incomplete scheme... is that what you were just thinking, Captain?" he asked with a brief laugh. "We just don't have room for irrelevant organizations. Take the Independent Association of Students, for example. They are quite vocal these days. But do they have any power? Just think of the student protests in 1968. We didn't even have a ZOMO back then with armoured personnel carriers and yet," he added almost cheerfully, "tear gas and night sticks did the trick. Gas and batons... and all within four days."

Menda used the intercom once more to call his secretary.

"Before we talk about the last box on the slide, we'll have some more coffee," he explained. He calmly pushed another button to make sure that the curtains were drawn up and the projector inside its container before the unsmiling and mousy-looking Miss Kowalewa brought in their beverages.

They sipped their coffee in silence. Zabłocki guessed that the most important information was still to come. No explanation for his transfer had been offered and he still hadn't come to any conclusions about the purpose of Menda's little game.

Menda sighed and passed him another cigarette. He suggested that they cover just one more item before lunch. The same slide appeared on the screen and the colonel pointed to a large box labeled 'Grunwald'[13]. Zabłocki noticed that it was connected by two dotted lines to the dark section of the Party block, the group that he was supposed to join.

"What do you know about Grunwald?" Menda asked.

Zabłocki pondered the colonel's question briefly. He had heard of the organization but he was sketchy on a number of points. 'The Patriotic Association Grunwald' was opposed to Solidarity and had nothing to do with trade unionism. For the most part it was comprised of people who professed the Communist ideology but didn't associate with any coterie in the Party and the government. At the same time, the organization pretended to be a nationalistic group. It had gained some points in its bid to erect a plaque to pay homage to the thousands of Home Army soldiers, Anders Army veterans and other people who were eliminated by the U.B. Secret Service between 1948 and 1956. He was sure that Menda wouldn't be pleased with the possibility of his past surfacing. He smiled at the colonel.

---

13. Grunwald (or Tannenberg) the name of the battlefield where the united Polish and Lithuanian forces defeated the Teutonic Knights in 1410. Here, it denotes the name of a political organization.

"Grunwald is a strange organization," he stated. "They claim they want to see revenge on former U.B. and Public Security Ministry officials but, on the other hand, they call themselves both Communists and Polish nationalists..."

Menda smiled. "So, comrade Captain, can you derive any conclusions about this strange association?"

"Not really, and I can't understand why you have put Grunwald on the diagram so close to your group either."

"As smart as you are, comrade, you should avoid being too simplistic," Menda warned. "Grunwald condemns the slaughter of patriots during the Stalinist period because the Poles take that issue very seriously. However, the most important thing to remember is 'who' they blame for the tens of thousands of people eliminated during the 'Fifties. Do they blame good soldiers like Lt. Colonel Kliski and myself?" He paused. "No, comrade Captain, they blame only... the Jews." He burst into hysterical laughter. "Just imagine, we have Jewish scapegoats even though those who had indeed been involved, left Poland a long time ago or are no longer alive..."

As quickly as his mood became joyful he turned in the opposite direction.

"There is a problem though," he said gloomily. "Our countrymen don't seem to give a shit for anti-Semitism anymore... Nevertheless, a good percentage of Grunwald members work for us."

The colonel rapidly put the room back in order and opened the curtains. Zabłocki blinked several times trying to adjust to the bright sunshine streaming into the room from outside.

"We're going to lunch now, Captain," Menda said, easing him toward the door. "We have had a busy morning and the afternoon is going to be even more exciting."

The lunch room at the Central Political Command was larger than the club at the 17th Regiment and offered a much more lavish menu.

Their waitress brought them a tureen of pea soup and when they had finished, the two officers enjoyed thick slices of roast beef with cooked beets, mashed potatoes and tomato salad. Chocolate ice cream completed the meal.

"So, do you think that you'll be happy with us here at the GZP, comrade?" Menda joked after the captain wiped his mouth with a napkin and sat back with contentment. Zabłocki yawned and nodded.

"Don't worry, Captain," Menda said with a smile. "We'll get some coffee in my office."

When they passed the colonel's secretary she disconnected an already boiling kettle.

"She knows that I always have a craving for coffee after lunch," Menda said, sitting behind his desk. "Kowalewa is a good girl. If only she smiled a bit more," he said with a deep sigh.

The secretary entered the office.

"Is there anything else you would like, comrade Colonel?" she asked stonily.

"No, thank you. Just leave us alone and remember... I am not to be disturbed by anyone unless there is a call or a visit from my superior."

"Yes, comrade Colonel, you told me about it yesterday," she answered and left the room.

"Do you think that we can start now, citizen Captain?" Menda said as he pushed his empty glass to one corner of his desk.

"Yes, I am ready, citizen Colonel," Zabłocki answered, sitting up in his chair.

Again, the drapes were drawn and the screen uncovered. A new slide appeared in front of them. It was a large box divided in two by a dotted line. The top half of the square was designated with a #1 and connected to a red circle labeled 'Forum'. The lower half was clear and had a simple #2.

"As you might suspect, citizen Captain, this diagram represents 'us', and as you can see, there are two factions in our group..."

Captain Zabłocki listened with interest.

"First, I would like to talk about the group as a whole," Menda said. He circled the box with his pointer. "We are the Communists who are trying to avoid any modifications to the political system of this country. We want a strong government, a strong Party and powerful military and security forces. We are prepared to fight for the principles of the Socialist system, meaning: no opposition, central planning and, above all, Soviet supremacy over this country and its people both politically and economically. As you can see, Captain," Menda said as he began his habitual walk back and forth, "our group is determined to save and preserve what my generation took such pains to build during the 'Fifties."

The sound of the tall man's solid steps were subdued by the thick carpeting underneath. "To you, my mother organization, the U.B., is just one part of the grandiose past of Polish Communism," he added, looking squarely at Zabłocki.

"I'm sure you think that myself and other agents spent most of our time tying Home Army soldiers to door handles by their balls. Well... sure, it was amusing at times... but do you know how hard it was to get one of those S.O.B.'s into prison?"

Zabłocki cringed but the colonel continued undaunted.

"People your age probably think that our prisoners just made us feel powerful, but that is wrong. Despite the amnesty, many Home Army soldiers refused to lay down their arms. They did not recognize the Warsaw government and they remained faithful to the Polish Government in London even though it had been abandoned by its Western allies... From 1948 to 1956 we had to fight regular battles with the underground. In the cities, we had control... but in the villages and the forests? Did you know that Kliski once had a twin brother?" Menda asked. His voice was a thick hiss. "Kliski's brother was the commander of a U.B. post in Wonbolice. In 1952, the partisans attacked his outfit. They killed the guards and released all of the prisoners. Then they took Wiesław Kliski into the forest with them."

Menda paused and abruptly took a cigarette out of his package on the desk and lit it. Zabłocki watched him in silence.

"... When Błażej Kliski, the man you met this morning, found his brother he was already stiff. The partisans had followed their usual routine. They had forced him to eat and swallow his Communist Party ID and then they hanged him from a tree... but not before they court-martialled him. Beneath his corpse, Błażej found a notice. It read: *Lt. Wiesław Kliski, an officer of the U.B. Secret*

Service, has been found guilty of torturing and killing 235 Polish patriots. Convicted to death by hanging in the name of the Republic of Poland."

Zabłocki avoided looking up at the colonel's face. He heard the officer take a deep drag from his cigarette.

"We are going to fight for what we have now, Captain," Menda said decisively. "We're not going to let anybody dismantle Socialism..."

The captain tried to concentrate on the slide in front of him. Menda stood in silence for a moment, and then, noticing Zabłocki's apparent interest in the topic at hand, he stalked over to the screen and picked up his pointer.

"All right," he began. "why don't we look at Faction #1," he said and pointed to the upper half of the square. "This group consists of those comrades who would like the Russians to come in as soon as possible, do the job and install them at the top."

Suddenly, Menda began laughing.

"How naive and unimaginative they are... listen," he said, turning to Zabłocki. "If you are weak enough to scream for help and cause quite a bit of trouble and expense to the Soviets, you wouldn't expect to be rewarded for that. Yes," he said, nodding, "the Russian invasion could happen, and then a brand new power structure would emerge in the country, one that wouldn't involve them or us. As for who 'they' are," he continued impatiently, "I would say that most of the Central Committee's hard-liners, or 'hard-headed', as some people commonly call them now, belong to this category. Many functionaries with the S.B. Secret Service also favour the Russian solution. They are furious because the agency's power has been weakened considerably by Solidarity's various actions and demands... As far as the military is concerned, I would estimate that some 30 to 40 percent would like the Soviets to come. Any questions?"

"What about the low-ranking civilians in this group?" Zabłocki asked.

"Well..." Menda said with a smile. "Most of the local Party bosses who are being replaced by Kania's crowd could probably be included in this group. However, most of them are so scared that they could not be depended on for real support. They are petrified because they think they might be charged and put on trial for mismanagement of government funds." Menda coughed slightly and then placed his pointer on the red circle on the screen.

"This represents the now famous 'Katowice Party Forum'," he said. "This didn't even exist six months ago but now it is an 'ultra hard-line' faction as the American press would say. This informal Party group is doing a good job... what do you know about them, Captain?"

Zabłocki had a hazy idea about the Katowice Party Forum which seemed to be a club of some sort. He remembered hearing that the group had some native Russians. It was best known for the statements it had issued in the Communist press condemning counterrevolutionary developments in Polish society. It had also gained some coverage on television with its violent reaction to alleged desecration of graves.

"It is a puzzling organization," he told Menda. "I know there are a number of Soviet cemeteries in this country, in places where the Red Army fought with the Nazis. But what I find confusing, is the Katowice Party Forum's

257

complaints about desecration of Soviet tombs in areas where no fighting took place at all. Take Klusków Dolny, for example. I was born there and I know there are no Soviet graves anywhere near the town. Yet, on TV the Forum declared that Soviet tombs had been desecrated there. I don't quite understand..."

The colonel looked at him and began to bellow with laughter.

"Really, Captain," he asked. "What do you have in the centre of the Market Place Square in Klusków Dolny?"

"Well, just a monument to the Red Army. It was erected after the Nazis withdrew. But there are no tombs there. I'm positive..."

"Yes, in many areas there are no tombs," Menda conceded, "but in almost every town you can find a monument to Soviet soldiers, the liberators. The first so-called desecrations of tombs were, in fact, usually nothing more than the knocking off of a red star from one of the monuments. Nothing was done to any graves. These first few incidents were genuine. They were done by stupid, zealous teenagers months ago..."

"I did hear of them last week, the Forum called them 'desecration of tombs'..."

Menda smiled and sat down at his desk.

"In this nation, a 'desecration of a tomb' sounds much worse than a 'profanation of a monument'," he said quietly. "The latest incidents did take place, but it was necessary to orchestrate them so that the so-called liberal press would report on the events. The desecration of tombs is now being performed by agents working for Faction #1. This type of action creates tension and a suspicion that even sacred things are being abused by counterrevolutionaries... It is a good tool for psychological warfare and we fully approve of these acts and the publicity they generate... Anyway, so much for Faction #1," Menda said and rose from his chair.

"Now for the last group, Captain. This is comprised of a majority of generals, a good number of junior officers and it enjoys fair support in a few circles of the S.B. Secret Service. Among the civilians, the group is popular with some of the people in the present Central Committee. We hope this number will be increased at the Ninth Congress. Support at that level is not strong enough because of Kania's people," Menda said with disgust. "... Now, the main difference between the two factions is that the latter would rather not see the Russians come in. Number two is determined to solve this disaster domestically."

So this is the big secret of the comrade Colonel, Zabłocki thought. He couldn't help smiling. Yes, in 1968, the liberal leadership of Czechoslovakia was overthrown and the Russian army occupied Prague. The same might happen to Stanisław Kania, but without the Soviets who could challenge the popular First Secretary?

"If that was an easy task, we would have done it long ago, citizen Captain," Menda said without the slightest hint of a smile. "We need to get more support in the Central Committee, we must win the next Congress, not Kania's people, or our comrades from the first faction. We must also install as many people as possible into Solidarity..."

The words, 'we must, we must', echoed in Zabłocki's mind.

Menda began circling his desk once more.

"This isn't the time," he said earnestly, "but I am convinced that it will come in the foreseeable future. As ridiculous as it may seem, our immediate task is to constrain Faction #1. If the Russians cross our borders, the game will be over."

Why? Zabłocki kept asking himself. Wasn't the first option the most appropriate solution? It would teach the impudent people in the streets who was in real control.

"I don't know if you have much of a chance," he told Menda quietly.

"You should have said 'we', citizen Captain," Menda remarked sardonically.

"I am not with your faction yet, and I am not even sure if I want to join it," Zabłocki answered coolly.

The colonel smiled and sat down, swiftly opening a drawer and retrieving a thick file out of his desk.

"I am very sorry that I have to bring this up, Captain Zabłocki," he said "but if you aren't willing to cooperate with us, it is possible that in the course of Gapa's trial something about you might surface. I can list a number of possibilities... the coal quota, your endless praising of Gierek and his clique and of course, your weekly visits to Gapa's wild parties." The colonel leafed through a few pages in the file, and Zabłocki saw that it included a number of colourful photographs. "And the gifts Captain, we can't forget about them," Menda continued. "Do you, for example, remember the two expensive Italian dresses that your wife received? Did it ever occur to you that just possibly they were paid for with public funds?" Menda hissed. "You wouldn't like to answer to all of this in a court-martial, would you?"

Zabłocki sighed and sat back in his chair. He felt tired and Menda was a determined character. How stupid I was to assume he would be easy to manage, he thought angrily and turned to the colonel.

"Wouldn't this be considered blackmail?"

Menda's cold, blue eyes stared at him from across the desk.

"You can call it whatever you want, Captain. What is your decision?"

"I don't know," Zabłocki answered, shaking his head rapidly. "I would like to think it over... discuss it with my wife... can I call you tomorrow?"

Menda leant over the desk. "Yes or no?"

Zabłocki looked away and turned his head to the floor. His voice cracked. "Yes... Colonel."

Menda seemed satisfied. He sat back in his chair and put the file back in the drawer. Zabłocki grabbed a cigarette and inhaled it deeply. He had to calm himself down. The colonel sat and waited for his questions.

"All right. Now that I am a part of your faction, what do you want me for?"

Menda stretched his legs and placed his hands behind his head. He wheeled his chair around so that he faced Zabłocki directly.

"We would welcome your ingenuity and your connections," he said. "They may be needed as early as tomorrow."

"Surely, you could have found someone more useful than me..." Zabłocki said incredulously.

"Of course I could have," Menda answered with a smile. "However, we especially appreciate your friendship with our good comrade, General Nikolai

259

Ivanovich Lebiedyev. If you, or your lovely wife, happened to meet him I don't think we would mind if you tried to convince the general that an invasion would be a rather inefficient solution to the Polish crisis. You would do that for us, wouldn't you."

Zabłocki squirmed in his seat. He had no idea that his wife's affair with the Russian general was so well known.

"I don't... know," he answered haltingly. "I haven't seen him for more than a year. He is back in Moscow now..."

"I know that," Menda said sharply. "Lebiedyev is now with Warsaw Pact United Command. He is an aide to marshal Kulikov himself. Two weeks ago the marshal put him in charge of finding quick and accurate information on Poland in order to work out a strategy. He is coming to Warsaw tomorrow..."

Zabłocki hesitated. Already, it was obvious that Menda was deadly serious about implementing his scheme. He gritted his teeth and decided that he had to try to confront the officer.

"I don't know if Lebiedyev would be willing to meet me at all..." he murmured, "and I can't give you any guarantees that I will be able to discuss this with him."

Menda's steel blue eyes didn't leave the captain's face. Zabłocki felt increasingly helpless.

"What do you want me to say?" he screamed wildly, "Don't invade Poland, comrade?"

The plush, dimly lit room was deathly quiet. The colonel didn't respond and Zabłocki had no idea what to do next.

Menda got out of his chair and approached him. His nostrils had widened and he pushed his face right at Zabłocki; so close that he could feel his breath on his face.

"Listen, you little shit," he said with a tight grimace. "Don't give me that crap. Gapa's trial is starting the day after tomorrow. This is your last chance to stay with the army and out of prison..."

Zabłocki got out of his chair and backed up toward the far wall. He looked at the colonel with outright fear.

Menda cornered him and hissed, "Tomorrow, Lebiedyev arrives in Warsaw. He may not want to talk to you but, as far as I know, he will be more than willing to fuck your wife. You had better, " he shrieked, "be sure that she does a good job so that he gets the right message... understood?"

Zabłocki's head drooped from his body. He felt completely crushed and humiliated. His long awaited transfer to the GZP, Warsaw had materialized, and for what?

He managed to evade Menda and returned to his chair. His hands shook as he lit his last cigarette and smoked it quickly.

Menda opened a cabinet, took three cartons of Marlboros out and set them on the desk in front of Zabłocki.

"Here, take these," he said coolly. "You will get this many each week."

Zabłocki tried to smile. "Well, thank you, Colonel, but I don't need them. I can buy cigarettes in the street."

To his surprise, Menda began laughing loudly at his remark. "If I were you I wouldn't rely on cigarettes in tobacco stands just as you won't be relying on regular food stores. You will be shopping at military outlets, won't you?"

Zabłocki nodded.

"Good," Menda said. "I am glad about that. I never doubted your intelligence..."

Zabłocki had had enough of the colonel's riddles. "What do you mean, citizen Colonel?" he asked with a sigh.

"Come to the window, Captain." When Zabłocki joined him, Menda asked him to describe what he saw outside.

Zabłocki shrugged. "Well, I can see people in the street."

"Very good vision, Captain. Now, what do you see beyond the street?"

"Just a few construction workers sitting down and taking a break," he answered. "They are smoking cigarettes and chatting."

"Bravo Zabłocki, Bravo," Menda said and chuckled loudly. "Now, think about those people again. They are spending about five hours a day lining up for food. They work, queue for meat and other staples almost seven days a week. Most of them are tired and at times hungry... They are probably talking about all of this while they sit there and enjoy their smokes. Now - if," Menda's voice became very solemn, "the workers you see out there didn't have those cigarettes, if they had been smoking for years but there were none at all. Not at the newsstand... nowhere. What then?"

Zabłocki turned and looked at Menda. The officer seemed to be totally oblivious to his presence. He was simply enjoying his own thoughts. He gazed at the workers beyond the street and continued speaking. "So, they are going crazy without their daily dose of nicotine... then, the food supplies deteriorate even further and other essentials are non-existent. No soap, no cigarettes, finally no bread. Tensions increase and then the strikes erupt one after the other. Eventually, Solidarity proclaims a general strike and then..."

CHAPTER 4

The three storey building along Próżna street looked as if it had been around since Czarist times[14], with its peeling layers of worn plaster, flaking off on to the sidewalk, exposing bare areas of cracked, brown masonry. At street level, there was a neighbourhood barber shop, and to its right, a small grocery store with its characteristic tall, narrow windows and green shutters.

The store was run by the WSS state cooperative, but all its customers called it 'Blind Mary's', in honour of an elderly woman, with thick, heavy spectacles who had been store manager there since the war. She had been retired for a few years, but Budal employees still called her replacement by the same name.

Lately, grocery shelves had become noticeably more bare. Eggs virtually disappeared from state-run stores and private merchants began doubling and tripling their prices.

"We've got coupons, but where is the food?" an old woman who had joined Konrad in a queue remarked. "They think they can fool us forever, but they can't," she snapped. "Solidarity will put an end to this mess."

The woman's last sentence sounded decisive and her wrinkled face expressed a great deal of determination. She was Agata's age, and like his great-aunt, she sported a Union button. Konrad smiled, and told her about a meeting which had started in Bydgoszcz the day before.

"Solidarity is presenting its agricultural proposal to the local authorities. The main concerns are food production and distribution," he said.

"God bless them, God bless them," the woman murmured.

They were lining up for eggs, milk, and farmer cheese. The only articles on the store's shelves were vinegar, bread, margarine and poor quality tea, but the new 'Blind Mary' was expecting a delivery of dairy products. Stacks of gray plastic containers with empty milk bottles, stood beside the muddy curb.

About one hundred and fifty joined Konrad in the line outside on the street. The weather was relatively warm and the sun was shining.

A gentleman in his mid-seventies pouted. "This really is ridiculous," he said. "Poland has always been an agricultural country. Before the war we had fewer stinking factories but no problems with food..."

---

14. Czarist times - From 1815 until well into the First World War, Warsaw remained under the Czarist (Russian) administration.

"This situation has been building up ever since the war ended," Konrad remarked. "If private farms can't buy tractors, seeds or fertilizer, how are our farmers supposed to produce food?"

An attractive, brown-haired woman, who had been quietly preoccupied with her toddler in the stroller, began shaking her head. She explained that her relatives lived in the country and though they faced a number of difficulties, they were still selling many kinds of produce to the government collecting stations. The foodstuffs supplied by the farmers seemed to be disappearing before they even hit the local stores. "That's why Rural Solidarity has to be certified as soon as possible," she said decisively. "The two Unions will make sure that our food is properly distributed and they'll put an end to idiotic queues like this one."

Everyone in the crowd nodded.

Konrad left the line momentarily to look for the awaited milk delivery. The sunny street was quiet and there was no sign of a truck. When he returned to his place in the queue, he heard the same brunette telling the elderly woman with the Solidarity badge about the peasants' hunger strikes and a sit-in that was being staged at the United Farmers' Party headquarters in Bydgoszcz. The strikers were demanding the certification of Rural Solidarity.

"Well, at least we can be thankful that the Party officials are behaving themselves and not trying to force the peasants out," the old woman said with a sigh. "So many things have changed lately, perhaps the Farmers' Party will be more helpful to our peasants…"

Konrad shook his head. "We had better put our hopes on Michał Bartoszcze. He has been invited to meet with the National Council in Bydgoszcz. Maybe something will change for the better?"

"God will give his blessing to him and food to us. May Saint Mary support our farmers," the aged woman said and made a sign of the cross over her chest.

All of the queuers turned their heads when the salesgirl came outside. She shook her head. "I am sorry, but our expected delivery has been recalled. I'm told something might arrive this afternoon, possibly around three o'clock."

"It's the same every day," the young woman who was first in line said gloomily. "Come and go, come and go… How can we work if we have to hunt for staples all the time?"

The old woman sighed. "We have spent so much time in line and all in vain," she said quietly to Konrad. "And I was 20th in the queue. The next time I might be the 100th person and not get anything."

Reluctantly, she picked her bag off the sidewalk. The empty milk bottles inside clinked. Konrad looked at her shrunken, bowed silhouette and quickly left the line and rushed into the store. He approached the salesgirl. She too was wearing a Solidarity badge.

"Excuse me," he said, "but I think we should try to give everyone the opportunity to get their place back in the line at three o'clock."

"I would like to," she answered with some puzzlement, "but how would I remember who was where? New customers might come too."

Konrad winked at her and smiled. "Do you have a rubber stamp?" he asked. The salesgirl nodded with understanding and brought him a stamp and small scraps of paper. Within a few minutes, each customer had a numbered ticket and was told to return at three.

An old gentleman laughed. "I came with a handful of coupons and money to buy some food and, here I am, leaving with another piece of paper."

The young brunette in front of him scowled. "You shouldn't be so unfair, sir," she said. "It's a great idea. Now we won't lose our place and the time we have spent lining up."

"Oh, I wasn't complaining about the time," the old man said with a broad smile. "Our discussions this morning have been very instructive and I'm glad that I was here."

Engineer Smrodziński was waiting for him at his desk. Konrad noticed that his substantial belly wobbled underneath his boss' tight, non-iron shirt.

"I haven't seen you for over an hour," he said coolly.

"You are right, sir, I was lining up at 'Blind Mary's'," Konrad answered in all honesty.

The fat, oily face of his supervisor curled into an ugly scowl.

"But you are doing this during working hours," he said.

Konrad shrugged. He liked his work and he would have preferred to stay at his desk, but he had been forced to join the line-ups more frequently during the last few weeks. He decided that it was better if Eryk didn't venture out of his office, and Agata had almost reached the breaking point. Whenever she went shopping she became engaged in violent quarrels with the store employees and blamed them for the lack of food on their shelves.

"Still, you shouldn't do this when you're supposed to be working," Smrodziński insisted.

Maks and Małgosia struggled not to laugh, while Waldek stood behind Smrodziński and made circles in the air.

"I shouldn't, but we have to eat," Konrad argued.

Smrodziński let out a small giggle. "You don't seem to be dying of hunger," he remarked.

Konrad tried to ignore the comment although he knew that his boss was right. He had gained a lot of weight. He turned to Smrodziński and smiled mischievously.

"You are right, sir, I am not dying of hunger," he said with ridicule. "However, I do like to eat things like cheese and eggs, rather than the bread and potatoes that we've been living on lately..."

Smrodziński's eyes widened. "Cheese and eggs," he murmured. "Well, Mr. Dymowski," he said in a mild and kind tone of voice, "Would you be willing to sell some to me? I'd be really obliged."

Everyone in the office started to laugh; everyone, that is but engineer Smrodziński.

"Well, I just thought that if you had some to spare..." he added sheepishly.

Konrad smiled at him. "I could have shared my eggs with you if I had some. Unfortunately, I didn't get any. 'Blind Mary' says that they may bring something later in the afternoon. But..." he said, looking straight into Smrodziński's face, "I couldn't possibly leave the office again today..."

His boss smiled and his eyes brightened. "Oh, you shouldn't have taken my comments so seriously, Mr. Dymowski, " he explained. "I know you'll get your work done. You see," he said, lowering his voice and leaning toward Konrad, "I would like a half a kilo of cheese and six eggs. Then my wife could make some cheesecake."

The loudspeaker hanging from the ceiling in the office let out a loud squeak. Everyone in the room looked up and waited for a Union announcement. Through the public address system in the building, messages were conveyed to the staff almost daily.

"Solidarity to all staff," Adam Babinicz blurted out in an uneven voice. "May I have your attention please. This is an important communiqué." He paused and Konrad heard a number of papers rattle. "All right, now listen carefully," Budal's Vice-Chairman said. "... This is a message to all union members. Yesterday, the police attacked top representatives of the Independent Self-Governed Labour Union Solidarity. As you know, a delegation of Solidarity-Bydgoszcz was participating in an open session with that district's National Council. Solidarity's Chairman there, Jan Rulewski was invited by the Councillors who promised to give the Union the opportunity of expressing their views on the condition of agriculture and submit proposals to improve the food market situation in Bydgoszcz region.

However, before Solidarity even took the floor, one of the Councillors closed the session and ordered the hall to be cleared. Many of the other Council members opposed the move. Rulewski and the other Union representatives claimed that they had been invited to participate and they refused to leave."

The loudspeaker began squeaking loudly, and everyone in the office looked at each other in confusion. Even Smrodziński's face was drawn and pale.

Konrad was relieved when he heard Adam's voice come on again. His friend apologized for the delay and resumed his announcement. "A sizable group of Council members remained in the hall to support the unionists' stand and others left. Then the Vice-Mayor arrived and told everyone to leave. When the Union representatives refused, the police were called in. Jan Rulewski and the others were forced out of the hall and then badly beaten outside. Rulewski and two other men are in hospital now. One of them, 60–year old Michał Bartoszcze, is in very grave condition..."

Adam paused for a few seconds. The room was deadly quiet. Konrad shook his head with confusion. This, the first act of violence against Solidarity was a shock. Maks nervously lit his second cigarette in five minutes. All eyes looked at the small, yellow loudspeaker on the wall.

"... A nationwide strike alert has been called. All union members are instructed to obey directives issued by their Solidarity Locals. We will be maintaining communications with Solidarity-Mazowsze Region's headquarters. This afternoon, Lech Wałęsa and other members of the KKP are going to Bydgoszcz to investigate the incident. We may have to go on strike if a full explanation and apology isn't provided."

They could hear Adam taking a deep breath. "The situation is serious," he said in a grave voice. "Our Union has been attacked. Solidarity will stand behind those who have been beaten. All members must be ready and united."

A corner wall at a downtown intersection was plastered with scores of Union posters, each depicting crouched figures, their noses smashed and flattened by clubs, their faces bleeding profusely on the pavement, holding up their arms to ward off further blows.

Konrad joined the throng which had crowded around the ugly display. A sea of angry faces and voices was demanding justice. Many were cursing the government out loud.

"That's the way they talk to the nation," a tall, bearded university student shouted. "The SOB's speak of renewal and this is what they do. This time they've gone too far." He clenched his fists. Others responded by cursing the government and declaring that the situation was beyond compromise.

A thin and gray-haired woman, standing behind them shook her head repeatedly. "What they have done is horrible," she said, "but we must not overreact. Something will be worked out before the worst happens..."

Pointing at the image on the poster and raising his voice even higher, the student began insisting that the worst had already happened. "Decisive action is needed now," he added firmly.

Nearby, a stout man in his late fifties attempted to smile in a conciliatory manner. He peered at the young student with his gold-rimmed glasses. "Many more young people may be beaten if the Union is too aggressive," he pointed out. "I don't know," he said with a shrug, "perhaps it wasn't a good idea to put these posters up everywhere..."

Konrad turned and faced the older man. "It's not just young people, sir. The most seriously injured man is about your age and he might not pull through," he said, looking up at the photograph on the poster. "People have to see this, they must know what is going on. When student Stanisław Pyjas was killed because of his political activities, just before August 1980, many people found it hard to believe that the security forces were involved."

The young men in the crowd nodded in agreement and heckled. The bearded student threw his hands into the air emphatically, and warned that if the Union didn't appear strong enough, more violence would be inevitable. "If we do not solidly support the men who have suffered now, the whole idea of Solidarity will be lost and we will be finished... just like that..."

Inside the dim living room, enveloped in cigarette smoke, Konrad, Eryk and Agata sat glued to their chairs, watching their TV set that evening. The TV Daily reported that the country was in a state of pandemonium; that crowds were gathering in the streets and plazas, in the schools, universities and factories. Enraged workers around Bydgoszcz had walked out right after the incident.

The TV cameras revealed Polish banners waving over a red brick building, as well as neighbouring trailers and small bungalows. The massive steel gate was shut, wrapped tightly with a rusty chain and padlock. Tall, black letters on an enormous billboard atop the gate read 'STRAJK'.

For a few seconds, Wałęsa's mustached face appeared on the screen. His eyes were unusually bright, and profuse sweating pearled on his forehead. Mustering all his authority and will, he urged the angry unionists to halt the strike and wait patiently for a government-appointed inquiry to produce its findings.

Some film footage was released to the media by the government task force showing Rulewski and a group of his Union colleagues forming a human chain and singing the Polish national anthem in a dreary corner of the National Council Hall in Bydgoszcz. A short, corpulent police major, repeatedly ordered them to leave the building in a robot-like voice.

The beating itself was not shown and the government commission claimed that it was not able to find out who had done it.

The police head denied that he had issued the order to attack the unionists. "They were forced to leave the area but not beaten," he said. "Perhaps these unionists were injured by their own people to implicate us and cause social unrest," he added, and flashed a brief, sarcastic smile at the television camera.

Liberal newspapers like Życie Warszawy, demanded that the perpetrators be found and punished as well as those who had issued the orders in the first place. Polish television took the opposite stance, blaming Rulewski and his colleagues for the outcome.

Despite the disappointing performance of the government investigators, representatives of the KKP Country's Commission agreed to hold talks with Vice-Premier Rakowski in Warsaw. Union presses gave daily accounts of the negotiations between Solidarity and the government. Wałęsa and the other Union representatives quickly became frustrated. "Mr. Vice-Premier," Wałęsa told Rakowski. "We have talked long enough. You know what we want – we want the guilty exposed and punished. We also want a guarantee from you that union members will not be harassed in the future..."

The military's Żołnierz Wolności published translations of articles from other Eastern Bloc newspapers like Pravda, Rude Pravo and Neues Deutstchland. Solidarity was given labels like *'revisionist'* and even *'fascist'*. The Polish government was also censured for allowing *'the overt counterrevolution'*.

The Voice of America reported on suspicious activity by the Soviet military poised on Poland's borders. American AWACS[15] in West Germany were ordered to monitor the situation.

After exhaustive talks with the government, Solidarity issued a statement to its members. Konrad was at his desk when he heard the familiar squeak of the loudspeaker overhead. He nervously grabbed his cigarettes and lit a Sport.

"... Solidarity to all staff," Budal's Chairman, Wojtek Buliński announced in a slow and even voice. "The KKP conveys this message to all members. Negotiations between our Union leadership and the governmental task force headed by Vice-Premier Rakowski have ended. Despite our willingness to negotiate in good faith, the government has failed to propose any, I repeat, any acceptable solution to the crisis. However, we are going to be showing our good will once more, by staging a four-hour warning strike by all members. That will be our first response. If the crisis is not resolved after that, a general strike of indefinite length will be proclaimed on March 31st. The Regional Solidarity Chapters will be conveying precise instructions to all enterprises. It is important that all members solidly back the Union. Solidarity, and consequently our freedom, is in jeopardy. Everything depends on us."

Konrad sat back and inhaled from his cigarette deeply, drawing the smoke

---

15. AWACS - special early warning reconnaissance planes.

down into his lungs and stomach. Yes, it was a good feeling; his hands no longer shook and his mind had eased. Everything became clear. The short, mustached man, the clumsily-mannered electrician, had decided. They would just follow.

Within a couple of days, Regional Solidarity Chapters quickly transformed themselves into Strike Committees and moved their headquarters to shipyards, factories and other large enterprises.

On the scheduled day, from 8:00 A.M. to noon, the nation went on strike. Bus drivers parked their red vehicles by the side of the road. Construction sites were deserted and workshops quiet. Miners put their drills away and engineers abandoned their plans and drawings. Professors put down their lecture notes, and poets, their pens. At every enterprise, school or public utility white and red banners hung, proclaiming a strike in progress.

Konrad and Maks assumed guard duty in the front lobby of the building. They wore white and red armbands and made sure the glass door was solidly locked. Nobody was allowed to enter or leave the building during the warning strike.

Engineer Smrodziński approached the door just as they were about to hand their armbands over to their replacements. Smrodziński's shiny face was all smiles, but his double chin trembled nervously as he asked to be let outside. He claimed that his cigarettes were out in his car.

Konrad quietly took a package of Sports out of his pocket and passed one to his boss.

Smrodziński thanked him but still made a move towards the door.

"I really must go out," he insisted.

"I am sorry, sir, but it's not possible, not until after noon," Konrad warned and watched with fascination and genuine enjoyment as his fat boss stepped from one side to another. He kept the key to the entrance securely in his front pocket.

"Be realistic. What harm would I cause if I went out for a minute?" Smrodziński shouted.

Maks grinned impudently "I'm sorry, but we have to obey our Union directives. Go and talk to Adam or Wojtek. Perhaps they can help you."

Smrodziński's face turned beet red, he let out an abrupt snort and went back to his room.

Adam Babinicz beamed as he tossed copies of the Union newspapers on Konrad's desk the following day. The warning strike had proved to be a significant victory for Solidarity, with the walk-out affecting every part of the country. Only hospitals and power plants were exempted from the four-hour exercise. Solidarity's action was also supported by the Autonomous Unions, non-unionized workers, and even by some government-controlled Branch Unions.

"How did things go at your enterprise?" Konrad asked his father that evening.

Eryk smiled proudly. "Well, we posted a sign with 'strike' on the billboard, outside our front door, and we didn't do a thing from eight until noon. Everything returned to normal after that."

"Are you planning to strike on March 31st?"

"Yes. We have already hoarded food and there are sleeping bags so that we can stay on as long as required."

In Konrad's office, preparations for the general strike were under way as well. They had been informed that the city's transportation system would operate twice a day for two hours to allow people to get to and from work. In small companies like Budal, the bulk of the employees would sleep at home and union watchmen were organized to be on guard during the night.

Konrad sat in one of the purple armchairs in the Budal lobby and stared at the fragile, glassed front door that he and Maks had guarded just a few days earlier.

It was entertaining to make fun of Smrodziński in front of the rest of the company, he thought. Then he imagined standing by the door, guarding the dim, deserted building at night. It wouldn't take long for a police squad to smash the glass, get inside and do to Budal unionists what they had done to Rulewski.

He crossed his legs and lit a cigarette. It wasn't necessarily anger that he was feeling, or even fear. It was more like a sense of vulnerability and defeat. The idea of commuting to and from work is ridiculous, he murmured. Without a lot of people here around the clock, a general strike at this office has no chance of succeeding. Uncertainty was not to be shared with anyone else. The Union had to be strong and united. He did not feel strong inside, though. He wasn't a man of iron. He loved the Union, cherished freedom, and would do whatever Solidarity ordered him to do, but he realized that the beatings in Bydgoszcz upset him more than he had anticipated. He had to struggle just to be cheerful at work. At home, he had to calm Agata and try to encourage his father.

As he sat down at his desk, he felt nervous tension almost overwhelm him and he suddenly had the desire to talk to someone who knew him well, with all his imperfections and weaknesses. On the eve of the general strike, when even the macho Waldek was hiding quietly behind his desk, Konrad thought of someone who had been absent from his life for two years.

He quietly opened the door of his boss' office and peered inside. The newly-painted room was a refreshing sight, with bright, white walls and robust hanging plants. A solitary mug with a few dregs of coffee was the only object on Smrodziński's glass-topped desk.

Konrad picked up the telephone receiver and started to dial her number. After five digits, he put the phone down, only to pick it up again, a few seconds later.

He recognized her voice right away. It was just as deep and soft as he remembered it.

"Hello Klara, how are things?" he said cheerfully.

"Hello," she answered, "who is speaking please?"

"It is me, Konrad," he blurted out nervously. "We are going on strike tomorrow, you know."

"Yes, I know," she answered.

Pressing the silent receiver to his ear, he tried to imagine how she looked at the other end with her blue eyes, lavish hair and the jolly looking tip of her nose.

"Look, is there anything I can do for you?" she asked somewhat impatiently.

"Well, I was wondering if we could meet sometime," he answered sheepishly.

269

"Oh, really?" she asked sardonically. "After two years you tell me that you want to see me..." She attempted to make her voice sound cool and indifferent but Konrad wasn't quite sure whether the sarcasm was genuine. "I am sorry, Konrad, but I have to go. Good-bye."

"Good-bye Klara."

When he hung up the phone he was convinced that he didn't feel anything towards her, but at the same time, he couldn't deny that his mood improved significantly after their brief conversation.

Despite determination to go on strike, most people remained glued to their television sets that night, hoping that a head-on collision between Solidarity and the government could be avoided at the last minute. It was. Without placing the issue for a vote by the KKP, Wałęsa acted on his own and suspended the strike. People sighed with relief when he agreed to an apology and not too convincing guarantees from the government.

The move led to a split between Wałęsa and Andrzej Gwiazda, Solidarity's Vice-Chairman. Gwiazda was an engineer with a large Gdańsk-based electrical company. He had worked closely with Lech Wałęsa in the late 'Seventies when they organized the underground free trade unions and then during the strike of August 1980. It was apparent to most people, though, that Gwiazda was the tougher of the two men. He was known to have spent his childhood in a Siberian labour camp, and it was obvious that he didn't share Wałęsa's optimism and more conciliatory attitude towards the government. In an open letter to Wałęsa, Gwiazda questioned whether the Solidarity Chairman really had the authority to call off the strike on his own. Wałęsa responded that the Commission had given a mandate to Solidarity's government negotiators. He denied that he had acted autocratically.

Who was right? Konrad didn't know. The cancellation of the strike might have been a weak move politically, but most people were grateful that Wałęsa did it. Solidarity had to represent the people. And what kind of action would the government have had to resort to, he thought, if everyone had walked out? No, he couldn't blame Wałęsa, even though Gwiazda's arguments were reasonable.

The victims of police assault eventually recovered from their wounds and the posters displaying their bleeding faces faded and were torn off buildings downtown. A temporary lull followed that period of intense emotion and the Union agreed to return to a three month moratorium on strikes following a request by the new Prime Minister, General Wojciech Jaruzelski.

It seemed appropriate that the first signs of spring also began to emerge. A slight hint of green appeared on the slender limbs of the trees, and the earliest spring flowers bravely poked their heads out of the ground. Some adventuresome people even threw their winter coats away and paraded down Warsaw's streets, sporting T-shirts with the familiar, red Union logo.

Konrad was about to leave the apartment to go to his English class when someone rang the doorbell.

"It's Jolanta's mother," Eryk yelled. "She says there is a call for you. Hurry up."

Konrad climbed the double flight of steps and entered Mrs. Mackiewicz's apartment. Jolanta's mother passed the phone over to him. "It's a woman," she said with a discreet smile.

He was surprised and pleased that she had called. "Hello Klara," he said with enthusiasm. "How is everything?"

"I wanted to tell you that I was browsing through my books today and I came across one that belongs to you," she explained.

He felt a sudden burst of joy, and the patterns of the wallpapered kitchen began to circle around his head, as if he were riding a broken carousel. "Well, can I meet you?" he asked, forgetting to even mention the book.

"How about 6:00 P.M., 'under the cans'?" she suggested.

It had been their usual meeting place, a small confectionery in a downtown underpass which had a bright ceiling colourfully decorated with masses of shiny metal cans.

Konrad left his English class one hour early. He managed to buy a rose on the street and walked toward the underground tunnel close to Warsaw Central. He passed by a collection of 19th century buildings with their characteristic columns and sculptures, little vegetable stores, and a modern school building. He had only one more intersection to go. As he began to run, he couldn't help wondering if she had changed much.

CHAPTER 5

By early May 1981, deliveries of the equipment earmarked for Kenya Industries Limited were three months behind schedule and engineer Smrodziński's desk was covered with angry telexes from Mr. Mwamba.

Konrad sat across from Smrodziński and watched him scratch his head in distracted puzzlement and light up one cigarette after another, as he answered an overflow of calls from his superiors.

Electrical contactors were the problem. They were needed for the assembly of motor control centers, yet none were available. Budal's supplier, Elektra, simply refused to honour their order. Phone conversations proved to be futile and director Kossak-Roztworowski asked Smrodziński and Konrad to pay the factory a visit. It was situated in a town forty kilometres south-west of the capital.

A driver courteously opened the passenger door of his ancient taxi cab, parked on the driveway which encircled the lawn at the front of the train station, but Smrodziński waved him away. The smokestack of the Elektra compound was clearly visible and it seemed to be within walking distance. As they headed along an asphalt road in its direction, they passed a scattering of dusty, semi-opened crates full of carrots and parsley roots, all displayed in front of a vegetable store; further on, a green construction trailer and a work crew, digging a pit in the shoulder of the road. After crossing a bright, sun drenched meadow, they approached a five storey sandstone building.

The Elektra factory had been built in the early 'Fifties, and its interior decoration was representative of that period of Stalinist industrialization. Two life-like sculptures of human figures, a male and female worker, each holding a hammer and a trowel in heavily muscled hands, stood on either side of the main lobby, their silhouettes reflected on the well polished marble floor of the building.

The director of the plant, Józef Caban greeted them in his office and invited them to sit down and have some coffee and biscuits. He sipped his coffee slowly, obviously in no hurry to talk business with his two visitors.

Smrodziński put his glass down and smiled at the director. Konrad watched him search for a way to initiate a conversation with Caban. After a few minutes he sighed and, without pausing, explained that Poland would lose an important source of dollars if the company's contract couldn't be honoured.

He emphasized that he had recently received several calls from the Party's Central Committee urging Budal to expedite the foreign deliveries.

Director Caban smiled politely and continued to drink his hot beverage. The Adam's apple in his overly-thin neck seemed to wobble uncontrollably. He peered at Konrad and his boss through gold-rimmed spectacles.

When Smrodziński finished his breathless tale, the seemingly thoughtful company director cleared his throat. "I appreciate your commitment to Poland's export performance, but we cannot possibly help you out. Unless we get foreign exchange, we cannot buy what we need to manufacture the equipment that you want. We face a dilemma here too, as you can see," he added. He then flashed a cheerful smile which took both Konrad and his boss by surprise.

"Well, this is a ridiculous situation," Smrodziński said with disgust. "The Kenyans won't pay dollars before they get the equipment, and you can't make it without dollars..."

Director Caban nodded.

"A vicious circle," he commented and began laughing sarcastically.

Konrad was quickly realizing that their face to face meeting was not going to be successful. Their host was simply providing Smrodziński with the same easy answers that he had been giving them over the phone for weeks. Konrad decided to interrupt and asked Caban what Elektra needed to manufacture the contactors.

"Tungsten wire," the director said flatly. "Get me the wire and the contactors will be delivered to you in four weeks." He explained that while tungsten was a small part of the contactors, it was an extremely important component. He estimated that an adequate amount of the wire would cost Budal about five hundred US dollars.

Konrad's hands trembled as he informed the director that Kenya Industries Ltd. would pay a thousand times that amount on the receipt of their motor control centers.

Caban just shrugged. "I know the situation is preposterous, gentlemen, but this would not have happened two years ago. Foreign credit was not a problem back then, but..."

He paused and looked straight at Konrad, staring stonily at the Solidarity button pinned to his breast pocket.

"People like you," he said, pointing at the badge, "have altered economic conditions in this country significantly."

Konrad watched as Engineer Smrodziński's face curled into a wide, self-satisfied grin. Obviously, the director's comic indictment of the Union pleased his boss, but it just made him furious.

"We certainly did not ruin the economy," he said flatly. "Somebody else did it for us, and you, sir..."

His boss interrupted him in mid sentence and flashed a glare in his direction.

"Well, thank you, comrade director," he said quickly to Caban. "We will contact you next week. Hopefully, the situation will change in the meantime..."

"You can call but I wouldn't bother," the man said and accompanied them to the door. "I have been asking for foreign exchange for five months. The Minister of Foreign Trade says there is no money, period."

Smrodziński nodded with understanding and they left the office. Once outside he scowled openly.

"You should keep your opinions to yourself, Mr. Dymowski," he said angrily. "Now he's not going to help us, that's for sure," he exclaimed, throwing his hands up into the air. "I am fed up with your 'Solidarity.' I really mean it. Here you are, wearing that badge everywhere, even when it is inappropriate. You are an engineer, not a blue collar worker. You should understand the difference..." As Konrad was about to open his mouth, a voice from behind commented, "Well, someone stressing differences between Solidarity members? Very interesting."

Both turned around to face a tall, dark bearded man wearing a union button on the lapel of his beige suit. The corners of his mouth curled up in the slightest hint of a smile. "I am sorry, gentlemen, but you were talking so loudly that I couldn't help overhearing. I am the Chairman of Solidarity in this factory. Let me introduce myself. My name is Jan Mokulski. I am also an engineer." The man shook Konrad's hand and also greeted the embarrassed Smrodziński.

"You must be facing a serious problem," the Elektra engineer commented with a laugh. "Perhaps I could help you before you start fighting with each other again?" he added, gently placing his hands on their shoulders.

Smrodziński shook his head rapidly.

"No, thank you, sir. We really are in a hurry to leave."

Konrad grabbed him by the arm. "Why don't we talk to him?"

Jan Mokulski pushed both of them toward a door bearing the name *Solidarity Local #508*. A large white and red poster, depicting the Gdańsk Memorial, hung above the desk which was covered with neatly arranged piles of 'Daily News' and 'Independence'. The man encouraged them to sit down and Konrad quickly explained their predicament to him.

"Our comrade director told you the truth, there is no money," Mokulski said with a smile. "However, if he had really wanted to, he could have helped you out."

Smrodziński's lower jaw dropped.

"Do you mean you could deliver what we need?"

"Without tungsten wire we can't, but maybe we could locate some."

He opened the door to the adjacent room which contained a telex machine. A slight brunette, with a light complexion and green eyes, acknowledged their presence with an unpretentious smile. She wore a simple, but fashionable gray suit which was adorned with a large union badge.

"Monika, could you please telex Solidarity-Silesia and ask them if they know of anybody who might have some tungsten wire in stock?" Mokulski asked. He had hardly finished speaking, when the woman's slim fingers began moving quickly over the rows of telex characters.

Ten minutes later, Monika entered the office and handed a telex message to Mokulski.

"Ah, here we are," he exclaimed, "and much closer than anyone would have suspected. Huta Warszawa happens to have this wire in stock and we can buy it from them. They have more than enough to fill your order."

Smrodziński's eyes blinked rapidly and his mouth opened.

"We are... obliged," he said haltingly, "but I don't understand. We asked director Caban repeatedly if it was possible to do something and he said no."

He scratched his head and smiled with embarrassment.

"I imagine he grumbled about Solidarity and said that everything was in a shambles because of the Union, am I right?" the Elektra engineer asked.

He got out of his seat and began pacing around the room.

"You see, Mr. Smrodziński, there is no mystery behind this miracle. We don't want to destroy this country, we want to rescue it. People like comrade Caban figure that the poorer the economy, the stronger their own positions will be, but they are dead wrong. Comrade Caban is finished anyway," he said gravely. "He performed quite miserably during the 'Seventies and his anti-Union sympathies don't please our staff either. Our people are threatening to wheelbarrow him out of the plant themselves if he isn't dismissed."

Smrodziński said nothing, he just coughed and rubbed the side of his head above his ear, as he always did when he was unnerved.

On their way out of the factory compound, Jan Mokulski pointed to a large altar and cross in Elektra's loading area. The noon sun shone brightly on the pine structure. Hundreds of cut flowers sat in glass jars placed at the altar steps.

"This was built overnight in August 1980," he explained. "Our factory joined the national walkout near the end of the month. The first thing the workers did was erect this altar. During the sit-in, a mass was celebrated twice a day. Now, there is a service every Friday. Our lunch break has been extended by twenty minutes..."

Konrad thanked the man warmly. Smrodziński murmured an unintelligible good-bye and stalked off in the direction of the train station. He spat on the ground with disgust.

"It's unbelievable," he exclaimed. "I am happy that the problem is gone, but I wish it had been solved differently."

"Well, you did your best," Konrad pointed out. "You tried the Party line but it didn't work. The Union connection did."

"That might make you happy but not me," Smrodziński said. "Who the hell is running the country anyway? Directors, the Party or Solidarity? Devil knows. And the weekly mass in the factory yard? It's a bit much. Just like Wałęsa and the Black Madonna on his lapel. This will all have to be stopped one day..."

Listening to Smrodziński's angry comments, Konrad immediately thought of the two sculptures which adorned the lobby of the Elektra building. That was the way the Party wanted the workers to be - just crude, enthused followers of Communist ideals. It didn't take him long to respond to his boss' words.

"You don't like the cross, eh?" he asked. "Well, it has been with this nation since 966 A.D. Besides, your Party has been allowed to hold its meetings right on factory premises for thirty three years. Your Party? What has it done for you, anyway? Did your ideology live through August 1980?" he shrieked.

Konrad smiled to himself as he and Smrodziński waited inside the station for their train home. The dim waiting room was crammed with painted wooden benches in poor repair, and grimy steel ashtrays. The floor was squeaky and uneven. Yet, on the ugly yellow walls of the building, he spotted a series of Solidarity posters.

His relationship with Klara remained rather informal. It was nothing more than her occasional visits to his apartment. He treated her as a friend and did all he could to avoid talking about the past. But the issue was far from being resolved in her mind, he could tell.

Klara used the family car often to run her small toy-making business and whenever she drove up in her Polonez, Eryk was thrilled. He would walk around the blue hatch-back automobile, lovingly patting its hood and fenders, and reminisce about the cars he himself had owned many years before. Klara often allowed him to drive Agata to her brother Fryderyk's apartment. This gave her and Konrad some time together to talk in private.

On a Wednesday in May, they were sitting together on the couch in his bedroom; Eryk and Agata had just returned from a short outing and were watching TV in the other room.

Konrad found himself gazing at Klara closely, comparing her to the woman that he had met almost ten years before. Her hair was still lavish and full, but instead of a brash blond, she had allowed her natural colour, a warm, coppery blond to return. Minute wrinkles had begun to creep around the sides of her eyes, but the eyes were still striking. He embraced her and kissed her small nose.

"I still think that your nose is the prettiest I have ever seen. I really…"

Klara pulled away.

"It's very nice of you to say that," she interrupted dryly. "You didn't think so two years ago, however. Do you remember?"

"Yes," he said quietly, resting his hand on her shoulder, "but it doesn't matter anymore…"

"It might not matter to you, but it does to me," she said, abruptly brushing his hand away. "I will never forgive you."

Like an angry kitten, she leapt away from him, and sat at the far end of the couch, grasping her hands around her bent legs and resting her chin on her knee to avoid his gaze.

"Calm down. We're only friends now, aren't we?"

Klara was trembling.

"I will never forget," she cried. "You just left, without a second thought, because of that woman of yours. And I… I was pregnant by you…" she wailed, and began to weep uncontrollably.

He took her hand and kissed her fingers one by one. "Please, let's not talk about it anymore…" She hesitated and then laid her head on his shoulder and he caressed her hair tenderly.

Eryk suddenly knocked on the door. "Something terrible has happened," he shouted. "Come here right away."

Klara sat back on the couch with a depressed sigh. "Something always happens when we are together," she said. "Do you remember your grandmother's stroke?"

She followed Konrad into the other room. The glass ashtray on the coffee table was spilling with cigarette butts. Silently, his father lit another cigarette and passed the pack to Konrad, without taking his eyes off the TV screen.

It had happened during John Paul II's weekly general audience in St. Peter's Square. The incident was played back over and over again; the white robed man touching the wild array of hands reaching up to him from all directions, caressing children's heads, as his jeep moved slowly and majestically around the square, then the Pope's smiling face transforming into a painful grimace, his body falling back into the arms of an accompanying priest, while the crowd became a confused melee.

"He is in the hospital now," Eryk murmured.

Konrad asked Klara to drive him to church. When they arrived, a crowd had already gathered at the front entrance of the temple.

A priest rushed up to the solid oak doors and hurriedly opened them, allowing a stream of worshippers to enter the building. Konrad and Klara walked quickly into the dim nave toward the large cross at the back of the church which dominated the presbytery. Church bells began to ring and even more people flowed in, immediately kneeling on the floor, some right in the aisle of the church.

A slim priest, robed in a black cassock, told the parishioners that the Pope was undergoing surgery. He knelt and began praying. He was joined shortly after by Father Florian who announced the beginning of a 48 hour period of prayer.

Konrad remembered John Paul's triumphant return to Poland and the mass at Victory Square.

"Lord spare him. He cannot die," he murmured. "He can't leave us..."

Klara knelt by his side, clasping her head in her palms and quietly prayed.

The next day, prayers were even more intense. The pontiff was alive but there was no guarantee that he would survive.

When the media reported that the bullet which entered John Paul's abdomen, had not destroyed any major organ, people sighed with relief. While some continued to pray, others turned their attention to the would-be assassin. Many were convinced that the Turk, Mehmed Ali Agca was just a pawn. "But for who?" they asked. Who in the world could feel threatened by the philosophy of human dignity and love?

As Konrad stepped off the streetcar on Aleje Jerozolimskie street, he watched as a small gathering of light clouds soared above the white nineteenth century buildings on the north side of the avenue.

Just before leaving home that afternoon, Konrad had pinned a small image of John Paul II on the left pocket of his denim jacket, placing it right beside his Union button. Two years before, he had worn the same pin, during the papal mass in Victory Square.

Thousands of people were converging from all directions and marching toward St. Anna's Church for an open-air mass.

A short, blond-haired woman, a student he thought, beckoned him to join the column of people marching along Krakowskie Przedmieście, lined on both sides with three storey buildings in white or yellow with steep, tiled roofs. The gray-haired heads of aged peered down at the moving crowd from the open windows and balconies of their apartments above. They watched blue-jeaned young people with the Independent Association of Students parading under their green and white union banners.

The street opened into a narrow square dominated by a monument to poet

Adam Mickiewicz[16], surrounded by a low, wrought iron barrier and a neat carpet of grass. There, the students were joined by Solidarity members and representatives of many other organizations, carrying flags and large posters with the Pope's photograph.

Konrad managed to get a spot adjacent to the entrance of the St. Anna's Church, where an altar, specially constructed for the mass, was located. All of the streets and squares in the nearby area were densely packed with what looked like a field of waving hands, arms and flags.

He was able to identify a number of the figures on the podium behind the altar – Cardinal Macharski, Archbishop Miziołek and other members of the church hierarchy. With squinted eyes, he scanned the stage for Cardinal Wyszyński but the old priest wasn't there.

As the service was about to commence, Cardinal Macharski mentioned the Primate. He revealed that indeed, Cardinal Wyszyński wasn't able to attend because of a serious illness; an illness, he said, for which there was still no cure.

Konrad closed his eyes. The handsome, intense face of doctor Milewska, holding Julia's medical file emerged, and then faded from his mind, as the image of a pale, gasping Julia replaced it, her hand waving wildly in a dim hospital corridor.

As his thoughts returned to the sun-filled square and the altar in front of him, he realized that the gravity of the Cardinal's condition had scarcely even bothered his conscience before. My God, how unthankful I am, he cried to himself.

Suddenly, the calm and clear voice of the Primate filled the air, a taped address that he had recorded from his bed. He thanked his fellow countrymen for the prayers they might have said on his behalf but he was quick to ask them to focus on the Pope's survival.

"I convey all prayers to him. Yours and mine," the Cardinal said. "I am accepting my suffering eagerly so that he will survive. From now on, pray for him only."

Prayers continued throughout the country. In Cracow, the city with the closest ties to the Pope, students called off their traditional rag week entertainment gatherings and instead organized a White March on the Sunday following the assassination attempt. On television, Konrad watched thousands of Cracovians dressed in white converging in the city's market place.

Just when people were becoming confident about the Pope's survival, news of Primate Cardinal Stefan Wyszyński's death was released.

Again, Konrad stood amongst a sea of people in Victory Square, but this time it was not dominated by a triumphant Papal altar, but by an oak casket sitting atop a catafalque.

Words were being murmured over the coffin, but Konrad was so overcome by a sense of loss that he had to struggle just to be aware of the goings on around him.

---

16. Adam Mickiewicz, Juliusz Słowacki, Zygmunt Krasiński and Cyprian Norwid were the greatest Polish Romantic poets of mid 19th century. Adam Mickiewicz is often considered "the first among equals". His play "Dziady" ("The Forefathers' Eve") was banned by the Soviet Ambassador in 1968.

Over a hundred thousand participants came to pay homage to the late Primate. Leaders from virtually every Polish organization were involved in the funeral service.

"He was a unique Primate in our millennium of Christianity," Cardinal Macharski told the crowds as the coffin was lifted and carried down to the crypt of St. John's Cathedral in the Old Town. The government proclaimed an official period of national mourning.

Klara called him the next day and asked if he would be willing to go to a party with her that evening but he had to decline. The mourning period for the Cardinal had just begun and he had agreed to help Sister Maria at the parish church.

"What are you going to be doing?" Klara asked with interest.

Once a year, a mass and a meeting for the ill and disabled was organized by the parish. People who were unable to attend on their own, were provided with transportation. After the service, they were served a snack of tea and cake in the parish hall.

"I won't go to the party," Klara decided. "I'll drive some of the people to the church."

Dreary coated, and predominantly female, elderly parishioners filled the brightly lit church. Father Florian looked down on the crowd and smiled, blessing them several times. He then delivered a short sermon which emphasized that through their illness and suffering they were closer to Christ than most people.

"Your prayers go straight to God, the Lord of the poor."

Klara joined Konrad to help Sister Maria and the other nuns get everyone down to the basement. It wasn't easy, many of them could barely walk and they had to be supported firmly to get through the windy flight of steep stairs and into one of the large rooms which was normally used for religion classes. Tables were arranged in a circle around the room and covered with a gay tablecloth. Dozens of young people in colourful clothing helped the nuns to seat everyone and distribute cakes and tea. A small group of student musicians started playing some subtle rock variations of popular religious songs.

Agata, dressed in her favourite beige suit, smiled proudly and chatted with Sister Maria as she enjoyed her second piece of cake. She seemed to appreciate the sweet morsels more than usual, at a time when even the shelves in the bakeries were empty due to shortages of eggs, margarine and sugar.

An elderly woman with a flowered kerchief covering her head, leaned toward Sister Maria. She placed her trembling hand on the nun's arm.

"If it wasn't for you, sister," she said quietly. "Most of us would have died long ago. God bless you for your daily visits, God bless you."

Klara took Agata home and then returned to help transport the other people who were in need of a ride. She and Konrad received endless thanks and blessings as they escorted the shrunken and hesitating elderly people from the street curb to the doors of their apartments.

Klara smiled and reassured them repeatedly that she enjoyed doing it. Konrad watched proudly as the attractive woman walked slowly down the parish hall, guiding a very tiny old lady to the stairs.

The last woman to be taken home, was the most helpless of all. She was restricted to a wheelchair and lived in a nursing home run by nuns. Many memories flashed in front of Konrad's eyes, as he wheeled the woman toward Klara's Polonez. Just as he was about to lift her into the car, he noticed that she was wearing a Solidarity badge.

"So you are a member of the Union," he remarked with a pleasant smile.

The elderly woman grinned.

"Well, I wouldn't be called an activist," she said, "but I was admitted as an honorary member by Local 606, which was formed by the teachers and workers at a school close to my nursing home. I can't do much to help with the struggle but I pray for all of you."

Klara quickly encouraged the woman.

"That is very important," she said quietly.

"Yes, prayer is important," Konrad echoed. "Our Pope has survived because we prayed for his life. Faith can be very effective."

"It is," the immobile woman said, nodding in agreement. "But I also think that active struggle is important. The people with Local 606 come to our nursing home every day. They bring us the Union papers and we read them. Now, we feel a bit closer to young people like you. We know Solidarity was the first lay organization to bring up the issue of disabled people and our low pensions. They have embraced us along with everybody else in this nation," she said.

"To me, this badge," she added pointing at her breast, "is very precious. Almost as precious as this..."

She reached into her pocket and pulled out a string of black rosary beads.

CHAPTER 6

Agata greeted him at the door when he arrived home from work.

"You won't believe what I managed to buy today," she told him, rubbing her hands together with satisfaction and twirling around the hallway. Konrad guessed that she had bought some eggs.

"No, much better than that," she exclaimed. "You won't believe it."

Eryk emerged from the kitchen, wearing a pair of shorts and a T-shirt, his usual uniform for peeling the family's potatoes.

"Agata managed to get ham, smoked tenderloin, sausage and beef," his father said. "She used up all our coupons. The refrigerator hasn't looked like this since the 'Sixties."

"Unbelievable," Konrad said when he opened the fridge. "What has happened?"

Agata shook her head. "Nobody seems to know. Some people in the store said that it might be the beginning of a real improvement. They say Wałęsa must have managed to reach an agreement with the government on the food issue."

Konrad was puzzled. He hadn't heard or read anything about a new agreement between the government and the Union.

"And you won't guess who was in the line with me," Agata added with excitement. "For the first time there were some policemen and a few military officers."

"Our neighbour, Sgt. Klepka is furious," Eryk said, as he rinsed the potatoes in a strainer. "I met him on the streetcar this afternoon. His Polonez is in the garage, you know... He says the internal store at the Police Command is completely empty. Now he and his wife have to use coupons and shop like the rest of us."

They had a marvelous dinner that evening. Agata fried three enormous steaks and they had them with mashed potatoes and green beans.

"After a dinner like that, it's important to have a good cigarette," Eryk commented, sitting back in their old, blue armchair, and crossing his still muscular calves.

Cigarettes had been difficult to get since early spring and though the government had begun rationing them, the supply was unpredictable.

"You have used up your quota and Agata's," Konrad reminded.

"Yes, but they are only Sports or Klubowe. I thought you might have some Carmens or Marlboro."

Konrad teased his father. "Marlboro? Has anyone seen a single package since March?"

"Well, if you don't have any, I guess a Sport will have to do," Eryk said with resignation, "although I hate that brand. It's all we smoked in prison."

Konrad grimaced whenever his father mentioned his time spent in prison. He had paid Eryk two visits during his last term. He remembered the massive steel gate, which was the prison's only opening into the street. A much smaller door, actually a part of the gate, acted as an entrance and exit for prison visitors. A gray uniformed officer had collected his ID card, and unlocked the door, allowing him and other visitors to enter a cavernous yard, behind the administrative portion of the premises. Led by another guard, they encountered another, less imposing gate in a second fence, this one decorated with barbed wire. Men, standing in elevated guard booths, equipped with reflectors and machine guns watched from above.

The small building set aside for visitors was simple, with a plain white interior and one long table, which was designed to prevent the passing of money, food and cigarettes to the shaven and uniformed inmates.

However, when one of the turnkeys wasn't looking, banknotes were put over the table's barricade, and passed to the convicts, who swallowed them immediately. Passing through a guard search, they would return to their cells and force themselves to vomit. The bills were then cleaned and used to make purchases in the canteen such as cigarettes, onions, bread or margarine to supplement the meager meals provided at the prison.

Konrad looked at his father, got up and went to his bedroom where he opened his cupboard and took out a package of Marlboros. Eryk accepted them gratefully and passed a cigarette to Konrad. Sitting back again in the comfortable armchair, he skillfully brought his Ronson lighter up to mouth. Konrad observed his movements. He seemed to be relaxed and contented, his face was well shaven.

"These are Polish Marlboros, aren't they?" Eryk remarked, inhaling the smoke with delight. "I didn't think they sold them anymore."

"They still do in Pewex if you have dollars..."

"We can't even buy Polish-made cigarettes with our own currency," Eryk exclaimed. "What has happened to the usual supply? They seemed to have disappeared overnight."

Konrad shook his head and shrugged.

"It's the same with razor blades," his father continued, sending puffs of bluish smoke around the room. "I saw an interview with the director of the Polish Gillette company yesterday. The man was swearing that they were operating at full capacity... but just try to buy a razor blade."

"More and more people that I queue with..." Agata interjected firmly, "are saying that distribution should be handled by Solidarity so that goods will be taken right from the factories to the stores."

"I hate to be pessimistic," Eryk commented, "but we all know how much the government opposes that."

Konrad had to agree with him. Despite Solidarity's spectacular victories in some areas, in many ways the Union was helpless. Provisions of all kinds were vanishing.

"I bought one more thing today," Agata said. She was all smiles. "I bought a cake."

"Really?" Eryk asked, getting out of his armchair. He had a love for sweets just like his aunt.

They both opened their mouths in disbelief when Konrad told them he wouldn't be having any dessert. Shaking her head rapidly, Agata tried to convince him that the cake was delicious and not to be missed.

"You and Eryk go ahead, I am going on a strict diet. Now that I have finished my English studies, I really have to do something. No more potatoes, bread, cakes or sugar of any kind."

"Are you crazy?" Eryk asked. "What will you eat then?"

Konrad looked down at his fat-lined stomach and squirmed.

"Milk, cheese, carrots and apples will have to do. I weigh 93 kilograms. I can't squeeze into any of my clothes any longer." Eryk looked at him sternly.

"You're going to make yourself sick if you do that," he said. "Why don't you just exercise? I met your friend Irian the other day. He was jogging. Why don't you run with him?"

Konrad pondered his father's suggestion, and decided that it would be nice to see Irian more often. They could exercise together, yes, but he also hoped that contact with his friend would do him some good. He just didn't feel himself. Sleep evaded him most nights and he spent hours smoking and staring at the ceiling of his bedroom. His thoughts weren't pleasant. They always brought foreboding and apprehension, yet he had difficulty defining what was causing his anxiety.

The next day he went down into the basement and unlocked his bike. It was covered by a thick layer of dust. He wiped it off and added some air to the tires with his small handpump.

From the busy downtown street, lined with tall, pre-war buildings and travelled frequently by speeding streetcars, he pedalled out of the city. A few kilometres out, the traffic had dispersed, and the street shrunk to a narrow, asphalt road. Just beyond a grassy meadow, drenched by the golden-hued sun of the late afternoon, he could see a new subdivision dominated by box-like gray buildings.

The housing situation in the city was so bad that the tenants had moved in before the outside of their building was finished or any grass-sod had been laid down on the muddy ground. Traces of construction materials were littered around the front.

He locked up his bike and climbed to the second floor where Irian, dressed in a green track suit, greeted him at his doorstep.

"You have just come at the right time. My enthusiasm for jogging is disappearing quickly."

Konrad was encouraged by Irian's appearance. His friend was even more overweight than he was. His still bright eyes seemed to be enveloped in overly fleshy cheeks and that, along with a massive neck, made him resemble a bull. Irian laughed when he noticed Konrad scrutinizing his protruding belly.

"How can you refuse when you have a wife who cooks like mine. Ela knows over a hundred wonderful dishes with potatoes."

In contrast to her husband's wide girth, Ela was a slim, almost skinny woman with a youthful, short haircut and bright, deep-set eyes which had a hint of mischievousness about them.

Their apartment had two small bedrooms. In one of them, Konrad saw a crib and a large pile of toys in the corner.

"Be quiet please," Ela whispered. "If Irena wakes up now, we'll have her for the rest of the evening."

He looked down at their little daughter breathing regularly under a fluffy, white comforter and withdrew into the hallway. Irian and Ela's bedroom was furnished with a small set of drawers and an old, green upholstered sofa bed which he recognized from Irian's parents' apartment. In their fair-sized livingroom, Konrad looked down at a simple blue rug.

"This is a wedding gift from my uncle," Ela explained. "It's nothing special but it's a carpet nevertheless."

Two large armchairs faced a television in the room. Konrad hesitated for a few seconds before sitting down. It was obvious that one of them would have to remain standing.

"Sit down please," Ela said. "I have work to do in the kitchen."

She returned with two glasses of clear tea and a bowl full of green apples.

"I didn't bring any sugar," she pointed out with a short giggle. "You two are on a diet, aren't you?"

They discussed the Union. Irian, who was an engineer with a construction company, told him that more than half of the employees had joined Solidarity. He was a Solidarity boss at Warsaw Construction North.

"What about those who didn't sign up with you?" Konrad asked.

"They're Branch Union people mainly," Irian explained with obvious disgust. "Most of them belong to the Party and we don't get along with them very well. Things have gotten worse since the four hour warning strike too…"

Konrad remembered watching coverage of the event on television. One news story about the warning strike on construction sites, gave the impression that Solidarity people were beating workers who were refusing to join the walkout.

Irian shook his head and let out a brief, sarcastic laugh.

"Albin Siwak and his Branch Union boys are liars. I was there. From eight to twelve we walked out. Meanwhile, the Branch Unionists worked as hard as they could. Normally, they're the last to show up for work and the first to take breaks. Our guys called them rats and bastards and the Branch Unionists started throwing rocks. I got one, right here," he said, pointing to his shoulder. "But I told our people to stay in the locker room after that and they did. There was no beating of Branch Unionists."

Konrad was intrigued by Albin Siwak. Nobody seemed to be able to decipher the man's motives. During his several public appearances, he had fiercely criticized Lech Wałęsa and then turned around and done the same thing with Vice-Premier Mieczysław Rakowski.

Irian's face curled into a grimace. "The man is an idiot," he said, stretching his trunk-like legs in front of him. "His speeches are as ridiculous as his grammar. What I especially don't like, is his preoccupation with 'order'. We both know what this word means when it's coming out of the mouth of a Communist in this country. "

Ela came into the living room. "What are you joggers debating now?" she asked with an amused smile. She burst into laughter at the mention of Albin Siwak's name.

"Do you know that university students joke about him all the time? I saw posters in a student club the other day. It read, 'the most intelligent man in Poland, Albin Siwak, needs no ticket – entry gratis'. Some students though," she continued with a wink, "predict that he may have a great career ahead of him in the circus. He's better than a clown..."

"Who needs a circus?" Irian asked in a more serious voice. "We have the Central Committee. But, we shouldn't disregard Siwak. Someone is using that guy. He's too stupid to do anything on his own."

"Enough," Ela said with a distinct clearing of the throat. She showed them to the door. "You are supposed to be jogging."

Konrad found that he was in worse shape than he had suspected. After only 200 metres, he started to gasp and he slowed down to walk. Irian looked behind and chastized him.

"Come on. You can't give up so easily. According to my jogging guide, the first half hour is the worst. After that, you'll be able to run as long as you want."

Konrad gritted his teeth and started to pick his feet off the ground again. The pavement beneath changed from soft, new asphalt to hard, uneven cobblestones and he joined Irian on the soft shoulder. They left the new subdivision and found themselves on a suburban country road. Potato fields, meadows and a few wooden, one-story farmers' buildings were on either side. The only sign indicating that they were still in the city was the red transit bus that passed them. The driver tooted his horn and waved through the window. "That's right, run you fat guys. It's good for you," he shouted.

Konrad kept his head down and tried to concentrate. The salty sweat that was streaming into his eyes was uncomfortable, and a layer of dust was slowly settling on his forehead, but the jogging was definitely starting to get a bit easier.

The sun was just setting. As they ran in the direction away from the city, the wide wheat field on their right, was illuminated by a deep, red glow.

Konrad's enthusiasm for his diet and jogging routine didn't wane. Every other day, he cycled to Irian's apartment and the two of them would go jogging along their usual route towards a small forest on the outskirts of the city.

One day, in the middle of a jogging session, Konrad noticed that Irian was picking up speed suddenly. All he could do was try to keep up with him.

"We have to run faster, Konrad. I forgot, *Opole* is on tonight."

Opole was an annual Polish song festival held in the city by that name. Rumours circulated through the country that it was going to be very political and freedom-minded that year.

Ela greeted them at the door. "Hurry up, it has already started," she exclaimed.

They rushed into the living room and threw themselves in the armchairs in front of the television. The brightly lit stage of the Forest Opera in Opole filled the screen. It was dominated by a sculpture-like representation of a pear tree, set right in the centre.

The first song told the story of a Polish girl who was lured out of the country by the promise of a foreign career and money. The witty song generated genuine laughter. It was an obvious reference to the notorious 'Cipex' affaire. In a quest for foreign cash in the late 'Seventies, enterprising directors of some Polish entertainment agencies started to recruit young women for promising singing careers in the West. As it turned out, the girls were promptly delivered to brothels in Italy. Their passports were often confiscated and most of them found themselves threatened by local pimps. The affaire was uncovered after Edward Gierek's demise in 1980.

After a short break, a small group of young people assembled on the stage. Their faces were solemn and that suited the song they began to sing. It was intense and disruptive to the ear.

"He stands on the tribune, ovation persists
The Leader is greeting his subjects below...
'Let's make a giant leap,' he strongly insists
Let us build a future like you've never known.
When someone keeps asking, 'Where are we to go?'
His voice isn't heard, claque's clapping their hands
The Leader is greeting his subjects below
The Leader is saying, 'Let's have bread and games!'
The bread is for Him, the games for the people
The faithful follow the Leader!"

Guitars in the background played passionately for a few minutes before the song continued.

"And more ovations, games follow the games
But where is the bread? Has it all been eaten?
The claque are still clapping, the tribune still stands
But where is the Boss? Where is our Leader?"

The performers were looking straight into the camera and singing in a loud, challenging chorus.

"Don't ask silly questions. The Leader is sick.
He's in the hospital, he is sad and poor
'But where is the bread?', the people repeat.
We want him to answer, we mustn't be fooled."

Again, the guitars played vigorously and the last verse followed.

"He's now left the tribune. He's pleading for silence.
Yes, something went wrong, but be quiet folks
The people are looking at the void behind Him
And they see only a hoax
The Leader... and behind... a hoax!"

The last sentence was nothing more than a loud shout.

Hoax - an act intended to trick or dupe. Something that only imitates the truth. The four letter word which summed up the entire decade that had just passed; ten years during which words such as 'motherland' and 'nation' had lost their original meaning and significance, and were uttered repeatedly by those who believed in nothing spiritual.

Despite the exercise he was getting, Konrad knew he was becoming more tense by the day. He realized that unless he shared his problems with someone else, he would sink even deeper. He had often tried to talk to Irian, but he always felt somewhat intimidated by his friend. Irian worked hard, enjoyed his family and was fully engaged in Union activities. Often these things were nothing more than a duty to Konrad.

He thought of Albert. Since their vacation together, they had only seen each other a few times, but he sensed that Albert was the right person to talk to. He was carefree and straightforward and Konrad didn't have to worry about him being too 'perfect'.

When Albert first opened the door, Konrad backed up as if he was confronting a stranger. His friend's hair was cut short and he had a lavish mustache. His eyes gleamed as he looked at Konrad.

"What's wrong? Did you take me for Lech Wałęsa?" he asked, obviously enjoying his friend's surprised response.

Konrad chuckled. "Not exactly, but your mustache is a lot like his..."

Albert led him into the livingroom which was virtually covered with scattered pieces of paper. A typewriter was sitting on the table near the front window. Konrad was intrigued by the papers strewn around the room.

"It's supposed to be a cabaret script," Albert quickly explained, poking head out of the kitchen. "You didn't know that I have become a great writer, did you?" he asked with an excited grin, and then promised to explain everything after he had prepared their tea. While he was in the kitchen, Konrad quietly leafed through the papers and scanned through some of the text.

The Students:

"Albin... take it easy... if you killed all of the Solidarity members, there would be 10 million fewer Poles."

Albin Siwak:

"And that's exactly what we need... There will be plenty of food and apartments for the remaining 26 million..."

Albert grabbed the paper out of his hand.

"You shouldn't read it now, Konrad. It needs a lot of polishing. It won't be ready for another month, but then it will be premiering at the Stodoła Student Club. I hope you will come and see it."

"It looks interesting..."

"It had better be. I've been working on it for weeks. It's going to ridicule all the bastards who oppose the renewal," he explained with excitement.

Konrad looked at Albert's bright eyes and his long mustache.

"I can't believe it," he exclaimed, "when you and I went to the mountains just a year ago, all you talked about was your mother's new Polonez..."

Albert grinned and sat down beside him.

"You see Konrad," he began, "Everything has changed. Eleonora didn't get her talon and about three weeks ago the government stopped supplying meat to her Ministry. She shops in normal stores now."

Konrad shook his head with disbelief.

"You're kidding..."

"Not at all. It's true. I don't think anyone expected it to happen. Isn't it great?"

Konrad was stunned.

"You are happy that you don't get your daily ham?"

Albert shrugged.

"It doesn't matter any more. All of us have to be given the same opportunities. The Gdańsk Agreement called for equality... besides, how could I write my script if I didn't line up for meat like everyone else? A bit of malnutrition helps my art," he added merrily.

"You certainly seem to be happy these days," Konrad remarked.

Albert looked at him squarely.

"I am," he said. "I was working on this project and well, two weeks ago Henia came down to visit me. She liked the idea and the script. Then she proposed to me. Can you believe it?"

Konrad's couldn't help thinking that everybody else's life seemed to be progressing logically to fulfill its destiny. As he inquired further about Albert's wedding, he knew that his voice was tinged with sarcasm and jealousy. Albert however, continued to talk as if nothing had happened.

"Henia wants to attend the First Solidarity Delegate Congress. She has to win a delegate position. She is very popular where she works now but if she changed jobs, she wouldn't have a chance of winning. That's why our wedding is scheduled for Christmas Day."

Konrad congratulated his friend. He realized that things had changed dramatically since their school days. The sense of purpose that had driven him since his stint in the army was exhausted and he knew it.

Albert must have read his thoughts.

"You don't look good, Konrad. You seem to have lost some weight. Are you sick?"

He attempted to smile, and then told Albert about his diet and exercise program.

"But yes," he said, looking at Albert with all seriousness. "I don't feel like myself. I don't know if I can handle what is going on right now much longer. That's why I've come.."

Albert passed him a cigarette.

"Tell me everything. What are you feeling?"

"I really don't know, in the middle of the night I hear noises and I open the window. When I look outside, the street is always calm and silent. Then I go back to bed and I can't sleep for hours. At work, I can hardly keep myself from blowing up at my friends. Then, I return home from work and I wonder if Eryk is going to be there. I always run from the bus stop back to the apartment. I worry about him, about everything..."

Albert looked with concern at the dark circles which rimmed Konrad's eyes and his waxy complexion.

"You should see a doctor," he said firmly. "I don't think I've seen you like this before. Something is definitely wrong."

Konrad shrugged.

"No doctor can do anything for me," he said grimly. "Can he just make all of our problems disappear in a flash? Make Eryk a responsible person?"

Albert took a sip of his tea and set his cup down.

"You have problems," he said quietly, "but the rest of us do too. It looks like everything is just too much for you."

Konrad sighed, looked at his watch and told Albert that he had to leave.

As he descended in the elevator, he chastized himself for not telling Albert the whole story. It was true that he was still worrying about his father, but that wasn't the primary reason behind his incipient paranoia. The noises he heard at night were recognizable, like tanks rolling down the street. They woke him up every night and he hated himself for hearing them.

Eryk and Agata also noticed his anxiety.

"You should stop starving yourself," his father told him. "Why are you so tense? If it's because of me, you won't have to worry. I'm going on a four week vacation on Friday."

He had just sat down in a livingroom armchair and happily lit up a cigarette, when Konrad began shouting at him.

"Do you want to ruin everything?"

"No," Eryk answered quietly, "but I deserve a vacation just like anybody else. I'm going on a holiday, not a drinking spree."

The station platform was congested with travellers heading south. A large group of blue-jeaned teenagers, wearing hats and Solidarity shirts, leant against their backpacks and played guitars, while mothers chased after their scrambling children.

Eryk and Konrad managed to get a seat on a bench beside an oval, green painted kiosk. The stand used to sell cigarettes and candies but its display shelves were completely empty and it was padlocked shut.

As the large, chrome-bumpered locomotive, pulling about a dozen passenger cars, arrived at the station, people began shouting to each other, grabbing their luggage and running along the tracks in preparation for a contest for compartment seats. The train emitted a loud blast of its horn.

Konrad grabbed the rail beside the car door before the vehicle had even stopped, jumped inside and, after finding a vacant seat in a second class compartment, he opened the window. Eryk groaned as he strained to lift his luggage up to Konrad and then he climbed on to the train. They kissed each other quickly and Konrad struggled through the narrow, dim aisle and made his way on to the platform.

Eryk waved at him from the window and smiled. As Konrad looked up at his father, he felt his throat tighten.

"Don't let me down," he said, in a hoarse voice.

Eryk grinned.

"Don't worry about me. You should see Klara and enjoy yourself more."

The train began pulling ahead and he found himself surrounded by the crowd of onlookers. He could barely see Eryk's gray head through the waving hands, as it disappeared into the red sunset glow in the distance.

The unusual meat supplies the family had enjoyed two weeks earlier, seemed like a passing dream. Sitting in front of the television set, sipping some tea from her large, white mug, Agata complained about the lack of food in the stores that evening.

"A week ago at least there was vinegar and cheap tea on the shelves. Now, they bring in bread once a day, that's all."

She asked him to check the stores near Budal to see if they had any food and he agreed, although he knew that 'Blind Mary's' shelves had been empty for over a month.

The next day after work he began walking toward the grocery store, expecting only to see the pretty eyes of the salesgirl. After passing a hedge which separated Budal's muddy parking lot from the street, he stopped and stared with surprise at the scene in front of him. A fair-sized queue was forming in front of 'Blind Mary's' and he watched as people left the store carrying bags filled with with their purchases. It didn't take him more than five seconds to join the line and begin questioning the other queuers. He listened with surprise, when the tall, well-muscled man in front of him explained that the store was selling all sorts of things, including cigarettes, biscuits and sweets.

"A Solidarity van brought a huge truckload of stuff in ten minutes ago. Some Union members discovered an underground stash of food. It was in the forest, not far from the city."

Konrad shook his head repeatedly.

"I've heard stories about clandestine food caches but I thought they were just gossip."

"Gossip," the man shouted, and cocked his head to the side, "You should have been here earlier. The guy with the Union told us all the details. They found an entire pit full of food!"

Other people in the line nodded and loudly confirmed the account.

Konrad was grateful that he had his food and cigarette coupons in his wallet as 'Blind Mary', proud as a peacock, put biscuits, two kilograms of cereal and five packages of Carmen cigarettes down on the worn, wooden counter.

Lech Wałęsa was reluctant to initiate any strike action for political reasons. The Party's Ninth Congress was convening in July and the Union's first national convention was scheduled for early September.

"We must let the two congresses take place in peace. We'll have ours, let them have theirs," he said. It failed to stem a public outcry.

"Our children are hungry, our husbands are hungry and we can't buy anything in the stores. They are starving us to death," many women protested.

The Union press and even some official newspapers began to report on incidents of the deliberate disposal of food products in municipal dumps near several small towns. Some militants threatened to act on their own, without the Union's consent. Hunger demonstrations sprang up all over the country and people chose to leave the protection of factory fences and pour into the streets, shoving their placards and banners into the air, oblivious to the past, deaf to the warnings, and confident that the whole Union was on their side.

In the middle of preparations for its first national congress, Solidarity assumed sponsorship of the protests.

A shaky transit bus stopped abruptly, sending a few passengers sprawling along the central aisle. The centre doors jerked open with a loud hiss and Konrad jumped down on the pavement.

A row of red streetcars lined Marszałkowska street. Motionless, they stretched all the way from the Saski Garden, past the glassed-in Centrum department stores, down to Warsaw's main intersection. Hundreds of placards and banners waved above the columns of protesters who marched beside an impressive convoy of trucks and vans, all decorated with Solidarity flags and sending a noisy chorus of horns into the air.

Konrad found himself walking behind a blond woman who was carrying one pole of an enormous painted banner which read, *'You Are Starving Kids'*.

Initially, the plan was to turn on to Aleje Jerozolimskie Avenue and demonstrate in front of the Party's Central Committee headquarters, which were located in a large, narrow-windowed building called 'The Party House'. From there, the demonstrators were to disperse. But, as the marchers edged closer towards the intersection, angry voices began demanding that the demonstration continue past the 'Party House' and proceed towards the Soviet Embassy.

The intersection near the Forum Hotel, proved to be the end point of the march. Cool, silent rows of steel-gray uniformed police stood behind the roadblocks which cut Aleje Jerozolimskie Avenue in half. Some zealous youngsters threatened to stone the policemen unless they allowed them to proceed, but the human barricade didn't move.

The voice of Zbigniew Bujak cut through the turmoil. The Solidarity-Mazowsze leader climbed on an improvised podium on the top of the truck, decorated with Polish and Union flags. He announced that the roadblocks would not be crossed, but the city centre would remain occupied for forty eight hours. "The 'Party House' is only two blocks away. They'll hear us."

At about ten o'clock that evening, Konrad quietly slipped out of the apartment, being careful not to waken Agata. He felt exhilarated as he walked toward the site of the sit-in. The whole area was brightly illuminated by orange-tinted street lamps and a few floodlights. Colourful summer shirts and dresses filled the street and adjacent sidewalks and lawns. It was like a field of blossoming flowers that had mysteriously been sown right in the very core of Warsaw.

Large, steaming pots sat beneath neatly spaced linden trees in the middle of the manicured lawn of the white balconied Metropol Hotel. Volunteers ladled out cabbage soup that had been provided by the Farmers' Union to the protesters, who sat on empty crates, pails, blankets or whatever else was available.

By the following day, the mood of the gathering had changed dramatically, from anger to joyfulness, as people turned their attention to the idea of freedom. Famous varsovian actors and performers entertained the crowds from an improvised stage. White and red Polish flags mixed with Solidarity placards and green Rural Solidarity banners. Members of the Independent Association of Students played guitars and sang political songs, some of which Konrad remembered from the recent Opole Festival. Soon, they all began to chant, "So-li-dar-ność, Spra-wie-dli-wość; Solidarity - Justice."

When the forty eight hours had passed, the crowds peacefully dispersed, the police removed their barricades and the city's transit system began operating normally again.

The sprawling branches of the majestic oaks cast a pleasant shadow on the series of green-painted benches; their grooved trunks resembling the filigreed motifs of classical columns, giving the space a temple-like effect.

The sunny June afternoon was exceptionally warm; the air fresh and inviting after a brief spring shower.

They got up and began walking down Aleje Ujazdowskie Avenue, passing by the intricate wrought iron fence of the city's botanical gardens. Konrad slipped his hand around her waist. He could feel Klara's shapely body through the thin layer of her silk dress. He could smell her sweet make-up and perfume as he kissed the woman's lips and nose.

At the front entrance of Łazienki Park, two painted buckets, filled with roses and tulips, were strategically placed. An overweight woman sat on a stool behind the flowers.

Klara's lips touched his cheek with a brief, delicate kiss, when he handed her a bunch of sweetheart roses.

"They are beautiful," she whispered. "I only wonder how I'm going to be able to take them home with me..."

Agata greeted them anxiously in the hallway.

"I'm so glad you have come back," she said.

Konrad looked down at his great-aunt's hands. They were shaking violently. He embraced her and asked why she was upset.

Still trembling, Agata explained that something had happened in Otwock. She talked quickly, raising her hands in exasperation, but from bits and pieces of her chaotic monologue, Konrad and Klara managed to find out that some people have been beaten by the police, that a jail had been set on fire, and that Solidarity activists had arrived on the scene.

"The newsman insisted that it was all the Union's fault," Agata added, shaking her head.

Klara and Konrad followed her into Julia's old bedroom, where the television set was blaring.

On the screen, a long, concrete platform was crowded with people. In the background, a slim trace of smoke was emanating from a pile of rubble nestled beside a row of tall poplars, planted along the railroad tracks.

The TV camera was focused on the figure of a short, slightly overweight reporter with dark, unkept hair and fleshy cheeks who was talking rapidly and waving his hands around violently for emphasis.

"Ladies and gentlemen," he shouted into his microphone, trying to overcome the uproar behind him. "Otwock has never experienced violence like this. Hundreds of people are gathered here, at the town railway station." He extended his arm back toward the crowd in the background.

"At this point, the police station is in a shambles, two youngsters are in the hospital and representatives with Solidarity-Mazowsze Region are involved... Otwock is not a quiet little town anymore. Tension and unrest persist. We will be monitoring the situation closely and will return in half an hour."

The TV broadcast hadn't given them any new information. Agata slumped in her chair and stared up at Konrad and Klara with her faded green eyes. She looked very unhappy, with her chin resting on her palm; her thin fingers with their arthritic joints moving nervously.

Klara walked over to Agata and gave her a hug.

"We'll have to wait and see," she said. "Maybe nothing serious has happened at all."

She left the room, walked into the hallway and returned carrying her own bouquet of roses.

"Here, these are for you," she said to Agata, laying them on her lap.

"Oh Klara," the elderly woman marvelled. "Thank you."

She smiled and left to put the flowers in the family's favourite crystal vase.

A small, one-story building, with charred, empty window frames, filled the screen as the TV broadcast resumed. The same newsman stood by a large bench on the station platform, surrounded by a handful of people.

"Ladies and gentlemen," he said in a high pitched voice. "As you can see, tension is Otwock persists..."

"Everything looks quiet, as far as I can see," Klara commented.

The reporter announced that he would be interviewing Adam Michnik, one of the Solidarity-Mazowsze top advisers investigating the incident. Konrad was thrilled; he had never seen Michnik before.

"Who is Michnik?" Agata asked. "His name sounds familiar but I can't place him."

Konrad moved his chair closer to hers and thought for a moment about the man who had almost become a legend for his generation. Back in March of 1968, Konrad and Irian were in the streets during the riots but they were too young to join the student sit-ins. They admired Adam Michnik, one of the two students arrested for organizing meetings at the University of Warsaw. Michnik and the other student, Szlajfer, condemned the Russian ambassador's interference in Poland's cultural affairs and demanded freedom of speech.

"That's when Gomułka sent the police on the campuses," Agata remarked with a nod.

The television camera left the reporter and focused in on a group of people who wore Solidarity buttons.

A blond-haired man was making his way through the crowd toward the newsman. The reporter pointed his microphone into Michnik's face.

"Mr. Michnik, is there any chance of a peaceful solution to the crisis?"

Klara shook her fist at the reporter in exasperation.

"What is this idiot talking about?" she gasped. "He's making it sound like we're going to war..."

Konrad didn't comment. Instead, he concentrated on the slim, unimposing figure of Adam Michnik who, despite being in his mid thirties, looked very young, almost like a boy. The man stuttered slightly when he first began to speak.

"Well, I don't think that we have a crisis here, sir, but... let me explain the situation as I understand it now. At about three o'clock, we received a call from a Solidarity member in Otwock, telling us that two youngsters had been brutally beaten by the police and put in jail there."

He pointed behind him to the pile of rubble beside the train station. A small whisper of smoke was rising from the ground.

"Who set the fire?" the journalist asked.

Michnik's face tightened and a smile briefly flashed on his face.

"That happened while we were driving here from Warsaw," he said. "It seems that many people gathered around the police station. They started to demand the release of the two boys so that they could be taken to the hospital. When I arrived, the police station was already ablaze."

"Well, what did you do then?" the reporter shrieked. His voice was a strong contrast to Michnik's calm, matter-of-fact manner.

"The people put the fire out and entered the jail to get the boys. They were badly bruised and semi-conscious. We sent them to the hospital and their parents were contacted. We also called the Minister of the Interior and advised him to conduct an investigation to find out just what the boys allegedly did and whether the police had abused their authority. We also asked the crowds to go home..."

"But the people didn't do that," the newsmen cried. "Instead, they set the station on fire once again."

Michnik seemed to be unnerved by the journalist's aggravating manner. He hesitated in his next answer and again, he started to stutter.

"The policemen were no longer in the station... at that time. The crowds were aroused by the initial brutality of the police but... most of the people left... after we asked them to go home..."

"But who started the fire?" the newsman cried.

"Who started the fire?" Michnik repeated. "I don't know, maybe you do?" he said, looking rather gloomily into the reporter's face.

"What are you alleging?"

"Nothing," Michnik answered firmly. "Let me just tell all your viewers that we need peace across the country. Quiet is of primary importance right now." His voice grew stronger. "Whatever happens, purely emotional reactions such as Otwock has experienced today must not happen again. Thank you." He left the platform and most of the bystanders followed him.

It was obvious that the reporter wasn't satisfied with Michnik's answer. He faced the camera and continued in an anxious, high-pitched voice.

"Our nation is being torn apart by violence. The police no longer seem able to maintain order."

That night, sleep eluded Konrad. He flicked the light switch on and shivered. After throwing a sweater over his shoulders, he got out of bed and opened his window. It was calm and quiet outside, just as he expected. He lit a cigarette and looked out at the clear, star-spangled sky above him.

The images he had seen on the TV screen flashed in front of his eyes; the serious, determined face of Adam Michnik, responding to the newsman's questions. He analyzed the day's events again, carefully. First the police brutally beat the youngsters, while hundreds of people gathered at the railroad station during rush hour. Then, Solidarity got involved, a fire was set and TV cameras happened to arrive on the scene. The mysterious chain of events reminded him of the Bydgoszcz incident, the one that had put almost the entire country on strike just three months earlier. There were also the deliberate food shortages to consider and the recent appearances on television of Albin Siwak, the Central Committee member who appealed to people to put the country 'back in order', by whatever means. As he stood by the window, he thought he heard a rattling sound coming from the street although he knew it was just his imagination. Everything was clear to him then, it all fitted together... but can we stop it from happening? he wondered. Can I stand the noise every night? My foreboding?

Lying back in bed, he realized that if the worst happened, the Poles would be quite helpless. We have no way of defending ourselves, he thought bitterly. He started to laugh hysterically when he recalled an article he had read in Newsweek. The author of the story claimed that a majority of the Polish military would fight any invading East German or Soviet troops. How naive the Americans are, he thought to himself. The draftees might want to fight the invaders but they won't be let out of the barracks.

He remembered the various characters he had met during his army service... Captain Zabłocki, Colonel Gapa... Menda. Maybe they have more of a role than we think, he thought fearfully.

Eryk had been on vacation for three weeks when Konrad finally received a postcard from him. His father wrote that the weather was decent, the meals poor and he swore to his son that he hadn't touched a drop of liquor.

As his father's return approached, Konrad became more uneasy. Suppose he has been drinking, he thought. Maybe he just won't come home. Maybe he's gone on a drinking spree and everything will be lost.

His bout of insomnia passed, but strangely enough, continuous nightmares began to disturb his sleep. In his dreams, he saw Eryk's face, reddish and swollen, grimacing down at him from a moving train. Its path, over rails laid down on rough, cobblestone pavement, led straight into a closely guarded prison yard. He was struggling to keep up with the train, jogging alongside on the soft shoulder, but the train's speed always increased as it neared its destination. The steel gate slammed shut with a loud crash, just at the moment when he was less than three meters away. He was always awakening in a flood of sweat which began streaming down his face.

On the eve of Eryk's scheduled return, Konrad took his bicycle and pedalled to the Lutheran cemetery. Leaving the bike propped up against the cracked and decrepit fence, he entered, and began walking towards his grandmother's grave. Darkened sarcophagi, elevated on granite pedestals and surrounded by massive steel chains, sat in the shadows of the elderly, gnarled trees which sprawled overhead, in the oldest part of the cemetery. Some of the old stones were speckled with bullet holes, dating back to 1944, when the Lutheran cemetery had been an insurgents' stronghold during the Warsaw Uprising. He left the shaded area and made his way along a sunlit gravel road to an open meadow with a sparse assortment of trees, bushes and graves. A polished red granite cross, set inside a white stone plaque, signified his grandmother's tomb.

Julia Dymowska, née Wittig
Born 5.09.1903 - Died 17.11.1980

He knelt down and prayed. Tears began flowing uncontrollably down his cheeks but he didn't try to stop them. He was with her, he could cry, he told himself. She knew what he was feeling, she understood how weak and uncertain he was. He prayed for strength to help him sustain what was ahead. Eryk returned home tanned and relaxed. "Here I am, as sober as hell. What did you expect?" he asked, teasing Konrad.

"I expected you to be sober," Konrad answered, realizing that he was incapable of hiding his joy.

The long awaited Ninth Congress of the Polish United Workers' Party was convening in Warsaw. Brezhnew decided not to attend and lower ranking Soviet officials were expected. Many observers felt that this was a direct message to the Party, 'get rid of the revisionists'.

The most outspoken proponent of reforms, Stefan Bratkowski, head of the Polish Journalists Association, was expelled from the Party for having published the freedom-minded 'Open Letter to the Party Rank and File'.

The movement towards a Horizontal Party Structure had been tamed and the Congress was attended by the centre and hard-line groups. Still, one-third of the delegates were Solidarity members.

Changes were seen in the voting procedures of the Congress. Unlike during the previous conventions, four candidates for the position of First Secretary were nominated.

Vice-Premier Mieczysław Rakowski declined as did another nominee. That reduced the choice to the two important candidates, Stanisław Kania and Tadeusz Barcikowski. Barcikowski was the man who had presided over the government commission which negotiated with striking workers in Szczecin, the year before. In a secret ballot, Stanisław Kania defeated Barcikowski, by a margin of two to one.

Most Poles were relieved. They weren't crazy about Kania, but then again, they didn't dislike him either. He and Solidarity had managed to co-exist for almost a year. Overall, the convention allowed for a relatively uncontrolled exchange of viewpoints and opinions. Representatives of the Party vowed to pursue a line of renewal and national reconciliation. And, for the first time ever, delegates promised to monitor the Party leadership's adherence to guidelines established at the Congress.

The newly-elected Central Committee proved to be a mixture of old and new faces. One of the Politburo members to be reelected was Albin Siwak. Many wondered how such a rough character had managed to make it through the Extraordinary Congress. People were also disgusted at the election of Stanisław Kociołek, the man whom many held responsible for the killing of shipyard workers in Gdynia in 1970.

The Poles noticed that the honeymoon with reform and concessions was over. Immediately after the completion of the Congress, the official Party newspaper, Trybuna Ludu declared, 'Our Party has regained its credibility with the Polish people. Now is the time to rule...' Albin Siwak, Mieczysław Rakowski and most of the media, echoed the same sentiments.

A seemingly impenetrable wall of people crowded around the seven-storey building on Krucza Street. Konrad had just picked up the latest issue of Newsweek at the Grand Hotel newsstand, and was going home. He sighed with relief when he finally began to make his way through the crowd.

A short passerby bumped into him. Konrad excused himself and continued on, but the man grabbed his arm.

"Hello, how is it going," he asked.

The protruding eyes and wide grin of the stranger were slightly familiar, but he hesitated.

"Don't you recognize me? Short memory," the man said with a loud laugh.

Konrad nodded.

"Comrade Sroka," he said. "Well... how are you?"

The former First Secretary of the Party Committee at United Enterprises smiled and handed him a Marlboro.

"I'm fine," he said and flicked his lighter. "I was just filing my passport papers."

"Where are you going?"

"First to Austria, " Sroka replied. "And then... who knows... How about you, have you applied for your own yet?"

Konrad shrugged.

"No, why should I?"

Sroka's eyes widened with disbelief, and he burst into laughter. When he had calmed down slightly, he tapped Konrad's shoulder and winked.

"They're giving out passports to anyone who asks for them now, but you never know how long that is going to last," he said with a mischievous chuckle. "You can apply for one and just keep it at home. If I were you, I would. You never know when it may come in handy."

As Konrad continued to walk along Krucza Street, he wondered why Sroka was leaving Poland. He recalled that the man had been quite well off, had owned a profitable greenhouse, occupied a well paid position in the Party, and driven a BMW which was now replaced by a cheap Fiat. He has probably sold off everything and is going to be playing the part of a poor Polish refugee when he arrives in Vienna, Konrad concluded. Poles were reported to be flooding into Austria by the thousands. How many of them, he wondered, have lavish bank accounts and had once been Party officials, perhaps dismissed after the events in August 1980? What does it matter anyway, he thought dismally. All rats flee.

That night, he looked out his bedroom window once more. The street was dark, and very quiet. He thought about the passport. How could he even consider leaving? The country was more free now than it had ever been before. He tried to clear his mind, to rid himself of emotions. What was he afraid of? His mind became focused and he thought of Czechoslovakia in 1968. After the invasion of that country, its borders were sealed for almost a decade. If a similar crackdown were to happen in Poland, he would no longer be allowed to see the West, to walk along Montréal's St. Catherine street, with its stores, restaurants and McDonalds. Was this what he wanted, the luxuries of a colourful, capitalist city? Was it more important to him than the freedom he was experiencing at home?

"No," he cried out, into the empty street. "No, for God's sake..."

The next afternoon though, after bidding Klara good-bye near her apartment building, he walked the single block to Krucza street and surveyed the enormous throng crowding the sidewalk. He left quickly, but he knew that he would be back.

The line-ups weren't any better when he finally returned. It took three hours just to reach a wicket and file his application.

A guard controlling traffic going in and out of the first floor office, opened the glass door for him. He pushed his way through the mass of anxious queuers, and took a large gulp of air.

All of a sudden, he saw Klara standing there, right in front of him. She looked down at the papers in his hands.

He watched as two tears began running down her face and he swallowed quickly. He felt an intense pain enveloping his stomach.

CHAPTER 7

The morning express train between Gdynia and Warsaw sped quickly out of the city and into the Polish countryside. A tall, 30 year-old American reporter, dressed in tan canvas pants and a brightly coloured shirt, put down his magazine and gazed out of the window. Rows of sand dunes randomly covered with clumps of grass and solitary pine trees, gave way to a substantial beach, lapped by pearly waves reflecting the pink-hued colours of dawn. The reporter sighed, remembering that the beaches in Gdańsk Bay were closed to the public. Large billboards posted along the seacoast read, *'Bathing prohibited – Water Pollution'*.

"I can't believe how much this place has changed," he marvelled. "Just last year, during the strikes, we were still swimming in the bay."

His German companion smiled sardonically.

"It had to happen one day," he said and shook his head. He peered at his friend through his silver-rimmed glasses.

"I have relatives who live in Silesia. The air pollution there is so bad that you probably wouldn't be able to breath at all if you went to the region."

The American looked away from the window.

"What about the people who live there?" he asked with astonishment.

"Lung cancer has reached epidemic proportions in Silesia, Mr. Brubecker," the German visitor said. "The man who ruled this country until 1980, Edward Gierek, cared only about coal and steel output. In some areas, where there is pressure from free trade unions, smelters have been shut down for a while."

"Do you mean there are more strikes, Herr Heller?" the American asked with curiousity.

"No, just excessive air pollution in some areas. As Solidarity saw it, the only possible solution to the problem was... to shutdown. That's not the main cause of the idle factories, though."

"What are the other reasons then, Herr Heller?" Brubecker asked. "The Poles I met on this trip weren't complaining about meat shortages like last year. There isn't any meat on the market but they have even more serious problems now. I am told there is no soap, no washing detergent and no sanitary napkins for women. Even bread is hard to find. The family I know in Gdańsk, has collected food coupons from June, July and August. The new rationing system doesn't seem to be working because there is no merchandise. Why is that?"

The gray-haired Heller lit a cigarette and coughed.

"I am not an expert on Polish politics," he said, clearing his throat, "but as a businessman, I can see two major reasons for the plant shutdowns. Most of their new industries require raw materials from the West but because Poland has no foreign exchange reserves, these factories are idle. Some other plants could be running but often there's not enough electricity. That fellow, Herr Gierek, had a number of new factories built during the 'Seventies... but he forgot about providing enough power plants..."

In the midst of the acute shortages, Konrad's family unexpectedly found themselves in a privileged position. Their Aunt Alice from Chicago began sending them food parcels twice a month.

"Noo... God Bless her," Agata exclaimed. "I wonder how she knew, we didn't ask her for anything," she remarked as she happily pulled a ham out of the box.

"She probably heard about it through the media," Konrad said. "If Newsweek was any indication, the situation in Poland must look grim to outsiders."

He looked at his most recent issue of the magazine. It was published almost exactly one year after the 1980 strikes had erupted. Solidarity marchers covered its front. *Have they won?* was the cover story headline. Before he opened it and started to read the West's opinion on the Polish situation, he tried to answer the question for himself.

In the year following the 'Polish August', the country had undergone a number of dramatic transitions. Solidarity had become a 10 million strong organization, with enormous prestige and respect among Poles. 'Renewal' had brought a relaxation of censorship and many new independent organizations were formed. Others which had been dormant for years, were revived and searched for a place within the newly emerging democratic environment.

The United Farmers' Party and Democratic Party decided to become political partners with the powerful P.U.W.P on the basis of equality and independence.

Poland's parliament, the Sejm, passed a number of remarkable bills, complying with the Gdańsk Agreement. Before August 1980, an act determining limits to censorship was not possible within the Soviet sphere of influence.

And people felt free. Perhaps often hungry and exhausted, but liberated like never before.

Konrad glanced at the Solidarity banner on the magazine's cover and sighed. In spite of several significant achievements, there were still two crucial issues to be resolved. One was the question of food. Solidarity demanded that food production and distribution come under the control of the blue collar and farmers' unions, but the government wasn't anxious to negotiate.

"Whoever has the food has the power," Vice-Premier Rakowski declared. "If Solidarity wants to control food supplies, it must become a political force... however, that contravenes one of the guarantees the Union made. It would not become political."

Another issue was the overall economic reform of commercial enterprises. The government proposed a program of reform which, it said, would stabilize the market and help to overcome the crisis, however, the system still prevented employee control of planning and management.

Solidarity's economic advisors made an alternative proposal. They suggested that a majority of businesses become, 'self-governed enterprises, owned by the society', with an elected Employee Council and free competition for high level positions. Such an enterprise would take care of its financial health and produce marketable merchandise that could be sold on both domestic and foreign markets, according to the law of supply and demand.

If the Union had its way, government control would be limited to taxation and credit policy.

The economic scenario that Adam Babinicz had outlined for Konrad almost a year ago, had been worked out to the last detail. The Union also initiated the, so called, Network Plan. It led to the formation of Employee Councils in many large factories and businesses throughout the country. These organizations, Solidarity hoped, would communicate with each other and evolve into a movement which would lead to a new, more efficient management structure of the national economy.

Konrad was aware of the concept of 'Society owned enterprise' because of his regular reading of the Union press, but Albert had also told him a lot. His fiancée, Henia, was elected to the Employee Council at her factory, and she was also chosen to be a delegate to the first Solidarity Congress scheduled for September.

"The system has collapsed," Albert insisted. "There are just too many factories which are wasteful. Now, if the Network Plan was successful in having Employee Councils take over the management, they could decide what goods to produce or not produce."

Konrad marvelled at Albert's apparent transformation.

"What does your mother think of all of this? Here she is, working for a Ministry and her son wants their role eliminated. There must be a conflict of interest in your family," he added with a chuckle.

"Not really," Albert said with a smile. "Henia explained the Network Plan to Eleonora and my mother found it very interesting. I just wish the government would react the same way. So far they've ignored every proposal for the new economic deal..." Albert said as he began pacing between the sofa and the front window of his apartment.

"The Union can outline the Network Plan, but if the government still opposes it, the Employee Councils will have to take over anyway. If they don't, we'll all die of hunger in the near future."

Albert finished his preaching and glanced at his friend. Konrad looked unusually pale and thin, with dark circles etched under his eyes.

"How are you feeling?" he asked. "Are you any less tense now?"

Konrad surveyed Albert's face, with its playful eyes and somewhat comic, drooping mustache.

"I have applied for a passport and I am leaving for Canada," he said finally. He watched Albert's reaction. The man's forehead wrinkled and he rubbed his chin methodically.

"Why?" he asked.

"Don't you remember? I told you about my nightmares..."

"Yes, and I told you that you weren't alone."

"You mean, you have the same sensations?"

"Quite often. But, I suppose, I'm lucky. They don't bother me as much," he said gravely.

Konrad thought he was calling him a coward but Albert denied it.

"It's your decision. I just hope you won't forget about your friends here. You won't, will you?"

He went jogging with Irian the next day. When they had passed through the outskirts of Warsaw, he stopped suddenly and told Irian about his decision to leave. They walked for a while along the quiet country road, which intersected a harvested wheat field, and discussed the move.

"There is one thing I would like to ask you," Konrad said.

Irian encouraged him to explain.

"Well, you see Eryk is doing very well now. I was wondering if you would be willing to keep an eye on him and Agata. He's not drinking now but anything could happen when I leave. Since my grandmother died, his brother Bib hasn't been around much. And, when I get to Canada, I will start sending you food parcels. Will you do it for me?"

"I don't mind your request, but there is something about the way you said it," Irian answered coolly. "We have done a lot for each other over the years. Why didn't you ask me to look after Eryk as a friend, instead of offering me a deal? Is it because you feel guilty about leaving?"

Irian smiled briefly and then patted Konrad on the shoulder.

"It's all right. I'm not going to say anything more. You seem to be feeling bad enough already without me. Of course I'll help you. I'll do what I can."

The First Solidarity Delegate Congress convened in Gdańsk. A large indoor sports arena that went by the name of 'Olivia', was rented to accommodate the representatives of ten million people.

Posters all over the country advertised the event. The poster had a picture of a smiling toddler, wearing a Solidarity T-shirt and walking through a meadow. The toddler held a raised cane in its right hand, suggesting that although friendly, it could wield authority and power too...

Before the Congress commenced, the government agreed to broadcast interviews with the outgoing Solidarity leaders. However, the coverage was censored and the Union was portrayed as a bunch of militant radicals. Television and radio concentrated on a statement made by the leader of the Solidarity-Szczecin Region, Marian Jurczyk.

"People like Vice-Premier Rakowski only sour relations between the nation and the government. Mr. Rakowski is not the right person to negotiate with Solidarity. Genuine goodwill is needed, not a skillful politician."

Television commentators called Marian Jurczyk an 'irresponsible extremist'.

Solidarity retaliated immediately and barred Polish television crews from the First Congress.

302

As a result, the only glimpses of the meeting's activities came from Eurovision. Polish TV purchased some of the footage of the scenes inside the hall. Outside the meeting hall, Polish TV crews waited in vain. A white inscription painted on the pavement near the front door read, 'TV Lies'. Konrad kept a close eye on the Union press. All of the delegates at the Congress had been elected through secret ballot and they spent the first day just working out the procedures for the convention.

"Today, Poland is giving us a lesson on democracy," some foreign newsman reported.

The first part of the Congress was devoted to an analysis of the past year and the extent of the government's compliance with the Gdańsk Agreement.

Many delegates from the smaller, less industrialized regions, reported that Union activists were being harassed and Solidarity initiatives blocked by local authorities.

"What they pledge on television doesn't materialize," one delegate was quoted as saying. "We don't have a hospital in the area but when we suggested that they convert a newly-constructed ZOMO Riot Police barracks into a hospital, the authorities were strongly opposed. We eventually had to proclaim a regional strike, which received a lot of bad press. Negotiations began but no solution at this point is in sight. Meanwhile, we still have to drive our sick eighty kilometres to the nearest hospital. The government builds barracks, posh Party Committee headquarters and, consequently, there are no construction materials left for hospitals and kindergartens.

Other delegates stressed the sad state of existing health care facilities.

"Despite a pay raise there are still not enough nurses in our hospitals," one female delegate, a nurse herself, said. "It would help a lot if the government allowed nuns to work in some hospitals. They are often well qualified and very eager to help, especially with disabled patients. There is one other thing I should mention. Our supply of drugs has improved significantly thanks to Western donations via the Solidarity Health Fund."

Soon the delegates stopped complaining about the past and moved on to the future. "If the situation doesn't improve quickly, many Poles aren't going to survive the winter," one elderly delegate said. "The government should submit some kind of plan to cater to the food and heating needs of those most prone to suffering; the ill, old and incapacitated."

He was widely applauded for his suggestion and many of the delegates agreed that Solidarity had to establish organized aid for the most needy when the temperatures started to dip.

"Our friends from Rural Solidarity, the Independent Association of Students, as well as the Boy Scouts, have promised to help us," one Union leader said, "but we have to ask the government what plans it has made for the winter. It still distributes our coal and food so we have to know how they are going to improve delivery during that particularly crucial season."

The Congress started to pass resolutions on a number of subjects. One of them was an appeal to East European Nations. It stated that despite the efforts of governments in neighbouring countries to portray Solidarity as a destructive, revisionist force, the Union was a genuine labour organization representing a majority of Polish employees. The appeal encouraged other East Europeans to form truly independent trade unions, following the example of Solidarity.

The Convention recessed, with plans to reconvene in two weeks to elect a new Solidarity's National Council, the KKP[17].

The official media reacted with vehemence to Solidarity's appeal to East Europeans. They claimed that the Union was interfering with the internal affairs of Poland's neighbours. The official press in Warsaw Pact countries defined the appeal as 'an act of war'.

In the Soviet Union, rallies were organized in many factories to publicly condemn Solidarity. In one of the largest truck factories in the USSR, the workers reportedly protested against Solidarity's contention that they needed free unions. "Our Unions are free, but not revisionist and destructive, and not sponsored by Western organizations. We don't need to follow those agents of the CIA who call themselves Solidarity," the official communiqué from the rally read.

The employees at Ursus Tractor Works near Warsaw responded with an open letter. "How can you condemn Solidarity if you don't know what it is all about? There are 10 million of us here, in this country. Please come and see for yourself what we are trying to achieve."

The invitation was ignored.

During the period between the two sessions, the government began distributing its own version of Solidarity's Congress poster. This time, however, the baby held a box of matches in its hand, and the inscription underneath read, *Don't Play with Fire*. Although most Poles agreed with the spirit behind the decision to make the appeal to East European nations, few took the message on the new posters lightly.

When the Solidarity Congress reconvened, two major problems had to be resolved. One was the election of the National Commission (KK), the Commission of Audits (KKR), and the Union Chairman. The other was the compilation of a document that would spell out the Union's policies for the following two years. According to the Solidarity charter, the conventions were to be held bi-annually.

The delegates tabled a resolution to fight for the protection of the rights and cultural development of minorities. Another document addressed the state of the country's judicial system, demanding that its powers be deemed separate from that of the government. Others expressed the Union's views on national culture and called for the immediate release of all political prisoners.

The Union's program declaration was different again. It was an in-depth study of some of Poland's most vital issues and contained a number of proposals for healing the country's failing economy. It stressed the need for a restoration of the market. Some of the Union's economic advisors conceded that price increases were inevitable. However, the program declaration stressed the need to protect the poor from any hardship that might result from price hikes.

The declaration tabled a comprehensive program for the rejuvenation of all vital forces in society in order to overcome the crisis and build a *Self-Governed Republic*, the final goal of the movement. *"It will be a free society, living in a free country,"* the document concluded.

---

17. In fact, at the First Solidarity Congress, the official name of Solidarity's national council was changed from Country's Commission for Consensus to National Commission. Its acronym, therefore, was abbreviated to KK from KKP.

Konrad held the latest issue of Solidarity Weekly in his hand. On the paper's front page, there was a photo of the final message to all delegates. The words, 'Solidarity – See You at the Next Congress', were flashed on the arena's score board.

The Congress had just finished. Wałęsa was re-elected and became the Union's Chairman for another two years. Many well known leaders were also brought back for a second term on the National Commission. Regional Union Chapter bosses automatically became members of the National Commission (KK) upon their re-election to Regional Chairmen posts. New names could also be noticed amongst the eighty two members of the National Commission. The composition of a nineteen seat Presidium was very much different than before, not including either Marian Jurczyk or Andrzej Gwiazda who had once been a Wałęsa deputy.

Konrad folded the newspaper and put it in his drawer. In many ways it was difficult for him to think about the Union's work anymore. Its leaders were prepared to stay and fight but he wasn't. He went out into the street. It was an exceptionally mild afternoon for the time of year and many people were out. Most of them discussed the Congress and its outcome. Solidarity buttons seemed to be everywhere. Konrad looked down at his and sighed.

For the last few mouths he had been hinting to Agata and Eryk that he might be leaving to work on a contract abroad. He told them that nothing was decided but that he might be leaving for at least a year.

One evening, he opened his desk calendar and began leafing through the months of autumn. He intended to leave sometime in November, and decided that a Sunday in the middle of October would be a good time for a farewell party. In a short note to Roman and his wife, he invited the couple to come for the celebration, but stuck to the explanation that he was going abroad with his company. I'll tell him the real story when we meet, he thought, recalling their conversation at the wedding party.

He was expecting his passport in a month, six weeks after he filed the application.

The wait at the office of Polish Airlines was almost two hours, and when he finally did reach a wicket, he was told that flights until the 15th of December were completely booked.

"There is a single reservation for October 23rd, however," the airline representative said. "We just received a cancellation. Would you like to take it?"

Konrad hesitated. He had hoped to spend November 1 st, All Saints Day in Poland.

"Do you want to take it or not?" the woman asked again, as the angry queuers behind urged him to hurry up. He nodded and collected the reservation slip.

The next day, he began to prepare for his departure.

The two suits he had were in good shape, but neither of them fit at all because he had lost so much weight. He went to two tailor shops before he was able to find one that would accept a last minute order. It was located on the sixth floor of a dreary, pre-war apartment building.

He offered the tailor 1000 złoty extra because it was a rush job, but the old man shook his head and pushed the money away.

"I will do it at the regular price. I am busy with other orders but I can't refuse a man who wears a Solidarity button..."

Konrad thanked him and left the tailor's shop. Once outside the darkened oak door, he looked down at his button and was tempted to take it off right there, in the hallway. He didn't deserve the favour the old man was doing for him. I don't have any right to wear this at all, he thought angrily. In the end, he decided taking it off that wasn't a solution; it wouldn't calm his conscience and Solidarity needed whatever support it could muster with the Party vowing constantly to 'rule' the nation.

He stared up at the massive flight of wide, granite steps to the church's arched portal entrance, and slowly entered the quiet, dim building. There, he knelt at the confessional. As the priest looked at him through the grating, he thought for a moment that it was Father Florian, but quickly realized he was mistaken.

He confessed openly about his decision to leave Poland.

"Every man has the right to chose the country where he wants to live. If you have decided to leave, that is your right," the priest replied in a calm voice.

"I know, but I also believe that what I am doing is cowardly. I am weak." He could feel the warmth of the priest's breath as the man leant over and whispered into his ear.

"We are all weak. It is a part of human nature. The fact that you recognize this, proves that you are sensitive. You should never lose that..."

"But I am fleeing a country in need," he pleaded in a cracked, broken voice.

"But you have made a decision to do so," the priest said quietly. "It was your choice."

"Can I be forgiven this weakness, this lack of courage? Can God forgive me? Please tell me, father."

The priest considered his answer for a few minutes. "All humans are weak," he said in a gentle voice. "We all fall and get up again every day. But Jesus comes to the rescue of the weak too. Remember St. Peter? He was also weak and uncertain. He eventually obtained strength from the power of the Holy Spirit and gave his life for his faith. The Lord grants you absolution. Go in peace now. Perhaps you will be stronger one day. Just make sure that you retain your sensitive conscience. It brings you closer to Jesus."

On the day he was supposed to pick up his passport, he went to his local police station. A blond, crudely-featured man, sitting behind a small desk in a closed office, told him that the passport wasn't ready.

"Does that mean that I have been refused a passport?" he asked the officer.

The man closed his eyes briefly and yawned.

"If you had been refused, I would have given you a formal notice weeks ago. Come back in two weeks."

Konrad asked him if there was any way to speed the process up and the officer, who seemed anxious to see him depart, told him to contact the director at the main passport department.

Konrad looked with disgust at the sidewalk in front of the Krucza Street Passport Office, crowded with people, all apparently wanting to see the director.

He spotted Zdzisław Sroka leaving through the building's double glass doors, sporting a green passport in the breast pocket of his jacket. The man nodded and extended his hand in greeting.

"So you took my advice," he remarked.

Konrad nodded, but pointing the throng in front of the passport office, he explained his predicament.

Sroka was aghast.

"I wish you had told me earlier," he said. "I could have helped you. Is it urgent?"

"Quite, or I wouldn't be lining up here."

Sroka took him by the arm and steered him away from the crowd toward his car, parked a small distance down the street.

"Have you been refused by your local office?" he asked in a in a whisper.

"No."

"Well, what did they tell you?"

Konrad repeated the police officer's words.

Sroka shrugged.

"Do you want it tomorrow or can you wait two weeks?" he asked in a casual tone of voice.

"I guess I can wait."

"O.K., I won't be leaving before the end of next month. If you don't get your passport in two weeks, call me."

He tore a page out of his date book, jotted down his phone number and stuffed the sheet into the breast pocket of Konrad's jacket.

Before he walked away, Konrad asked him why he was making such a generous gesture.

Sroka laughed briefly and then his expression hardened.

"Don't think that I'll do it for free," he said. "It will cost you 50 'papers' just to speed it up," he said dryly. "In the case of a refusal, 100 'papers'. This is pure business, no charity."

A 'paper' was a new slang word for an American dollar.

Quite unexpectedly he received the passport. It was valid for three years and allowed him to travel to any country.

His friends in Canada had made the necessary arrangements with the Immigration Department, but to obtain a visa, he still had to have an interview with a consular official. He arranged for an appointment with the Canadian Consulate in Warsaw. Seated behind a long table and facing a pudgy, gray-haired man, he took pains to appear trustworthy and relaxed. After a number of brief questions about his reasons for travelling, and Konrad's answer that no, he was not going to Canada to seek employment, his visa was approved.

The same evening, he purchased his airline ticket and withdrew all his money from the bank. The teller issued a certificate which entitled him to carry US $1,300 across the border. He was ready to go.

307

The following day, he met Klara in a gas station queue. She was sitting glumly in her Polonez. About fifty vehicles, parked bumper to bumper sat in front of her car.

"I'm lucky today," she told him. "Yesterday, I was 97th in line and the gas ran out after the 90th person. Can you believe it?"

After finally filling the tank up, Klara started the engine and they drove towards the Trasa Łazienkowska expressway. The roads were virtually deserted.

The rural highway was lined by dark, newly harvested fields, from time to time accompanied by solitary straw-roofed farm houses. Klara turned off on to a muddy country road and drove toward a small grove of trees.

"I can't go too far, Konrad, I have to do some driving for my business tomorrow."

They sat there together, the silence interrupted only by the songs of birds overhead.

"So you've got it now, don't you?" she asked eventually. "Can you show it to me?"

Konrad took the passport out of his pocket. After browsing through the small booklet Klara handed it back to him.

"Your pass to freedom, " she said. "Soon, you'll be far away from all of this."

Konrad looked down at his lap in silence.

"... After a while," she continued, "you will forget that there was ever anything like a food or cigarette line. You won't remember the gas shortages and the Communist propaganda. You'll be far away from all of these troubles." She turned her head and looked straight into his eyes.

"You'll be far away from me too," she whispered.

He embraced her and gently kissed her lips and eyes. He couldn't stop crying.

When his emotions subsided, they left the car and entered the autumn tinged woods.

They walked, holding hands, looking far into the heart of the forest.

"When I met you, I was married," Klara said quietly. "You always insisted that I get a divorce, but you were just a kid then, you didn't consider the consequences. Now you are grown up and you know."

She smiled and they sat down on a thick layer of soft moss. She caressed his hair. Then she bent down and kissed him more tenderly than she had ever done before.

"Kocham Cię, I love you," she kept saying. "I love you like nobody else in the world."

Ten days before his departure, he began the task of packing up his belongings, explaining to Agata and Eryk that he was being sent to a Polish construction site abroad for at least a year.

"A whole year," Agata said sadly. "That is a long time."

"Well, he has to go and make some real money at last," Eryk told her. "Don't worry, we'll stay together all right."

The airline specified that he was allowed to take only two pieces of luggage with him on the flight. The problem was, he didn't have any suitcases at all. He set out toward the complex of three department stores on Marszałkowska street, 'Wars', 'Sawa', and 'Junior', recalling that they were always well stocked with merchandise.

Inside 'Junior', he watched crowds of people milling about, buying practically every piece of clothing they could find. The shoe stand was completely empty and so was the luggage department. When he asked one of the salesgirls if any more were in-stock, she laughed loudly.

"Are you kidding? They were all gone two months ago."

He managed to find a large suitcase in the basement of his building. It was an old canvas thing, reinforced with cardboard fittings which had come from Wilno when his grandmother immigrated to Warsaw in 1945. Both locks were broken and the handle was torn off, but a nearby shoemaker managed to fix it. Unfortunately, it wasn't large enough for all of his things.

"Why don't you take the 'Anders' bag'?" Eryk suggested.

"What bag?"

"The large, military roll bag we have. It is on the shelf near the bathroom."

Konrad managed to find it in the back of a closet, under a pile of worn out curtains. It was about eight feet long and three feet wide, made of khaki canvas and it had two solid looking leather belts.

"It looks brand new. This is marvelous."

"You bet it is. Good old British production. Robert used it only once, when he was given his demobilization papers from the Anders' Army[18]. The bag was packed in London and unpacked here. Ever since then it has been on the shelf."

Konrad opened his dresser and took all his remaining clothing out of the drawers. He took about half of it and stuffed it into the bag.

"The rest is yours," he told Eryk.

"Are you crazy? It's good clothing and you may need it abroad."

"No. Most of it is too big now. You can use it, though. All you have to do is shorten the pant legs."

Eryk didn't say anything for a few minutes. He embraced his son and kissed him. Later, he took all of his unexpected gifts and left for his small room.

The bag was almost filled. On top of the clothing, Konrad put two engineering handbooks, his grandfather's wartime edition of Polish-English dictionary, Henryk Sienkiewicz's trilogy[19] in paperback, a prayer book and a volume of Julian Tuwim's poetry. Then he called Eryk in to help him close up the bag.

His farewell party was held on the Sunday before his departure. Klara had to stay home. Only Irian and Albert knew that he was leaving for Canada and not for a foreign contract. He didn't want to tell the others the truth until the last moment.

---

18. General Władysław Anders (1892 - 1970) was a Commander in Chief of the Polish Army formed in the USSR. It was later converted into the Second Polish Corp known for its victorious Battle of Monte Cassino, Italy.

19. Henryk Sienkiewicz (1846 - 1916) won a Nobel Prize in literature for his novel Quo Vadis. However, to the Poles he is best known for writing a trilogy 'With Fire and Sword', 'The Deluge' and 'Pan Michael' (sometimes translated as Fire in the Steppe) which described the wars Poland waged against Cossacks, Tatars, Swedes and Turks in 17th century.

There was nothing to buy in the stores, but the family had a few cans of ham stored from food parcels. Eryk prepared sandwiches and Konrad set to work to bake two large chocolate cakes. They had cocoa left over from holiday parcels from their American relatives and Agata had stocked up on sugar and flour.

Roman couldn't come. He lived almost 300 kilometres southwest of Warsaw and his car was in the garage for repairs. 'But don't worry, I will definitely come to see you before you leave,' his letter read.

Everyone at the party wished him good luck, especially Albert and Irian. They knew that Konrad was taking a risk by leaving for overseas, perhaps forever. Yes, he did have a place to stay and his English was good but he was leaving for a country thousands of kilometres away.

"Good luck, Konrad, good luck…" Irian said and shook his hand. "Don't worry, I won't forget about your request," he added quietly, as he and Ela stood at the doorstep, about to leave.

Albert was the last to say good-bye.

"Well, there isn't much beer left for you and me to drink," he said, "but I am still sorry that you're going anyway."

Before Albert left the apartment, Konrad asked him for a favour.

"I need a lift later today. I just found out that my great-uncle Fryderyk had had a stroke and is in the hospital. It's raining like crazy outside; not the kind of weather for a bike…"

Albert shook his head and murmured, "Your poor great-uncle. Sure, I'd like to give you a ride. The only problem is that I am low on gas. If I can fill up, I'll be over."

When Konrad finally spotted Albert's bright yellow automobile coming down the street, the darkness of evening had already begun to set in. He ran and jumped into the car.

"Terrible weather, eh?" he said, wiping the rain off his forehead.

Albert turned his attention to the road. After Konrad gave him the directions, he pushed the accelerator and they moved quickly through the flooded streets. They didn't talk along the way.

Albert stopped the car at the hospital gate. Konrad told his friend to wait in the car, explaining that the visiting hours at the hospital had long passed. Albert nodded.

"Convey my greetings to your uncle and be back soon. Do that for me, OK?"

Konrad turned and looked at Albert with surprise.

"Are you angry with me?" he asked.

"No, I am not. But I'm just not in a joyful mood either. Are you?"

He shrugged, explaining that he was sad about his uncle's stroke and his impending departure, but he was still puzzled about Albert's angry demeanour.

"You're not in a bad mood because you're almost on the plane. You just don't give a shit about what has happened today!" Albert yelled.

"What has happened?" Konrad shouted back at him.

"Weren't you listening to the radio or watching the news?"

"No, I was washing dishes after the party and then I fell asleep. What has happened for God's sake?"

Albert looked sadly at Konrad.

"I am sorry," he said and turned the radio on.

"Today's decision by the Central Committee of the Polish United Workers' Party should put an end to the anarchy and stop the process of disintegration of the Polish State. This has been the evening news... Next on our program, the Rhapsody in Blue by George Gershwin from the Metropolitan Opera in New York City, 1981."

"I'm still not clear on what happened. What was the announcer talking about?"

"There's no Kania anymore," Albert replied solemnly.

"What do you mean? He was elected by a majority of delegates at the Congress, the only democratic Congress the Party has ever had."

"I meant what I said. Stanisław Kania left the post after a violent meeting of the Central Committee. Many radicals, including Albin Siwak, accused him of allowing for an unprecedented disintegration of the State and loose policy with respect to 'anarchy', as they put it. He resigned an hour ago."

One glance at the solemn expression on Albert's face, confirmed for Konrad that the unbelievable story was not fictional.

"But the Congress elected him," Konrad repeated in a numb voice.

"The Central Committee has accepted his resignation, though, and have already approved of a new First Secretary."

"Who?" Konrad asked quickly.

"The Prime Minister – General Wojciech Jaruzelski."

Konrad sat back in silence.

"I wonder what's next?" he murmured finally.

"I think the more correct question would be, 'When'," Albert said dryly. "I just hope it doesn't happen before you flight takes off... Just think, Jaruzelski was approved unanimously," he said sarcastically. "Already the Ninth Congress belongs to the past and I'll tell you frankly, that today's developments prove that the Congress was much less democratic than we were led to believe. I heard that following Jaruzelski's nomination, Rakowski got up and welcomed 'the new era in the history of the Communist Movement in Poland'. I sincerely hope you'll be able to leave before this 'New Era' begins for good."

Konrad stepped out into the moist evening air.

"I won't be long, just a half hour."

His great-uncle lay still in his bed. His skin looked very thin, almost like paper, his eyes were closed. Konrad placed two cans of orange juice on the night table, and sat himself down on a metal hospital stool. The ill man opened his eyes slowly and looked at him.

"Hello, Konrad," he said slowly. "It was nice of you to come to see me."

"How are you, uncle?"

"Well, I have survived the stroke, but for how long, God knows."

"Can you walk?"

"No, but I can sit up in bed and I can look after myself a bit. He pointed to the bed-pan standing beneath his small night table.

"The guy over there is much worse," he added, nodding at the red-haired man in the adjacent bed who seemed to be unconscious.

Uncle Fryderyk pointed to the two cans of orange juice.

"Where on earth did you find them?" he marvelled at the gifts. "Thank you very much."

"I got them at a restaurant. The waitress wasn't going to sell juice for take out at first, but when I told her it was for my sick uncle, she said OK. Would you like some now?"

"Yes, please," Fryderyk answered and struggled to sit up in bed. Konrad looked sadly at the motionless left hand, wrapped in a sling, remembering the beautifully carved wooden boxes that had been his great-uncle's life long hobby. He poured a glass of juice and handed it to Fryderyk.

"So you are going abroad soon," his great-uncle remarked. "When?"

"This week," Konrad answered.

The comatose patient in the other bed uttered a series of snorts and then became quiet again.

"Well, I hope you will do all right. Are you happy about leaving?" Fryderyk asked and handed his empty glass back to Konrad.

"I am not happy but I have to go."

His great-uncle nodded with understanding.

From the corridor, Konrad could hear the nurse on duty calling on visitors to leave the floor.

The ill man managed a cheerful smile and kissed Konrad.

"I hope that you will succeed with your work abroad."

"God knows."

"I will be praying that you do. Good luck."

Konrad kissed him once again and looked down at his pale, ashen complexion.

"Don't worry, uncle. We'll see each other in a year's time."

"Good-bye, Konrad," Fryderyk said sadly. "Thank you for coming and God bless you."

He wished the corridor had been shorter, but it was long and winding and he had trouble finding the exit. Long before he was able to step outside, the tears had begun to flow.

On his way to the bus stop the next morning, he noticed a number of new posters affixed to poles and walls of buildings. A quick examination left no doubt in his mind about the distributor of the propaganda. One poster displayed a hand with the index finger pointing down. People were depicted on top of the finger, sliding down and falling into an abyss. 'The way indicated by Solidarity', the inscription on the poster read. The placard beside it was no more subtle. It had the representation of a priest blessing a Solidarity banner below which Ronald Reagan was sitting on a neutron bomb.

"Are we going to turn the clock back and return to July 1980?" a man at the bus stop asked his companion.

"It looks like they badly want us to," his friend muttered.

"But we mustn't," Konrad blurted out. Then he stopped himself. He realized that he no longer had a right to speak on the subject. I am leaving and they are staying, I have to shut up, he thought miserably.

312

He called Tina that afternoon and they arranged a meeting at her apartment. He sat down on the red sofa in the livingroom and gazed at the family's bookshelf, its mahogany shelves densely packed with scores of volumes, some of them his own. His face tightened when he spotted Tina's ornate pewter candlestick on the top of the cupboard.

"I hope Artur isn't here," he remarked, noticing that her kitchen door was securely closed.

Rather than flying into a rage, as he had expected, Tina responded in a hushed tone of voice.

"No, he went out with his friends. I told him that I wanted to talk with you in private."

She brought a tray with a teapot and two mugs from the kitchen and placed them on the coffee table in front of the sofa, then sat down beside him. She carefully surveyed his face.

"So tell me the truth," she said. "I know you aren't going abroad with your company..."

His eyes widened with astonishment, thinking that his mother was the first person to see through his secret.

"... I am your mother after all," she remarked, noticing his surprise. "You can't fool me like Eryk or Agata."

He told her then that he was leaving for Canada. They sat in silence, Tina wiping her eyes with a handkerchief, inadvertently ruining her mascara and makeup. He got up to leave, telling her that he still had to say good-bye to Xenia.

"She doesn't know yet..."

Tina nodded and followed him to the front door. They kissed each other without saying a word.

The miserable weather improved slightly on his last day in Warsaw. The rain subsided and it was sunny, though cool. He took his bicycle and pedalled to the only place that he had to visit before he left.

The cemeteries were very calm. Konrad was surprised that he was the only visitor that day. He lit candles and put cut flowers on the graves of his grandfathers and great-grandmother and prayed quietly. Then he rode toward the Lutheran cemetery. Julia's grave was the last he had to visit.

He knelt and prayed beside her.

"Please Babcia, ask St. Mary and Jesus to take care of Agata and Eryk. Forgive me that I am leaving..."

Tears blinded his eyes and he could no longer control himself. His chest heaved as he wept loudly. After a few minutes he stood up and lit a candle. He placed his last bouquet of flowers on the stone step at the front of her grave.

As he sat down at a bench nearby, scenes from his childhood reappeared before his eyes. It was as if he was watching a silent movie about his life. Julia was smiling and talking to him, leading him for a walk through the park. Then he saw the same park, but she was in a wheelchair... they met Eryk. He was in the hospital chapel with her, nailing the coffin up himself.

He took a deep breath and set off towards the front entrance of the cemetery. At the outside gate, he turned around and ran back to the grave. There he knelt and cried for another hour.

Eryk was sitting in his armchair smoking a cigarette. It was late evening. Agata had already taken a bath and she was wrapped up in her dressing gown. There was no better time to tell them where he was going.

"For Canada? That far...?" Agata murmured sadly. "When do you think you will come back?"

He didn't answer. Instead, he looked at the old woman. Standing there in her nightgown she looked more frail than he remembered.

"Are you leaving us forever?" she asked, still looking straight at him.

"I don't know," he answered quietly, trying to avoid his great-aunt's faded green eyes. He turned to his father for support. Eryk seemed to understand.

"Don't worry, auntie," he said, trying to soothe her. "Konrad is going to the country which offers the best living conditions in the world. He deserves it. Don't you think?"

"Yes, he certainly does," Agata whispered, sitting down at one of the chairs beside the television.

"I'll be sending you food parcels and both of you can come to visit me," he said, wanting his voice to sound firm and convincing. "You will come, won't you?"

"Oh yes, we will," Agata answered, half cheerfully.

He tried as best he could to control his emotions. I must not cry now, he told himself. I mustn't, he repeated.

He went into his bedroom and brought out a bank book.

"This is your money," he said, handing it to his father. "I have been saving it for you for over a year. The account is in my name but you can draw out any amount you wish. You see, your name has been entered in this box," he said, pointing to the front inside cover of the small booklet.

Eryk leafed through the book, glancing at the stamps of the PKO Popular Savings Bank. He closed it with a flap, put it in his back pocket and embraced Konrad.

"Thank you," he said quietly in a strangely solemn way. Then, shaking his son's hand, he added in a reassuring tone of voice, "Don't worry, we'll be all right, Agata and I."

Konrad woke up in the middle of the night and switched on the small table lamp beside his bed. He dressed quickly and silently opened the front door, slipping into the dark, empty stairwell. A drowsy caretaker emerged from the apartment gatehouse following his ring. The man unlocked the heavy entrance gate and mumbled something unintelligible when Konrad squeezed a twenty złoty coin into his hand.

He proceeded quickly across the main boulevard, and then down into a dimly illuminated side street where asphalt pavement soon gave way to cobblestones intersected by a set of rusty steel rails, leftover from the electric train that used to pass along the route fifteen years before.

Facing the bending tracks was a tired-looking, brown brick building which housed a grocery and dyeworks. The street outside was dry, but he could remember being fascinated years before, by the colourful sewage which oozed out to the gutter and then facing Tina's scolding when he came home, his clothes covered with ultramarine spots. He had decided, nevertheless, to return the next day.

The small grocery store used to sell bottled beer, and construction workers often drank it inside, throwing beer caps into a cardboard box on the floor. Outside the shop, he met Irian who had shown him how to place a row of caps on one of the train rails. They would sit and wait impatiently for the resounding sound of the yellow and blue electric train to roll the metal flat. After removing the cork inserts of the caps, the shiny disks were ready to use. Sometimes they played *Gazda*, tossing the flattened caps into a chalk drawn rectangle from a distance, or they tried to trade their stock with the older boys for permission to play soccer behind the unpainted board fence which surrounded the rubble of a deserted cigarette factory. They never succeeded. Their schoolmates from the higher grades played *Gazda* with real coins and always ignored their offers. By the time he and Irian were old enough to make their way to the makeshift playground, the bulldozers had demolished the remains of the factory and a large high-rise building had been erected in its place.

He shivered, realizing that it was after midnight, and that he was standing alone, in front of the dreary glass windows of the bare shelved grocery store.

Minutes later, as he was ringing the bell at the entrance of his building, he remembered Klara's last words of warning. No, I will never forget, he told her in his thoughts. It doesn't have to happen...

Sitting in Julia and Robert's old room in the darkness, he lit up a cigarette and struggled to get a hold of his emotions. Both Eryk and Agata heard his weeping and came into the room.

"Don't cry, try to relax," his great-aunt said, leaning over and caressing his hair. "You are going on a long trip tomorrow. Try to calm down, my little boy."

His weeping became loud, spasmodic wailing.

By the time Klara came to pick him up, he had calmed down significantly. His eyes felt tight and sore, and his throat was raw, but other than that, he felt able to make the trip. Using all of his strength, he lifted his large, khaki rollbag and threw it into the car trunk.

Agata walked from one room to another, following his every step. She didn't talk much that morning, she just looked at him closely, as if she were trying to remember his face forever.

It was time to go. He kissed her numerous times and handed her a chocolate bar and a bouquet of flowers. As he headed toward the backyard gate, he turned to look back at the tiny figure in the window, holding the roses and watching after him.

Their small group stood by the yellow airline counter, having just made their way through the milling crowd of passengers carrying a multitude of suitcases, trunks and crates.

He kissed Eryk, Irian, and Albert, and then he embraced Klara, burying his face in the woman's hair and staying close to her for over a minute.

"You have to check in," she said. "... farewell, Mój Kochany, my love."

After passport control, he proceeded to the customs. The officer ordered him to open his bag, and then began examining his luggage in detail. A few minutes later, he sighed and set to work, rolling his bag up again and fastening it tightly. Then he put it on the luggage conveyor and passed through the security gate, walking from the terminal building toward a blue airport bus that would carry all of flight passengers to the aircraft.

He turned around and looked up, seeing Eryk and the others waving from the outdoor terrace above. "Eryk, Eryk," he shouted, "remember..." He pursed his lips, knowing that his father couldn't have heard his words.

The plane began to accelerate before taking off. He clutched a silver shield, he had received on his baptism and looked out of the window. He watched as the terminal buildings rapidly decreased in size. Seconds later, he could see the entire district, then Warsaw, then only clouds.

He looked down at the familiar medal in his hand, fingering the outline of St. Mary of Ostra Brama, and a stylized image of a white Polish eagle. The contours of the engraving became foggy as he felt a warm sensation in the corners of his eyes.

CHAPTER 8

It was before dawn. Roman climbed into his icy car and took care starting the engine. It often protested on bitterly cold mornings. Shivering, he watched his warm breath dance around the inside of the tight, frozen little box before he finally pressed his foot down on the accelerator and the car took him out of Kępno to the main route toward Warsaw. Descending from a steep hill, he blinked, his eyes coming face to face with the rising sun. Skeletal poplars lining the highway yielded to the strong gusts of wind which whistled around the speeding car.

Half of his trip completed, he turned off the main highway, drove along a rural route, and pulled up beside a gas station in a small village. During the gas shortage, the operator of the station, whom he had befriended, was usually willing to fill up his Fiat for two hundred złoty extra.

Making his way back to the highway, he prayed that he would be as lucky on the way home. It was risky making the three hour drive rather than taking a train, but he could stay in Warsaw for only two days. He planned to spend some time with Konrad, visit with his parents and, if possible, see a couple of movies. The few cinemas in his town offered only a limited number of second rate films. His last stop before leaving Warsaw was going to be the Solidarity-Mazowsze office. Living in Kępno, he was relatively isolated from important union strongholds and it was difficult to get up-to-date information on the situation in the rest of the country.

After Solidarity's First Delegate Congress had ended, relations between the Union and the government were strained. The government controlled media had launched a concerted campaign to discredit the movement. It blamed Solidarity for almost all of the nation's problems, ranging from the poor state of the economy to a purported increase in the crime rate.

Little attention was given to the revelations released by the Central Office for Statistics that fall. The agency's data demonstrated that during the first nine months of 1981, the number of working hours lost due to raw material and energy shortages was almost forty times the corresponding figure resulting from strikes and sit-ins. The statistics digest also indicated that per capita alcohol consumption had dropped by a factor of three, when compared to the same period in 1980.

Yet the official media continued to go haywire, claiming that anarchy was rampant in the country.

317

"Due to Solidarity extremists, our motherland cannot even provide basic services," Ryszard Kwapień cried on a TV Daily broadcast. The newscaster, once closely affiliated with Gierek's clique, had been sent on a one year assignment to Bulgaria shortly after the departure of the former First Secretary. His recent reappearance on the TV screen had infuriated many people and gave rise to widespread suspicions that many other hated officials may stage a similar comeback.

Roman parked down the street from Konrad's apartment building, crossed the narrow yard and entered the stairwell. He wasn't quite sure if the doorbell was working properly. He pushed it down repeatedly but there was no response from inside. Perhaps Konrad is out, he thought. His great-aunt's is getting deaf, maybe she just can't hear the bell.

The door slowly opened a few minutes later and Agata looked up at him with surprise. Roman greeted her with a 'good morning' and kissed her hand.

"Is Konrad in?" he asked.

"Good morning Roman, please come in," she answered.

He followed her into the dim front hall of the apartment. After pointing him in the direction of an armchair, she went into the kitchen and returned with a glass of hot tea.

"I'll bring you some strawberry jam too," she said.

"No, thank you very much. I don't want to cause you any trouble" Roman protested.

Agata shook her head.

"What trouble? I am glad you have come to visit. It is homemade jam. Everyone helped to make it, Eryk, Konrad and myself."

She marched out of the room. Roman watched after the tiny woman and sighed. She seemed to be lost in the large apartment. Years before, it was almost crowded. There was Agata of course, Julia and Robert, and the most senior member of the family, Konrad's great-grandmother Luba. They also had a pet then, a dog called Lady who always barked happily when a visitor she knew arrived at the door.

As Roman looked around the quiet apartment, he sighed. The room was dull and dreary with a table lamp providing the little light there was in the small cubicle. And Agata... she was the only one left. How she has aged lately, he thought.

Konrad's great-aunt returned from the kitchen with a plate and a jar of strawberry jam. She also carried a mug of tea for herself. She smiled and watched as Roman helped himself to the sugary fruity preserves.

"So how are you, Roman?" she asked. "Are you happy? It must be difficult living so far from your parents, from Warsaw?"

Roman shook his head.

"Well, I'm not lonely," he answered. "My wife Krystyna and I keep each other company. We're doing fine."

"Well, that makes a difference," Agata conceded with a nod of the head. She paused for a moment, deep in thought. "I always wanted Konrad to get married, but he loved Klara. As you know, she had a husband, so it was impossible... but she's a good girl. She drops in to see me quite often. Not many people visit Eryk and me these days," she commented with a resigned smile.

Roman smiled back and continued to sip his tea. He was in a hurry to find Konrad, but he didn't want to hurt the old woman's feelings, and the jam was delicious. As he sat back and savoured a large spoonful, Agata surprised him with a question.

"Roman, what do you think is going to happen to us? Will the Russians invade?"

He sat up quickly.

"Well, I don't think so," he answered, trying to reassure her. "I think that if they were going to invade Poland, they would have done it after August 1980."

Agata let out a long, drawn-out sigh.

"Eryk says the same thing," she said, "but other people swear something is happening. Our neighbour's son has been serving his two-year term in the army since 1979 but he hasn't been discharged yet. In his last letter, he told his parents that no one was being released from the draft. He also told them that fewer new recruits were coming in."

Her face became strained with apprehension.

"I'm suspicious, Roman. If there was a war they would need those trained soldiers, they wouldn't want to contend with new recruits... "

Roman didn't know how to answer her. He too had heard strange stories about the military.

"... I have lived through three wars and the Soviet revolution which we barely survived," the old woman continued. "I wonder if there will be tanks and troops in the streets again. Tell me, Roman."

He was hesitant about frightening Konrad's great-aunt, but he also felt that she deserved to know the truth. He looked down at his tea while he answered her question.

"I don't think we will face an all out war, madam," he said slowly and deliberately, "but I have heard that a state of emergency might be announced and then... God knows what will happen. There might be tanks in the streets..."

Agata stared at him with horror, as if her worst thoughts had finally been confirmed.

"But please, don't be worried too much," Roman added quickly. "Solidarity is strong and Wałęsa must know what is going on. An agreement with the government is still possible. Remember last March in Bydgoszcz? Everyone thought that there would be a general strike and a Russian invasion, but Lechu found a solution at the last moment."

Agata nodded.

"Yes, he is very wise," she admitted.

Roman smiled pleasantly and leaned closer to the elderly woman. He told her he was in a bit of a hurry and asked her when Konrad was expected to return.

"When will he be back?" she repeated in a distant voice. "I wish I knew myself. Perhaps never."

"Do you mean he has already left to work on his foreign contract?"

"He left for Canada, Roman," she answered sadly. "He was only telling us that he was going to work abroad because he didn't want us to suffer more than we had to. The day before he left, he told us the truth. He is in Montréal now."

Agata got out of her chair and approached a wall calendar. One date had been outlined with a black, felt-tipped marker. Roman noticed that while it was November, the elderly woman's calendar hadn't been updated. Time must have stopped for her on that day in October, he thought.

"If I had only known..." he murmured.

Agata's pale, green eyes looked at him with sympathy. "Konrad was hoping to see you, even up to his last day..."

"My car was broken... "

Agata waved her hands in the air.

"Noo, what has happened, has happened," she said philosophically. "At least he is safe now, away from all of this. You can't imagine how terrible he looked before he left, Roman. He was thin and sickly. His last night here, he cried for nearly two hours. Nobody could calm him..."

Roman looked down at his watch and told Agata that he had to go. In the hallway he inquired about Eryk.

"He's doing well," she answered. "He hasn't been drinking for months and he goes to work every day."

As he drove along the almost traffic-free Aleje Jerozolimskie Avenue, he couldn't help feeling badly about missing his friend's farewell party. Since their last meeting at his wedding party, he had wondered about Konrad's thoughts and plans. He glanced down at his watch, and realized that he had a few hours to kill before his family got off work.

Within five minutes of parking his car in front of Warsaw's Palace of Culture, he was inside a movie theater and settling down to watch a newly-released film called 'Coup d'Etat'. The principal actor and director of the film was the controversial Ryszard Filipski, a member of the Patriotic Association – 'Grunwald'. Some of the actors and cinema directors who belonged to the group made Poland's pre-war years the subject of their films. It was a period in the country's history which had been condemned and deliberately overlooked by successive Communists administrations, and despite Roman's dislike for Filipski, he was eager to see the movie.

Coup d'Etat was almost exclusively devoted to Marshal Józef Piłsudski, a popular figure in Polish history. An organizer, and the first Head of the resurrected Polish State of 1918, Piłsudski was most revered for his defeat of the Soviet army in the crucial Battle of Warsaw, a victory which ensured Poland's success in the 1920 war against Russia.

The lights dimmed and Roman sat back in his seat as the first film on this national hero shot in post-war Poland, filled the screen.

In the leading role, Filipski portrayed the late Marshal as an autocrat who was preoccupied with order and discipline. The least memorable chapter of Piłsudski's political career was the major focus of the film. It recreated his actions of May 12th, 1926, when the Marshal, thinking that the country's very existence was being threatened by parliamentary instability, toppled the democratically-elected President Wojciechowski and his government. The military coup was quickly organized but a number of soldiers faithful to the President were killed.

The film was biased, Roman knew that. He watched and listened, hoping that at some point Filipski would reveal that the May Coup was in fact, welcomed by a majority of Poles, including leftist parties. He didn't. Where the film was most interesting though, was the way it demonstrated the army's determination to take over the government. The action quickly moved on to the 'Thirties. He watched as the trials of opposition members of parliament ensued, and how, despite insufficient evidence, they received stiff sentences. The final scene of the film showed a spirited meeting of leftist parties in Cracow's Market Place. Roman thought immediately of the rallies and demonstrations that Solidarity had organized during the past year.

To him, the intended message of *'Coup d'Etat'* was clear: military force crushed the opposition, dissidents were tried, sentenced and imprisoned unfairly and protests were futile. The military-controlled government triumphed.

By the time Roman had left his seat and was making his way out of the theater, he was in a foul mood.

A rather corpulent man dressed in an army uniform got out of his seat near the front of the cinema. By chance, Roman glanced at his face. He recognized the officer immediately. It was Captain Zabłocki. Roman stopped in his tracks and stared at the man with wide-open eyes.

"Good day, sir," Zabłocki said without hesitation. "So we meet again. Company Zero, wasn't it?"

Roman nodded. "Citizen Captain has a good memory," he said, standing more erect.

At that moment he could have been back in the barracks.

"Well, you still remember how to address an officer, very good... very good... So you came to see Piłsudski," Zabłocki remarked. "I liked the movie," he added, not waiting for Roman to answer. "I am not on the same side of the fence with the old Marshal but a number of his actions were well-calculated and quite instructive..."

The captain then glanced at his watch and quickly bid Roman good-bye. "I was pleased to meet you and to find that you still remember some of your military training. You may need it yet... in the meantime, think about what you have just seen, good-bye."

Before Roman had time to say anything, Zabłocki was outside in the street.

Colonel Alfons Menda opened a large map of the country and pointed quickly to the city of Gdańsk.

"This is the first circle," he said.

Then his finger moved swiftly over the map and made the same sweeping motion over the location of Warsaw.

"The second..." Zabłocki remarked.

Menda nodded. "And the third circle is here," he declared, pointing to Silesia in the south. "As you can see, we still have Wrocław, Szczecin and Poznań to cover."

The two officers were sitting in the quiet office at the GZP, the place where Zabłocki had begun his new career ten months before.

His first assignment had proved to be easier than expected. As planned, his wife Emma spent a fruitful weekend with the Russian general and soon after, Lebiedyev accepted Zabłocki's invitation for a drink.

The captain approached his task cautiously at first, but as the two men made their way through voluminous amounts of vodka, he found it easy to steer the conversation toward the desired subject of discussion. He learned that despite the fact that Soviet divisions were deployed on the Polish border, an invasion hadn't even been contemplated.

"Western credits..." Lebiedyev grumbled. "The entire fucking Eastern Bloc is so indebted to the imperialists that we could hardly go ahead and invade Warsaw like we did to Prague in 1968. Personally, I think we should, though..."

Seizing upon the right moment, Zabłocki casually mentioned that Poland's own 360 thousand-strong force would be able to handle the problem on its own.

General Lebiedyev began to laugh and he looked at the captain with ridicule.

"I would like to know how many of these 360 thousand repeated the words of the military oath properly," he remarked.

The captain got up to fetch another bottle from the refrigerator and then refilled their glasses. He pointed out that, despite the turmoil the country was experiencing, military cadre were in full control of the People's Armed Forces and were deeply committed to the cause of Socialism.

"As Suslov[20] would say, actions and not rhetoric count, comrade," Lebiedyev said sardonically. "Soon I'll see if the people you praise so highly fulfill your expectations."

The following day, Zabłocki gave his report to his superior. However, that was just the beginning. Since the captain's transfer to the GZP, he had surpassed Menda's expectations. It had been his idea to temporarily withdraw meat supplies from internal stores in some government ministries, police, security forces and the military in early June and, as he had predicted, the move did provoke more antagonism towards the Union and its advocates.

Now, just a few days before the deployment of *Operation Three Circles,* Colonel Menda was confident that the plan could be carried out smoothly, with few repercussions. The Soviet military divisions, sitting at the border, would not have to fire a shot. They were useful as a tool of intimidation more than anything else. Marshal Kulikov, joined by Lebiedyev and other Soviet generals would be in Warsaw during the Operation, but everything was to be carried out by Polish security forces and the military itself. Menda smiled at Zabłocki.

"You must have noticed that as it stands now, the plan is supported wholeheartedly by our group. The two factions have united," he declared proudly.

Zabłocki nodded in agreement. In spite of Menda's rather unorthodox methods, he had to admit that the officer was shrewd. Despite his own inclination months before, it was obvious to him now, that asking the Russians for help could have meant political suicide for the Polish military.

That afternoon, the colonel informed Zabłocki that he would be promoted to the rank of major shortly. "You will have to wait until a State of War has

---

20. Mikhail Suslov (1902 - 1981) - a Kremlin ideologue, creator of the Brezhnev Doctrine which called for armed intervention in satellite countries when Moscow's interests were threatened.

been proclaimed, though," he added. "According to peacetime regulations, you haven't been wearing your captain's insignia long enough for a promotion. When the State of War starts, we can both look forward to some extraordinary opportunities." Zabłocki looked closely at Alfons Menda. So the rumours I've been hearing aren't exaggerated, he thought. He is going to be promoted again. "When will I be able to call comrade Colonel a general?" he asked with a wide smile.

Menda waved his hand.

"We mustn't be premature," he answered quietly, "but don't worry about yourself. Your promotion is almost certain. I can't see why you wouldn't be rewarded for your exceptional performance."

Zabłocki looked at the man with overt suspicion and Menda reacted with a brief chuckle.

"No, Captain Zabłocki, believe me. You have earned the promotion. By working on general Lebiedyev, you have helped to assure Poland's future relations with the West. The promotion though, is not because of your wife's charm, you have earned it yourself."

Zabłocki felt proud and at the same time puzzled, by his commander's comment. Menda laughed heartily.

"My dear Zabłocki, listen," he said, leaning forward in his chair. "The fact that the Soviets are just sitting at our borders will undoubtedly result in the West's silent approval of our moves. They don't want the Soviets to invade. The West lost face in Hungary in 1956 and in Czechoslovakia in 1968 and they will welcome any excuse not to take any serious action. Operation Three Circles will be an internal Polish affair, much better than a Soviet intervention. The West will perceive our general Jaruzelski as the saviour of the nation, you just watch."

Zabłocki still wasn't convinced.

"I hate to be pessimistic," he said slowly, "but I can't imagine that damned cowboy actor, or that old bitch on Downing street welcoming Operation Three Circles."

Menda burst into hysterical laughter and began chastizing the captain.

"How can you call the Prime Minister of her Majesty's government an old bitch?" he said with a wink. Minutes later though, his face became solemn.

"The worst we can expect is rhetoric," he added. "Look at the French and British in 1939. Did they want to die for Gdańsk[21]? Nor will anybody go to war for Gdańsk now."

Zabłocki nodded, but he still wasn't sure that a ten million strong union would fold as easily as the colonel expected.

"You are forgetting, Citizen Captain, that these ten million people, are barehanded. We are the ones with the guns... " He got out of his seat and began pacing around the room. His furrowed face revealed a high degree of concentration as he continued to speak. Zabłocki's presence in the room had become irrelevant.

---

21. France and Britain did declare a war against Germany in 1939 but no military action
    followed. They actually went to war in 1940 after Belgium and Holland had been invaded.

"I don't underestimate Solidarity, but we will break its backbone easily. By cutting off phones and telex lines, by banning sales of gasoline, we will remove all important means of liaison between the Union regions. We must make sure that there is no bloodshed for the first 48 hours. That amount of time is needed to clear the country of all Western reporters and journalists. After that, there will be a complete news blackout. That's when we have to act. There will be strikes all over the country and we'll have to work quickly to break them. We won't use machine guns in the large cities, but we must use force to frighten the population and make them refrain from forming any post-union organizations. There must not be an underground. On the other hand, in areas where there is no danger of Western surveillance, we will spill as much blood as possible... I know that some of our close collaborators think that everything can be done cleanly and smoothly with gloves, without brutality. That is bullshit," Menda cried.

Zabłocki began shuddering in his seat.

"Brute force is needed," the colonel hissed. "If the miners go on strike, we'll open fire right in the shafts. We must erase hope. Do you understand what that means, Captain? We have only a few days before the West re-establishes its spy network of journalists and the like. Before that, the Poles must be intimidated. They must see blood and mass arrests. Only blood will wash away the rebellious mood they've been in since August '80. There will be no more 'Pole talking to fellow Pole'." Menda sat down in his chair and quickly lit a cigarette.

"Yes," he said firmly, "there must be a lot of blood... and then... higher food prices, tripled prices, tanks in the streets and hopeless calm..."

"That is all very well," Zabłocki said as he scrutinized Menda's words, "but we may face a number of obstacles..."

"Yes... someone with Solidarity's National Commission might escape. However, we intend to get them all at once in Gdańsk."

Zabłocki looked straight at Menda and asked the question that he had been pondering for months.

"How can we predict that Solidarity's leadership will meet in Gdańsk and provide the necessary pretext for Martial Law?"

The colonel got up from his chair and flashed a broad smile.

"We will provide them with a reason to act. There is a sit-in at the Firemen's College going on now. We will storm their strike headquarters and make sure that we are brutal. That, and continuing hysteria in the media should do the job. They will be provoked. A meeting will be called and our man on the Commission will make a suggestion to the Unionists."

"What if they don't vote for a general strike?" the captain asked.

For a few moments, he watched the colonel go around his armchair in silence. Then he heard a calm, solemn voice coming from behind his chair.

"This time, it won't be a general strike. This will be a national referendum on the legitimacy of the current government including its international alliances..."

"They'll never vote for that..." Zabłocki said with disbelief. He then felt a firm grip on one of his shoulders.

"They will, comrade," Menda said with determination. "Many of them are hot-headed and volatile. Take Jurczyk, Rozpłochowski, Gwiazda or... think about Rulewski? The bunch of them on the National Commission think that the government is really going to collapse... They will react so strongly to the helicopters on the roof of the Firemen's College that they will do the job for our people, without even realizing that..."

Menda stood motionless behind his desk and Zabłocki sensed that their meeting was over.

"Watch the TV tomorrow," his superior advised. "You will see a beautiful finale to the fireman cadets' sit-in."

At first, Albert just turned off his alarm, and contemplated spending a little more time in bed. Then he noticed the numerous piles of university books that had to be taken down to the basement and remembered that Eleonora had also given him the task of washing and polishing the apartment's floors.

"A busy day," he murmured and pulled himself out of bed.

He sat down at the kitchen table and his mother put a plate of ham in front of him.

"I'm glad they have started to supply our store with food again," she commented. "Without that, we wouldn't be able to have even a modest celebration on your grand day."

Albert nodded. It was Sunday, December 13th, just two days before Henia was expected to arrive in Warsaw to prepare for their wedding.

He picked up a piece of ham, folded it, and popped it quickly into his mouth. It was down his throat in a flash. Eleonora smiled at him and shook her head.

Her expression changed quickly when she heard a strange grinding noise, coming from outside. Albert rushed to the window. He gasped, seeing three armoured personnel carriers inching their way along the dark street below. Eleonora joined him at the window. The cup she held in her hand fell and crashed on the floor. When she looked up, after surveying the shattered pieces of porcelain, her son was already out in the hall, putting on his sheepskin jacket. He jerked the front door open. Eleonora's face turned completely white as she stood at the doorstep and begged him not to leave the apartment.

Two Union flags in front of the regional office of Solidarity flapped in the penetrating December wind. Albert pulled his collar up around his neck and tried to turn the knob of the office's front entrance, oblivious to the locked bolts on the door. He cursed and went down the steps to the snow-covered sidewalk, now crowded with other people searching for some news about the Union.

The Solidarity-Mazowsze office had been moved to the Ursus tractor factory as soon as the first military patrols were spotted on the highways leading into the city.

This was the message passed through the worried crowd of Solidarity supporters.

"A strike committee had been formed and a general strike proclaimed," one woman close to Albert yelled.

"Did everyone manage to get to Ursus on time?" he asked.

"I don't know," she answered and burst into tears.

Albert gazed up at the locked door of the Union's Mazowsze headquarters and clenched his fist in the air. Just a few months earlier, he had bought his first Union button there. He remembered lining up in front of the small Union store located inside the building. He was watching the young men and women who were milling around him, grabbing Union tabloids right off a printing press and bundling the still warm issues up on a large table in the hallway so that they could be sent to Solidarity locals in the region. Their fervent devotion had infected him with the Union faith, much more so than Henia's constant preaching.

Henia? Albert's eyes widened and he felt his body begin to shudder. My God... what has happened to her? He knew he had to call his fiancée immediately.

He started walking across the street and after a few steps, almost stumbled over an elderly woman crouched down on the pavement. She was praying rapidly, trying at the same time to swallow the flood of tears rolling down her cheeks. Beside her, another woman with a blue knitted cap on her head, lit a candle on the street and prayed for a miracle.

"Saint Mary, Mother of God, save Solidarity..."

He stood there, mesmerized by the women's hysterical pleading, their chorus of supplication.

A strong hand planted itself on his shoulder. He swung around and saw Konrad's father Eryk.

"Albert, what are you doing here?" he asked.

"And what are you doing?" Albert repeated, still gazing at the feeble light of the candle stuck in the snow.

Eryk grabbed him by the shoulders.

"Listen Albert," he yelled. "Irian is here too. We all have to get out of the area quickly. I saw ZOMO Riot Police forming up near the corner of Piękna and Mokotowska streets."

"ZOMO, so what?" Albert couldn't care less.

"So you are back!"

Eleonora's eyes filled with tears when he returned home. She placed his face in her hands and kissed his cheeks and eyes.

Albert shook his head.

"I have to call Henia."

Eleonora watched in silence as her son picked up the phone and then slammed it down seconds later.

"All the phones have been disconnected, Albert," she said quietly.

"Well, then I'll drive there," he answered and strode into the hall to put his coat on once again.

"You can't drive, Albert. Movement out of the city has been prohibited. Gas sales have been cut. There is a curfew and every city, town and village is sealed off by military patrols..."

Albert eyed her suspiciously.

"How do you know? Did you find out about all of this beforehand?"

"How could you?" Eleonora cried. "It was on television. He announced all of it."

Albert felt helplessness overcome him.

"Who?" he asked weakly.

"The general."

He flopped down on the sofa and closed his eyes. Neither he nor his mother said anything for a few long minutes. Then he sat up and looked at Eleonora.

"Mother, you can have your phone restored, can't you?" he asked hopefully. "Please ask to have it reconnected."

Eleonora felt a flood of tears streaming down her face.

"… Mother, do it. You aren't an average person. You work for an important Ministry. Tell them, whoever they are, to reconnect your phone. Go to the Central Committee or wherever, but get the phone working. I beg you - do it for me…"

Eleonora looked down and tried to wipe the tears away from her swollen eyes. Then she began speaking slowly and decisively.

"This is Martial Law. The ruling Military Council for National Salvation issues the orders. All others must obey, the troops, the Secret Service, the police and the Central Committee. This is war, Albert. Whatever connections I once had, no longer exist."

Konrad did not experience a feeling of relief when his plane landed in Montréal. In the weeks that followed, he wandered through the streets and malls crowded with Christmas shoppers as if in a daze. He hardly noticed the almost endless amounts of food, lavishly displayed on supermarket shelves, or the opulence of the merchandise in department stores.

He looked closely at faces, at expressions and movements. Most of the people he passed in the street were smiling; to him they seemed unnaturally relaxed and unconcerned. There were no leaflets, no posters, no flurry of political discussion.

He would speak to anyone about Poland. Anyone who cared to listen, and they would smile politely and nod their head when he gave them detailed descriptions of empty stores and his Union's political struggle. Inevitably, they would ask him if it had been difficult to leave his country and he would feel a rush of anxiety overtake him as he tried to explain that his departure was not important. What was significant, he told them, was the fate of his nation. He was often emotional.

"People are still there. Leaving is no solution."

"But you have left, nevertheless…" they would point out.

He knew that he must have seemed a little crazy to them as he talked incessantly about his cowardliness and told them that the true patriots of Poland were the ones who stayed behind to fight to the very end.

The weather grew bitterly cold on December 13th. An icy wind swept around the Polish Consulate and chilled the faces of the Montrealers converging on Pine Avenue to protest against the imposition of Martial Law in Poland.

"Souvien total de Solidarité! Long live Solidarity! Solidarność!" the people chanted.

Konrad watched the Polish flag being stripped off the consulate flagstaff. It was replaced with a white Solidarity banner which bore the Union logo in red.

A few hours later, when the demonstration dispersed, he walked slowly down a quiet downtown street, carrying his ragged cardboard poster over one shoulder. The day that he had most feared and apprehended had arrived but, as he had wished when he stood at his open bedroom window back in Warsaw, he was far away, secure. He shoved the placard stem into a pile of dirty snow outside the brightly lit entrance of a Métro station.

A flimsy piece of paper with clumsily written words 'Solidarność-Mazowsze' fluttered in the wind.

Deep River, Ontario
December 1984